THEORETICALLY DEAD

A MYSTERY BY TINKER MARKS

NEW VICTORIA PUBLISHERS
NORWICH, VERMONT

Published by New Victoria Publishers Inc., PO Box 27 Norwich, Vt. 05055
A Feminist Literary and Cultural Organization founded in 1976

Cover Design Claudia McKay

Printed and bound in Canada
1   2   3   4   2003   2004   2002   2001

Library of Congress Cataloging-in-Publication Data

Marks, Tinker.
    Theoretically dead : a mystery / by Tinker Marks.
      p. cm.
    ISBN 1-892281-16-3
     1. Women philosophers--Fiction. 2. Artificial insemination, Human--Fiction. 3. Lesbians--Fiction.   I. Title.

    PS3613.A37 T48 2001
    813'.6--dc21

                       2001030539

To Maura and Johanna, with love and gratitude.

Acknowledgements

Quite a few people made valuable contributions to this book. We are most grateful to Deb Cafiero, our once-and-future literary agent, for editorial guidance and general encouragement. Many thanks to our editors at New Victoria Publishers, Beth and Claudia, who have done so much to improve this book. A number of friends and colleagues sent us comments on early drafts of the book, including Edyth Montgomery, Kathy Krynski, Johanna Meehan, Maura Strassberg, Barbara Azeka Powell, Liz Savoca, Tony Rodrigues, Ginny Baldwin, Paula Smith, Barb P. Powell, and Kate Callas. We received helpful advice from at least two Ellens: mystery writer Ellen Hart and literary agent Ellen Geiger. Our daughter Mary Powell read the first draft at age nine, and suggested we list her as 'editor' on the cover. Though we declined this offer, we admit that she made some very useful comments. Our son Kurt Montgomery made absolutely no contribution to the book, but is nevertheless a pretty cool guy.

CHAPTER ONE
Hammond, Iowa 1991

Imagine you were on your way to a party where people would talk about things like "Conceptual Traditions in Agnostic Ontology" or "Existential Dilemmas in Cartesian Dualism." Would you be in hurry? Well I wouldn't either, but it happens that on this particular occasion I was. Emma's now-famous philosophy conference began on a Monday, the third Monday in January I believe, and I was late for the opening reception. It was probably about 6:30 PM when I walked from my office to the College Inn to join Emma and the other philosophy professors. I am not—and I'd like to emphasize this point—a philosophy professor myself. I had agreed to come to dine with these philosophers merely as a courtesy to my partner, Emma.

On a winter evening during semester break, the campus at Hammond feels acutely empty, like a beach on a rainy day in November. On any given Monday in the fall, the whole place teems like an ant colony, the sidewalks full of students gabbing and laughing on their way to class. But on that January night, as I crossed the campus, long brick buildings with dark windows surrounded the great open quads. I was surprised, in fact, to meet another person. I was even more surprised that the person I met was lying on the sidewalk.

I had just reached the pedestrian bridge across what our admission brochures like to call a river, when I came across his crumpled form. By my fifth winter in Iowa I had learned to walk with my eyes focused down in front of me, especially at night. Though the college keeps its sidewalks meticulously cleared, there is always the possibility of some rogue patch of ice lying quietly in wait on the dark cement. So I nearly stepped on the man's chest before I saw him. The sight of him almost made me yelp. (OK, the sight of him *did* make me yelp.) He lay on his back, the eyes in his grey head closed and the stubbled jaw hanging slightly off-kilter with his mouth open.

I dropped down beside him and put a hand on his shoulder. "Mister! Mister! Are you all right?" That, of course, was a pretty stupid question, because a man lying on a sidewalk on a winter night in Iowa is, by definition, not all right. He is either dead, or on his way to being dead from hypothermia. The man's overcoat was unbuttoned and I saw a suit jacket and pants underneath, and a white shirt with no tie. Was he alive? I couldn't tell. While I frequently deal with people who appear dead—my 8:00 a.m. theory class springs to mind here—I rarely encounter an actual body. Gingerly, I pressed my fingers against his skinny, whiskered neck, feeling for a pulse. I couldn't find one, but then I wasn't sure I was looking in the right place.

What to do? Obviously, I needed to call an ambulance. I had to get to an emergency phone and call the night watchman. I looked around the deserted quad, but saw none of the little blue lights that shine above the campus emergency phones. I thought I remembered one in the lobby of Goddard Hall on the far side of the quad. I took off in that direction, running as fast as I could in my mid-heeled dress shoes. By the time I reached the double glass doors at the main entrance to Goddard, I felt the cold air burn my lungs as I puffed and heaved. Goddard Hall is a good place to run in an emergency because it's a computer center whose facilities are in constant demand by students writing term papers (the night before they're due, naturally) and therefore open around the clock. Unless, of course, the college is on break. Which it was. I cursed myself for forgetting that as I stood panting in front of the lobby door. Where is there another emergency phone? I thought. I remembered: back the other way, on the east side of the chemistry building.

I started running again, back around the corner, across the quad back toward the bridge where I had found the old man. I would stop to check on him, button his coat up and put his hands in his pockets before going off to find the other phone. The clap of my feet on the sidewalk echoed off the windows of Prospect Hall as I passed it. By the time I approached the spot where I'd left the old man, I felt myself sweating in spite of the cold. When I reached the bridge I stopped running. There was no old man there.

For a few seconds I had to bend forward, my hands against my knees, puffing hard. Usually I make it a point never to go running when the temperature is below fifteen degrees. I also make it a point never to go running when the temperature is above fifteen degrees.

I straightened up and looked around, squinting in the darkness. I couldn't be in the wrong place, could I? No, I had found him at the foot of the bridge on the east side of the river, it was definitely the right place. The man just wasn't there anymore. I had only been gone for a couple of minutes. Had he regained consciousness, gotten up off the sidewalk, pulled himself together and walked away? In that little bit of time I had been running across the quad?

I called out. "Hello? Is someone here?" I looked around, straining to listen. No answer. Louder this time, I called, "Hello, is anyone hurt?" only to hear my own voice echo back from across the square.

I walked to the top of the bridge's shallow arc to get a little higher and looked around. I saw nothing moving, no one on the sidewalks running in either direction from the river, no one visible across the quad, though, as I said, it was quite dark.

I unbuttoned my coat and flapped the sides in and out a few times. I would feel awkward enough at the reception where I was headed without having sweat stains under the arms of my blouse. The cold air felt soothing. A light wind stirred and a small piece of green paper flitted across the sidewalk a foot or two from where the old man had been lying. I picked it up. It was from a Hammond College memo pad and the words "Someone called for you, 555-8519" were scribbled diagonally across the page. I recognized the scratchy handwriting immediately.

Now, as a rule, I'm always proud and happy to pick up a stray bit of trash now and then to do my part in keeping our beautiful campus litter-free. But picking up that piece of paper was a really big mistake.

CHAPTER TWO

The philosophy conference had officially started the morning before that cold evening when I found the old man. I knew Emma's behavior would eventually show signs of stress that day, but I thought she'd be OK at least until some key milestones had been passed. Breakfast, for example. But I was still toweling off from my shower when Emma stormed into the bathroom in her frayed blue robe holding a white plastic tube between thumb and forefinger. It was short and fat and had a wide round top. She thrust it at me.

"Do you see this?"

Since it was three inches from my face, I could honestly say, "Yes, I do."

"The top is all white. Do you know what that means?"

That was slightly less obvious. I'd have to take a guess. "It means you're not ovulating?"

"That's right, I'm not. So now what do I do?"

Boy, these questions kept getting harder. I got my terrycloth robe from the hook behind the door. "Do about what?"

"About inseminating, Claire! The sperm comes today. I'm going to be tied up with this conference day and night for the next three days, when am I going to do it?"

With the sleeve of my robe I wiped the fog off the bathroom mirror. "Oh, you'll probably ovulate tomorrow morning." I made a monster grin and examined my front teeth.

"I'd better." She sat down on the edge of the claw-footed bathtub. "I don't even know how to keep the stuff. What do you store sperm in, anyway?"

"Normally, a husband."

She glared at me. "At what point in this conversation do you plan to become helpful, Claire?"

"Look," I turned to her, "there's nothing to worry about. You can inseminate tomorrow before the paper sessions. You're just all worked up about the meeting."

"Well, maybe." She held up the uncooperative little tube and examined it in the light from the steamed-up window. "But the last thing I need is to get up in the middle of someone's presentation and say, 'Pardon me, ladies and gentleman, I need to go get pregnant.'"

I laughed. "I bet that'd be the most interesting thing anyone says at that philosophy conference." She tilted her head back and gave me a thin, insolent smile.

"Yes, I shouldn't wonder that among the Philistines in your discipline, it might well be the only sentence they could comprehend." The tube hit the bottom of the waste basket with a pop.

We went downstairs for breakfast. My house, our house, is a big white Victorian built by a mill owner in the 1890s, the kind of house young academics can afford only in places like rural Iowa. There is an inevitable sequence of events when you move from a tiny, big-city apartment, in my case in Chicago, to a small town in Iowa. You see the big houses, you find out how cheap they are, you quickly buy one, you feel euphoric. The euphoria sometimes lasts a full week before you are crushed by the realization that a house that size and age requires approximately as much maintenance as the USS Nimitz. After five years in that house, I still had a lot of renovation to do, but at least the first floor was in pretty good shape. I had replastered the walls, refinished the floors in the living and dining rooms, put in new kitchen cabinets, and replaced the picture window. Now, with Emma living there, I planned to do more. There wasn't a lot of furniture for such big rooms, but we'd keep working on it if Emma stayed at the college. And if she didn't? Well, on that frosty morning that the conference began I had few doubts that she would be staying.

On my way to the kitchen I stopped to check the thermometer outside the dining room window. Twenty-one degrees, a little warmer than I'd expected. I opened the window and shook some sunflower seed into the birdfeeder on the outside ledge. Through the bare maple sapling in our side yard, I could see our next-door neighbor carefully spreading salt on his front sidewalk. Ice is ubiquitous in the Iowa winter, and people his age need constant vigilance against slipping and falling.

Through the open window I called, "Good morning, Mr. Leach," my voice brimming with sunshine and birdsong. The grey head turned toward me. His lips curled up into about twelve per cent of a smile, which lasted for maybe two-thirds of a second, then he went back to pouring the salt.

"Claire, stop torturing that poor man."

"Torturing him? I'm extending the hand of fellowship across the great gulf between our lifestyles."

"Of course you are, dear, and I am the Grand Duchess Anastasia Romanov."

Emma's present for my thirty-second birthday had already done its job; the kitchen air was delicious with the smell of a new vanilla coffee I was trying. Emma stared glumly into the refrigerator while I went to the cabinet and pulled out coffee cups. I started toasting a bagel and Emma got her hot dog buns out of the breadbox. That's what she likes to eat for breakfast: hot dog buns. Sometimes with butter and jelly, sometimes just plain. This is a woman who won't eat a fish that's more than twenty-four hours out of the water, who refuses to cook with any wine that is domestic, who lectures waiters on the preparation of her toast. There are many swirls and eddies in Emma's personality. I had been aware of this for all the years I'd known her, but only now that we lived together had it really become clear to me.

My bagel had just popped up when I heard a heavy thud, thud coming from the rear of the house. Just outside the kitchen door stood a tiny old man, alternately scraping and whacking the icy back steps with a garden shovel. He paused, poured some salt over the top step, then moved down to start whacking the one below it. He wore a ratty green parka, green work gloves, and green rubber boots unsnapped at the top. With a silver goatee on his little chin, he looked like he was here on sabbatical from Santa's Workshop.

I opened the door. "Hey, Cubby, you're making a lot of noise out here."

He looked at me sideways, still pounding the ice. "If you don't clear off the snow right away, the sun melts it. Then when night comes it turns to ice." He smoothed out the salt with the tip of the shovel. "How many times I gotta tell you that?"

"How many times have you told me?"

"About fifty."

"Well, I think fifty-five ought to do it."

He leaned the shovel next to the back door and came into the kitchen. Cubby lives in a small blue house across the alley between our back yards. "I don't think you girls are gonna make it as Iowans," he said. He's about the only person who can get away with using the word "girls" like that around Emma, who is the Kendall Professor of Feminist Thought at the college. He hung his parka on a peg and stepped out of his boots. I heard Emma in the dining room talking on the cordless phone.

"Want some coffee?" I said.

"Isn't decaf is it?"

"Hell, no! I wouldn't offer decaf to a farmer."

"Ex-farmer." He wore blue jeans and a denim shirt buttoned all the way up to the neck. "Truth is, at night decaf's all I drink now." He shook his head at this sorry state of affairs. I handed him his coffee, milk but no sugar. He sipped it and nodded, "You made this, right? Emma's is always real weak." He took another sip. "Hell, her coffee's too weak to come out of the pot."

Emma came in from the dining room, writing down some notes on a little yellow pad. "Hi, Cubby."

"Hi, Em." He stuck out his thumb in the direction of the door. "You gotta clear off those back steps, Em, I was telling Claire. You don't clear 'em off, you get ice every time."

"OK, Cubby," she said. "Claire, that was Maria on the phone." Maria is the secretary for Emma's department at the college, Philosophy and Religion. "She needs to go to the bank this morning and straighten out something with her son's student loan. My suggestion that a trip to the bank could wait until tomorrow fell on deaf ears, of course, since absolutely anything that threatens to inconvenience her son can immediately be classified as a national emergency." True, Maria was positively obsessed with her son.

Emma paused and looked at me. "So anyway, this is…kind of a problem for me."

"Yes," I said, "that does sound like a problem." Here it comes, I thought.

"Maria was supposed to go to the airport this morning to collect one of my …ah, visitors." Her eyes wandered away from my face.

"Oh, a *visitor*," I said brightly, "An old college roommate? A maiden aunt from Toledo, perhaps?" I folded my arms across my chest.

"OK," she said, "It's Roger Stuhrm. Could you pick him up at the airport for me? I wouldn't ask if I weren't in a bind."

"Who's Roger Stuhrm?" Cubby asked.

"Just some guy I used to date," she said. "You can take my car to the airport if you want."

"Emma, I do not have the time to go all the way to Des Moines to pick up Roger Stuhrm. I have a lot of work of my own to do."

"You used to date guys?" Cubby said.

"Come on, Claire, Maria can't do it and I don't have anyone else who can do it."

In my Iowa-schoolmarm-circa-1860 voice, I said. "That is a contingency for which you should have prepared."

"How about you, Claire, did you date guys?"

Emma turned her back on me, strode to the counter and started pretending to butter a hot dog bun. "It's a very small thing I'm asking of you, Claire. I should think you would recognize the importance of this conference for our future together and be willing to make a few tiny sacrifices for it."

"Hey, I'm already making quite a few *tiny sacrifices* for this conference. I'm going to dinner tonight, I'm helping with the party tomorrow—lots of stuff. It's not fair to ask me to do more."

"Did you date this guy before or after you met Claire?"

"It wouldn't take long, you'd be back by 11:00."

"That isn't the point."

Emma sighed dramatically and slapped some jelly on her bun in a way obviously meant to express frustration. After a brief moment she turned back to me. Emma has a strong repertoire of pleading looks, and she gave me a particularly cute one that I call Beagle-Puppy-with-Hurt-Paw. "I wouldn't ask if I didn't really need it. Please?"

I waited a respectable three seconds before caving in. "Oh, all right," I said. We'd both known all along that my resistance was merely token.

"Thanks, honey." She smiled at me. It struck me at that moment how gorgeous Emma is, an odd reaction to her appearance in the morning, which is certainly not the peak of her beauty cycle. Before she showers, her close-cropped, dark-brown hair is always jutting out at some improbable angle. She has few wrinkles, but at thirty-four her tall, slender form has started to soften at the edges. On her way to class, in one of her clever skirt, blouse and scarf ensembles, by conventional standards she is definitely attractive. But in the mornings she wears that hideous blue bathrobe she kept from her eight months at Marlborough House. It's ratty and frayed with blue threads and little beads of terrycloth hanging off it. Why does she keep it? She told me she'd felt safe at Marlborough House and maybe some of that safe feeling still clings to the bathrobe.

Cubby tugged at my sleeve. "So, how long ago did she date this guy?"

I frowned at him. "What guy? What're you talking about?"

The back door opened and someone called in, "Hello?"

"Colin!" Emma said. Colin Jensen, the newest member of Emma's department, was fair-haired, handsome, and twenty-six years old, though he looked nineteen.

"How're you doing?" he said. "I came over to get a copy of the Bailey paper."

"Hey, I'm glad you're back. I was starting to worry you wouldn't make it." Emma gave him a big smile. He took off his coat and threw it on the counter. Underneath he wore faded jeans and a red rugby shirt with tan and black stripes across the chest. He crossed to the table, bent down to let his lips briefly touch Emma's, then went back to the counter to pour himself some coffee.

"Hi, Claire."

"Hi, Colin. Colin, this is our neighbor Cubby MacIntosh." The two men exchanged nods.

"So when did you get back, Colin?" Emma asked.

"I didn't get in until almost midnight," he said. He began to describe his trip back to Berkeley. Cubby leaned over and whispered to me.

"Do they do that in your department?"

"Do what?"

"Kiss each other all the time."

"In Economics? Certainly not! It's those people in the humanities who are always kissing each other. They're really into the touchy-feely stuff."

Colin came over and joined us at the table. "Had a great talk with Matt Rosen," he said to Emma, "about a paper I'm hoping to cut out of my thesis. He thinks I could get it into *Annals of Philosophy*."

Oh, God, I thought to myself. Please don't start this already, Colin. Not this early, not today.

Emma said, "That's terrific," but I could see the muscles in her face tighten up. Conversations about research always flick her compulsion switch because she's constantly worried about her publication rate. This is a woman who has published two books, three monographs and a score of journal articles, and whose obsessive devotion to scholarship is admired by practically everyone who doesn't have to live with her. I went over to the counter to get one of the pears that were ripening on the window ledge.

"Of course, I want to get this conference paper out first," Colin was saying. "You know, I've thought of a way I can get two pieces on Weber out of it."

Erik Weber was the philosopher whose work was the subject of Emma's conference. His name was German and Colin pronounced it *vay bur*, rhyming with labor, which Emma had told me was the correct pronunciation for people in the know.

"One piece will be for your book, don't worry," Colin said. He laughed. "But I'm pretty sure I can do a second for *Ethics and Society*. I think the editor likes my style." Emma's hands began massaging her coffee cup. "Of course, God knows when I'll find time to write this. I still have to make final revisions on my chapter for Hal Chapman's book." Emma's shoulders made a slight twitching motion. "Still, if I'm lucky…" Colin's hands did a little drum roll on the table, "this year I should get three, maybe four articles published." Emma's left eye flickered a couple of times.

I looked down at the little knife I was using to peel my pear. Colin was so young and handsome, so filled with the earnestness of youth, that a jury might not understand why I felt compelled to drag that knife across his throat. You kind of had to be there, I'd explain to them. Well, maybe instead of killing him, I could just change the subject.

"So, Colin, you think it's going to stay sunny for this conference?"

"I hope so, Claire. I'm presenting the best paper I've ever written." He got up, came over and stood across from me at the counter, his face beaming.

"It's a new twist on an old subject," he told me, almost as if I'd actually asked. "You know that Platburg accused Weber of plagiarizing his *Discourse on Rationality*, right?"

Having never heard of Platburg, I was naturally somewhat fuzzy on what he'd accused Weber of, but I said, "Uh huh."

"Well, that's a really old debate, whether Weber plagiarized. But I'm doing something no one's ever tried before. I compare Weber's early writings in the original German with his later stuff in English, looking for any inconsistencies that would bear on the plagiarism charge. See that's where Morrison and Perkins failed—they looked at translated works instead of the original." He pushed his coffee cup toward me as if he were pointing. "I can prove that Weber plagiarized."

"Ahhh," I said.

"Now take, for example, *Hermenutics, Verstehen, und Wahrheit.* The original German conveys a much different meaning than Halberstam's translation."

As he told me this, I realized with growing horror that Colin was on the verge of describing his entire paper to me. Perhaps, I reflected sadly, it's time to draw this knife across my own throat.

Emma stepped in to save me. "I'm sorry to interrupt, Colin, but Claire has to go to the airport in a few minutes."

"Oh." Colin's expression sagged. "Oh, OK."

"Sounds good though, Colin," I said. "You'll have to tell me about it later." Yes, later, I thought, so much later that while you're telling me you can put flowers on my grave.

"Come on, Colin, I've got your copy of Bailey's paper in my study."

"OK." Colin perked back up and followed Emma out of the kitchen. "Hey, have I told you my theory about why Weber disappeared? I think he may have gone…" his voice trailed off as they went up the front stairs. I sat back down at the table with Cubby.

"Who's this Vadar?" he asked me, "Sounds like the guy from Star Wars."

"Not *vay dur*," I said, "his name's *vay bur*. It's spelled like Weber, but it's German."

Cubby ambled over and picked up the coffee pot. "And he's disappeared?"

"Who's disappeared?"

"This *Vaybur* guy," he said, "didn't that young fella just say that?"

"Did he? I'm afraid my attention wasn't riveted to that conversation."

Cubby made a swirling motion with the coffee pot; only a quarter inch of brown liquid swished around at the bottom. He opened the cabinet above the sink where he knew we kept the coffee beans. "So today's the big conference she's been in such a tizzy about," he said. "Why's this such a big deal?"

"Emma's chair expires next year; she's hoping this conference will get her more money."

He looked at me. "How does a chair expire, exactly?"

"You know what an endowed chair is, right? Well, her chair is funded by a three year grant from the Kendall Foundation. The college is trying to raise money to make the chair permanent, it's part of the big capital campaign. This conference is supposed to be a sort of showpiece for attracting donations."

"Why can't they just give her a regular job like yours?"

I waited for the screeching of the coffee grinder to stop. "Well, first of all there isn't a job open, not in Philosophy, anyway. And second, Emma's way too expensive. To get someone as prominent as she is you need a chair. Big salary, lots of research money."

"So how come you aren't helping with the conference?"

"What do you mean? I am helping with the conference, Cubby. Besides, she doesn't have anything to worry about. This is just Emma obsessing as usual."

Cubby filled the glass pot with water and poured it into the coffee machine. In a few seconds drops of coffee plip, plipped into the pot. With a sponge from the sink he swept escaped coffee grounds into his hand and deposited them in the wastebasket under the sink. He took a cigarette out of the pocket of his shirt and glanced nervously at the doorway to the living room. In a loud whisper he asked, "Think she'd notice if I smoked in here?"

"I think she'd notice if you smoked in Des Moines." But I waved a hand. "Screw her, smoke if you want to."

Cubby put a cigarette in his mouth, turned on the front burner of the stove, then bent low and pushed the tip of the cigarette into the blue flame. I held my breath. I was sure his hair would ignite like a cotton ball.

"So," he said, "Emma's worried this conference'll mess up and you two'll have to live apart again. That what it is?"

"Yeah, that and the other thing I mentioned to you."

"What other thing?"

I lowered my voice. "You know, that thing with the package? That's coming today?"

"Package?"

I glanced at the kitchen doorway. "The S-P-E-R-M." What the hell was I spelling for?

"Oh, the Baby!" he practically screamed across the kitchen.

"Jeez, Cubby, keep it down; she doesn't know I told you."

"She doesn't?" He walked over to the table and picked up the little pitcher that held the cream. "Is it a secret or something?"

"Well, she wants it to be. For the time being anyway."

"Why?"

I shrugged.

"Cause you're both girls?"

I shrugged again.

He filled the cream pitcher with half-and-half from the refrigerator and put it on the counter "That's not so weird nowadays, is it? Two ladies raising a baby, I mean." He put the pitcher back on the table and picked up my empty mug. "If you guys have a baby, then the kid'll just have two mothers is all."

I didn't say anything while he poured some coffee into both our cups and came back and set mine in front of me.

"I suppose it's two mothers, right?" he said. "I mean, you'll be the mother, too, won't you?" For the third time I simply shrugged.

"Well, what else would you be?"

"I don't know, Cubby." I stood up, took a perfunctory sip of the coffee he'd given me and pulled my robe tight around my waist. "Well, I guess I'd better get ready to go to the airport."

Upstairs, dressing in front of the full length mirror, I wondered how much I'd changed since last seeing Roger. Staring back from the mirror was a tall, statuesque brunette, the morning sunshine brightly gleaming in her thick mane of chestnut hair. Astonishingly blue eyes sat above high cheekbones and full sensual lips. Her figure curved downward from ample bosom through slender waist, to thighs as sleek and graceful as those of a gazelle.

OK, so that's who I wished had been staring back at me. The woman who was actually there was short and her frizzy mane of brown hair was showing little streaks of grey. While her bosom was ample enough, those thighs would need to shed five or ten pounds before she could hang out with any gazelles. Still, it could have been worse at her age. She was OK-looking, I guessed. On a good day, with a tailwind, she might make it all the way to cute.

I put on jeans, a white turtleneck, a purple cardigan, and my no-longer-white tennis shoes over heavy wool socks. So the sperm's coming today, I thought, but Emma's not ovulating. If she couldn't inseminate this cycle and had to wait a month to try again, she'd be really disappointed. Me, on the other hand, I could definitely wait another month. Yes, I could wait another month, and many more.

CHAPTER THREE

I was a few minutes late leaving for the airport. Emma wanted me to stop at Maria's house on my way to get Roger, but I didn't have time, so I'd have to do it on the way back to Hammond. I hoped Maria would still be there. See, that's how it is when Emma gets me involved in one of her projects. At first it was, "Can you please meet Roger at the airport?" Now it was, "Oh, and on your way to Des Moines, could you stop at Maria's and get the registration packets?" Probably at the airport a loudspeaker would say, "Claire Sinclair, please come to the courtesy counter for a message," and I'd get instructions to pick up maraschino cherries. It's a slippery slope, I'm telling you.

I always find the drive to Des Moines relaxing. The land undulates softly with miles of open fields dotted with farm buildings and small stands of trees. Left untouched by human hands, the land would change from hardwood forest along the Mississippi to tall grass prairie as it rolled west to the Missouri. Farther on, in Nebraska, the grass would grow short and the trees would disappear. Out there the land would appear flat, though it was really climbing toward the Rockies with infinite patience.

To me there seemed a sort of paradox about the Iowa prairie. The deep black soil, scoured from rock by advancing glaciers, is as rich and fruitful as any on earth. Yet in a natural state it hosts mere grass. By contrast, the Amazon rainforests, those bursting cornucopias of every sort of life, have dreadfully poor soils, leached of fertility by constant rain. Rainforests have to keep their organic matter alive and busy, up in the plants above the forest floor. But prairies hide their organic riches. The treasure is underground in the dark rich earth, safe from winter cold, grazing buffalo, and the fires that swept through the grasslands in autumn. In the mid 1800's American farmers discovered the prairie's secret. By 1851, the land that had once been considered 'only fit for Indians' was all in the hands of white settlers.

Roger Stuhrm was on a 10:15 flight from Chicago. I sat waiting nonchalantly in a chair in the gate area. Somehow I felt that my usual habit of peering down the ramp in search of my party would make it seem like I was, I don't know, anxious for him to arrive or something. Like I was happy to see him. I wasn't happy to see him and I didn't want him to think I was happy to see him. I'm not sure why that sort of thing would matter to someone who wasn't wearing braces on her teeth, but there I sat.

On his flight, Roger had sat in the very back of the airplane because I was waiting for him, and that's where everyone I ever wait for apparently has to sit; it's like an FAA regulation or something. Roger is tall with a narrow waist and broad shoulders. His black hair forms tight little curls and his eyes are a milky chocolate brown. As a grad student Roger was rarely without some coed tagging along, her books clasped across her chest, gazing moon-eyed at him as he pontificated about Nietzsche. I had no doubt that as a professor he drove his students even more ga-ga. Roger didn't dress like a professor, though, he dressed like a bond trader at Lehman Brothers: a steel-grey pin-striped suit, a light blue shirt, and a yellow power tie. I'd have bet long money that under the jacket was a pair of suspenders, probably red. I hadn't seen Roger since graduate school in Chicago, but ten years had done little to abrade his youthful appearance. He carried a leather flight bag in one hand and a laptop computer in the other.

"Roger."

He turned toward where I was sitting and looked at me, surprised at first, then smiling in that self-satisfied way he has. "Claire. Fancy meeting you here. Emma told me to expect some flunky with my name on a sign."

"Did she, now? How odd, Emma rarely uses words like 'flunky'." He smirked a bit at that. I gave him the short version of why I was doing Emma this favor and suggested we go get his luggage.

"No, this is all I have," he said, hoisting the two bags. We headed down the gate concourse toward the main terminal, which, in Des Moines, is the only terminal.

"Is it cold out?" he asked, "I hear Iowa is brutally cold."

"It's not that cold. About what you were used to in Chicago. Jeez, Roger, living in DC must be making you soft." Roger taught at Georgetown University.

We were out of the airport and cruising up Fleur Drive when Roger said, "So, after all these years, you and Emma are back together again. And living in Iowa of all places. My, my. How big is this little town of yours, anyway?"

"About six thousand people."

"Six thousand? Good Lord, how can you live in such a tiny place? What do you do there? I mean, to keep from dying of boredom?"

"Well, Roger, Emma and I have developed a new hobby that keeps us kind of busy. We call it 'working-for-a-living.'"

"Six thousand people." He shook his head. "You're never going to keep Emma happy out here in these boondocks."

We were heading east on I-235 and I felt a keen urge to change the subject. "There," I said, automatically pointing out to my visitor one of the few landmarks Des Moines could offer. "That's the state capitol. It's the only state capitol in the US with five domes."

"Lovely," he said flatly. "And it seems to be on a hill. Now what would a hill be doing in Iowa?"

"Iowa is not flat, Roger. People think it is, but it's not. And now that you mention it, that 'hill' you pointed out is actually kind of interesting, " I said. "It's called a terminal moraine. It's a huge mound of rocks and soil pushed ahead of a glacier. During the last ice age the glaciers came south as far as Des Moines and then retreated."

"Who could blame them?" he said. "I imagine this place seems pretty dull even to a glacier."

My watch said it was only 10:40. That meant that in the decade since we'd last met, Roger had shaved about twelve minutes off the time it took him to get on my nerves. Remarkable. What had Emma seen in this guy? I asked myself for the four hundred and fifteenth time. When we'd all been grad students there had, I suppose, been something captivating in Roger's good looks and suave arrogance, and maybe it had even bewitched me for a time. In any case, Emma and Roger had only dated for six weeks or so before Emma and I had gotten together.

Never mind, I wasn't going to let Roger make me mad already.

"So what's this big conference about anyway?" I asked him.

"You don't know?"

"Well, I know it has something to do with Erik Weber."

"My dear, it has everything to do with Erik Weber. This will be the definitive conference on his life and writings even, if it is held in the wilderness, and he'll be viewed ever after as he never was before." His enthusiasm seemed so genuine that I was tempted to point out that the number of people who had heard of, read, or cared about Erik Weber could easily fit into a good-sized school bus. I restrained myself. I knew from Emma that inside that bus the man was a god, one of the first conservative philosophers to embrace feminism. She'd written her dissertation on his early writings. Emma, however, unlike most people coming to the conference, was generally very critical of Weber.

"Is this thing being held because Weber just died or something?"

"No. Well, theoretically I suppose he could be dead."

What the hell did that mean? "He could be theoretically dead?"

"No, I mean that as far as I know he hasn't died. But, of course, I can't be absolutely sure."

"Excuse me? On the eve of the 'definitive conference' on Weber's life, you don't even know if the guy's alive?"

"Weber disappeared two years ago. No one's heard from him since."

Disappeared? I wasn't getting this. "What do you mean, he 'disappeared?' Are you saying he just vanished without a trace, a la Jimmy Hoffa? Was he kidnaped or something?"

Roger sighed in apparent weariness at having to indulge my ignorance. "Weber makes a habit of disappearing from time to time. It's part of his carefully manicured mystique. He vanishes without a trace for months at a time and then emerges suddenly with a brilliant new manuscript. I think he means it to imply that insights as great as his can be arrived at only in some isolated transcendental state."

"So you're saying he didn't disappear, he's just hiding somewhere?" I asked. "Still in Germany presumably?"

"Germany, Siberia, Katmandu." Roger waved his hand. "The jerk could be here in Des Moines for all I know."

"*The jerk*?" I laughed. "You're attending a conference celebrating this man's work—I was sort of under the impression that most of you people admired the guy."

"Oh, I admired him a great deal until about four weeks ago."

"Four weeks ago?"

"That's right, four weeks ago."

I waited for him to explain. He didn't. I waited a little longer and he still didn't. Now, I realize that an even slightly less petty person than I would have at least given Roger the satisfaction of asking him what happened four weeks ago.

"Well," I said, "I'm sure Weber will be sorry to hear you've stopped liking him."

We sped down Interstate 80 in silence.

Maria lives down a gravel road about a mile east of town in what used to be a big old farm house. It's still a big old house but it's no longer connected with the fields that surround it. They were absorbed long ago by a larger enterprise when the family that lived there gave up the struggle. Economies of scale, we economists call it: larger farms can produce food at lower cost than smaller farms. That simple fact bears relentlessly down on family farms, crushing them slowly, but as surely as if the glaciers had come back.

I pulled off the gravel road and went down a little hill to where the house lay a hundred yards or so back. The house was missing a couple of shingles and its white paint was flaking off at the base of the roof and under some of the window shutters. The enclosed porch sagged a few inches toward its middle. Roger waited in the car while I walked up the icy walk and knocked on the door.

Though her hair is mostly grey, Maria is a large, stout and healthy-looking person, about five-foot-eight with broad shoulders. Standing in a pink dress with a floral print, a bandanna on her head, she looked a lot like a Slavic peasant woman. She is, in fact, originally Hungarian, I believe. She and her son came to Iowa from Europe many years ago, though her accent is still quite noticeable.

"Hi, Maria, do you have some conference materials I'm supposed to pick up?"

"Yes, the registration packets," she said. "I was stuffing them last night." She ushered me up the steps and into the enclosed porch at the front of her house. "I was going to leave you a note that I had put them in the mailbox. I am just about to leave." She closed the door behind me. "I am sorry you had to come out here, Claire. I have an appointment at 11:30 and I was afraid if Dr. Stuhrm's plane was late I would not get back in time. There was a mix up about my son's student loan and I have to go to the bank in Parmley. I will go get the packets."

I knew that Maria's son was way old to be getting a student loan. He was what, at the University of Chicago, we used to call an 'nth year' grad student, someone who had been working on his Ph.D. so long that no one could remember when he had started. I noticed that on the shelves to my left were what amounted to a shrine to Maria's son. There were various toys and whatnot: a trophy with a baseball on top, a pair of black leather baby shoes, a silver mug engraved with a winged football and 'Hammond Regional High.' There was a brown wooden horse with red polka dots and next to it a graduation picture. I picked up the photo. In the picture Maria's arms were around her son's neck, and they were both smiling broadly, the joy and pride in her face unmistakable. I knew that Maria doted on her son, that he was practically her whole life. But what would happen if Emma had a son? If Emma had a baby, and if we stayed together, there would someday be a picture like this on one of our shelves. Would I be in it? How would a son describe that picture? Would he say, "Here are my moms and me at graduation?" or "Here are my mom and Claire and me at my graduation?" I wouldn't really be his mother, after all. I'd be raising him, changing his diapers, driving him to school, reading him stories in bed at night, just like his mother.

But I wouldn't actually be his mother. I'd be something less. I might even be something a lot less, something like those two women my Dad had married after my mother died of cancer.

Maria came back and caught me looking at the picture, which made me feel unaccountably embarrassed. "Sure is a handsome boy," I said. "Well, man."

"Yes, he is all grown up now, thirty-three next May." She looked at the picture and smiled, but a little sadly I thought. "I just wish he were not so far away," she said. Experience had taught me that if I made any response, I might spend twenty minutes listening to Maria go on about her son, which I am perfectly willing to do on occasion, but was not in the mood for at this particular moment. Besides, Roger was in the car.

"Well, I'd better get going," I said.

She handed me a stack of manila envelopes. "You have not been home yet?"

"No, I'm just coming in from the airport. Why?"

"Emma called. She said you should get home quickly, there is something being delivered that she wants you to wait for." So the sperm hasn't shown up yet, I thought.

"I thought Emma was home waiting for it."

"She had to leave. The president's secretary called about some problem with the dinner for tonight and Emma had to go to the administration building and straighten it out." No surprise there. That woman had been hassling Emma about every detail of this conference for the last month and a half. "This delivery," Maria asked, "is it something for the conference? Do I need to make copies?"

I wanted to laugh at that. "No, I'm pretty sure Emma isn't planning to distribute this stuff at the conference," I told her. "Well, gotta go." I opened the porch door and started down the creaky wooden steps. Maria saw Roger sitting in the front seat of my car.

"Is that Dr. Stuhrm?"

"Yeah, I told him I'd only be a minute."

"I have to ask him something." She came out of the house, hugging herself against the cold air, and stepped carefully across the icy gravel driveway to Roger's side of the car. She bent down to his window and gave him a formal semi-smile, like the receptionist in a dental office. "Dr. Stuhrm?"

Roger rolled down the window about an inch. "Yes?"

"Hello, I am Maria, the secretary for the Philosophy and Religion Department. I am afraid we never received a copy of your paper."

"I couldn't help that, it wasn't ready."

"Do you have it now?"

"Yes, I brought it with me."

Maria held out her hand. "If you give it to me, I can make copies and give them out to the other professors."

"Thank you, but that won't be necessary. I have copies with me and I'll hand them out at my session."

"Well…" she said, "that is not the way we have been doing it. The other participants sent their papers in beforehand as requested in the letter of invitation. I am afraid yours is the only one that has not been passed out yet."

"As I said, I'll distribute it myself, at my session."

Even ever-polite Maria had to frown at that. "You do not want your colleagues to read the paper before the session begins?"

"No, I really don't." Roger rolled up the window, turned away, and sat gazing calmly toward the front of the car. Maria kept staring at him for a second, then straightened up and looked at me over the roof of the car. Why was Roger being such a jerk? All I could do was shrug my shoulders at Maria. Still, I wanted to say something to balance his rudeness.

"Thanks a lot Maria, I hope you get everything sorted out with the loan." She nodded and forced a little smile.

I turned the car around because I didn't want to back all the way up that long driveway. In my rearview mirror I saw Maria still watching us as we lumbered over the snow covered ruts on our way up to the main road. I asked Roger why he wouldn't hand out his paper.

"I'm not going to release my findings until I'm ready."

"Findings?" I said. "Roger, microbiologists have findings, you philosophers have thoughts."

"You may be surprised, my dear." He gave me a smugly sweet little smile. "I'm going to blow the lid off this conference."

"Ohhhh," I said, "so you have a big philosophical scoop, huh, Roger? Did you discover that Weber is really an empirical phenomenologist instead of a phenomenological empiricist?"

His smile became a little less sweet. "You'll see, smart ass."

CHAPTER FOUR

It was past noon before I finally got home and I was making myself a bologna sandwich when Emma came whooshing in the back door. "Did the sperm come? Were you here in time to get it?"

"I just got here. I haven't seen it."

"Damn." She ran a hand nervously through her hair as she looked at the big white clock above the sink. "Do you think we missed the UPS person?"

"Nah, I don't think so, there wasn't a note or anything. He probably hasn't come yet."

"But he should've been here by now." She dropped her satchel on the kitchen table and slumped into one of the white enameled wooden chairs. "They ship the stuff express, packed in dry ice. And whereas I don't have the foggiest notion of how long it will last, I'm certain it's not more than a day or two. Oh, what am I going to do, Claire?"

"Look," I said, "it doesn't seem likely that the shipper would just drive away without leaving a note or anything, especially with something so perishable. He's probably just running a little late. I'm sure we didn't miss the delivery." Her eyebrows rose a half millimeter, my argument having apparently ignited a flicker of hope.

"Well, maybe you're right." She stood up to pull off her lambswool coat, poured herself some of the coffee I'd made, then came back and sat at the table. "Listen, Claire, I appreciate your collecting Roger at the airport."

"No problem." I slathered some hot mustard between two slices of bologna.

Emma watched me eat for a few seconds and then said, "So." She looked at me slyly over the top of her coffee cup. "Is he still as cute as ever?"

I pointed a finger at her. "I don't think that's any of your concern, young lady." I wagged the finger. "Don't forget that I'll be watching you." Her eyes crinkled up. "And yes," I said, chewing on my sandwich, "I have to admit he's still really cute." And still a jerk, I thought. That reminded me of something. "By the way," I said, "what happened, that you couldn't wait here for the sperm? Maria told me you had to go someplace."

Emma sat bolt upright. "That…that WOMAN in the president's office—she moved my opening dinner from the inn to Benning Hall! Without even asking me! I set this dinner up two months ago." Emma stood up from the table, leaned toward me and held up two fingers. "Two months ago! All of a sudden, today, she discovers she needs the dining room at the inn?" Emma started pacing back and forth in front of the counter, gesticulating with her arms. "And she can just claim my facilities, without even consulting me? I have to plan my events, but she doesn't? The temerity of that woman."

It was obvious that the little red arrow on Emma's mood meter had swung all the way over and was pointing at RANT. When Emma's in that particular mode, one confines one's responses to sympathetic noises and short statements of support. It's especially important to avoid attempts at soothing like, 'Well it's not so bad,' or, 'I'm sure it will all work out.' To do so is like throwing water on a grease fire.

"Changed your dinner?" I said. "How dare she do that!" I tried to sound suitably shocked at the woman's gall. If one hazards an opinion on whatever Emma's ranting about, the smart choice is to absolutely agree with her.

"She said there's some trustee meeting to plan for the big capital campaign. 'Very important friends of the College are here,' she says. It figures. Let some rich trustees show up and the administrators act like lap dogs, but for mere 'academics'? We'll just send them to Burger King."

Oh, if only this little town had a Burger King, I thought wistfully.

"But it isn't really so bad, though, is it?" I said. "Benning Hall has a decent dining room."

That, as I believe I explained above, was one of the things it would be imprudent to say at this point. Emma went up like a Molotov cocktail.

"It IS a big deal! These conferences aren't usually held at tiny colleges in the middle of nowhere. I need to entertain these people properly, Claire. Do we want to look like hayseeds in front of distinguished colleagues from other institutions?"

"Mmmmm," I said. A sympathetic noise.

She put two fingers against each of her temples, rubbing them around in little circles, and I knew exactly what that foreshadowed. Given her emotional state, I'd been wondering when a migraine would show up. In a quiet, tired voice she said. "I wish John were here. He'd never put up with any of their nonsense. I miss him, Claire."

John Marchak had been the head of her department, the person, in fact, who had pushed the administration to hire Emma. John was himself a Weber enthusiast from way back. The conference was actually his idea and he had promoted it, helped organize it, and gotten the administration to kick in some money to hold it at Hammond. But all the while he was dying of cancer and didn't live to see the project realized. Emma had liked John very much. We both had.

There was a knock at the kitchen door, which opened slightly while someone said, "Hello?"

"Come in Sara Grace," Emma said.

Sara Grace Harper had been to our house enough to know to come to the back door because we would very likely be in the kitchen. Since Emma started living here it seemed as if there were always a half dozen philosophy majors like Sara Grace hanging around our house, which is only two blocks from campus. It gets on my nerves sometimes. What I mind is not so much that they're there, but the reason they're there, which is that they positively worship Emma. How come my econ majors don't worship me? OK, maybe I'm not as passionate as Emma, maybe I'm not as witty in class, maybe I'm a little tougher on grades than she is. Well, I suppose that's enough to explain it, actually. And I admit that there may be the occasional student who would rather study Sexual Identity and the Historical Roots of Women's Oppression than Econometric Applications of Linear Regression Analysis. Personally, I can't imagine why, but some would. Anyway, the bottom line here is that, grouchy as she may sometimes be with them (not to mention me), Emma really and truly cares about her students. For many of them she feels genuine love. And genuine love is what they give her back.

Sara Grace came in and pulled off a jean jacket that was not nearly heavy enough for Iowa's winter, because among the students, being warm is not cool. A native Iowan and the child of an interracial marriage, Sara Grace is slender and beautiful with short, dark curly hair and deep brown eyes. She was wearing navy blue chinos and a yellow turtleneck that looked wonderful against her olive skin. I knew Emma thought her to be the brightest of the current crop of philosophy majors, and her intensity and passion reminded me of Emma as a student.

Sara Grace handed Emma a list and said, "These are the ones who've arrived so far, about two-thirds, I guess. I left Justin in charge of the registration desk." She looked at me and smiled.

"Do you want a soda, Sara Grace, or some coffee?" I asked her.

"Sure, thanks, I'll get a pop." From behind the refrigerator door she said, "I checked Dr. Stuhrm in at the inn, Emma. He seems really nice." Quite a few of Emma's students call her by her first name, a fact which may also help account for her popularity.

Emma frowned at the list, "Renee Amundsen isn't here yet? She was driving up from Champaign-Urbana." Renee had been Emma's thesis advisor at the University of Chicago. She was now at Illinois. Renee was a good friend and mentor to Emma and had been instrumental in getting Emma her chair at Hammond so that Emma and I could be together. I asked Emma why she'd arranged to put Renee at the inn instead of having her stay with us.

"I thought it would be better that way. I don't have time to be a good hostess. Plus we have that other stuff going on here at the house."

"What other stuff?" She gave me her don't-be-stupid look and I remembered about the sperm. "Oh, I forgot, we're expecting the swim team."

Her eyes narrowed to little slits. She asked Sara Grace a question before the girl had time to wonder what the hell we were talking about.

"So, you got Roger Stuhrm settled?"

"Yeah," she said, "he's so nice I couldn't believe it. He asked me what kind of philosophy I was interested in and what my future plans were and everything. I told him about my seminar paper on Weber and he offered to read it and give me comments. He said he might be able to help me get it published." Her eyes fairly danced at the prospect.

Emma and I exchanged a look. "Yeah, he's a sweetie, old Roger is," I said. "You know, speaking of Roger, he told me in the car that his paper has some big revelations about Weber. They're such a big deal he wouldn't even give Maria the paper to make copies. He was really a little rude about it, too."

"Yes, I've about had it with his antics," Emma said.

"What's his paper about?" Sara Grace asked.

"That's the problem, we don't know. Last summer he agreed to submit a piece on Weber and ethical theory. But this fall he went on sabbatical in Germany. He apparently found something over there, because two weeks ago, a week after his paper was supposed to have arrived here, he writes and tells us to cancel his old paper. He has a new one with exciting findings, he says. But he wouldn't even give the title of the new paper."

"Wow! What kind of stuff do you think he found?" Sara Grace said, "Maybe an unknown manuscript? Wouldn't it be cool if something like that was announced at our conference?"

I snickered. "Bear in mind, Sara Grace," I said, "that these are big revelations by philosophic standards. Roger probably 'discovered' that Weber's writing was far more influenced by the death of his cat Fluffy than was heretofore suspected."

"Oh, well now," Emma said, "I'm sure it won't be as exciting as your last paper, Claire. What was it called, 'Omitted Variable Bias in Recreation Demand Functions?' Yes, that was a real page-turner."

I raised a scornful eyebrow. "It was interesting to those of us who appreciate analytical rigor."

"Oh, yes, of course," she said, "analytical rigor. If you stick a bunch of numbers into a computer what emerges must naturally be rigorous, right? It must also be The Truth. You economists are so ridiculous."

"Well what do you people do?" I said. "All you talk about is, 'When Kirkegaard said this, did he really mean that?' Who cares? The guy is dead!"

"Well, at least we don't pretend to be a science. Do you really think economics could ever be like—"

In a loud voice Sara Grace said, "Maybe Dr. Stuhrm found someone in Weber's family." We were obviously making her quite uncomfortable. We had seen this in graduate school days when we'd argue for hours at Jimmy's Bar in Hyde Park; people can't always tell whether Emma and I are really fighting or just shooting our guns in the air.

"Oh yeah, that reminds me," I said, "that's something else Roger told me, that Weber disappeared. No one knows if he's dead or alive."

"Oh, that's no big deal," Emma said. "He does that from time to time. He vanished for a year while I was writing my doctoral dissertation about him. I kept thinking that if he turned up dead, I'd be sure to get it published as a book."

Sara Grace's eyes got wide at that.

"She's joking," I assured the girl untruthfully.

"Weber sounds like he's pretty strange," Sara Grace said, "for someone who is so, you know, so brilliant and all."

Emma sat for a second contemplating her student. "Actually, quite a few of the 'brilliant' types are borderline psychotic, in my opinion," Emma told her. "And, in Weber's case, rather nasty to boot."

"So how is Weber crazy?" I asked. Now that the topic had switched from philosophy to gossip I was mildly interested.

"He's paranoid, for one thing. He was always afraid the East German authorities were going to kidnap him and drag him back to East Germany. Maybe he's over that now that East Germany no longer exists, but I wouldn't bet on it. He's even paranoid about his name: constantly worried that people will confuse him with Max Weber, the famous sociologist." She looked up from her list and glanced at Sara Grace. "And that's not even the worst of it."

"By all means," I said, "let's hear the worst of it."

"He drinks constantly. As a professor he was a notorious lecher, and his proclivities ran to the youngest undergraduates. And there are rumors he routinely beat his three wives."

"Wow," Sara Grace said, "did you know him personally?"

"Well, I took a course from him at Freiburg during my junior year abroad. My roommate talked me into taking his seminar on Kant."

This roommate, I knew, was Karen Kling, Emma's first love. She was an American who, like Emma, was taking her junior year in Europe—from Swarthmore, I think. Emma cut short her trip when Karen committed suicide that spring.

Emma changed the subject. "Has Maria made copies of all the papers, all except Roger's?"

"Yes, they're in the registration packets."

I looked at Sara Grace and tried to imagine her as Karen; she was about the age Karen was when she died. Young, beautiful, full of promise. I felt a twinge of irrational jealousy.

"Your paper is on Weber and Spengler, right?" Sara Grace asked.

"Yes, Weber and Spengler on the Ideology of Language." Emma was looking at the list again.

"That's great," Sara Grace said. "I love the stuff Weber wrote with Spengler. Oppression and the Sense of Self, that was so moving and all."

"Uh huh." Emma was making check marks on the paper. "I find the Weber-Spengler work much more persuasive than Weber's other writings, which says to me who the real genius was in that duo."

As hard as it was to wrench myself from another episode of Philosophy Kitchen, I had a lot of things to do that afternoon. I put my napkin down on my plate and stood up. "Well, I think I'll go into my office and do some work. Unless, of course, you're going to make me pick up Spengler at the airport, too." They both stared at me. Sara Grace leapt at the chance to show her erudition.

"You can't."

"Oh no." I said, "Don't tell me he's disappeared, too!"

"Spengler was shot in 1965 while escaping from East Germany," Sara Grace said, apparently not sensing that I didn't care. "Weber's speech at his funeral has my favorite line in it: 'We must not mourn this tragedy, but embrace it, for tragedy and loss are the comrades of true freedom.'" She darted a glance at Emma to see, I assume, if Emma was impressed.

"Well, then," I said, adding my plate to the pile in the sink, "with Spengler gone there's nothing I can do but get on with my life."

"Ah...Claire," Emma said, "haven't you forgotten something? Someone has to wait here for the delivery?"

"What? Oh, come on, Emma, I thought we agreed that we already missed the delivery."

"Missed it? Claire, you were the one who said..." She stopped and glared at me.

"Well, why can't you wait for it?"

"Because I have to go to the inn and—"

"You know you don't have to wait here for a delivery," Sara Grace said.

"We don't?"

"No. You guys aren't used to small-town Iowa yet, are you? If you're not home, the delivery guy will just leave the package with your next-door neighbor. It happens to my Mom all the time."

Emma and I looked at each other wide-eyed—the sperm went to our next door neighbor?

CHAPTER FIVE

A short time later I was walking to my office, after arguing with Emma about walking to my office. She had wanted me to stay home all afternoon and wait for her delivery. We'd even argued about my using that phrase: "My delivery, Claire?" she'd said, "Not our delivery? You don't want us to have a baby?" Which gave me another good reason to go to the office; I sure didn't want to have that argument again. And when she couldn't get me to stay home and wait, she asked me to stop next door at the Leaches' house to see if the package was delivered there. The Leaches, septuagenarian heterosexuals who spent half their time in some church with a name like the First Cavalry Pentecostal Church of the Charismatic Nazarenes or something. The Leaches who were appalled even by the dandelions in our lawn, never mind our lesbian lifestyle. The Leaches, upon whose door I was supposed to knock and say, "Hi there, do you have some sperm that was meant for us?" She had to be kidding, right?

But the argument had depressed me, and I walked in a funk along the river that runs through campus, behind the library, toward the bridge to East Quadrangle. I like the walk into work, especially at times of the year when there is hardly anyone around. Ice clung to the big rocks that lay in huge piles along the embankment by the river. The East Campus bridge is made of great chunks of granite. Both bridge and stone were donated by a Minnesota alum in memory of two classmates killed in the Ardennes in 1918. Three weeks ago the bridge had been crowded with students walking to class. When the weather gets warm there are students hanging out on it until late in the evening, reading, sunning themselves, sitting and talking. Occasionally some frisbee types will show off by playing catch from opposite ends of the bridge, trying to avoid hitting pedestrians or sailing their frisbee into the muddy water. But today the bridge was entertaining only one guest besides myself, a young woman pushing a toddler in a big blue stroller. The child herself was all but undetectable amid the bundle of coat, hat, scarves and snowpants. As we passed on the crest of the bridge I smiled at the mother, who looked to be ten years younger than I. I assumed she was the mother. People would assume that about me when they saw me out strolling with Emma's baby. Oh, you have such a sweet baby, they'd say. And what would I say? Thank you, but she isn't really mine.

I have an office in Alumni Hall just over the bridge on the East Quadrangle. Emma's office, across campus in the Humanities building, has art posters on the walls, carefully arranged bookshelves, and a hand-woven rug she bought in Mexico. It's usually very tidy. My office, on the other hand, looks like the drop site for the Computer Paper Recycling Program. Stacks of computer printouts are everywhere, some of them three feet tall. In my bookshelves periodicals and books mix randomly, and little stick-on reminder notes cling to my walls like lichens on a tree trunk. Papers cover my desk to a depth of four inches. Normally I don't mind working in such a messy place, but when my mood is foul, as it was at that moment, I find the place pretty depressing.

I removed the bunch of papers piled on my chair, sat down at my computer and logged on to the electronic mail system. I don't get much e-mail during winter break. There was only one message, from a student surprised by his low grade in Microeconomics who wondered if he'd done badly on the final exam. I was tempted to respond, 'No, your final was a masterpiece of economic analysis; I gave you a D because your shirt was untucked.' I assured him that he had definitely done poorly on the final and said that I would put his exam in campus mail. I logged off my account and logged back onto Emma's to check her messages, as she'd asked me to do earlier. Her password is the name of some dead existentialist and it took me two tries to spell it right.

Emma had lots of e-mail, she always does. Several students thanked her for a 'wonderful semester,' or a 'course that changed my life.' Yak, yak, I thought as I scrolled past those messages. There was a note from the president's secretary reminding Emma about proper accounting for conference expenses. I felt sure Emma would appreciate her advice. A notice from the library demanded the immediate return of Russell's *History of Western Philosophy*.

There was also a message sent over the Internet from Georgetown University. It was from Cindy Stuhrm-Lawson, Roger's wife. Cindy had been part of that graduate school crowd that included Emma and Roger and me for a time, and I knew her slightly. Cindy's message was really for Roger; she was asking Emma to pass it on. She had finally finished writing some huge grant proposal to the U.S. Department of Education. She said her boss had thought it the best proposal he'd ever read and thought the chances for funding were extremely high. Cindy was apparently ecstatic. I liked Cindy and the message made me happy for her. She also said she was changing her plans. She was going to fly out and join Roger here in Iowa, and then go on to San Francisco with him after the conference. I copied the message to a file, downloaded it from the mainframe to my PC and printed it out on my inkjet printer. I was ripping off the printed sheet when someone behind me said, "Knock, knock."

There was a short, slightly pudgy man standing in my doorway. He had a round face, thick dark hair and a mustache with a few strands of grey in one corner. His paisley tie was loosened at the open collar of a white dress shirt. He carried a puffy rust-colored down coat.

"Marshall. How are you? You're on the wrong side of campus, you know."

He gave me an embarrassed smile and came into the office. "Well, I knew I was lost." He settled into my beat-up chintz guest chair. "I was taking a walk around campus and got a little disoriented. The sign outside said the economics department was in this building, so I thought I'd, uh, come in, and, uh, see if you were here, maybe ask directions." The embarrassed smile again.

"Well, lucky for me you did," I said with polite insincerity. "How've you been?" I knew Marshall from those long years when Emma and I were occasional lovers and we'd fly out to spend a few days together at a professional conference, hers or mine. I met him at some philosophers' meeting or other and I suppose I'd had dinner with him a few times. I only 'suppose' that because at those academic meetings we tend to go out to restaurants in big groups, and Marshall is not the type to stand out in a crowd.

"I'm good," he said. He nodded and looked at his shoe tips.

"Did you fly in from Lansing?" Marshall taught at Michigan State.

"No, no, I drove. Had some business in Chicago." He looked at me for a second then down at his shoes again.

A pause.

"So, you're here for the conference, right?" That question sounded stupid, but I didn't know what else to say.

"That's right. I came in this morning." He smiled again and looked back at his shoes, where someone must've been showing a film or something. So far this was painfully typical of my conversations with Marshall Udall. He was a very hard guy to talk to. This was a problem only because he always seemed to make a point of coming over to talk to me.

"So, did you come by yourself?"

His head came up quickly. "Oh, yes. I'm divorced. I have been for some time now."

"Ah, yeah, I know. I was thinking you might be traveling with a colleague."

"No, no, just me. A lone scholastic pilgrim, as it were." He smiled nervously and loosened his tie a little further. "It's a little warmer here than in Michigan," he said. He took a handkerchief from his back pocket and wiped his brow.

I thought Marshall a very nice man, but I am really not good with conversations that are full of lulls. For some reason they make me incredibly anxious.

"Marshall, I have to take a message to Emma at the inn. Why don't I walk you over there?" Cindy's message could have waited until later, but it was a good excuse to shorten his visit.

"OK, I'd like that very much."

I logged off the PC and locked my door as we left the office. We walked in awkward silence down the stairs and out the front of the building. I couldn't think of anything to jump start the conversation, so in desperation I stated the obvious.

"I assume you're giving a paper on Weber, like everyone else?"

"No, actually I'm not here presenting research, I'm conducting it."

I pounced on that opening like a starving cheetah. "Conducting research? Really?" I tried hard to sound intrigued.

"I'm writing a biography of Weber. A number of the presenters here knew him personally, so I'm going to do some interviews."

"Then I guess this conference will really come in handy for you." We made a left and walked across East Quad toward the river.

"Yes, I'm quite excited about it." He relaxed noticeably as he warmed to his subject. "So much has been written about Weber's work but almost nothing about his life. And he's had a very interesting life, you know."

"Yes, I've been hearing about it." Too much, actually. "It sounds like his life would make an interesting book." I relaxed too, this conversation seemed to have cleared the trees at the end of the runway. "Whom do you plan to interview?"

"Oh, well, let's see. Kurt Burghoff was a close friend of Weber's. They were at Goettingen University together. In fact, Weber was instrumental in getting Burghoff out of East Germany after he was arrested."

"Really? I didn't know that." I had no idea who Kurt Burghoff was.

"Oh, definitely. And there are a few fellows who'll be here who knew Weber as a student. Actually, your late colleague John Marchak was a boyhood friend of Weber's."

"Was he? That's very interesting," I said, exaggerating wildly.

"And, let's see, I suppose I'll interview Renee Amundsen. She and Weber were lovers at one time."

What? Emma's mentor? My gossip detector began buzzing loudly. "No kidding? Renee Amundsen had a thing with Weber?"

"Sure. Of course, it was a long time ago, in the late '60s when Renee was still his student." Marshall chuckled. "Yeah, there are plenty of ex-student-lovers of Weber's around, at least the ones who haven't killed themselves."

Suddenly Marshall stopped dead in his tracks. He turned toward me, his face pale and strained, and he reached out to hold my elbow.

"Claire, I'm so sorry, what an awful thing to say." Looking at his horror-struck face I nearly laughed.

"Marshall, why're you so upset? It's me, Claire, remember? The Mid-western Queen of Tasteless Humor."

My reaction calmed him a little, but he was still visibly upset. "Yes, thank God it was you and not Emma. What if I'd said something like that in front of her?" He shook his head.

That seemed an odd thing to say. "Why? Emma wouldn't joke like that herself, but she isn't so much of a wet blanket that she'd get mad at you for doing it." We started walking again, climbing up the bridge over to West Campus.

"I was thinking of her roommate at Freiburg," Marshall said, "the one who committed suicide—"

"Oh, I see."

"—after her affair with Weber ended."

That knocked the wind out of me.

After a few seconds I said, "Marshall, are you saying that Karen Kling killed herself because of Weber?" Holy shit, I thought, Emma never told me that.

"Well…yes. At least that's the speculation; she didn't leave a note. But she and Weber were definitely sleeping together—that came out after the suicide. He apparently dumped her for some other student and Karen killed herself. It was a scandal at the time. She was thirty-five years his junior and that's the reason Weber left Freiburg." Marshall gave me a puzzled look. "Claire, didn't you know all this?"

I felt very embarrassed not to have known. "I knew about the suicide, I didn't know the rest of the story. Emma had told me about Karen, but she'd never said anything about a Weber connection." This certainly explained a lot about her professional hostility towards him.

"Listen, Claire. I'm really sorry to have surprised you like that. I assumed you knew."

I patted the back of his puffy coat. "No, no, Marshall. It's no big deal. It was a long time ago. She probably told me and I forgot." Could that be true? I certainly have a reputation for forgetting things Emma told me; every trip to the grocery store gave testimony to that. No, I thought, this I would definitely have remembered.

We walked in silence for a time, and then I said, "So anyway, tell me more about your book." Marshall was happy to do that as we walked behind the library and across West Campus.

In a few minutes we turned up the walkway to the inn. It's a large 19th century brick house, not quite a mansion, which was originally the home of the college president. Now it mainly houses visitors to the college. It was busy on this day, with all sorts of well-dressed people coming and going. Most of them were probably trustees and alumni here to plan the big capital campaign the college was set to launch in the spring.

"Here you are, Marshall, safe and sound."

"Aren't you coming in?"

"No, I have to run some errands." I really didn't feel like going in there, I was in no mood to talk to Emma. I also wanted to get back to work.

"OK, well, thanks Claire."

"See you later Marshall." I smiled at him and turned back up the sidewalk, still thinking about Karen Kling.

The message from Roger's wife sat in my pocket, undelivered.

CHAPTER SIX

I was late as usual when I started getting ready to join Emma and her colleagues for dinner. I was supposed to meet her at the inn and walk over to dinner at Benning Hall with the conference group. It took an exasperating fifteen minutes to find the purple blouse that went with my black skirt, a blouse I was certain I'd washed on Friday in anticipation of this dinner. I'd searched my closet twice and Emma's closet once, and was about to go mad when I realized that I could remember putting the blouse in the dryer but not taking it out. I went down to the basement and looked in the dryer where my poor blouse had spent the weekend. Then I had to spend ten minutes ironing the damn thing, ten minutes I'd allocated to cleaning the scuffs off my black dress shoes. All this is by way of saying that my mood, as I hurried to rejoin Emma and the Weberites, could not be accurately described as 'festive.' Walking as fast as I could in mid-heeled shoes I'd be lucky to make it to the inn before they left for dinner.

And then what happened? On my way across campus I'd found that man, that fellow lying unconscious on the sidewalk at the campus bridge. And so I ran around trying to find an emergency phone to call help, only to return to that spot and find the sidewalk empty. All I found was a scrap of memo paper that said, 'Please call 555-8519' in Emma's handwriting. I decided that the man on the sidewalk must be part of the conference, which explained his having a note from Emma, and that he had regained consciousness after a fall to the sidewalk and made his way to the inn. I planned to check on him there to see if he was all right.

The inn's main living room, which serves as a lobby, was crowded with people talking and drinking. The opening speech must have run long because they were still enjoying pre-prandial cocktails. There were, I would guess, about forty people milling around. I scanned the room for the fellow from the sidewalk. I saw Emma standing by the portable bar talking to a grey-haired man in a dark suit, but it wasn't my grey-haired man. I hurried over and interrupted the conversation. "Will you excuse me one second," I said to the fellow she was talking to. He nodded politely. I leaned over and whispered to Emma about the fellow I'd found lying by the bridge. Her brow knitted and she looked around the room.

"I don't think anyone's missing," she said. "What did he look like?" I described the old man to her. She frowned and scanned the room again. "I don't know who that could be, it doesn't sound like one of our people."

The man she'd been conversing with smiled at me and said, "I am sure that it is I who represent the elderly at this conference. That is what I believe you Americans call affirmative action?"

Emma gave a high-pitched laugh that seemed affected and said, "Oh, I'm sure you will bury us all, Professor." To me she said, "Why don't you check with Sara Grace, she has the conference list. Besides, she has a message for you."

"OK." I turned and walked only three steps before running into Sara Grace, bright and beautiful in that yellow turtleneck.

"Hi, Dr. Sinclair, I have a message for you."

"So I heard."

She gave a giggling sort of laugh and looked around. "It took a while to find you, with all these professors in here." Her eyes were alert and excited; it was obvious how happy she was to be part of this conference. That made one of us.

"Who's the message from?"

"Emma. She wants you to call the liquor store on Main Street and check on the bottle of…" She looked at a slip of paper in her hand. "…porte…fino. It was ordered special. And if it's come in, could you run down and get it?"

So Emma tells me that Sara Grace has a message for me, and the message is from her, I thought. I considered sending back a message about relocating that liquor store somewhere besides Main Street.

"All right, Sara Grace, I'll take care of it. But I need you to check on something for me." I asked her to go around looking at name tags to verify that all the men on the conference list were here in the room. I sighed and walked to an end table on the far side of the lobby where there is usually a telephone that can make local calls. There is also usually a phone book sitting there, but on this particular occasion, I noticed without the slightest surprise, it had arranged to take a leave of absence. Colin Jensen was standing a few feet away talking to a couple of youngish women. I called to him and he came over.

"Colin, what's the number of Jake's Wine and Spirits on Main Street?" He stiffened his back and gave me a look of mock umbrage.

"Now what makes you think I'd know that number?"

"You're young, single, and stuck out in the cornfields in the dead of winter, so you must be on intimate terms with the liquor store." He laughed, his dark eyes crinkling up at the corners.

"As it turns out, I do just happen to know that number."

"I thought so."

"It's 555-2970."

"Wait a minute, could you write it down for me?"

"Write it down? You economists are supposed to be so quantitative—you can't remember seven digits?"

"That's the problem, Colin. I've got a lot of numbers crammed in my head: GDP, the Consumer Price Index, the elasticity of demand for sweat socks. There's no room in there for mere phone numbers."

"I see."

He took a pen out of one pocket of his jacket and felt around in the others for something to write on. Out came a stack of business cards an inch thick. He wrote the number on the back of one of them and handed it to me. The card had red and blue lettering on heavy grey paper and was embossed at the top with the seal of the college.

"My, my, what's this?" I said, admiring the card. "Colin Avignon Jensen, Ph.D.," I read aloud. "Assistant Professor of Philosophy, Hammond College. Boy, you even have a fax number on here." Colin looked embarrassed, and I suppose I was being a trifle mean. It's by no means unusual for professors to have business cards. But Colin, I knew, was passing these out for a special reason. "So, Colin," I said, "doing some serious networking at this conference?"

He looked over his shoulder to see if anyone had heard. I patted the cushion beside me on the couch and Colin plopped down while I dialed the number.

"It's OK," I said while the number was ringing. "Everyone knows you have ambitions to get out of Hammond. No one's going to hold that against you." (I was lying, some of the senior faculty might well hold it against him.)

"It's not like I don't like the people here," he said.

I held up my hand as a woman at the liquor store answered the phone. I asked about the order and she went to check.

"It's just that Hammond is oriented so much toward teaching," Colin said. "I need a place that emphasizes research. If I want to get anywhere in this business I need to be around people who are publishing like I am. Emma's great, but the truth is she's about all this school has." He shrugged. "Hammond's a nice place, I just think maybe I can do a little better, that's all."

I nodded. It was true, Hammond isn't one of the stops on the academic fast track.

"It isn't there yet?" I said into the phone. "Do you think you can tell me when it will come in?...I see, OK, thanks a lot." I hung up. "I understand, Colin, really," I said. "You and Hammond may not be a good match, that's all."

I changed the subject. "Listen, why am I calling about one bottle of wine, anyway? Why did Emma order this stuff?"

"I'll bet it's for Kurt Burghoff."

"Who's Kurt Burghoff?" I thought I'd heard that name before.

"He's a big name philosopher Emma invited to the conference." Colin looked around the room, apparently scanning for this Burghoff guy. "I haven't had a chance to meet him yet."

"But...," I said, brandishing his business card, "I bet you will, won't you Colin?" He lowered his head and smiled sheepishly. I put his card in the pocket of my skirt and stood up to go look for Emma.

"Claire."

"Renee!" She stood a few feet away with a young man I didn't recognize. "So you finally made it up here." I hugged her. "You look pretty smashing for such an old broad." This was not idle flattery. For a woman of almost fifty years, Renee Amundsen was strikingly handsome. Trim and tall, she had a smooth face with high cheekbones and deep blue eyes. Her hair was sandy-colored and the accumulating grey hairs, which she made no attempt to disguise, nicely complemented her mature, elegant features. She held both my hands and tilted her head to one side as she smiled at me. It was really good to see Renee.

"Claire, this is Fritz Mazowski from San Jose State. Fritz, this is Claire Sinclair, Emma's partner. Claire teaches economics."

"Ah, an economist," he said. We shook hands. "What sort of economist are you?" Fritz had a thin beard and dark hair and looked like a gangly teenage boy. He wore brown corduroy pants and a green shirt with no jacket. On his head sat a black beret. Really.

"I teach environmental economics and econometrics," I said. "My research is mostly on environmental issues."

"Environmental issues? Really? I thought you economists only cared about economic growth. You know, the other day I was reading a paper about how the so-called 'victory' of capitalism over socialism is sure to accelerate the pace of environmental degradation. That seems inevitable to me, don't you agree?"

There were only two sensible responses to this question: 1) 'No, actually I think that's bullshit,' and 2) 'Will you excuse me? I have a dental appointment.' Years of hanging out with Emma's friends had taught me that when talking to a philosopher, response #2 was the preferred option. Arguing with these people is maddening. The argument will rarely ever really make any headway because the philosophers don't necessarily want it to. They are professional arguers, it is the process of discussion that interests them most, not the conclusion on a particular topic. And, needless to say, you can never *win* an argument with a philosopher. Even if you make a couple of good thrusts and parries in debating your point, they can always fall back on some off-the-wall defense like, 'Your argument is valid only if the universe exists, and we can't be sure it does.'

"Well, ah, I don't know," I said to Fritz. "We should talk about it sometime."

"But you will agree," he held up a finger, "that a social system based on profit will never value a clean environment because it has no market value?"

I shrugged. "Well, that's an interesting question. Maybe after dinner we could..."

"It's undeniable," he said, "that by assigning everything a price, as capitalism does, we degrade the sanctity of the natural environment. You economists are partly to blame for this."

"Excuse me?"

"Your discipline has provided the social justification for environmental destruction."

"Oh, we have, have we?"

"Absolutely. Your theories have extolled capitalism's efficiency while ignoring its moral illegitimacy."

"I see. Well if capitalism is the problem, Fritz, how do you explain that socialist countries like Poland, Czechoslovakia, and East Germany degraded their environments much more than the capitalist West?" Ha! That'll shut him up.

He smiled. "I don't consider those countries to have been socialist."

"Not socialist? You must be joking."

"Not at all," he said. "What you had in the former Soviet Bloc was not true socialism but a form of state-based capitalism. See? You economists don't even know the nature of true socialism."

I set my phaser on full sarcasm. "Please correct me if I'm wrong, Fritz, but it was my impression that in the Soviet Bloc there was state ownership of all the means of production—"

A glass started tinkling somewhere.

"—prices were set entirely by fiat—"

The tinkling got louder.

"—and production output was centrally planned. Now if that's capitalism, I'd like to—"

Renee put her hand on my arm. I stopped sputtering and turned toward the sound of the tinkling, which had now turned into Emma's voice.

"Madames et Messieurs, bonsoir et bienvenue. Wilkommen und guten Abend." Her smile was radiant, as though she couldn't be more thrilled than to host this conference. "Most philosophers will acknowledge that the mind cannot be stimulated if the body is not sustained. In other words, it's dinnertime." A smattering of laughter. "Spinoza said, 'All things excellent are as difficult as they are rare.' We have an excellent dinner for you, but we must all face the difficulty of walking to it." The crowd chuckled. "I assure you, however, that the beef will be rare without being difficult." Laughter all around, a few hands clapping. "So if we could all put on our coats, we can walk over to the dining hall as a group. It's not a very long walk."

I marveled once again at the Great Emma Paradox. The public Emma was so poised, so witty, so confident. Why was the private Emma such a cathedral of insecurity?

People started moving toward the coat closet by the front door. "That was an interesting discussion," Fritz said. "We should continue it sometime."

"Yes…it was." I felt really stupid for having become so vehement. Fritz walked away and Renee took my arm as we moved toward the door. She put her mouth close to my ear.

"Emma told me she wants to get pregnant," she said.

"Yeah, she's supposed to start trying this week. It's kind of a secret, by the way." Renee nodded. "I'll tell you, Renee, that and this conference have her in an absolute, force-five tizzy."

"That's Emma all right. Not at her best under this kind of pressure."

I watched Renee put on a snug-fitting suede jacket and remembered what Marshall had told me about her affair with Weber. I tried to imagine her as a young graduate student. She would've been gorgeous, no doubt about it. I wondered if Emma had known about that relationship.

It was pretty cold outside by this time of evening, but Emma's people, still warm and jolly from liquor and companionship, were chatting merrily as we started across campus. Sara Grace had gotten the point and Emma was walking back along the column counting her sheep. She worked her way down to Renee and me at the tail-end of the party.

"Hi, Claire," she said.

"Hi." I had time to remember our fight this afternoon and I still felt some residual anger.

Renee obviously sensed the tension. "Emma, I need to talk to Arnie Cohen before his session tomorrow," she said. "I'm going to move up and see if I can find him. I'll see you guys at dinner." She walked off.

In a near whisper Emma asked, "Was there any word at home about the package?"

"Yes," I said, not looking at her. "Mrs. Leach left a message on our machine. It's at her house. We can pick it up in the morning." I kept my voice level—not warm, not cold, just matter-of-fact.

"Good," she said. "Thank you."

"You're welcome."

We walked along in silence for a while. "Is something the matter, Claire?"

"No."

The troops entered Central Quad and proceeded west toward the river. Cold, hungry, and unfortified with alcohol, I personally would have liked them to move a little faster. My fellow travelers seemed quite content, however. Eventually Emma said, "Roger asked me to thank you for picking him up at the airport."

I doubted that very much but I appreciated the gesture of conciliation. "No problem," I said.

Again we walked in silence for a while. The troops were moving along the river behind the library.

"Marshall told me he went to your office," she said.

"Yeah, Marshall came by. Talked my ear off." That reminded me of the business about Karen Kling, but this certainly was no time to bring that up.

She leaned close to me. "Did he propose?"

"What!" I whipped my head around and stared at her. She was giggling.

"He has a crush on you, Claire, can't you tell?"

"Oh, be quiet!" I had to laugh a little. "How many glasses of wine have you had?"

"Too many, that's for sure." Her hand came out and held me lightly by the arm. We were on the west side of the river approaching the bridge to East Campus. I'd adjusted to the cold by now and the still night air began to feel good to me.

"Oh, speaking of Marshall, Emma, I remember now. I walked him over to the inn so I could give you a message that—"

At that moment someone shouted. A sudden commotion erupted up at the head of the column, as two men in the front ran over the bridge and down the opposite bank of the river. For a second people froze in place as the men climbed off the river walk and down onto the large rocks that lay at the base of the bridge. There are not many streetlights along this river walk, something campus women have complained about more than once, but there was enough light to see the men bending over someone lying across the

43

rocks. The form was on its left side with its head against a large boulder and its arms out in front. The hands looked almost as if they were folded.

Everyone moved ahead quickly. Emma yelled to Sara Grace from the top of the bridge.

"Sara Grace, run and call security. Tell them to send an ambulance."

We rushed down to the opposite bank. The crowd parted for Emma, and I moved through in her wake. We both climbed down onto the rocks where two men were squatting by the injured person. I recognized the man instantly; it was the fellow I had found on the sidewalk earlier. One of the two discoverers turned from the body and said to me, "I'm pretty sure he's dead. I can't find a pulse."

A pang of nausea shot through my stomach. He must have been alive when I found him and then wandered over here and fallen again. Should I have done something more than I did? Should I have looked around until I found him again? I turned to tell Emma that this was the guy I'd told her about, the one I had found on the sidewalk earlier.

Emma wasn't there. I looked up and down the riverbank for her. She was standing over by the far end of the crowd, holding Renee's hand as the latter climbed down off the river walk onto the rocks. The two of them came over, stepping carefully on the small boulders, and looked down at what I was already thinking of as 'the dead body.'

"Sweet Jesus," Renee said. It was almost a whisper. "You're right, that's Erik Weber."

CHAPTER SEVEN

Having grown up in Brooklyn, I can point out many advantages of small-town life over that bumper-to-bumper endurance test one faces daily in cities and suburbs. But good ethnic restaurants are not among them. To make a profit, a good ethnic restaurant requires a certain critical mass of local humanity, and little towns like ours usually can't provide it. And many academics, at least academics of the snootier sort, which is a large fraction of the total, take great pride in claiming to have palates so sophisticated they must have steady access to ethnic cuisine. Without it, survival is impossible. Quite impossible.

The point here is that Emma was worried about feeding her conferees. There were few local restaurants that would suit her needs, so it was decided that for most of the conference meals would be provided by the college's food service. Unlike most colleges, Hammond doesn't contract its food service to outside vendors. It owns and operates the system that feeds the dormitories and runs the campus snack bar. The results, in my opinion, are surprisingly good. The students complain about the food some, but that goes without saying. College students would no more praise dormitory meals than an eighth-grader would say, "My parents are really cool, and their views on teen fashion are right on the money." It just isn't done.

But on this occasion the campus chefs were supposed to feed two score of Emma's most influential colleagues, all of whom would judge this conference partly on the basis of what showed up on their plates. She had told me earlier how anxious she'd be as she led the crowd into that first meal of the conference. It turned out that Emma was spared that anxiety. By showing up dead near the river walk, Weber had relieved Emma of the need to even attend the opening dinner. (Though that was probably not his motive.)

After the discovery of Weber's body, the police had been summoned, of course, and I had told them about finding him earlier, a few yards away at the foot of the bridge. It seemed obvious that after I found him he had recovered somewhat and tried to walk away, only to stumble fatally over the stone wall of the bridge and onto the rocks below. At first I felt awful, if I had only looked down from the top of the bridge, I might have seen him and could have helped. But a paramedic assured me that his head had been so damaged by the fall that he had probably died by the time I returned there. In any case, as soon as Weber's body was taken to the hospital, Emma and Renee went off to the police station and Sara Grace and I led the rest of the participants to dinner at Benning Hall. It was not, perhaps, the ideal time for a meal, but there really wasn't much else to do with them.

The mood at dinner was hard to describe. Perhaps we could call it *pseudo-somber*. From every table came voices that were hushed and respectful, but also clearly animated. An important scholarly figure, one who'd influenced each of their lives, was dead. A sad event, certainly. But still, within the small circle of academic philosophy, his death was pretty hot news, and they had been present when it happened. Obviously, in general, they found this exciting.

"The irony of this is staggering," said someone named Arnie Cohen, sitting at my table. "Classic Weber: full of surprises, right to the end." Arnie appeared to be in his early fifties. His nametag didn't identify his university. There were four others at the table besides Arnie and me. These included Marshall Udall, the guy who'd come to my office that afternoon, and young Colin from Emma's department. I didn't know the other two. "The man dies attending a conference on his own work," Arnie said. "A conference he wasn't even invited to."

"That's right, isn't it, Claire?" Marshall asked me. "Emma didn't invite Weber, did she?"

"Well, my involvement in this conference is extremely peripheral," I pointed out firmly, "but I don't see how Emma could have invited him. She told me nobody knew where he was."

"He could quite easily have found out about it," said a plain-looking woman in her mid-thirties sitting beside Marshall. Her name tag said Melanie Hollister: University of Connecticut. "He probably saw an announcement in one of the professional journals."

"I don't think there was one," Arnie said, looking at me for confirmation.

I exaggerated my shrug to assure him that I hadn't the foggiest idea whether there was or not. "Well, I never saw one," Arnie said. "Did anyone else?" No one else had.

A hand touched my shoulder. Maria, whispering in my ear, asked if I knew where Emma was. Maria must have come to the dining hall early to work on dinner preparations. When I explained to her quietly about Weber's death, she held a hand to her mouth. The table conversation continued around us as I sketched out the basic circumstances of the accident.

Maria just shook her head when I finished the story. "Oh, Emma, the poor dear," she said, "I hope she is all right." She looked down at a clipboard she was holding. "The reason I need her is that someone has to sign the form charging this dinner to the right account." She handed me a clipboard, which had a Food Service form on it. I stared at the form helplessly.

"I don't know the account number, Maria."

"I wrote it down already."

"Oh. Yeah. Um…listen, can't you sign it, Maria?"

"No, it needs to be a faculty member."

With a deep sigh, I signed my name and my department. My contribution to this conference was supposed to have consisted of going to a reception, eating a meal or two, and making a little small talk. Now here I was signing things. It did not bode well.

"Do you think they will cancel the conference now?" Maria asked. Her eyes were intense, her brow furrowed. I knew she'd been working for weeks with Emma to set this thing up, and now it looked like it all might collapse. I feebly tried to reassure her.

"I don't think so. I'm not sure, but Emma didn't say anything about canceling it."

"Well, all right then, thank you." She took the clipboard and walked away, not looking very reassured.

I turned back to the table conversation, Melanie was talking.

"…and anyway, who knew where Weber was? How to contact him? Does anyone know who was still in touch with him?" Head-shaking all around. A student waiter came over and refilled one or two wine glasses. Not surprisingly under the circumstances, the crowd was fairly swilling the special Chardonnay Emma had chosen for this dinner. I started worrying that we might run out.

"This situation is not looking good for Hammond College," said an Indian or Pakistani fellow with a wispy black beard whose name tag read Rupesh Kapur: UC San Diego. "I am predicting that there will be a very big lawsuit."

"Oh Lord," I groaned, "I hadn't thought about that. Will the college be held liable for Weber's death, do you think?" Now there was a depressing thought. Emma, for whom it's a short walk from anxiety to paranoia, would worry that if some legal problem resulted from her conference the college would blame her. Even more depressing was my suspicion that her fear would not be entirely unfounded.

"Why isn't there a railing along that bridge?" Melanie asked me.

"Oh, they've been trying to put one up for years, but the students always protest. They say the administration is being paternalistic."

"That sounds like students, all right," Arnie said.

"Well, I think Weber was drunk," Melanie said. "I could smell alcohol when he went past me on the stretcher. That should eliminate your liability, shouldn't it?"

"It goes without saying that Weber was drunk," Arnie said. "He always was. But that won't help your case much. No," he added cheerfully, "sounds like a lawsuit to me. You'd better hope that Weber was murdered."

"Are you thinking that is a serious possibility?" Rupesh asked.

"Of course!" Arnie said.

"Who would want to kill a man like Weber?"

"Who'd want to kill him? Are you serious?" Arnie said. "Look, if the police need a murder suspect, I suggest they put everyone who knew Weber in a large room and toss a rock up in the air, it will land on someone who wanted him dead." He took a big gulp of wine. "Weber had all kinds of enemies. Disgruntled colleagues, jealous husbands, ex-wives, you name it. Hell, didn't Platburg threaten to kill him over that plagiarism thing?"

"No, Arnie, he did not," Colin said from the far end of the table. "Come hear my paper tomorrow. That supposed threat was fabricated by Weber to cover up his own guilt."

"You know, I don't agree with you, Colin," Marshall said. "I think Platburg did have a vendetta against Weber. That's why he made up the plagiarism charge."

"He didn't make it up," Colin shot back. "When you look at the writing—"

"Doesn't matter." Arnie waved a dismissive hand at Colin. "The point is that the man had enemies. There must be a dozen suspects in this dining room alone. Marshall, you're Weber's biographer, tell them."

Marshall looked uncomfortable. "Well, certainly a number of people here knew him, but you can't seriously suggest someone here would—"

"Of course I can suggest it!" Arnie put a large hand on Marshall's shoulder. "In fact, Marshall here is my prime suspect." Marshall's eyebrows rose.

"What makes you suspect him, Arnie?" I asked. "Is it that sense of quiet menace lurking beneath his calm demeanor?" I smiled at Marshall; his cheeks colored.

"Well, that too, of course," Arnie said. "But I was mainly thinking how much Marshall will benefit from this untimely 'accident.'" He took a bite of salmon from his plate. "First of all, there will be no further years of Weber's life to report. That should significantly cut his research time. Second, the biographer can now claim to have been present at his subject's death, that will look very good on the book jacket. And, in general of course, biographies of dead people are always more satisfying than those of people still living. With live subjects the book seems so…premature, you know?"

"But are you not forgetting, Arnie," Rupesh said, "that Claire found Weber on the sidewalk before he fell off the bridge? He could not have been murdered."

"The perfect ruse!" Arnie said. "That was the plan, you see: Marshall lures Weber to a remote part of campus and knocks him cold. He hides under the bridge, waiting for someone to come along and find Weber. He knows that the person who finds Weber will have to run off to call an ambulance, at which point Marshall jumps out, whacks Weber again and tosses him off the bridge. Voilà, everyone concludes he had to have recovered, then stumbled off the bridge." He took another drink of wine. "Damned ingenious, Marshall, my hat's off to you."

"But what about motive, Arnie?" Melanie said. "With Weber dead Marshall has no chance to write that second volume, *Erik Weber: the Declining Years*."

"Oh, now that's a good point, Melanie, I'd missed that." Arnie patted Marshall's shoulder again. "But don't worry, Marshall. This murder should boost sales enough on your first volume to make up the difference. No doubt you have already calculated that." He raised his wine glass at a passing waitress. She poured Arnie some more Chardonnay, then made several stops around the table.

Marshall smiled throughout this exchange, but was clearly embarrassed by all the teasing.

"There's a significant problem with your murder theory," I told Arnie. "The conference participants all have an alibi, they were at the opening talk when the murder was committed."

"Hmmm, you're right," Arnie said. He stroked his chin. "By God, you are diabolical, Marshall. However did you pull this off?"

"Well, you know, we can't be sure Marshall was actually at the opening talk the whole time," Colin said. "He could've shown up at the beginning, sneaked out and murdered Weber, then popped back in time for the cocktail party. People would just assume he'd been there the whole time."

"Of course!" Arnie said. Wine sloshed onto the tablecloth as he pointed at Colin with the glass in his hand. "That's how he did it. Brilliant. An airtight alibi." He slapped a hand against the table. "Oh, Marshall, if only your genius could've been used for the good of mankind instead of for evil."

At this point Marshall was staring down at his plate and shaking his head. Others at the table were in various states of amusement.

"What I don't understand, Marshall," Melanie said, "is how you knew Weber would be coming to the conference at that precise moment? How did you arrange for him to be walking through that part of campus in the middle of the opening talk? If he'd arrived at the beginning or the end, your plan would've been ruined."

"Don't you see?" I answered Melanie. "It must have been Marshall who told Weber about the conference. As his biographer, he discovered Weber's secret hideout and invited him to come. I say 'invited' though it was more likely blackmail." (Marshall rolled his eyes at that.) "But he gave him the wrong time. Weber thought the conference started later than it did and he was walking up to register when Marshall jumped up and shoved him off the river walk."

"Fiendishly clever." Arnie raised his wine glass to signify a toast. "My friends, I give you biographer Marshall Udall. He may be a ruthless killer, but the man sure knows how to end a book."

We all clinked glasses and said, "Here, here." Marshall kept shaking his head while Melanie patted his back affectionately.

I noticed that people at other tables had turned to stare at us.

"I hope you get away with this Marshall," Sam Dawson said. "Claire, does Iowa have the death penalty?"

"In Iowa, death is not a penalty." That came from someone standing directly behind me. "Anyone stuck here would welcome execution." It was Roger Stuhrm. He put a hand on my shoulder and bent down next to my ear. "Could I speak with you a minute?"

He stepped back and motioned me away from the table. We wove our way among the crowded tables and went over to the side of the dining hall. On the way I noticed that the room had gotten louder, conversations seemed more relaxed and laughter floated up from a number of different places.

"There's some speculation that the conference will be canceled," Roger said. "Do you think it will?"

"I have no idea, Roger."

"Well, I think cancellation would be a big mistake. This conference is an important event, even more so now that this accident has occurred. I hope you'll use your influence to keep it going."

"My influence? Jeez, I don't know Roger, I was saving up my influence to bring about world peace."

"I'm serious, Claire. Emma listens to you. I want you to tell her that the people in this room do not want the conference canceled. In fact, now that he's dead, they see the conference as a fitting tribute to Weber's memory." I didn't ask Roger how he knew what all the people in the room were thinking.

"I don't even know if Emma can make that decision, Roger. This accident might cause the college legal problems. The administration could step in and cancel the conference for reasons of its own." That prospect seemed to enrage him.

"Why the hell would they do that? It would be damned lousy public relations to bring all of these people out to the boonies, then send them right back for no good reason."

I shrugged. "College administrators react conservatively to crises, you know that. Look, all I'm saying is that lobbying Emma may not do much good in this circumstance. But I'll be happy to pass on your message, if that's what you want."

He frowned at me for a moment. "Fine," he said. "Thank you."

There was a loud tinkling of glass. At a table near the center of the room a man was standing at his chair and tapping his knife against a water goblet. The room fell silent. I recognized this man as the one I'd seen talking to Emma earlier at the inn. He was tall, silver-haired and distinguished looking, at what I guessed to be seventy or more years of age. He wore a white shirt and blue tie under a dark suit. Rather a striking figure, I thought. His accent, when he spoke, was heavily Teutonic, probably German.

"My many friends and colleagues, tonight we have witnessed the tragic passing of a great man and scholar, a man whose work we have gathered here to admire. This comes as a great shock to us all. Could I ask you please for a moment of silence in memory of Erik Weber?"

All around the room people bowed their heads, and most closed their eyes. I bowed my head too, but my eyes searched the room surreptitiously. Someone in here must have known Weber was coming, because one of them apparently told him about the conference. I supposed that whoever had informed him would tell everyone soon enough. Why wouldn't he?

After a moment the silver-haired man said, "Thank you," and sat back down.

"Who was that?" I asked Roger.

"That's Kurt Burghoff, Professor Emeritus at Ohio State. I don't know how Emma got him here, but it was certainly a real coup."

"Is he a big gun?"

"Very. He's an old friend of Weber's."

And that, apparently, was enough chitchat for Roger. "Please remember to tell Emma what I said about canceling the conference," he instructed me. He turned and walked away.

"Why certainly, I'd be happy to," I called to his back.

"Claire?" Maria stood behind me wiping her hands on a dishcloth.

"Everything is set now. The students will clean up. I think I will be going home, if that is all right."

That statement filled me with unreasoning dread.

"Maria," I said, grabbing her elbow. "Emma isn't back yet. What am I supposed to do with all these people?"

"Nothing," she said. "Just take them back to the inn. There will be night-caps served at nine o'clock if anybody wants one." She looked at her watch. "If you are really worried I suppose I could stay."

"No, no," I said. "That's OK, you go home. I'll be fine."

She said goodnight and went out through the kitchen. I considered what to do next. The situation was momentarily stable, dessert and coffee were being served. There was a payphone in the hallway by the door and I decided to nip out and make a quick call home. There was a slight chance that Emma would go there directly from the police station.

As I expected, no one answered at our house. When my own voice invited me to leave my name and number, I pressed '3' to play back our phone messages. I figured Emma might've called home from the station knowing I would check our messages.

There was only one message. A man's voice said, "Hello, this is Oscar Lamb of the *Cedar Rapids Gazette*. I'd like to talk to Dr. Emma Harrington about the death of Erik Weber. My number is 555-2770, and I'll be here all evening. If possible I'd appreciate a call tonight so that I can make the deadline for the morning edition. Thanks very much."

To say I was 'surprised' by this message would be like saying Weber was 'inconvenienced' by the injury to his head. How in the world did the *Gazette* find out about this already? The body was discovered only an hour before, and almost everyone who knew about it was in the room behind me. Why would any of them call a newspaper? I was sure Emma had informed the president's office by now, but they wouldn't blurt the news out quickly, they'd want to control how the information was released to the press.

I felt around in my skirt pocket to find a piece of paper to write the reporter's number down, and pulled out a small piece of Hammond College memo paper. The sight of that paper hit me like a slap. I stared down at it for five or six seconds trying to comprehend its meaning, trying to understand its very existence. Please call 555-8519. Emma's handwriting is unmistakable: frail, thin and terribly squiggly, like a prescription from a ninety-year-old doctor who's had seven cups of coffee. I had found this note by the old man's body, Weber's body. He must have had it on his person, probably in his hand when he fell. How could Emma say she didn't know him? How could it be the case that she didn't invite him? The man was carrying a note from her.

CHAPTER EIGHT

The philosophy troops had hiked safely back to the inn and were peeling off coats, scarves and winter hats when Renee walked through the front door. Emma wasn't with her. I was standing at the desk, waiting to inquire about the refreshments Maria had mentioned. Renee came right over to me. People crowded around us to hear whatever news she had, but I first wanted to know where Emma was.

"I made Emma go home," Renee said. "She's very upset and needs to get some rest." There was a general murmur of understanding from the group. "The news is this: that was, in fact, Erik Weber who was found, and he was dead when we found him. Apparently he fell and hit his head on those rocks he was lying on. They haven't done an autopsy yet, but it seems clear that he'd been drinking heavily."

"I'd better get home then," I said. I turned to retrieve my coat from the coat rack. Renee stopped me.

"No, Claire. Emma wants you to stay here and serve as host to her guests. It was a condition of my getting her to agree to go home."

Damn. "Oh. Well, all right," I said. "At least I'd better call her."

Renee held up a hand. "She doesn't want you to. She's OK. She would rather you attend to her people here at the conference, that's what she's most worried about."

Terrific. At a time like this I wanted to go home and be with Emma. Now I was not only trapped like a rat at this stupid conference, I'd just been appointed acting director. I was really having a rotten day. Not as bad as Weber's, maybe, but pretty rotten.

The inn has a series of sitting rooms just off its main lobby. These rooms are relatively small but are connected to each other by large open doorways. Each has a fireplace flanked by bookshelves, and a sofa and armchairs surrounding a coffee table. The bookshelves hold mainly items of local interest: faculty publications, college yearbooks, books about famous college alumni. Emma's guests had distributed themselves comfortably among these cozy rooms in a matter of minutes. A few gangs of trustees and alums were also scattered here and there, and a student waiter wandered among the sitting rooms pushing a cart full of wines and whiskeys. He was greeted with enthusiasm at every stop.

I resigned myself to having to stand in for Emma as host. There was no choice but to walk from room to room and introduce myself. I made sure they all had drinks, inquired as to everyone's comfort, and explained that if anyone needed anything, anything at all, they had only to tell me and I'd say, 'Hey don't come whining to me pal, this isn't my conference!'

One person did ask if she could switch to a nonsmoking room. I wanted to send Sara Grace to ask at the desk, but I couldn't find her, so I asked myself. It turned out that the inn doesn't have any. Other than that things were pretty quiet all along the front and I started thinking that maybe I could just be sociable for a few minutes more and then sneak away home.

At the end of my rounds I found Renee seated with Marshall, Fritz, that fellow with whom I'd argued earlier, and the elderly man who made the toast at dinner. Fritz had taken his beret off. I wasn't anxious to join a group with Fritz in it, but at least I was friends with Marshall and Renee. I was also slightly curious about the older man, whose name, I remembered, was Kurt something or other. He had the general aura of someone important. I ordered a wine cooler from the drink cart and sat between Marshall and Renee on the teal sofa. Kurt and Fritz sat in large armchairs facing the couch, with Kurt nearest the fire. No one seemed to be talking much, presumably because of the lateness of the hour and the shock of the accident. Only one lamp burned in the room, and the firelight gave a warm, soft glow to this quiet gathering.

"Kurt," Renee said, "I don't think you've met Claire Sinclair. She teaches economics here and is Emma's partner. Claire, this is Kurt Burghoff, Professor Emeritus at Ohio State." We smiled at each other. Since this guy was a heavy hitter I wanted to say something polite.

"Welcome to Hammond, I know Emma feels very lucky to have you here." Of course I didn't actually know this, I just assumed it based on what Roger had told me. But among economic theorists it's quite common to take a bald-faced lie and relabel it a 'simplifying assumption.'

"Oh, I would not have missed it," Kurt said. "It is nice to be back in Hammond after all these years."

"Oh, you've been here before? When was that?"

"Well, let me see," he looked up at the ceiling. "It must have been '79 or '80, I think. John Marchak invited me to a symposium here on…oh, I think it was Ethics in the Public Sphere or something." He took a sip of wine. "I was sorry that I could not come back for John's funeral, I was in Holland at the time."

"I didn't know John well," I said, keeping up the small talk. "He seemed like a wonderful man. He was very popular with the students."

"Yes, it was very sad when John died," Renee said. "I learned a lot about teaching philosophy from him."

Renee looked over at the fire and was quiet again. For a few seconds no one else said anything either. We were rapidly approaching one of those conversational lulls that drive me crazy, so I had to say something.

"Well, at least John wasn't here to see Weber die at his conference." Something stupid as it turns out. Oh, God, I thought.

But Kurt made a quick and gracious response, "Yes, John and Erik had known each other for a long time. They were students together when the war started." He took another sip from his glass.

There was that silence again.

After a few seconds I said, "I, ah, realize that everyone here knows about this but me, but do I understand correctly that you and Weber were also friends back in Germany?" He smiled a little at that question.

"Yes, we were friends." His tone was mildly ironic. "To the extent that anyone could be friends with Erik, I suppose I was."

"What was he like as a young man, Professor?" Marshall asked. Kurt smiled again.

"You are not going to quote me in your book, are you Marshall? I have had too much wine."

Looking embarrassed (as usual) Marshall held up both hands as if to show he had no weapons. For a minute Kurt stared into his glass.

"Well," he said, "some people think Erik was less difficult as a young man, but I do not remember him quite that way. At that time he could be every bit as selfish and petty as he was in middle age. But I think in those days one was simply distracted from these peccadilloes by his brilliance. He was fiercely ambitious, of course, but in a young man at the time ambition was a compelling virtue." Kurt crossed his legs by lifting one leg with his hands and placing it on the other. "Erik really was a kind of charismatic figure. Even as an undergraduate he had a group of what can only be described as followers. And they were not all women, either, though of course he had no shortage of adoring females."

I involuntarily shot a glance a Renee. She had no apparent reaction to this comment.

Marshall stood up. "While you're in a nostalgic mood Professor, I wonder if you'd mind commenting on some photographs I've gathered for my book. I'll be right back." He hurried out of the room and everyone turned to watch him go.

"Marshall sees this conference as a golden opportunity for a biographer," I said, as if anyone needed an explanation for his exit. Everyone smiled but no one said anything. The conversation seemed perilously close to another lull, so once again I sprang into action. What to say? I remembered the discussion in our kitchen at lunchtime.

"And did you know Spengler, Professor?" I asked. I hoped like hell that was the name of the guy Sara Grace had mentioned. I wanted my question to serve two purposes with respect to this conversation: to keep it moving, and to fool them into thinking I had some idea what it was about.

"I did not know him well," Kurt said. "I met him only once, a few months before he died. I was arrested myself after Spengler's death. Erik had made it over to the West by then." He placed both hands above his left knee, then slowly stretched that leg out straight. "It is quite amazing, what has happened in Germany, is it not? Reunification, I mean. For the first time in decades you can speak your mind, do what you want, leave the country. The secret police are gone. I am an old man, yet for almost all of my lifetime people in my home country lived under one form of oppression or other. First the Nazis and then the Communists. And even before that there was the economic chaos of the Weimar Republic and the First World War. In this entire century East Germany will have enjoyed only two decades of real peace and freedom, the first and the last."

"Political freedom, yes," Fritz said, "but how much economic freedom can these people expect under capitalism? With communism they at least had some economic security; they had freedom from the fear of poverty, if nothing else."

He asked this question of Kurt but he was looking sideways at me. Now only a hopeless dimwit would fall for such baiting a second time, but Fritz had the good fortune to be sitting across from one. Before I could leap into the trap, however, I felt Renee's hand on my arm.

"Claire, will that wine cart be coming back this way?" She held up her empty glass and smiled at me with exaggerated sweetness. I laughed.

In my Suzy Homemaker voice I said, "Renee, why don't I just go freshen that drink for you?"

"That would be lovely, dear."

"Anyone else need something?" Fritz and Kurt shook their heads. I had the impression that Fritz was smirking, but maybe I was imagining it. I went off in search of the drink cart.

It was getting late now and the sitting rooms were emptying out. I could hear the murmurs of only a few conversations lingering around the big armchairs. I found the cart parked in the corner of the room farthest from the lobby. I didn't think anyone was there until I heard what sounded like a giggle from one of two chairs facing the fire. The high chair backs made the occupants nearly invisible but it sounded to me like Sara Grace. Apparently she and another student were getting cozy by the fire, so to speak. I thought that was pretty cute.

I poured some red wine into Renee's glass and tried, not very hard I admit, to pay no attention to the students in the chairs. But I couldn't help seeing the hand that crossed the gap between the chairs. It was a left hand and there was a wedding ring on it.

That wasn't another student with Sara Grace, it was Roger Stuhrm. I thought this much less cute.

For a moment I considered going over and making some disapproving noises, but quickly decided against it. Hell, I'd already done too many jobs at this conference, I wasn't about to volunteer for camp counselor. Still, I would say something to Emma about this, that was for sure.

I returned to our sitting room to find Kurt on the couch next to Renee, while Marshall, sitting on the arm of the sofa, passed photographs to Kurt from a large album. Renee, sitting sideways with her stockinged feet tucked under her, looked on from Kurt's left. Fritz was gone. I came over and stood in front of Renee, handing her the glass of wine I'd refilled. She wriggled to her left making room for me on the couch between her and Kurt. At that moment, tired, worried about Emma, distracted by thoughts of Roger and Sara Grace, I made a foolish and inexcusable tactical error: I sat down.

The second my bottom touched the sofa I realized what I'd done. I had lighted on the flypaper. If I had just thought for a few seconds I could have made a graceful exit before sitting down on that couch. They didn't need me anymore; most of the conferees were already in bed. But there I sat, awkwardly squeezed between Kurt and Renee, like the new fiancee who has to pretend she's interested in pictures of people she's never heard of.

I cursed myself.

"This is Weber and his mother, circa 1925," Marshall said, holding the picture by its edges. Kurt took the picture in his left hand. In his right was a set of glasses which he held a few inches from his eyes as he studied the photograph. In the picture stood a boy of about eight or nine next to a short, slender woman in her mid-to-late thirties. On her other side was a white-haired woman wearing an ankle length skirt and long-sleeved blouse with a high collar. The boy had on Tyrolean trousers buckled at the knee. The younger woman, who wore a short-sleeve print dress, was scrawny-looking with limp hair. The boy, on the other hand, was quite handsome.

Kurt peered at the picture for a moment before commenting. "Yes, I remember Erik's mother. Everyone called her Mitzi. A very kind and gentle woman, so different from his father. She died shortly after the war, I think, '46 or '47."

"It was '47," Marshall said. "She had a stroke. Do you know, Professor, if the older woman is Weber's grandmother?"

"By appearance she certainly could be. But I cannot tell you for sure, Marshall, I never met her."

Marshall handed another photo to Kurt, who passed the previous one on to me. I held it up, pretending to study the picture, but really trying to get a look at the old man's watch. It was 11:15. I really have to get of here, I thought. I gave the photo to Renee.

In the next picture there were two men seated at an outdoor table. It appeared to be on an open terrace of a large home, or maybe some kind of hotel. The men, one of whom was obviously Weber, were mustached and in shirt sleeves. On the floor between them was a small boy in short pants, maybe two or three years old. The child was oblivious to the camera, busily pushing a little spotted horse on wheels across the floor. Between the men was a bottle of something, probably wine, and two small glasses.

"This is Weber and Spengler, of course," said Marshall, "and the boy is Spengler's son. I got this picture from a friend of Weber's late sister. She wasn't sure of the date. Given the boy's apparent age I would guess the year to be 1964. What do you think, Professor?"

Kurt studied the photo with and without his glasses.

"Again, I am sorry, Marshall. I cannot be much help there because I did not know the Spenglers. I know that when Spengler got shot in the tunnel the boy was still very young. It was thought remarkable that he and his mother kept crawling and got out. That was in '65, so 1964 is plausible for this picture. That is all I can tell you."

I was inspired by that story. If this little boy could crawl through an escape tunnel while being shot at, surely I could find the courage to escape from this couch.

Marshall pulled another picture out of the photo album. Good Lord, I thought, is he going to show us every one of them? I would have to make a break for it. Soon.

"How about this one?" Marshall asked. This picture was an 8 X 10, a group photo on the steps of a university building. There were seven young people, apparently students, and Weber, who stood at the back and left. The season was probably fall because a nearby bush was bare of leaves but the students were wearing only light jackets, the men with ties. "This is Weber with a group of students at Freiburg. I got the photo from the university archives.

Can you, Professor, or you, Renee, identify any of these students?"

Kurt released an almost inaudible sigh. He shook his head at the picture and handed it to me to give to Renee.

Something in that picture caught my attention. One of the women on the lowest step of the house was wearing a sort of blazer with a patch at the left breast. The jacket's color was indeterminate in the black and white photograph, but the patch was distinctive by its unusual shape: a tulip. I'd seen that patch before, maybe even that jacket. Emma had such a patch on a green wool blazer she'd had since before I met her. She never wore it and I didn't know where it was, but I knew it had been packed when she moved into my house. The woman wearing the patch in the photo might have been Karen, the roommate of Emma's who killed herself at Freiburg. With this in mind I held the picture and looked hard at that girl. Emma had never really described her to me. The girl in the picture was thin and of medium height, with blond, shoulder-length hair. I felt a sharp stab of jealousy. Even in a group photo you could see she was a knockout. Had Karen really been that gorgeous?

The woman might not have been Karen, of course and probably wasn't. Still, as a matter of curiosity, I studied the details of the patch, its shape and size, its position on the jacket. I would compare it with the patch on Emma's jacket if I ever happened to see it again. I mean, you never know, even if it was buried way up in the attic in one of a dozen unlabeled clothing boxes, I might just run across it some day.

Possibly even tomorrow, I thought.

I didn't know how many more of these pictures Marshall had in his album, but I was completely sure I'd seen enough of them. I had to get up my courage to leave.

"Listen folks," I said, "I'd really like to stay and talk some more, but I think I should get home now and check on Emma."

To my relief, there was immediate widespread agreement. It was that simple, and no one shot at me.

"I'll see you out, Claire," Renee said.

We walked to the lobby. I got my coat from the coatroom and began bundling up for the walk home.

"You tell Emma that everything will be fine," Renee said. "Everyone thinks she's doing a wonderful job."

"I'm scared Renee. This conference was already a big strain on her, and now this guy Weber shows up dead? I don't know if she can handle this."

"Oh, I don't think you're giving her enough credit. Emma didn't get to be who she is without being a strong woman."

59

I didn't answer Renee, but she could tell what I was thinking.

She shook her head. "She's not going to have another breakdown, Claire. That's behind her. She's taking her medicine, isn't she?" I nodded. "OK, then, you don't have to worry about that." She smiled and wrapped my scarf around my neck and kissed me on the cheek. "Besides, she has you now. You'll take care of her."

I wanted to tell Renee. I wanted to tell her that when I had seen Weber lying on the sidewalk, I had found that note from Emma beside him, that I knew something more than I was letting on. But I didn't tell her. I wanted to believe what Renee had said, that Emma was fine now and there was really nothing for me to worry about.

"Will you be safe walking home?" Renee asked.

"Around here? Sure. Nobody would try to bother me except Jack Frost, and I can handle him. Good night, Renee, and thanks a lot."

Outside, the town was deep-winter quiet and I heard nothing but the clop, clop of my own shoes as I walked alone down the sidewalks on Main Street. I figured it was down near zero degrees because the night air felt tingly against my face. I'd been told that thirty years ago Main Street was an arching tunnel of giant elms towering above the Victorian houses. But Dutch elm disease had come in the '60s, and now I could plainly see the clear sky above me.

I wondered if Emma would be awake when I got home. I knew she'd be pretty badly undone by Weber's death, but at least I could report that the rest of the philosophers were nestled snug in their beds back at the inn, everybody safe and sound.

CHAPTER NINE

Day two of the conference dawned sunny and not as cold. I woke up when I heard Emma clumping around on the second floor. I'd been sleeping downstairs on the living room sofa. My sleeping there had nothing to do with anger, hurt feelings, or marital discord. It's just that when I'd gotten home from the inn, Emma was already asleep, a fact which testified strongly to her nervous exhaustion. Had I climbed into bed with her I would have woken her. Within the first weeks we'd been sharing my house I had come to recognize Emma's sleep as a sacred and inviolate thing, fragile, delicate, not to be tampered with lightly. Under the best of circumstances a sleepy Emma is a grumpy Emma, and her current circumstances were not the best. And keeping Emma asleep is like preserving the Mona Lisa: it requires strict control over light, temperature, humidity, every environmental variable you can think of. So I sacked out on the couch.

When I heard Emma's bare feet trudging slowly down the stairs, I sat up and pulled my blanket around my shoulders. The house was still chilly. She came over and slumped down next to me on the sofa. She was wearing that frayed blue bathrobe over a flannel nightshirt. Her eyes were red and slightly puffy, and her hair jutted out at two places in the back so that she looked like My Favorite Martian.

"Are you OK, Emma?" God love her, she gave me a little smile. The smile, however, was shot through with exhaustion.

"Yes, I'm fine. I appreciate your sleeping downstairs, Sweetie. But I hardly slept at all, anyway."

"I can imagine. I wanted to come home but Renee said you didn't want me to."

"I didn't. Thanks for taking over for me at the inn, Claire, it was really a big help. Did everything go smoothly? Did anyone seem annoyed that I didn't come back?"

"Absolutely not. Everyone agreed with Renee, you needed to come home."

"Well that's good," she said. Emma sighed deeply and leaned back until her head rested on top of the sofa back, face pointed at the ceiling, eyes closed, her hands stuck in the pockets of the grungy robe. "This is a nightmare, Claire. Positively a nightmare. For weeks I've been worried that something or other would go wrong with this conference. But this? No, this I was not worried about. It hadn't occurred to me that Erik Weber might unexpectedly show up dead." She gave a short, bitter laugh. "You always tell me that I worry too much, Claire, but you see now? It's the things you don't worry about that clobber you. Good Lord, I haven't been thinking about tornadoes either—maybe we should hurry down to the basement."

It was good to see her sense of humor peeking out from under the rubble.

"What happened at the police station? Renee didn't tell us much."

"It was relatively straightforward, actually. We were asked to verify his identity, but he was carrying a wallet so that was really pro forma. Then they asked us what Erik was doing here, so we explained about the conference."

"From what I heard at dinner, Weber wasn't even invited to this conference. Didn't you say yesterday morning that no one knew where he was, that he'd disappeared again?"

She looked at me. "It's true, he did. I tried explaining that to the police but they seemed very unpersuaded. It was clear that, in their experience, when people disappear it isn't done as an academic exercise. We spent a long time talking about that."

She had brought up the exact subject I wanted to broach. The skirt I'd worn last night lay on the floor next to the couch and I reached down into the pocket. I was fumbling around for the note I'd found next to Weber when Emma took her right hand out of her robe pocket and extended her arm towards me. She held, between her fingers, the tyrannical white tube of the ovulation test.

"And now," she announced, "to begin this fun-filled sequel to yesterday's adventures, I wake up to discover that I'm still not ovulating." Little tears welled up in the corners of her eyes.

"Jeez, I'm sorry, honey." I left the note in my pocket; this was not the right time to start interrogating her. I reached over and patted her on the knee. "But look, at least you know the sperm is here. You can get it from the Leaches today."

"Oh, that's right." She brightened up for nearly a full second. Then she slumped back in the sofa again. "Well, I don't know what good that will do, it's been sitting around for a whole day, and it's extremely perishable. Once it thaws it goes bad very fast. Even if I ovulate tomorrow it will probably be too late." Her eyes started filling up again. "Two hundred dollars wasted and another month of waiting."

"Can't you just stick it in the freezer until you ovulate?"

"No, it has to be kept extremely cold. They pack it in dry ice, which melts quickly, and where could I get more dry ice in a place like Hammond?"

I thought for a second. "The science people are always freezing stuff, aren't they? Call Steve Penski. Maybe the biology department could freeze it for you."

She gave me a doubtful look. "I'd have to tell him what it was for."

"Steve's a good guy. If he knows it's important to you he would never blab."

This idea seemed to elevate her mood from hopeless despair to semi-hopeless despair.

"Do you really think Steve could freeze it for me?"

"It's worth a phone call."

Emma chewed her lip for a few seconds. Then she stood up and walked determinedly to the phone in the kitchen.

Meanwhile, I started thinking about showering and getting dressed. Thoughts of clothing reminded me of the jacket with the tulip emblem. Could that really have been Karen I was looking at in the picture? I wanted to ask Emma. I wanted her to tell me about Karen, about Karen's relationship with Weber, about the cause of Karen's suicide. I would really have liked to talk about these things, but I knew it wasn't the time, not with all Emma had to deal with today. I decided to keep my mouth shut. For once I would act in a mature, sensitive, and responsible fashion. With luck I wouldn't have to do it again for four or five years.

By the time I'd rolled up my bedding, Emma came walking back in from the kitchen.

"Good news. Steve says we can put the sperm in liquid nitrogen. That stays at 320 degrees below zero. Steve will arrange for us to get some from the chemistry department." She started up the stairs. "You can go get it after you pick up the package from next door."

"After I what? Hey, come back here!"

In half an hour Emma was on her way to breakfast at the inn, and I was headed back up the walk of the big white house next door to get the parcel containing the sperm. This was ridiculously unfair, of course, since I was no more qualified for this assignment than Emma. If I asked one of the Leaches, "Do you have a package for us?" and the Leach in question replied, "Yes, we do," it would be the longest conversation I'd ever had with either of them.

No exchange of words was required for the Leaches to express their distaste at living next door to a pair of lesbians.

The Leaches have a white Cape Cod with blue shutters on a quarter acre of carefully tended land. The five inches of snow on the ground parted over their sidewalk as crisply and evenly as a sliced wedding cake. Come summer that sidewalk would have a tidy border of petunias, daisies, and tulips, and a family of wooden ducks would take up residence on the lawn. It was only 8:15 but I knew the Leaches were early risers. At least I was pretty sure the Leaches were early risers. Were they really early risers? Doubts about their morning habits began popping up the second my finger pressed their door-bell. A long moment passed. I was wondering whether to press the bell again or make a dash back to our house when Mrs. Leach opened her front door. I noted with relief that she was fully dressed. She wore a dark brown skirt and white blouse under a beige cardigan sweater.

"Good morning, Mrs. Leach. I hope I'm not disturbing you. I'm here about the package that was delivered yesterday." Mrs. Leach is a small woman with short salt and pepper hair and a thin face. It's a nice sort of face; she doesn't wear that permanent scowl I've noticed on her husband.

"Yes, come on in," she said, which slightly surprised me. I stepped care-fully into her living room. She seemed almost ready to give me a smile, but the smile faded nervously, as if she thought it out of place. "I'll just go get it for you," she said.

I stood waiting in the foyer. The inside of her house was very much as I'd pictured it. The love seat and sofa were in a matching pink floral pattern. Their wooden armrests gleamed as did every other surface in the room. Above the sofa was one of those oil portraits in which Jesus looks more like Leif Ericson than a Levantine Jew. The wall next to me had professional pho-tographs of two young men, one of them in naval uniform, and on a small table was a picture of two little girls I had sometimes seen playing in the Leaches' yard. Grandchildren I guessed. At the back of the house I heard the sound of organ music coming out of a TV set.

"Here you are," Mrs. Leach said. "The package was cold on the outside, so I thought I'd better put it in the refrigerator."

"Oh…well, that was kind of you." The express-mail package did feel cold.

Mrs. Leach hugged her arms as if she too were cold, though the room felt fairly warm. She smiled at me, though she was clearly very nervous. She looked back over her shoulder toward the sound of the television for a sec-ond.

"Is it some kind of fruit?" she asked.

Technically, I suppose, it was the fruit of someone's loins, but I was pretty sure that wasn't what she meant. "No, it isn't fruit." I tried to think fast. "This is some special medicine that Emma needs to take." Fast thinking all right, like medicine ever comes in the mail, Claire. Well, that definitely made it time to leave. "Thank you Mrs. Leach, for keeping this for us."

"Yes, well," she was still hugging herself, "you're welcome…um…"

"Claire," I said, "I'm Claire."

"Claire."

I turned to go.

"Listen, Claire…" She glanced over her shoulder again.

"Yes?"

She just looked at me. "Well, ah…oh, it's nothing," she said, "never mind." Her smile was very thin and uncomfortable. "I'm glad you got your package."

I nodded. "Thanks again."

Out on the sidewalk, as I made the turn toward campus, I thought I glimpsed her still looking at me through the picture window in her living room.

Sperm package in hand, I headed toward campus. Along the way I formulated a plan, a plan of action, a strategic plan, a plan that was bold and daring yet elegantly simple. Here was the plan: I would go to the philosophy department, put the sperm package down on Emma's desk, and walk briskly out the door. That was it. Then I would go to my office where I would do my work. No more sperm, no more pick-ups, no more involvement with Emma's stupid conference. This whole thing with Weber was none of my business. If there was some mystery about how he got here, why he came, what Emma's feelings for him were, so what? It really wasn't my concern. I would drop off the package, walk away and forget about the whole conference. I knew my plan would require speed, agility, and flawless timing, but I was pretty confident I could pull it off.

History is littered with the detritus of such plans. ("Look, Josephine, I'm just going to zip in, take Moscow, and be right back.")

"Hi, Maria," I said, passing her desk on my way to Emma's office. "How're you?" I smiled cordially but I didn't slow down.

"I am fine, Claire." She looked at me curiously and followed me with her eyes. She seemed every bit as tired as Emma. Normally I would have stopped to commiserate, but my sympathy for her didn't weaken my resolve to get my buns out of there. "Claire," she said, "is that the box of transparencies Emma has been waiting for?"

"Ah …no," I said, "no it's not." I couldn't think of a good cover story for the package so I tried to distract her. I pointed at the 8 x 10 photo in the silver frame on her desk. "Have you told your son the big news yet? That a famous guy died here in little old Hammond, Iowa?" She didn't react and I felt a little foolish, so I said, "Have to hurry," and walked into Emma's office.

I set the package on Emma's desk. Little pink phone messages littered her desktop. I was surprised at how many. There was a message from Oscar Lamb, that reporter from the *Cedar Rapids Gazette* who'd called our house last night. Our local paper, the *Hammond Herald*, had called, the president's secretary had called, the police department had called, and the liquor store on Main Street had called. I wondered how the liquor store knew about Weber's accident.

I picked up the message from the *Gazette* guy and began thinking about how word of Weber's death had gotten out really fast last night. This reporter had to have been called either from the police station or from last night's dinner. Those were the only two possibilities. Maybe the *Gazette* had a contact in the police station, someone who alerts them on those rare occasions when something interesting happens in this town. It was either that or someone had called from the conference itself. But who would have wanted to do that?

Now, according to my strategic plan, the few moments I stood there considering these questions were supposed to have been spent expanding the distance between myself and the philosophy department. I'd squandered them. Instead of being a good three quarters of the way over to my own office, I was still standing next to Emma's desk when she came through the door of the department office.

"Good morning, Maria," I heard her say. I backed away from her desk and moved toward the wall. Maria started filling her in on all her messages, while I stood there wondering what to do. I suppose I could have pulled an I-Love-Lucy and hidden under the desk or climbed out the window. But those things were beneath even my dignity. Keeping my head in this crisis, I decided to fall back on Plan B: I would just walk out of the building. If Emma asked me to do something else for her I would politely refuse.' I'd like to help, Em, but I don't have the time. Sorry.' Courteous, but assertive, that would be me.

I strolled casually out into the main office where Emma was earnestly talking to Maria.

"Hi, Emma, I left the package on your desk. See you guys later." I smiled and headed toward the office door.

As I moved past her she reached out a hand and gripped my arm firmly.

"Claire," she said in a voice that sounded just a little too calm and pleasant, "could I see you in my office for a minute?" Damn.

We went in and she closed the door behind us.

"Surely you are not about to abandon me today?"

"What do you mean 'abandon you'? I got the sperm and brought it in like you asked." I pointed to the package on the desk as irrefutable proof of my valuable contribution.

"And what about the liquid nitrogen? That dry ice will have melted in a few hours, Claire, and I can't get the liquid nitrogen. I have a dead Weber on my hands, and this conference to deal with."

"Well, I assumed you'd ask Sara Grace or one of the other students to go get it."

Her eyes narrowed. "Are you being deliberately obtuse, Claire? How would I explain to them why I want liquid nitrogen without making a de facto campus-wide announcement that I am trying to get pregnant?" She stared at me for a few seconds, shaking her head slowly. "You just aren't going to help me with this, are you? If I want a baby, I'll have to do it all by myself."

She sat down in her chair and looked away from me, her eyes starting to fill with tears again. (It's amazing how fast she can fill them with tears, I swear she practices.)

I stood there looking down at her. If I had slept a little better, or gotten up a little later, or maybe even just had a little more coffee when I ate my breakfast, I might have gotten angry. As it was I just didn't have the energy.

"OK, OK, I'll go get the damned liquid nitrogen. Tell me what I have to do." I sighed heavily (on purpose) and dropped into the hard wooden chair in front of her desk. This was the chair where students sat when they came to this office to see Dr. Harrington and I prepared to take instructions, just like they did. She sniffed once and swivelled her chair back toward me.

"All right. Steve said to see the secretary of the chemistry department in Krynski Hall. She can arrange to have—"

Emma's phone rang. She picked it up.

"Hello?…yes." Her brow furrowed. She listened for a long time without talking. "All right…yes. I'll be right over, then." She hung up and looked at me wide-eyed.

"That was the president's secretary. They want me to go to the administration building and meet with the president and the police." She bit her lower lip. "Right now."

I knew her next line as surely as if we were dress-rehearsing for the junior-class play.

"Claire, will you please come with me?"

"Come with you?" I said. "Aren't I getting the liquid nitrogen?" I felt a sudden surge of enthusiasm for that project.

"You can do that afterwards, an hour or so won't make any difference."

"Oh, come on, Emma, jeez. It's not appropriate for me to go with you. I'm not affiliated with this conference. I'm not even in your department. How do we explain my being there? They'll know that I'm there only as your partner, for moral support." I threw up my hands. "It'll be like bringing a damned teddy bear."

"Please, Claire, I need you," she said. "Jack respects you more than he does me because you're a math jock." There was some truth to that statement. Like many hard scientists, the president was inherently suspicious of anyone who couldn't take the first derivative of X^2. Moreover, come to think of it, it wouldn't hurt for me to hear firsthand what the police were making of Weber's death.

"Oh, all right." I sighed again for dramatic effect. "I'll go with you." It was just a meeting, how bad could it be?

CHAPTER TEN

The office of the president of the College is on the second floor of the administration building, which also houses the offices of Admissions, College Development (the people who bring in money), and Public Relations, all offices that deal with the public. One result of this is that the decor and furnishings on that floor are an order of magnitude more plush than any other place on campus. Waiting in the president's office, Emma and I sat in two beautiful Queen Anne chairs in forest green fabric, while the secretary, who had directed us to them, studiously ignored us. I could tell that waiting was making Emma jumpy.

"Are the police already in there?" she asked the president's secretary.

Without looking up from her typing she said, "I'm sure the president will tell you whatever he wants you to know when he comes out." The secretary is a painfully thin woman in her late forties, whose medium-length hair is dyed dark brown. (At least that's what everyone says.) She reminds me of one of my former stepmothers. Actually, she reminds me of both of my former stepmothers, which is twice as bad as reminding me of just one of them. My dad had remarried twice after my mother died. My mother and father were only married for fifteen years, but their relationship spanned his entire adult life up to that time. They were high school sweethearts, college classmates, business partners in the auto shop he ran, and research collaborators in this great experiment of raising a child in a crumbling and increasingly frightening city. The marriage had worked. When the cancer took her he grieved, but did not despair, because he knew that with a little patience, a little luck, and just the right attitude, he could get another wife and find that kind of happiness a second time. In this, as in many things, my dad was too much the optimist. His marriage to Eleanor lasted ten months, and to Vicky three years.

Emma sat there kicking her foot up and down and I sat next to her staring into space. The air in the office felt uncomfortably warm. Feeling antsy I got up and walked over to a Plexiglas case sitting on a small oak table in the middle of the room. Under the case was a scale model of a one-story brick building in the shape of an L. The model was fully landscaped with little bushes, a few trees, painted-on grass, and even a little toy student walking into the building.

Jack Hathaway, the college president, came out of the door to his office. Jack is a tall, slender man with bushy eyebrows and grey at his temples. He wore navy blue pants with a crease that could slice salami. His shirt was a shade of salmon pink that picked up the floral pattern of his navy tie. The sleeves were rolled up to his forearms.

He gave us a warm smile. "Hello, Emma, hello, Claire. Thanks for coming over." If he was wondering what the hell I was doing there I saw no trace of it in his expression. He came over to stand next to me at the model. "Beautiful, isn't it? The new computer center. Just got the display yesterday. We have about a third of the money pledged already."

"So this is part of the capital campaign?" I asked.

"One of the big items, yes. Of course, we have lots of other things in mind, too," he turned to Emma, "like some endowed chairs, right Emma?" He winked at her and she smiled back weakly but her left cheek fluttered in a nervous tic. Jack's manner was as calm and assured as if we'd been there to discuss the faculty Christmas party.

He ushered us inside his vast office.

Before last evening, when he came to the scene of the accident, I had never met Peter Gammon, the chief of police. He was medium height and heavyset and he wore a blue policeman's uniform. A town the size of Hammond doesn't have the luxury of plainclothes police. The bare scalp on top of his head was covered with long strands of hair combed across it. I would have placed him in his early forties. He nodded amiably and shook hands with me as we were introduced. Jack made no attempt to explain why I was there, probably because he had no idea. Emma and I sat in burgundy leather chairs facing the great expanse of Jack's desk; he went around and sat behind it.

"Pete has been recapping the particulars of last night's accident," the president said to Emma and me. "And let me say how gratified I am to be getting such excellent cooperation from Pete's department." He smiled at Pete. "As usual, I might add." Jack sounded as if he were about to ask for a big donation, which is about eighty percent of what he does for a living. "Pete, would you mind bringing Claire and Emma up to speed on the situation?"

"Sure," said the chief. He leaned against the edge of Jack's desk and read from a little spiral notepad like the cops do on TV. "Dr. Harrington knows some of this already from last night at the station, but I'll start from the beginning." In an official sort of way he flipped back a few pages in the notepad. "Well, as you know, that fellow lying below the bridge was DOA when he got to the hospital. County coroner says he didn't die more than two hours before that, so we figure he wasn't dead more than an hour when you folks found him. Of course he could've been lying there unconscious a while before that, then died. But it was still light an hour and a half before, so somebody probably would've seen him." He turned a page in the notebook. "The ID in his wallet confirms what Emma said, the man was Erik Weber from Germany." He pronounced the name *Webber* rather than the German *Vaybur*. "Seems pretty clear Dr. Weber died of a blow to the right side of his head, just behind the ear. The coroner says there was a lot of alcohol in his blood, so it looks—"

"He was apparently quite inebriated," said Jack, who could no doubt already see the lawyers circling Weber's carcass.

"Ah, that's right," Pete said. "So anyway, it seems probable he accidentally fell off the bridge and hit his head on the rocks."

"Probable?" Jack said. "Why do you say probable, Pete?"

"Ah, well, that's the most likely explanation for his death."

"What other explanation could there be?" The presidential smile got a few watts dimmer.

"Well," the chief scratched his nose with the spiral of the notebook, "there's a couple a things that don't make sense yet. If it's an accident, I mean." He seemed embarrassed to be bringing this up.

"You're not about to suggest that this man was murdered, are you Pete?" Now Jack was wearing the first stages of a frown. "What possible evidence could there be for murder?" Apparently Jack didn't think a campus homicide was the ideal kick-off event for a fund raising drive.

"Well, if this was an accident, there's some things that don't fit right," Pete said. "For starters, I guess, his head injury doesn't look like it came from a fall. It's too small and sharp."

"But we know he fell." Jack turned to me. "Claire found him lying on the bridge. There was no one else there."

"Well, yeah, yeah," Pete said, "but that's the thing, there was only one head wound. And we can't figure out why he fell the first time, there wasn't any ice there or anything." Jack and Pete both looked at me for a second, a really long second, during which I was chilled by the recognition of an obvious explanation: I had murdered Weber, myself. I knew they didn't believe that, of course, because had I murdered Weber I would have had no reason to report finding him. Still, to be on the safe side I folded my hands primly on my lap and tried to look too-nice-to-kill-someone.

Jack turned back to Pete and gave a folksy sort of chuckle, though no amusement showed in his eyes. "Now come on Pete, this all seems a bit Agatha Christie doesn't it? We know he was drunk, we know he fell and hit his head on some rocks. There's nothing prima facie to suggest anything but an accident." He looked at Emma, then at me. "And why would anyone on our campus want to murder a prominent scholar?"

I gave a big shrug to assure the president that I could think of absolutely no reason whatsoever why someone would want to do such a thing.

Pete raised his hand to the halt position. "Now I didn't say there was a murder, you understand." His reluctance to annoy a powerful member of the local community was now very obvious. "I'm just pointing out a couple a loose ends, is all."

"Of course you are, Pete. I'm sorry, please continue." Jack leaned back in his chair. The fingers of one hand lightly tapped the big desk.

"And there's one more thing that seems pretty odd. We don't know how Dr. Weber got here," Pete said. He paused and looked directly at Jack.

"What do you mean, how he got here?"

"We don't know where he came here from. He lives in Germany, right?" A glance at Emma. "Well he didn't have an airplane ticket. And none of the airlines into Des Moines had him listed as a passenger. We checked the bus station down in Newton and nobody saw anybody like him. And it'd be strange to come in by bus when it's twenty more miles up to Hammond."

"So he drove in," Jack said.

"Didn't have a driver's license on him," Pete said. "We looked around town for out-a-state license plates and they're all accounted for. Plus we didn't find any luggage and he hasn't rented a hotel room in town."

"Couldn't he have caught a ride with another conferee?" Jack turned to Emma.

"Well, we're checking on that," Pete said, "but nobody's come forward to tell us they saw Dr. Weber. Of course we haven't talked to everybody yet."

Throughout this exchange between Pete and Jack, I tried to look at Emma without actually looking at Emma. I wanted to see her reaction to all this without letting anyone suspect what was going on in my head. In my peripheral vision Emma sat with her hands on her lap listening intently to the two men talking. Why wasn't she saying anything? The phone number on that piece of paper I found was local; Emma had written Weber a note to call a local number. She must have known something about where he was staying, about how he got to Hammond. Why would she withhold this information?

Should I mention the note myself? The question made my heart flutter.

The room was silent except for the rhythmic clicking, now much louder, of Jacks' fingernails on the mahogany desktop. "All right," Jack admitted, "these things seem to be mysteries, but rather minor ones. It's a great leap, don't you think, from a missing ride to deliberate murder."

He glanced at me, and I swallowed, afraid he'd be able to read my thoughts. But I nodded vigorously and he turned back to the police chief. Emma remained mute on the subject.

"Wouldn't you say so, Pete?" Jack asked.

"Sure I would, sure I would," Pete conceded quickly. There was a pause. "It's just that…well, we've still got a little ways to go before we wrap this thing up."

Sometimes the glad-handing style he affected as college president could make you forget who Jack Hathaway really was, an organic chemist of national reputation. At that moment he reminded us how quick and agile his mind could be. "I admire your thoroughness, Pete, but I hope you see that there are any number of explanations for these anomalies." He raised his index finger and said, "Weber got a ride from a local friend at whose house he was staying. That person doesn't know he's dead yet." He raised a second figure. "Weber rented a car somewhere in state and that car is sitting in town somewhere." A third finger went up. "Weber caught a ride with someone passing through Hammond. He didn't have luggage because he travels light." Jack leaned back in his chair and spread his hands in a gesture of appeal. "My point is this: naturally the college expects you to pursue a comprehensive investigation, anything less would be nonfeasance, but you will agree, I hope, that it would be premature to call what you're doing a murder investigation. There is not yet sufficient evidence for that. You're not planning to call it that, are you, Pete?"

"No, no. I'm not," Pete said. "Our department's gonna do a little follow-up on some of these questions, is all. In fact we're already checking the hotels in Cedar Rapids. But for now, the official cause of death is still an accidental fall."

The tension in the room relaxed noticeably.

"Great, Pete," Jack said. "I appreciate that. Naturally our faculty and staff will cooperate with your people in any way we can." He turned to Emma. "Emma, I expect that Pete will want to talk to some of your colleagues at the conference. You can act as liaison for him. Will you do that." It was not a question and he didn't wait for an answer. "Good. Well then," he said, "the only thing we need to resolve now is how to handle the press. We've been getting calls all morning from newspapers and TV. I don't know how the word got out so fast," a quick glance at Emma, "but apparently the death of a famous scholar is being considered news around here."

Pete showed us how well he knew how to deal with the college.

"Why don't I let your people take care of that?" Pete said. "I'll give you whatever information I have and you all can handle the press questions."

Jack seemed to think that was just a super-duper idea. His presidential smile was on high-beam again. "That would be terrific, Pete. We'll he happy to do that. All right then," he stroked his tie a few times. "I suppose we could hold a press conference and deal with this all at once. Emma, what do you think?" Another purely rhetorical question.

"Ah…yes. Sure. I guess we could do that. I could give Marlene any information she needs about the conference." Marlene Jastrow was the new head of public relations.

"Hmmm," Jack said. "I'm not quite sure that Marlene is the best person to handle this sort of assignment." Interesting. Apparently there was some truth to the rumors that Jack was unhappy with Marlene's performance. "I'd feel better if we had a faculty member handling the press. Someone connected with the conference. The logical person, of course, is you, Emma, but I don't want you to get bogged down with the press. You'll need to be helping Pete in anyway you can."

What he meant, of course, was that Emma was to keep an eye on Pete. If the latter had ambitions to become the Columbo of the Corn Belt, Jack wanted to know about it immediately.

Emma cleared her throat. "Well, I could ask someone else in my department. Colin Jensen's been involved in the conference."

Jack considered for a moment. "This is Colin's first year isn't it? No, I think we need someone a little older, with maybe a bit more experience. This matter has to be handled with some delicacy, I think."

Being by nature a helpful sort of person, I sat there racking my brain for them. Who on the faculty would be the best person to manage this press conference? Boy, that was a tough one. I thought hard for a few seconds before noticing that the room had become eerily quiet. Jack was looking at me, Pete was looking at me, and Emma was trying hard not to look at me. I had a really bad feeling about that.

"Claire," Jack said, "I guess that leaves you as the logical choice to talk to the media. Would you be willing to do that?"

I couldn't believe my ears. Would I be willing to run a press conference on the subject of Weber's death? Hell no, I wouldn't! I didn't have anything to do with Philosophy, I didn't have any knowledge of Weber's life, and I didn't have any experience dealing with the press.

On the other hand, I didn't have tenure.

"Well, uh," I stammered, "I guess…if you want me to I…" Think, Claire, think! "Well…you know, I could probably help Pete, and then Emma would be free to—"

"No," Jack said, "Emma's the one who knows these people. I think we'd better let her help Pete."

"OK…but, ah, but wouldn't it be better to have someone in Philosophy handle the press? Maybe Bob could—"

"Oh, I don't think field will matter here, the press won't know the difference." Jack was smiling at me. "I'm sure you'll be just right for this, Claire."

I saw that it was no use arguing with him; he wanted me to do it. I wasn't sure why. Maybe he wanted me because he thought an economist would sound less esoteric when talking to the press than would a philosopher like Emma. More likely he wanted me because my field is quantitative, and he has a scientific prejudice against fields that aren't. Of course this would make good sense if the reporters asked for a proof of Euler's Theorem of Homogeneous Functions, but what the hell were the chances of that?

"Well, OK," I said. Damn!

"Thanks, Claire, I knew we could count on you. I'll tell Marlene to have the PR office set a time and place for your convenience, but the sooner the better I should think. This afternoon would be best. After that, assuming Pete finds nothing untoward, which I'm sure he won't, I think we can put this whole thing behind us."

"Um, Jack," Emma said. She was avoiding, with good reason, all eye contact with me. "Are you going to tell me to cancel my conference?"

Jack took off his glasses and rubbed them on his handkerchief. After a second he said, "I guess I don't see any reason to, do you? Right now the official conclusion is that there was an unfortunate accident on campus. Canceling your conference will only draw more attention to it. If you and your colleagues feel up to it, I see no reason not to carry on as planned."

I could see the relief flood Emma's face.

Jack said, "So I guess we're done for now, right, Pete?" Pete nodded and Jack stood up from behind his desk. "I want to thank each of you for your cooperation. Please keep in touch with me about any new developments."

As Emma and I followed Pete out into the reception area, Emma leaned over and whispered in my ear. "I'm sorry, I'm sorry, I'm really, really sorry. I didn't mean to get you into this. I'm sorry." I didn't look at her. Outside the president's office she started following Pete but I just stopped and stood in the hallway. She turned around. "Aren't you going up to public relations now?"

"No," I said stiffly, "first I have to make a phone call." It was going to be to a local number.

CHAPTER ELEVEN

I still had that piece of green paper in my pocket and it felt like a hot coal against my thigh. The police chief was talking about a possible murder investigation, in which case that piece of paper might be material evidence. But that was only true, I told myself, in the very unlikely event that Weber's death wasn't accidental, and of course I would, I also told myself, eventually turn *the evidence* over to the cops. Very soon, in fact. But first I'd need to do two things: 1) call the number myself, and 2) dream up an excuse why I hadn't already given it to them. For #2 I might have to push the absent-minded-professor routine right to the very Wall of Credibility, but I didn't have time to worry about that now. First I'd call the number. I went to the little phone booth on the main floor of the administration building because I didn't have time to go back to my own office. And I certainly didn't want to be overheard.

My palms were moist as I dialed the number. What was I planning to say to whomever answered? Hi there, do you have a friend named Erik Weber? Yeah? Not anymore you don't! The number rang. It rang some more. I probably let it ring fifteen times before I gave up. What would I do now? I couldn't hang around calling this number all day, and the longer I waited to give it to the police the more culpable I'd be if there had been a crime. The tiny phone booth felt stuffy as I sat there thinking. Why don't you just ask Emma whose number it is? I thought. Yes, in this situation that was certainly the simple, direct, obvious course of action. Maybe I'd call that Plan B. Anyway, it wouldn't hurt to just wait a bit and call the number later maybe, just one more try. In the meantime I had this press conference to deal with.

Des Moines, Iowa's capital, is a small city by national standards, its population around four hundred thousand. Still, Des Moines rightly claims to have most of the amenities of her larger sisters in more populous states. There are ethnic restaurants, luxurious hotels, a convention center downtown, even a symphony. Once they held a Des Moines Grand Prix, in which formula racing cars sped through center city. Can Los Angeles top that?

What Des Moines doesn't have is news. Our little state capital is simply not capable of generating the news stories one hears every day in New York, Chicago, St. Louis or Detroit. The crime rate is low, there isn't much corruption, and this city has been spared the drive-by shooting as a daily feature of urban life. Nevertheless, Des Moines' TV anchorpersons are expected to fill the same half hour of local news as their more fortunate telebrethren in bigger cities. That isn't easy. The struggle to report thirty long minutes of local events in such an uneventful place sometimes gets a little desperate. They'll do five full minutes on parking problems at the annual State Fair, or maybe a graphical analysis of subsoil moisture. They'll have a complete film report on the burst seam in a grain elevator which, although there were no actual injuries, could have caused injuries had anyone been nearby, which no one was, of course, but certainly could have been. And just imagine if a bus full of school children had been parked next to that elevator! So to be on the safe side they'll do a follow-up story on how such tragedies can be prevented, just in case some day, one actually did happen.

One might think it more rational to acknowledge the limitations of the Iowa news scene and face them with dignity. At 10:15 the anchorpeople could say, "Well that's all we have for this evening, folks. While we wait for David Letterman, let's drop in on our pals Elmer and Bugs in that hare-brained adventure Wascally Wabbit."

At least that's what I would suggest if anyone asked me.

My point in describing the Iowa newscape is to make it clear that the death, even accidental, of a well-known philosopher on a local college campus was by no means beneath the attention of the Iowa press. The fact that he was well-known only in a narrow segment of academic philosophy didn't seem to bother them. They would have preferred, I'm sure, that he had died in a grain elevator accident, but no matter, every medium was interested: newspapers, television and radio.

Marlene Jastrow was supposed to brief me about this press conference. I didn't know her well, having met her only at formal college functions, but she seemed to me to be quite young to be heading a public relations office with four or five full-time staff. (I'm pretty sure she is not yet thirty.) An unmarried native of Hammond, she has short-cropped blond hair, a pretty, farm-girl kind of face, and a slender figure which she clothes more elegantly than anyone else on campus. As you would expect for a PR person, her manner is normally upbeat and cheerful. One might go so far as to say perky.

But today Marlene wasn't the least bit perky. Today Marlene had been given one hour to teach Press Briefing 101 to some snotty faculty interloper who was treading on her turf. It was profoundly obvious that Marlene thought she should be running the press conference, not me. The fact that I agreed with her passionately did not seem to improve her attitude toward me.

As we walked to the large conference room on the first floor of the administration building, Marlene read to me from a brown clipboard. She recapped the highlights of her hour-long briefing. I would read the short statement which she'd written about the accident. If there were questions from the press, which there certainly would be, I would keep my answers short and vague. The phrase, 'that's all the information we have right now' was to flow repeatedly from my lips like a Hindu mantra. Above all, on the express orders of the president, I was to ardently avoid anything that would raise the idea of murder in the minds of the press. I should stay away from words that even sounded like murder: merger, herder, girder, etc. Probably even 'sherbet' was too risky.

The conference room was filled to overflowing and my stomach muscles tightened the second I passed through the door. People sat everywhere around the edges of the massive mahogany table, while others stood behind them or occupied chairs along the walls. A score of simultaneous conversations made the room hum. I spotted some of Emma's colleagues here and there in the crowd. There was a faint whiff of cigarette smoke though a sign on the wall forbade smoking. Glaring TV lights and the crush of bodies made the room feel hot.

The whole thing seemed so unreal to me. Short hours before I'd been a reasonably content assistant professor of economics, and now I'd been turned into some kind of *spokesperson*. It made no sense. I mean, what were all these people looking at me for? I didn't know enough about accidents or philosophers or dead Germans on the rocks to be standing here hosting a press conference. I had a wild thought: maybe if I started talking about Hypothesis Testing in Multivariate Regression they would all just nod off to sleep like my students.

I walked to the front of the room where a dozen microphones protruded from the podium like thorns from a cactus. I tapped the largest of the microphones. It gave a thundering whump, whump that nearly made me wet myself. Standing right behind me, Marlene made a hissing sound.

Calm down, Claire, I told myself, you can do this.

"Good afternoon, ladies and gentlemen." That a feminist, lesbian academic would use the term *ladies* in this day and age gives you some idea how rattled I was. "I'm Claire Sinclair, a professor at the college. I have an unhappy announcement to make about an occurrence here on campus." I fought to control the quaver in my voice. "At approximately 6:20 yesterday evening the body of an elderly man was discovered lying on the rocks below the campus river walk. It was determined to be the body of Dr. Erik K. Weber, Distinguished Professor of Philosophy at Thurbingen University in Germany. Professor Weber died from a head injury apparently suffered when he fell from the river walk onto the rocks." (We'd decided to omit the fact that he was drunk as a skunk.) "Dr. Weber is very well known in the philosophical community for his work on ethical theory, hermeneutics, and other aspects of modern philosophy. The college has alerted German authorities about this incident. We wish to express our deepest condolences to Professor Weber's family and friends. He was a brilliant scholar who will be sorely missed in the academic world. Thank you. I will attempt to answer any questions you may have."

Several people put their hands in the air. I pointed to the one who looked the least threatening, a roly-poly guy with rosy cheeks and thick white hair.

"I assume it's been officially determined that the death was accidental?"

I felt an overpowering urge to answer 'yes.' But I was reluctant to begin lying to the press on my very first question at my very first press conference. I would guess that even Nixon had a better record than that.

"I don't believe there has yet been an official announcement to that effect," I said, "but we're expecting one soon." I surprised myself with that response, it sounded pretty innocuous but was still sort of true. Good one, Claire, I thought. I could tell that the reporters were disappointed with that answer, but that was perfectly fine with me. Maybe they'd all get bored and go home.

With slightly more confidence I called on another reporter. An attractive young woman in a black and tan pantsuit asked, "Was Dr. Weber here to give a talk on campus?" Whoa, I thought, easy one!

"Professor Weber was attending a philosophy conference here at the college."

"What was the conference about?" someone called out. Another easy one.

"The conference was being held to discuss Professor Weber's life and works," I answered congenially. I was beginning to get the hang of this spokesperson stuff.

A tall thin man in a brown suit stood up. "You mean that this man died at a conference that was held in his honor?" This caused a buzz of interest from the crowd, which caused my stomach to flutter up for a second.

"The, ah, conference was not specifically being held in his honor," I said, "but his work was the, ah, subject of the conference."

The chunky fellow I'd called on first asked, "What was the title of the talk he was to deliver?"

I wanted to ask him what the hell difference it made. It was a philosophy conference, for godsake; the Iowa news audience would not give a rat's patoot about the topic of any talk he was giving. What I said was, "I don't believe he was scheduled to give any kind of talk."

Unfortunately, this trivial bit of news piqued the interest of the tall guy in the brown suit.

"Are you saying, Dr. Sinclair, that Dr. Weber was invited to come to a conference on his own work, but was not asked to speak? Isn't that rather unusual?"

I wanted to scream, How would I know what's unusual at a philosophy conference? These people may tango in the nude for all I know.

"Ah…I don't believe that's especially unusual, no." I could feel my voice start to shake again.

"Was there some reason why he wasn't asked to speak?"

I felt beads of sweat break out along my hairline. What was I supposed to say to that? Well, you see, no one knew Weber was coming until we found him dead, at which point it seemed a little late to ask him to speak. Somehow that didn't sound like a good way to wrap up the press conference. Short and vague, Marlene had warned me, keep the answers short and vague.

"I don't have all of the details of the speaking arrangements at the conference," I said.

Just then a loud voice boomed out from somewhere over by the windows.

"Erik Weber was not invited to this conference." The crowd fell instantly silent.

I quickly scanned the room. Who said that? It was Roger Stuhrm. He was leaning against the ledge of a large window, his arms folded across his chest. Seated next to him on the window's edge was Sara Grace Harper, who concentrated intently on his face as he spoke. The room was so quiet I could hear my heart thumping.

"I'm Roger Stuhrm, Professor of Philosophy at Georgetown University and a speaker at this conference. Professor Weber was not invited to this conference because, until now, no one in the academic world even knew where he was." This elicited a buzz from the crowd. "Professor Weber's appearance here was a complete surprise." I stared in horror as the Iowa press started writing this down. TV cameras were hastily swung in Roger's direction.

Marlene's voice came hissing in my ear. "What's he doing? Why's he saying this?"

I gave my first truly honest answer of the afternoon: "I have no idea."

Roger now had the rapt attention of everyone in the room. Someone asked him to explain his statement.

"Professor Weber has a habit of going off alone for a time to write," Roger said. "He tells no one he is going, and doesn't communicate with anyone. Somehow he found out about this conference and decided to attend. That, by the way, is extremely unusual for Weber. He normally ignores what other people say about his work."

The crowd was scribbling furiously while a telegenic blonde in a blue dress asked, "Why do you think he wanted to attend this particular conference?"

I felt Marlene's fingernails dig into my arm. "You need to take back control of this thing. Quickly!"

"How? How do I do that?" Apparently she didn't have any ideas either.

It was obvious that Roger was delighted by the young woman's question and was savoring the opportunity to answer it.

"Well," he said. He paused and scratched his chin as if debating whether he should open Pandora's box. The crowd was eating up these theatrics. "This conference, you see, is going to discuss more than just Dr. Weber's theories. Recent archival work in Germany has unearthed some rather surprising, one might even say shocking, details of his early life. These findings will be revealed in a paper at this conference. Weber may have gotten wind of these planned revelations and decided to come to assess the damage to his reputation."

If the British royal family were to stroll through Piccadilly Circus in broad daylight in nothing but their underwear, they would be no more the focus of media attention than Roger now was at this stupid press conference. Death, scandal, secret revelations? All in little old Iowa? The crowd exploded in a cacophony of shouted questions. Something like fifteen people all asked at once about these newly-discovered details of Weber's life.

But having promised the starving reporters a downright, honest-to-God interesting local news story, Roger became suddenly coy.

"I don't think it's appropriate to release any of that information in this particular forum," Roger said. "These are, after all, research results, and should first be presented for peer review. I'm scheduled to deliver a paper on this subject tomorrow at 10:00 AM. After that I will be happy to discuss my findings with the press."

By now it was quite obvious why Roger, hereinafter referred to as 'that sleazy son-of-a-bitch,' had decided to take over the press conference. Clearly the SSOB was creating an audience for his paper about Weber. Now that Weber had suffered a mysterious death, Roger's paper would get the kind of media attention few academic studies could ever attract.

I wondered if maybe we could head some of that off by making Weber's death sound less mysterious. Was it too late to announce that Weber was drunk? I turned to ask Marlene.

"It's too late to say anything now," Marlene said. Her shoulders shook and her face was deep red. "Look out there! The press conference is over."

I saw what she meant. The reporters had gotten up from their chairs and were crowding around Roger while I stood ignored at the podium like carrot sticks on a buffet table. Roger was in the center of this large human mass fielding a barrage of questions. He had one arm around Sara Grace's lower back as if protecting her from the pressing crowd.

Marlene gathered up her papers and notes, all the while muttering to herself in a slightly demented way, "I should have handled this. Me! Not some scatter-brained Econ professor. Now we'll just see what happens." She stomped out of the room without so much as a glance at me. I hurried after her.

"What do you want me to do now, Marlene?" I felt really helpless.

"You? I don't want you to do anything. I'm going to go and have that bastard Roger what's-his-name thrown off campus."

"You can't be serious." She was walking so fast it was hard to keep up with her.

"I sure as hell am serious. Maybe I can't throw him off campus, but I'll be damned if he's going to present that paper tomorrow. Do you realize that those reporters are going to camp here overnight hoping like hell that this turns into a murder story?" We were whizzing down the hall toward the PR office.

"Look, the police will show that Weber's death was an accident. Does it really matter what the reporters suspect?"

She roared like a lioness who's been bitten by a snake. "Of course it matters! They can make a story out of just waiting to hear that guy's paper. Was Dead Professor Involved in Scandal? What was Weber's Big Secret? You don't think those are juicy enough headlines?" She shook her clipboard at me. "We're looking at three or four days of horrible publicity."

I was starting to get out of breath; I'd never met anyone who could walk so fast in heels.

"And now," she said, "I have to march into the president's office and get him to cancel this damned philosophy conference. That will be my last act as

PR director before he fires me."

Her statement made the little hairs on the back of my neck stand up. In my debut performance as a spokeswoman I appeared to have wiped out the most important conference of Emma's career and caused Marlene to lose her job. All in the space of about ten minutes. Emma's probable reaction to the closing of this conference was simply too hideous for me to contemplate.

Marlene crashed into the PR office, startling the staff who were sitting there. Muttering to herself again, she stormed into her private office. I followed her in and shut the door behind us. When she got behind her desk she turned and saw me standing there, as if for the first time. Her face showed astonished outrage that I, of all people, would have the nerve to be in her office. Like Jesse Helms finding Castro in his favorite chair.

"Marlene," I said. I felt my knees shaking. "You can't have Roger's paper canceled, and certainly not the whole Weber conference."

"Oh, no? Why the hell can't I?"

Good question. I had three-tenths of a second to come up with an answer.

"Because it will look like the college is deliberately squelching information about Weber's death. That will really look suspicious."

Having spoken this statement, I was amazed to discover that it actually made a modicum of sense. Marlene must have thought so too because she didn't try to refute it. For a long moment she just stared down at the neat stacks of papers on her desktop. Quietly, to herself, she said, "I wonder how long it will take me to clean this desk out?" It felt awful to hear her say that.

"Look, Marlene, you're not going to get fired. No one is going to blame you for this, I should never have been running the press conference in the first place."

"That's for damned sure," she said. (A little uncharitably, I thought.) Then she just sort of fell backward into her chair and put her forehead into the heel of one hand. To herself again, she said, "I just don't know why Jack doesn't have confidence in me. Why didn't he let me handle it?"

"Well, Marlene," I said, "maybe this will teach him a lesson."

There wasn't anything more to say to her. I turned to go. When I left I found her staff all standing outside her office door listening. I gestured for them to leave her alone for a while, and walked out of the PR office.

I wasn't sure where I was going. I felt too exhausted and depressed to go back to my office and try to work. I considered going over to get Emma's liquid nitrogen, not knowing what else to do. Maybe that would slightly dull the edge of her chagrin when she heard about how badly the press conference had gone.

Out in the hallway someone called out my name.

"Claire, Hi. They told me there was a press conference about the Weber meeting. I was coming to the public relations office to find out where it was." She smiled broadly and gave me a hug.

It was Cindy Stuhrm-Lawson, Roger's wife.

CHAPTER TWELVE

Cindy Stuhrm-Lawson is a pleasant-looking woman. She's an inch or two taller than I am, not slender but well-proportioned, with thick black hair framing a cherubic face. She was wearing a long black coat with brass buttons over a business suit in green and black plaid. A matching green scarf around her neck contrasted nicely with her dark complexion. It made her look very stylish.

I didn't know Cindy well. She'd been a first year philosophy grad student at the University of Chicago when Roger and Emma were well into their doctoral dissertations, and I was finishing mine in economics. That was long after Emma-and-Roger had turned into Emma-and-me, but Emma was still friends with Roger and we had socialized with them some. The night we met Cindy the four of us sat at a little corner table in Jimmy's Bar in Hyde Park. Emma and Roger argued about Nietzsche, or something, while Cindy and I drank our beers, listened to the juke box, and made some desultory small talk about movies and books. What sticks in my memory is that she had her hand looped around Roger's forearm. All night. I kept waiting for her to take it off, but it stayed there until the moment we got up to leave.

Like Roger, Cindy worked at Georgetown, but she wasn't on the faculty. For husband and wife philosophers to land teaching jobs at the same school would require, at least, the intervention of St. Jude. Cindy worked in the administration. It wasn't a bad job, associate dean of something or other, but I'd heard her lament that she wasn't using her Ph.D. in philosophy. Emma had told me that Cindy and Roger could each have had professorships within commutable distance of each other if Roger had accepted a job someplace less prestigious than Georgetown. But he'd been unwilling to do that.

Cindy was in a cheery and garrulous mood that afternoon. While we walked downstairs toward the press room she was merrily telling me about her decision to come out to Iowa.

"Anyway," she was saying, "we finished the whole proposal and mailed it off when Arthur, my provost, the man I work for, says it was the best proposal he'd ever seen! He asked if I was ready to take on more responsibility." Cindy gripped my arm and squeezed it with both hands. "Well I was floored by this, Claire. I didn't think he liked my work at all."

We were on the landing between the first and second floors of the administration building. I tried hard to listen to Cindy's story and express enthusiasm in appropriate places. It wasn't easy. I was too filled with anxiety over what we might encounter when we reached the first floor. In typical Claire-like fashion I'd forgotten to give Roger the message that Cindy was flying out here to join him. We were about to discover how serious an oversight that might have been.

As our feet hit the bottom step I was hoping against hope that Roger had left the press room. Or that Sara Grace had left the press room. Or, at an absolute bare minimum, that Sara Grace and Roger were not standing so close together that their proximity could be construed as more than geographic.

Did any of my three little wishes come true? Of course not. As soon as we emerged from the first-floor stairwell, Cindy enthusing about a possible promotion, we saw Roger in the corridor near the door of the conference room. He was facing away from us, still talking with a couple of reporters. Standing next to him, right next to him, was the young, beautiful Sara Grace Harper. Cindy recognized Roger from behind and we turned and started heading toward him.

Things might still have been OK had not Sara Grace chosen that particular moment to make a small but disastrous gesture with her hand. She lightly ran it up the back of Roger's jacket, just up and down for a second or two. Intent on his conversation with the media, Roger himself probably didn't notice it.

But Cindy reacted to that gesture as though it were a bolt of lightning, a sudden slap across the face. She abruptly stopped walking and stood there staring at the back of her husband, who was maybe twenty feet away. Her face went white, and her mouth hung slightly open. For a second nothing happened. I held my breath. Then, just as abruptly, Cindy whirled on her heel and walked off down the hall in the opposite direction.

Just like that.

I felt a quick wave of nausea as I turned to follow Cindy. What had I done? I had screwed up badly this time. I should have warned Roger or told Emma, or done some damn thing to let people know that Cindy was coming. God, now I could write in, '3) Cindy's marriage,' under, '1) Marlene's career' and, '2) Emma's conference' on the List of Things I Wrecked Today.

I raced down the hall to catch up with Cindy. (Apparently, Marlene was the second fastest woman I knew in heels.)

"Cindy, are you OK? What's wrong?" I figured that if I let her know I knew what was wrong it would only confirm her suspicions.

Cindy didn't answer. She just zoomed along the corridor headed she-couldn't-possibly-know-where, blinking rapidly as tears came to her eyes. I felt panic begin to rise in my throat and squeeze at my windpipe. What was I going to do?

Cindy came to the end of the corridor, made a random choice to turn left, and headed up the north wing of the administration building. I made a quick decision. When we passed a women's room on the right side of the hall, I grabbed her by the arm and pulled her into it. She offered no resistance. I looked to see that no one else was in there, then sat her on a wooden bench that stood near the doorway. She'd gotten a handkerchief out of her purse and was holding it against her eyes.

This was hideously awkward, to say the least. Cindy was more an acquaintance than a friend, and there seemed no logical reason she'd want to confide in me. Moreover, it wasn't clear that I'd be much help. As it happens, you see, relationship talks are not my special gift. I suppose I differ from most women in this respect, but for some reason they make me feel uncomfortable, even when they're about someone else's relationship. I don't know why this is, maybe because I was raised by my dad. On the other hand, Emma, needless to say, is deeply committed to relationship talks and never foregoes an opportunity to have one. She wants to talk not only about each and every little crisis, but also have routine maintenance talks, a sort of every-ten-thousand-miles kind of thing. For the first few months we lived together I strongly resisted. But I soon learned that my resistance caused fights, which led to even more relationship talks. My point here is that I didn't feel competent to talk Cindy through this crisis in her relationship with Roger. But I'd certainly helped get her into this situation; I had to do something.

"Cindy, tell me what's the matter," I said. "Is it that girl who was standing next to Roger?" She nodded tearfully, hand and handkerchief still pressed against her eyes. "Cindy, all I saw was her patting his back. She's just a kid flirting with one of these visiting professors, I'm sure it's no big deal."

"Claire," she waved the hand with the handkerchief at me, "believe me, when it comes to Roger and women students, I know what I'm seeing. I've seen it more times than you can imagine. And when he knew I was coming…"

A pause. She looked at me sideways. "So why am I still with him, right?" she asked. She gave a tiny self-mocking smile, then bent her head down, elbows on her knees. "It's all very complicated, Claire."

"Do you want to tell me about it?" I didn't know what else to say.

"No!" she said, then quickly added, "It isn't fair to burden you with this, Claire. I don't even know you that well." She sniffed, "And, of course, you're…" I could have finished the sentence for her: you're the partner of Roger's former lover.

For a few moments we just sat. I could hear the sound of water dripping somewhere in the room. With a queasy stomach, I felt a sudden compulsion to confess my own role in her marital disaster.

"Cindy, I have to tell you something. I think some of this is my fault." She looked up from her handkerchief. "I was the one who read your message to Emma, the one where you said you were coming out to join Roger. The truth is that I forgot to give it to her, Roger didn't know you were coming."

She looked away and sniffed a couple of times. "It isn't your fault, Claire. If he had known I was coming he would've just hidden it like he always does." She blew her nose into the handkerchief.

It took a few seconds for her to trace my confession forward to its logical implication. She looked at me. "But what you're saying, aren't you, is that I'm right. Roger has been carrying on with that girl."

In point of fact, there was no direct evidence of actual carrying on.

"In point of fact," I said, "there is no direct evidence of actual carrying…ah…" My chin dropped as she stared at me and shook her head. "Well, I guess I suspected it," I admitted.

For a while there was just the sound of the dripping water. I had not the faintest idea what to say to this poor woman. How could I have forgotten to hand over that message?

"Cindy, do you want to go out and talk to Roger? I'll come with you if you want."

She didn't answer right away.

Then she suddenly seemed filled with anger and determination. She said, "No, I don't want to talk to him. I want to go home." She stood up from the bench. "I'm going to get my rental car and drive back to the airport. Good-bye, Claire."

When she tried to take a step she pitched forward about forty degrees so that I had to stand up and grab her by the shoulder.

"Cindy!" I wrapped my arm around her. "Cindy, you shouldn't drive like this." Her body felt wobbly. "Listen, Cindy…ah, how about if I drive you back to the airport." A rash statement, when the hell would I be able to do that? I still had to fetch the liquid nitrogen. I tried to think.

"Look," I told her, "I have a really important errand to do now, but it will only take a half hour or so. Please stay until I'm finished. Then I'll drive you back to the airport. What do you say?"

Eyes closed, with a hand against her forehead, she considered this suggestion. "What about my rental car?"

"We'll get a student to drive it back." A student, I was thinking, other than Sara Grace Harper.

She thought for a few seconds. "OK," she said. "OK, I'd appreciate that Claire."

"And you're sure you don't want to talk to Roger, or let him know you're here?"

"No, I definitely don't."

"Well, all right then," I looked around, "let's get the heck out of here."

I kept hold of her as we walked out of the women's room. Was I really going to drag this poor woman around campus on a quest for liquid nitrogen?

The bright sun warmed us as we trudged north across campus toward the science building where I was supposed to get the liquid nitrogen. The temperature was in the mid-twenties, bright sunshine with no wind, and had I been thinking about the weather I would have described these conditions as just about perfect for a mid-winter day. Of course I wasn't thinking about the weather. I was thinking about how I would have preferred not to have Cindy tagging along. But it just didn't seem right to dump her somewhere and have her cry by herself while she waited for me to finish this stupid errand. Moreover, it was clear that she wanted someone to talk to. Even me.

Maybe there was some symbolism in my taking Cindy along to get the liquid nitrogen to keep Emma's sperm frozen, like a cosmic warning or something. I mean, Cindy's relationship with Roger was in some ways a lot like mine and Emma's. Although they'd spent more time living together as a real couple than Emma and I had, I had known Emma about as long as Cindy had known Roger. The four of us had met in the same place and we were all struggling with the great two-academic-jobs problem. I'd like to believe that my relationship with Emma worked better than her marriage to Roger, but otherwise there were key similarities. And now their marriage was in serious trouble. And Cindy and Roger didn't even have any children; surely children wouldn't have made things any easier for them. Especially if the child really belonged to only one of them.

"You probably didn't know this," Cindy was saying, "but I left Roger about two years ago." I held lightly onto Cindy's arm; she was still very tearful, and I didn't trust her to notice the patches of ice melting on the sidewalk. "He'd had a series of affairs with different students. I suspected it for a while, but never had any proof. Then he got into some trouble with his department. The parents of one student lodged a complaint and it almost got him denied tenure. And of course I was humiliated in front of the entire campus. So I left him."

"Hmmm," I said. I'd started thinking about the liquid nitrogen. Emma said Steve would call the chemistry people and arrange for them to give it to us. Had he done that? Did he tell them how much I was supposed to get? I certainly had no idea.

Cindy and I reached the chemistry building as a big pack of trustees and alums were filing in through the main entrance. At the head of this group was some science professor whose face I recognized but whose name I didn't know, describing some renovations just completed on the building.

Cindy continued her tale as I tried to decipher the building directory. I needed to find the chemistry department office, room 225.

"Roger and I were apart for six months."

"Six months," I said. The building directory made no sense. The hallway to our left had rooms 200-219 and 230-242, but none of the rooms in the 220s.

"Yeah. I was terribly depressed most of that time, but at the end of it I was determined to file for divorce."

"Divorce," I said. We walked a few feet down the corridor. The next hallway started at room 241 and ran to 260. Where the hell were the 220s?

"Yes, I figured I should get Roger out of my life. Find a new job, move to another place. I was scared as hell at this idea, but I had made up my mind to try it. But then Roger came and talked me out of it."

"Really?" I said. It was apparent that while renovating this building they had somehow misplaced all the rooms in the 220s. Or maybe they had sold them to Iowa State, I don't know, but they were definitely gone, that much was obvious.

"Yeah," Cindy said. "It surprised me too. Roger said he'd been miserable. He said he was sorry for the pain he caused me. He asked could we try again? He said he wanted us to have a baby."

"A baby," I said. We turned back toward the main entrance. Room 225 had to be on the other side of the building.

"Yeah. I'd wanted to have a baby for years, but Roger resisted. He said it wasn't the right time in his career. Of course, I knew it never would be. The right time, I mean."

"Uh, huh," I said. Back at the front door I saw that a sort of mini-hallway ran off to the right and at an acute angle. A sign said that the rooms 221-229 were clustered in there. Why, I don't know. The hallway was crowded with trustees listening to their tour guide describe the renovations. Cindy and I had to weave our way through them to enter the chemistry office.

The walls of the office of the chemistry department were covered with exhibits, mostly illustrations of department research projects. At the center of the room was a desk on which there were neat rows of pictures in gilded frames, an in/out basket, and two tidy stacks of documents. Behind the desk sat a small, white-haired woman in a lilac dress with a lace collar. She smiled at us as we came into the office. Noticing immediately that Cindy had been crying, her expression changed from pleasant greeting to grandmotherly concern.

"Can I help you?"

"Hi, I'm Claire Sinclair. I believe Steve Penski told you I'd be coming to get some liquid nitrogen."

"Oh, yes, that's right. I wrote out a supply-request slip after he called." She glanced at Cindy who was unable to suppress the occasional sniff. "Let me just get some billing information from you and then you can take the slip down to the lab manager." She got a pen from her pen holder and held it poised over the request form. "Now then, what department are you in?"

I was afraid she was going to ask that. "Economics," I said. Cindy got out a Kleenex and began daubing her eyes again.

"Economics? You're in the economics department?" She sounded surprised. I didn't blame her. "Well, all right then. Can you give me the account number of economics for billing?"

Oh hell, I didn't want this billed to the economics department. How would I explain it to my chairman? I was experimenting to see if demand becomes less elastic when you dip the buyer in liquid nitrogen?

"Um, I'd rather not have it billed to my department. How about I just write you a check?"

"A check?" Her eyebrows came together. "Well, I wouldn't know what to do with a check. Normally I charge supplies to a department."

"Yes, I know, but this liquid nitrogen isn't for a department, it's for personal use."

"Personal use?" Her eyes clouded over; I could tell she was furiously trying to imagine a 'personal use' for liquid cooled to minus 320 degrees. She glanced at Cindy who was sniffing again. Then I saw that she made a decision. It was clear to the chemistry secretary that for whatever reason, this poor woman crying beside me needed liquid nitrogen, needed it badly, and needed it now. "Tell you what," she said, "why don't I just give you a procurement slip and you can call me with an account number when you decide how to bill it."

"That would be very convenient, thank you." Beautiful. A classic Iowa matron, I felt like hugging her. She wrote out a requisition form and directed us to the supply room in the basement of the building. On our way downstairs Cindy resumed the tale of her marital troubles.

"Anyway, Roger agreed that we could try to have a baby. So I decided I'd give the marriage another chance. Bad reason, I know." We headed down the left hallway at the bottom of the stairs as the secretary had instructed. "In any event he didn't keep his promise long. While I was pregnant there was at least one incident with another woman. I didn't know what to do, I couldn't just leave now that I was pregnant."

"No, I guess not." There it was, just like she said: Laboratory Supply Room. From the room next door came the sound of some kind of lecture or presentation. Apparently the trustees were being shown the newly renovated labs. I knocked on the heavy steel door of the supply room and a young man wearing light brown work clothes answered. He had dark hair and a trim beard, and he ushered us into a windowless room with a bare cement floor. The walls were lined floor to ceiling with deep steel shelves loaded with tools, equipment, bottles of chemicals, and various pieces of electronic gadgetry. Bright fluorescent lights glared down from the ceiling. There was a faint but distinct odor which, if memory can be trusted twenty years after my last bio course, was the smell of formaldehyde.

"OK," said the young man, examining the request slip, "did you bring a container to put it in?"

A container? I hadn't even thought about a container. "Uh, I didn't, but I could go back to my office and get a thermos." He frowned at that suggestion.

"It says here you want twenty liters, that won't fit in a thermos."

Damn, damn, damn, I thought, now what am I going to do?

"Well," said the supply manager, looking around, "I'm sure we have something we could lend you. What will you be using this for?"

Oh, God. I didn't want to answer that question, I really didn't. I didn't want to tell even one person that Emma was trying to get pregnant because at a college this small the news would spread across campus like a grass fire on a dry prairie. But how could I avoid telling this man? I was up against the wall. I had no container, I had no means of transport, I had no other choice. Thinking to myself, I'm sorry Emma, I took a deep breath and let the cat out of the bag.

"I need it to keep some sperm frozen until it can be used for insemination."

He nodded. "Sure, we have a tank over here that's designed for that."

I was stunned. He walked over and picked up what looked like the water cooler that sat on the bench of my field hockey team in high school. The top was fitted with some sort of special cap that kept the tank sealed.

He said, "This is what most of them use to freeze sperm."

I nearly gasped. This is what most of them use? Most of whom? Was there a secret cabal of women on this campus performing ritual artificial insemination?

"Them?" I simply had to ask.

"The hog breeders," he said. "We picked this up at a farm equipment auction. There are fancier ones around, but this'll work fine."

Of course. He thought I was using liquid nitrogen to freeze hog sperm. What other kind of sperm would a God-fearing Iowan freeze?

"There is one problem, though," he said. "This thing didn't come with a cane."

"A cane?"

"The thing that holds the sperm vial in the middle of the tank. You can't just let it sink to the bottom, you know."

"Oh right, the cane," I said, trying to sound hog-breeder-like. "Ah…where could I get a cane do you think?"

"Oh, up at Henny's or Corval's, I guess. Any breeder."

I knew that as a hog breeder I shouldn't have to ask who Henny and Corval were, I should be pals with those guys. "OK, I'll check with one of them," I said. "Thanks."

The supply manager handed me some heavy gloves and pointed to a large, cylindrical tank protruding from the far wall of the room. "I gotta go help with the trustee tour," he said. "Holler if you need me." The lecture from the next lab got louder as he disappeared through a side entrance leading to it.

All this time Cindy stood near the door we'd come through and stared down at the cement floor. The peculiarity of our surroundings seemed to mean nothing to her. Her mind was in another place, another time, struggling with an altogether different problem. All of a sudden she started to cry again, softly to herself.

"Cindy, it'll be OK, honey. Let me just get this tank filled and we'll talk some more."

As quickly as I could, I dragged the container across the floor and put it under the spout at the bottom of the tank. I donned the gloves and, with some difficulty, turned the round handle on the spigot of the tank. There was a gushing sound.

Instantly the room filled with steam-like vapor. Evaporating nitrogen rose up like fog as it poured from the spigot into the container. This provoked from me the sound you hear when you accidentally step on a poodle's tail. In the lab next door the lecture abruptly stopped. Nitrogen vapor was flowing under the door. Oh, shit!

"Is everything all right in here?" It was the science professor giving the tour. He poked his head through the supply room door and looked at me curiously. I was sure he recognized me as a faculty member but knew I didn't teach in any of the sciences. Then he noticed Cindy crying. Alarm spread across his face and he stepped into the room.

"Did someone get hurt?"

I wished he had said that a little more quietly. In seconds the doorway was thick with trustees, mostly middle-aged men in dark business suits, all pressing forward to get into the room, their faces full of concern at this apparently serious laboratory mishap. One could imagine members of the Buildings and Grounds Committee resolving to review campus safety procedures.

"No, no, we're fine, we're fine," I assured them loudly, waving my hand to blow away the fog. "We're very sorry to interrupt."

The trustees and the professor gave me suspicious looks, but the latter could see what had caused all the fog. "There's no problem here," he said. "Shall we go back to the lab and continue the demonstration?" He shepherded his flock out of the supply room and frowned at me before shutting the door behind him with a bang.

I closed the valve and took a full minute to figure out how the sealing cap on the top of the tank worked. Then it was definitely time to leave. I hoisted the heavy container with both hands and tried to walk toward the door. The result was a ridiculous staggering waddle that would have embarrassed a pregnant duck. I set the tank down. Impossible. There was no way I could lug this thing a quarter mile across campus down slippery steps and over icy sidewalks. There was only one thing to do, and I only did it with great reluctance.

"Cindy, I know how lousy you feel right now, but do you think you could help me carry this thing?" Nice, Claire. You won't let her drive to the airport, but you will make her drag this tank around campus.

Listlessly, Cindy said, "Sure," and reached down to take the other handle of the container. Lifting it between us we left the supply room and headed back up the stairs.

I felt guilty for having, first, paid so little attention to Cindy's story, and then having roped her into helping in this ridiculous enterprise. I tried to make amends. "I'm sorry for the interruption Cindy. Why don't you finish telling me about what happened between you and Roger." She resumed the tale as smoothly as if she'd never stopped talking, as if we hadn't looked foolish in the laboratory supply room, as if she wouldn't feel silly lugging supercooled liquid across a frozen campus in the dead of winter.

"So, anyway, after I got pregnant I hoped things—"

"Pregnant? You got pregnant?"

She looked confused. "Yeah, I told you. When we got back together he agreed we could have a baby."

"Oh, right. Sorry."

We had made it to the first floor and were trying to maneuver the tank out the main door of the science building.

"Anyway, Roger started acting in a way that made me suspicious again. He was having long meetings in the evenings with one of his 'protégées,' a student in his senior seminar. When I confronted him, told him how suspicious I was, he denied everything. We had a huge fight."

We started across East Campus toward Emma's office, Cindy telling her tale and me watching for patches of ice. The air was less cold now and there was still no wind. The exertion of dragging this heavy tank around made us warm in the winter sunshine.

"Anyway," Cindy said, "that night I lost the baby."

I stopped. We set the tank down on the sidewalk and I straightened up to look Cindy in the face. I started to reach over to squeeze Cindy's hand, but suddenly feeling embarrassed, I let my arm drop to my side. "Good Lord, Cindy, I'm really sorry."

She turned her head and looked away for a few seconds. By the time she looked back at me tears had started rolling down her cheeks again. She grabbed the tank handle determinedly, as if to say, let's keep going. We hoisted it again and she continued.

"Well, after I lost the baby, Roger acted like he was very sorry. He seemed moved by it. He swore to me things were going to be different, and I believed him." She sniffed. "That sounds stupid now, of course."

"No, it doesn't." Actually it did, but I was trying to, you know, say something nice. It was getting harder and harder to do that because my arm was beginning to ache.

"When Roger went to Germany this fall I could only go for two weeks in October. He was very solicitous, he acted like he missed me."

We made the turn toward Emma's building and Cindy paused in her story as we negotiated the tank through the double doors at the front entrance. We made a sharp left into the main philosophy office. Maria saw us struggling with the heavy container and immediately came over to help. I introduced Cindy and Maria while Maria held the door to Emma's office for us.

"What is in the tank?"

"Oh, nothing much," I said, "just some stuff we need at home." Maria was too polite to press for a better answer.

We set the tank down on Emma's floor with a thunk. My arm was killing me and I was out of breath. Cindy, who showed no effects of exertion, resumed her story, not seeming to even notice Maria. "Roger wrote me sweet, long letters from Germany. And when he found something interesting in the Stasi files, he was all excited about it. We had a wonderful time when I was there in October."

"What are the Stasi files?" I asked, genuinely curious. Maria stood behind Cindy listening to our conversation.

"The Stasi were the East German Secret Police. They had a huge amount of material and Roger went through it this fall looking for background material on Weber."

"Weren't the files secret?"

"Since reunification, most of them have been opened up."

"So," I said, "is this where Roger found his big surprise about Weber? The thing his paper is about?"

"Yeah."

"So what was it?"

Emma banged in loudly through the main office door. Maria and Cindy and I all turned to look at her.

"Cindy!" she said, "What are you doing here?"

CHAPTER THIRTEEN

When I explained to Emma why Cindy's visit was unannounced, she gave me a pretty icy stare, I can tell you. If she'd looked at the sperm that way we wouldn't have needed liquid nitrogen. But I was way past being cowed by nasty faces from Emma. In a single day I'd been humiliated in front of television cameras, had made a fool of myself to a group of trustees, and had lost all feeling in my favorite arm, all on Emma's behalf. No, at this point I figured I should hold the local monopoly on giving dirty looks, especially after lugging that stupid tank across campus. Emma did, I admit, act grateful to Cindy and me for doing that and seemed relieved to see the liquid nitrogen. I explained to her that we still needed the metal cane that held the vial in the center of the tank.

Anyway, in Emma's office, with the door closed, Cindy repeated her story as we all drank the coffee Maria had brought us voluntarily (the Kendall Professor of Feminist Thought would not ask a secretary to bring her some coffee). Eventually it was decided that Cindy would not return to the airport, she would stay the night with us. We were hosting a party for the conference that evening and Cindy could meet Roger there and confront him if she wanted to. This was Emma's idea, and one which I thought perfectly insane. I didn't want them fighting in our house, during a party, for God's sake! But Emma is nothing if not a loyal friend. Cindy agreed to this plan only after extracting a solemn promise from each of us that we wouldn't tell Roger she was here; she said she wanted time to think about what to say to him.

Finally Cindy left with Maria, who'd offered to drive her and the liquid nitrogen tank back to our house. Before she left she told us what supportive friends we were, gave my hand a little squeeze, then hugged Emma around the neck and kissed her on the cheek. (She and Emma were both trained in the humanities.)

When Cindy and Maria were gone, Emma asked me, "So, do you think Roger's really carrying on with Sara Grace?"

"Well, I can't be sure, but it looks pretty bad." I told her about seeing them by the fire at the inn the night before.

She shook her head. "What do you think I should do? I'd like to go tell him off. Tell him that Hammond does not tolerate sexual exploitation of innocent students by adulterous faculty lechers. But Cindy won't want that."

"Could you at least keep Sara Grace away from him, maybe keep her busy with conference work?"

"Yeah." She nodded slowly. "Good idea."

"Ah…by the way," I said. "While we're on the subject of bad things Roger did…" I proceeded to tell her about the press conference and Roger's little coup in hyping his upcoming paper to the reporters.

Her pretty blue eyes burned bright with anger. "Boy, he is such a contemptible toad. All this media attention is just what he wants."

"Whoa! I just came up with a theory, Emma!" I leaned across the desk and raised my eyebrows. In a whisper I said, "Maybe Roger clunked Weber on the head so the press would come out here to hear his paper." Actually I was only half-joking.

Emma smiled a bit. "I wouldn't put it past him. Nevertheless, I'm afraid I must say something that I expect you economists hear rather frequently: your theory is a pile of pigeon poop."

"Why?"

"Because Roger couldn't have done it. Neither could anyone else. That's what Pete and I spent the morning doing, finding out where everyone was between 5:00 and 6:30 yesterday."

"So is Pete satisfied now that it was an accident?" This thought brightened my mood considerably.

"I don't think so. He was very cheery and polite with everyone this morning, but there was always this, I don't know, police-chief look in his eyes."

She said this while rubbing each temple with the tips of two fingers like she does at the onset of a migraine. Oh Lord, don't let her get one of her migraines, not on top of all this.

"Well, what's Pete's problem?" I asked her.

"I don't know what his problem is. It couldn't possibly have been a murder, you found him lying on the bridge, didn't you?"

"True," I said, "though that doesn't rule out someone hitting him before I came along. Someone who ran off when he heard me coming."

"And just who might that someone have been? Everyone was accounted for when Weber died."

"Everyone was at the opening talk?"

"As far as we can tell, yes. Kurt came in just before five and we started his

98

talk immediately. We didn't take attendance or anything but I'm pretty sure everyone was there. I was in and out some of the time checking on arrangements with Food Service."

"So you can't be sure that someone didn't leave? Besides yourself I mean."

She stopped rubbing her temples and leveled her eyes at me. "As a matter of fact, Miss Marple, I can be sure no one left. Sara Grace was standing at the doorway the whole time handing programs to everyone who came in."

"And she confirmed that no one went out?"

That look again. "Yes, Claire, no one came out." Tone: a little on the testy side. "No faculty, anyway, just a couple of students."

"Did Sara Grace know who the students were?"

"She didn't know all of them but she said they looked familiar, she'd seen them around campus. They were too young to be professors."

"What about the other little mysteries Pete mentioned in Jack's office? Did they ever find Weber's car and luggage? Did you figure out how he heard about the conference?"

These questions provoked more fatigue than annoyance. She leaned back in her desk chair and closed her eyes. "I don't know about the car, the police were checking on that. No one admitted to telling Weber about the conference, but I don't think that means much." She sighed a heavy sigh. "I'm in hell, Claire. In hell. Thank God John Marchak isn't alive to see how badly I mangled his conference."

"For heaven's sake, Emma, none of this is your fault." I reached over and rubbed my hand along her arm. Eyes still closed, her mouth formed a slight, weak smile and she put her hand over mine. "How's everyone taking it?" I asked. "His death, I mean. Weren't some of these people his friends?"

"Well, everyone's pretty shocked." Her head still leaned against the back of the tall chair. "The odd thing is though," she opened her eyes and looked at me, "his death has made the whole conference more…I don't know…more interesting. Livelier. People think it's exciting that the inn is crawling with reporters interviewing everyone about Weber." She shook her head. "I think I'm the only one here who isn't having a good time." She leaned back and closed her eyes again.

For a moment neither of us said anything, and in the silence I remembered that little piece of paper in my pocket. I took it out and reached across Emma's desk with it.

"By the way, is this yours?"

She glanced at it. "It looks like my writing. Why? What is it?"

"You don't remember writing this message?"

"No, I don't." An inquisitive look. "Why?" When I didn't answer she looked at the message again and her voice became a little impatient. "What is it?"

"It's just something I found, that's all," I said. A pause.

She stared at me, waiting. "So?"

"So…nothing," I said.

Now she sounded irritated. "Well, where did you find it?"

That was a very simple question to which I did not want to give a simple answer. I had told her at the reception last night about finding the old man, the old man who showed up again dead at the river, the old man who turned out to be Erik Weber. So if I said I'd found this note next to his body, there was only one reason that I would be asking: I was suspicious about her relationship with Weber. You could figure that one out without being a Rhodes Scholar, and Emma, incidentally, had been a Rhodes Scholar. But maybe I could answer in a way that wouldn't make my curiosity sound like suspicion. Maybe, very casually, I could say I found this next to the body of the guy you said you didn't know even though he caused your girlfriend's suicide, and while I realize that you could never (ha, ha) do violence to anybody, you did get sent (hee, hee) to a mental hospital a few years ago, so if you could just explain…

Maybe not. So what should I say?

Some people are annoyed by a ringing telephone. But when Emma's phone rang, it sounded to me like the bagpipes of the Coldstream Guards arriving in the nick of time to drive off the attacking Boers. Emma picked up the phone, spoke for a few seconds, then hung up.

"That was Sara Grace. I have to go back to the inn and dig up an overhead projector for Arnie Cohen's talk. It was supposed to have been there already." She groaned softly and stretched her shoulders as she got up out of her chair. She had buttoned up her coat and was pulling on her gloves when she asked, "Will you be back in time to start the hors d'oeuvres for the party?"

"Back from where?"

Casually, thoughtlessly, she tossed that last little straw onto the camel's back. "Back from getting the cane for the liquid nitrogen."

That statement set me off like a stick of dynamite. I exploded with the righteous fury of the brutally oppressed. "I can't believe this! I'm not going to get that cane. I've had it with your little errands. I've spent two days doing things for you, hosting dinners, holding press conferences, chasing sperm all over central Iowa, I'm going to work for myself now." I stood up, grabbed my coat and prepared to stride theatrically out of her office.

Before I could leave she tried to manipulate me with the sort of cheap, adolescent, utterly transparent trick that I fall for every time: she started crying. As I turned to fling out some dramatic exit line I saw that she was leaning on her desk staring out her window, tears starting to run down both sides of her face. Yeesh.

"Look, Emma," I tried to swallow my irritation. "Why don't we just get a student to go get the cane? You don't have to tell him what it's for. You call ahead, he gets it, he brings it back, that's it. This isn't such a big deal." Emma kept looking out the window.

"It isn't the cane, Claire, that's not why I'm crying."

Well, of course I then had to ask, "Why are you crying?" the sort of question that leaves you wide open for a relationship talk.

"It isn't so much that you won't cooperate on my trying to get pregnant. It's the reason you won't cooperate."

"I have cooperated, Emma. The reason I won't cooperate endlessly is that I have a lot of work to do."

"No, Claire, that's wrong." She turned to look at me, her eyes full of accusation. "You still don't want to have a baby with me. You say you do, but you really don't. It always comes back to the same thing."

She came swishing around her desk, yanked open the door and made the big theatrical exit that I was supposed to have made. I wanted to run after her, answer that accusation, tell her she was wrong, at least say something in response.

But what could I say?

CHAPTER FOURTEEN

No one who knows me would be surprised to learn that I ended up going to get the cane. From Emma's office I called one of the places the lab manager had mentioned and they did indeed have a cane I could buy. The place was ten miles northwest of town on Highway 58. I decided I would go out there and get it. Getting the cane, I assured myself, would by no means constitute admission that what Emma had said about my feelings was true. Nor would it diminish my claim to have already made huge sacrifices for Emma's conference, for Emma's pregnancy, and for Emma in general. Going to get the cane, I decided, would merely be one more example of how I'm a selfless and devoted partner. A cooperative and supportive partner. Hey, let's not mince words, this made me practically a saint of a partner.

So I started trudging back home to get my car. On the way I had to pass the library, except I didn't quite pass the library. I slowed down in front of the library, I stood for a moment staring at the library, and then, on a whim, I went into the library. It had occurred to me that the library subscribed to one of those CD databases that have every phone number in the United States. Maybe I could search that database to see whose phone number was written on that slip of green paper I'd found. Emma's note told Weber he should call this person, and if I knew who it was it might tell me something. Exactly what it would tell me I didn't know, but what the heck.

The whole process only took a minute or two. The name on the terminal screen in the library basement said Regina Daly, RR 1, Hammond. No street address, someone living out in the country. I turned off the terminal and headed up to the reference section on the main floor. I glanced over my shoulder to see if anyone I knew would see me here, but the only other person was a student clerk stamping books over at the circulation desk. I pulled out the Jesop County Plat book and looked in the index under Daly, Regina. She lived on a farm on the Newton-Bascom Road about six miles northwest of town. I guessed that she was a farm widow. I closed the book. Why in the world would Erik Weber, an internationally known European scholar, need to call some farm lady in the middle of Iowa?

A cheery thought occurred to me. Maybe the note had nothing to do with Weber. Maybe it was just a random slip of paper floating around campus that I happened to pick up near where Weber fell. Maybe my worries were entirely fantastic. Emma could have written that note to someone besides Weber, someone who dropped it, and the wind blew it to me just after I found Weber. A simple coincidence. Improbable perhaps, but that's the way coincidences are. What I should do, I decided, was to stop being silly and ask Emma again, this time more directly, what the note was about. Or, better yet, forget the damned thing altogether. It meant nothing. Why was I bothering with something so trivial?

I put the plat book back on its shelf. My head felt a bit giddy with relief as I walked out of the library into the waning winter daylight and headed back home to get my car.

It was almost four o'clock when I drove past West Campus on my way out of town to get the cane. I saw a familiar-looking man coming toward me down the sidewalk. He was walking very slowly and seemed to be limping, both hands stuck in the pockets of his overcoat, his head looking down at the sidewalk in front of him. I realized it was Kurt Burghoff, the professor from Ohio State who had opened the conference. He was a long way from the inn, and was almost certainly missing a talk at this time. I pulled up next to the curb and rolled down my window.

"Professor Burghoff? Hi, I'm Claire Sinclair, we met last night."

He seemed a little startled, but gave me a weak smile. "Yes...how are you?" He also looked the slightest bit embarrassed. I guessed that he was lost and couldn't find the inn because he was certainly headed in the wrong direction. It seemed impolite to ask. I was loath to accuse a distinguished philosopher of wandering around aimlessly, even though that's pretty much my opinion of what they all do professionally.

"Can I give you a ride back to the inn, Professor?"

He hesitated for a moment, looking up at the trees as if trying to decide. "Yes, thank you, that is kind of you."

I watched him step slowly and carefully around the front of the car and open the door on the passenger side. He leaned against the door frame and used his hands to put his left leg in before lowering the rest of himself into the seat. His grey wool overcoat came down past his knees and he smelled a little like tobacco.

He gave a slight grunt as he buckled the seat belt across his chest. "I am afraid that you caught me, Ms. Sinclair."

"Caught you?"

"Yes, I was taking a stroll, playing hooky from the conference."

That made me laugh. "Professor Burghoff!" I said.

"Yes, it is shocking." He smiled. "But please call me Kurt." He was quite handsome for an elderly man, very distinguished-looking, and with a disarming smile. "The sunshine was so lovely I just had to get outside."

"Well, your secret's safe with me." His eyes were wrinkly and looked a little bloodshot. I could imagine how he must be feeling, having lost his old friend Weber yesterday. To the others at the conference, Weber was an academic subject, a field of study, a means of advancing their own careers. But here was a man who'd known him personally for, what, forty years? Fifty years? Longer than Emma or I had been alive.

I turned the car around and headed up Park Street.

"You teach…ah…history, Claire?"

"Economics."

"Economics, yes. I do not know much economics, I'm afraid. Not besides Marx, anyway." He gave me a sly look. "And I am told that these days Marx could not even get tenure."

"Well, not if he kept spelling 'capital' with a K." Kurt laughed.

I slowed the car as we passed Maple Street. "There is a very nice arboretum about a quarter mile that way. You might consider that for your next stroll."

"Ah." He looked in the direction I was pointing. "It is very pleasant walking here. The big old homes remind me of the town I lived in as a boy. It was almost entirely destroyed by bombs in the war."

"The neighborhood by the college is the oldest part of town. Most of the houses are about a century old."

At the corner of Park and Lincoln I waited while two women escorted a band of toddlers, all puffy and cute in their thick winter outfits, across the street to the day-care center. One little boy stopped right in the middle and tried to line up his snow boots with the yellow line in the center of the road. The teacher smiled apologetically at me as she shooed him on. I could still hear the kid's excited babbling as we turned up Lincoln toward the inn.

"I hope I am not taking you out of your way, Claire."

"No, no, I'm just on an errand. I've got to drive out of town a few miles."

"Ah, well I envy you," he said. "The countryside is very lovely around here."

"Yeah, I'm looking forward to the drive." That was a lie.

"Much better than being stuck at a philosophy conference."

"I'm sure it is." That was the truth.

The inn appeared on our right and I pulled the car up next to the curb. "Well, here we are," I said. I recognized the dean of the faculty walking up to the front door carrying some stiff white posters under one arm. Probably charts and graphs to show the trustees, the dean was very big on charts and graphs.

Kurt unbuckled his seat belt and it snapped back into its holder. But he made no attempt to open the car door. He just sat staring through the window at the face of the inn, as if he needed some more time to get up the energy to go in. In that instant there occurred to me an improbable idea and I blurted it out without thinking.

"Want to come with me?" I said.

Without a hint of hesitation, he turned to me and smiled. "A charming idea." He rebuckled his seat belt. I smiled back at him, put the car in gear, and a second later off we went.

Outside of town, the sun was sinking so low that the stubble of corn stalks left shadows on the snowy fields. A few warm days had been followed by a cold spell, so that the top layer of snow had turned into ice. The fields looked as if they'd been shellacked.

"What is our mission, if I may ask?" Kurt said.

Oops. When I said I had blurted out my invitation without thinking, this is what I meant. How would I explain to Kurt what we were doing? More importantly, how would I explain to Emma why I had explained it to Kurt? Well, whatever the consequences, I was unwilling to lie to Emma's most distinguished guest.

I took a deep breath. "We're going to get a long metal cane that holds a vial of frozen sperm in a tank of liquid nitrogen." He didn't look at me, but his lips formed the slightest trace of a smile. I gave a short nervous laugh. "I suppose you'd like to know why we're doing that?"

"Not if you do not wish to tell me."

"No, I don't mind. It's kind of a secret, though, so if you could…for the time being at least…"

"We Germans are very good with secrets. That has been one of our problems in this century."

"OK, well, you see, Emma is trying to get pregnant. By artificial insemination, of course. I mean, not the regular way, you know, because she and I are a couple, so…that wouldn't work." Déjà vu from last night: I was babbling like a lunatic in front of this man. "Anyway, some semen arrived from a sperm bank yesterday, but Emma hasn't started ovulating yet. We have to keep it frozen until she's ready to, ah, use it." It seemed awfully strange to be having this particular conversation with a distinguished gentleman I barely knew.

"I see," he said. "Do you mind if I smoke, Claire? I should have quit years ago, I know, but at my age it is too late to bother now." He took out a cigarette and pushed in the dashboard cigarette lighter that I'd forgotten my car even had. "May I ask if this is Emma's first attempt to become pregnant?"

"Yes, it is."

"Then I wish you the best of luck. My late wife Greta and I were unable to have children, though we tried for many years. That was very hard on her."

"I'm sorry to hear that."

He nodded. "At my stage of life one should be playing with one's grandchildren, not writing more books." He held the lighter to the tip of his cigarette, then cracked his window a half inch. He blew the smoke toward the window, letting the speeding air suck it out of the car. "But work is a solace and a companion when you find yourself alone."

"How long ago did your wife die?" I hoped I wasn't being too personal with him.

"She died of a stroke five and a half years ago. Actually I have gotten used to being alone now. It has its consolations, one enjoys a certain freedom of movement, if you will. Renee Amundsen told me that I would adjust to it eventually, and she was right."

For some reason that statement tweaked a nerve of defensiveness in me. "Well, I think Renee has been happy that she chose not to have children. She's a very successful woman."

"Well, I am not so sure. She did not really choose it, of course," Kurt said. "Renee became sterile after an illegal abortion in the late 1960s."

Wow! I didn't know that. An illegal abortion. Boy, whatever else might be wrong with this conference, it was proving to be a fountain of juicy gossip.

We continued up the two lane country highway. I swung the Celica around a slow-moving semi, its big steel trailer full of holes like a cheesegrater. As we passed it, Kurt turned to watch the hogs inside, dark hunched forms huddled together against the cold. For a time we rode along in silence.

I started wondering—was it possible that Kurt knew something about Weber and Karen Kling?

"Kurt, were you by any chance at Freiburg with Weber?"

"No, I was in Berlin at that time. I had just made it out of East Germany."

"Did you have to sneak out? Escape, like that other man Spengler? Is that his name?"

"Actually Spengler did not get out. He was killed in the attempt. But no, when I got out of jail I was allowed to leave the country. It was partly thanks to Erik. He made a big fuss with the West German government and they put on pressure for my release."

"How long were you in jail?"

"About fourteen months," he said.

"What was it like?" I winced. Jesus, Claire, it was like summer camp in the Catskills, what do you think?

Kurt gave a sad smile. "Well, as you may have noticed," he tapped the thigh of his left leg, "I have never quite gotten over it."

"I'm sorry Professor, that was a stupid question. It's just that I find that sort of thing so hard to imagine. You know, people of my generation in the U.S. have lived in a country that has been, generally speaking, very safe and comfortable. Few of us have any idea what it's like to be afraid for our lives from war or hunger."

"Yes, you have been lucky," Kurt said. He reached down and put out his cigarette in the ashtray I only use to hold coins. "But we were lucky, too, in some ways. There in East Germany in the early sixties, life was exciting. We were on the front lines of the struggle between two great ideologies. We had a sense of purpose; we were publishing an underground newspaper. Very avant garde, very politically committed." He rolled up his window. "But as is so often the case with the young, our sense of the importance of our work was much too large, and our sense of its danger much too small."

"Because you eventually got caught."

"Yes, we did. We got caught just when we were about to get out. Erik had gotten out, of course." Kurt pushed back the sleeve on his overcoat to glance at his wristwatch.

"What happened?" I asked. Even I thought this was an interesting story.

"Erik had arranged for us to go out through a tunnel under the Berlin Wall. There were about twelve of us, I think, who contributed to the newspaper. Spengler was the head of this group, though I did not know that at the time."

"You didn't know Spengler was the leader of your group?"

"No, I knew only Erik and one other man. We did not all know each other, you see, that would have been too dangerous. Each member of the group knew only two other people in it. That way if you were captured and forced to talk, you could only divulge two names. It also made the group more difficult for the Stasi to infiltrate. The structure was much like the cell system which is still used by terrorist groups like the IRA."

From the inside pocket of his jacket Kurt pulled out a small plastic pill case. He took out a tiny white pill, placed it on the tip of his tongue and then swallowed.

"As it happened," he said, "Erik had made contact with a man who said he could get us out in three groups on three nights. It was enormously expensive but we all contributed what we could. The first group went out on a Thursday, I believe. Erik was in it, as was the other member of my cell. I was to go out on Saturday. But on Friday night, something went wrong, the Stasi showed up when the group was just entering the tunnel. They started shooting. The people in the rear were killed."

"And that's when Spengler died?"

"So I am told, I was not there myself. They started rounding the rest of us up almost immediately afterward." Kurt stared out at the empty fields. The setting sun gave a faintly purple cast to the white snow. I noticed Kurt's hand gently stroking the thigh of his bad leg.

"How do you think they found out about you? An informant?"

"Possibly, though I really have no idea who it could have been."

We rode in silence again until I saw, a few hundred yards ahead, a huge cinderblock building with a big hanging sign that said Henny's Hogs. The field behind the building was dotted with dozens of tiny hog shelters made of corrugated aluminum in an inverted V-shape. In front of the building was a bare dirt lot with two rusted pickup trucks sitting by the door. One of the trucks, though empty, had its engine idling. I pulled into the parking lot, jouncing a bit, cracked through the ice covering a huge pothole, and came to a stop a few feet from the cinderblock wall.

I had been thinking about the story of Kurt's arrest. "You know, Professor, there's something odd about how your group got captured," I said. I unbuckled my seat belt, and sat staring at the windshield. "If there was an informant in your group, why didn't the Stasi stop the first escape on Thursday night? On the other hand, if there wasn't an informant, how did they manage to round up the ones who weren't there on Friday?" I turned to Kurt. "Have you ever wondered about that?"

"My dear," Kurt's pale blue eyes looked into mine, "I have wondered about that for thirty years."

We got the cane without much fuss. No one at Henny's seemed to wonder or care why an un-farm-like young woman and an overdressed old man needed to buy hog-sperm paraphernalia. I didn't have to use the story I'd made up: that I was the State Department escort of the German Assistant Minister of Agriculture for Pork Production who'd wanted to see why Iowa's hog-sperm cane technology was the envy of farmers all over Europe.

On the way home we didn't talk much. Kurt seemed far away as he smoked another cigarette and looked out at the scenery. As we approached Newton-Bascom Road I began to think about that name I'd found.

"Professor Burghoff…Kurt," I said, "Can you tell me if Dr. Weber had a friend here in Iowa named Regina Daly?"

"I have never heard that name," he said. He flicked some ashes through the crack in his window. "I did not know that Erik had ever come to Iowa before. But of course he could have met her through your late colleague, John Marchak. She is a philosopher, I take it?'

"Actually, I have no idea who she is." Was I about to trust this man whom I'd only just met? Apparently I was, but not completely. I took a deep breath then told him about finding Weber on the sidewalk before the reception and about picking up the note that lay where he'd been. I did not tell him the note was in Emma's handwriting. I explained my question by suggesting that this person might be a friend of Weber's and might not have been informed about his accident.

"And you say this woman lives in this part of Iowa?" Kurt said.

"Well…uh…actually," I started to slow the car and pointed to my left, "she lives a couple of miles up that road there."

"Then I suggest you turn left," he said. I was definitely starting to like this guy.

The farm was a tidy modern-looking place with navy blue silos and steel grey Quonset huts. A large house, in the traditional white of the Iowa farmhouse, sat in front of the complex of buildings. A shallow slope ran up behind the house and on it were five rows of bare apple trees. A stoop-shouldered old woman in a tattered brown coat was pouring salt on the front steps. Kurt sat in the car and I got out and went up to the woman. She squinted at me as I approached.

"He ain't here," she said loudly, "haven't seen him since yesterday."

I was confused by this comment. "Ah…are you Mrs. Daly?" I asked.

She took a step forward and squinted at me harder. "Mrs. Daly? Regina's dead, honey, she died in April. Her son Jerry runs the place now. But he lives over to Parkville. I thought you was lookin' for the man who rents the place." She began spreading the salt again.

"Oh. Ah, well, maybe I am," I said. "What's his name?"

She straightened up, took a step toward me and squinted at me again. "I don't see too good anymore." After a pause she said. "Mr. Gustav lives here, Hans Gustav. But like I said, he ain't here now."

"Are you Mrs. Gustav?"

She laughed, it came out sort of cackly. "No, I just clean for him. Cook sometimes."

She stared at me so intently it gave me little goose bumps on the back of my neck. "Um, do you know when Mr. Gustav will be back?"

"I don't know. He ain't been here since yesterday and I don't know where he is," she said. "Of course his hours are kind of funny, you know. He's a writer. A foreigner too."

"Sure," I said. We Iowans all know what sort of bohemian shenanigans you can expect from a foreign writer. "Well, thanks, I'll try calling him." I started back to the car.

She called to me. "Want me to give him your name, tell him you was here?"

No, that I most definitely did not want to do. I just smiled and waved, got back in the car and scooted it out of there. Back on the road I asked Kurt if he'd ever heard of Hans Gustav. He paused to think about it for a very long time.

"Yes," he said, "I think I have heard that name." He had lit another cigarette and he puffed it thoughtfully. He shook his head. "But I cannot remember where I heard it."

I wasn't sure what I'd learned from that little side trip, but it somehow made me feel some relief. If there was anything sinister about the death of Erik Weber, it might well be attributable to Hans Gustav, the mysterious foreign writer who kept strange hours. (That's probable cause in rural Iowa.) I wondered if I should give his name to the police. Of course, they might be slightly curious about how I'd come up with it in the first place, which would be inconvenient to explain, especially if Emma found out. Maybe I could call in an anonymous tip. Good idea, I thought. If it turned out that Weber's death was not an accident I'd send in an anonymous tip about Mr. Hans Gustav. More likely, of course, Mr. Gustav had nothing to do with Weber's death and should probably be told about his friend's tragic accident. I could do that too. I'd call his number later to see if he'd come back.

Of course, I did not know then that Mr. Gustav wasn't coming back.

I dropped Kurt at the inn, then went over to Emma's office to deliver the cane Kurt and I had gotten from the hog breeder. Maria was nowhere to be seen, but I found Emma seated at Maria's desk in the department office. Just one look at her scared the wits out of me. Her face was gaunt and ashen, her eyes filled with fear.

"Emma!" I hurried over and knelt in front of her. "Are you all right?"

"Oh God, Claire, something terrible has happened. There's some kind of serial killer at this conference."

"What? Good Lord, has someone else died?"

"We think so. Kurt Burghoff has disappeared, vanished. He didn't show up at the four o'clock talk and no one can find him anywhere on campus."

I laughed with relief. "No, no, it's OK, Emma, Kurt was with me."

She looked at me blankly, uncomprehending. "What do you mean, Kurt was with you?"

"He went with me to get the cane." I held up the long metal cane and smiled, twirling it around in my fingers like a baton.

Expecting a look of joyous relief to flood Emma's features, I was cruelly disappointed when her face darkened, her lips pursed, and her eyes fixed me with a hard stare. I stopped twirling the cane.

"Why on earth would you take Kurt Burghoff with you to get the cane?"

"Well…he wanted to come."

"He wanted to come? That's it? He wanted to come? You scared the…bejesus out of me, do you realize that?"

At that moment Marlene from PR came bursting into the office, one gloved hand holding the strap of her huge shoulder bag, the other holding her ever-present clipboard. "Have you heard anything? Security says he's nowhere on campus."

"Yes, it's all right, Marlene," Emma said. "It turns out he was with Claire."

"He was with Claire?" she said. She stopped and glared at me with an expression that said she wasn't the least bit surprised to discover me at the bottom of whatever latest screw-up was making her life a living hell. "Where in God's name did you take him?" Both women looked at me with intense accusation.

I cleared my throat. "Well," my eyes went from one face to the other, "I had an errand to do and Kurt came with me." Neither of them said anything. "He wanted to come," I assured them. Silence. "I think he was, you know, a little bored with the conference." I instantly regretted the phrasing of that sentence.

"Bored?" Emma sniffed.

"Oh, he was bored was he?" Marlene said. "Gee, he should have stayed with us. We weren't bored, we were having the time of our lives. This campus is crawling with reporters, every one of them hoping that this guy's death will turn out to be murder, and then they hear rumors that another philosopher has disappeared. All of a sudden I'm in the middle of a feeding frenzy." She threw up her hands. "Oh, yeah, it was a barrel of laughs around here, I can tell you."

Marlene slammed herself onto the chair next to Maria's desk and started rummaging around in the bottom of her bag. I silently hoped she didn't have a gun in there.

Emma reached into the right-hand drawer of Maria's desk and pulled out a bottle of ibuprofen. "Need some of these?"

"Great, thanks, I can't seem to find mine." Marlene popped off the lid and shot down three tablets without even any water to chase them. Clearly Marlene, like Emma, was a heavy user.

"OK, listen," Marlene said, eyes closed, holding a hand to her forehead, "I'll call security and tell them what's-his-name is back. In the meantime we've got to start thinking about this party of yours tonight. You can expect that some reporters will try to get in."

"'Try to get in'? Are you suggesting we should keep them out?" Emma asked.

"No, that would look bad. But maybe we could put some spin on what they hear. I'll come myself and try to chaperon a little bit. That may not help much but I guess it's the best we can do." Marlene took a little round make-up case out of her bag and looked at herself in the tiny mirror. "Oh, and there's another thing you need to know about. I talked to the president, who, by the way, is not the least bit happy with the attention this is getting. We decided that the college should make some gesture of concern over Professor Weber's death."

Emma frowned. "A 'gesture of concern'?"

"A memorial service. We're going to hold a memorial service tomorrow in the college chapel. Nine a.m. I'll announce it to the press and you can tell your guests."

"A memorial service? Are you crazy?" Emma said. "Marlene, we can't just throw together a memorial service. Not on such short notice."

"We'll damned well have to," Marlene said, "because that's what the president told us to do." The makeup case snapped shut. She threw it in her bag and zipped the bag shut. "My people are already working on the arrangements and I've set it up with the college chaplain. You just need to get your colleagues to the chapel." She stood up, shouldered her bag and tucked the clipboard under her arm. "Nine a.m.," she said. "Sharp." She strode to the door, took hold of the doorknob, then turned around and looked back at us. "Oh, and naturally we'll need some speakers, an introduction, a eulogy, that sort of thing. I'll leave that to you. See you tonight." With a swish she was gone.

"She's coming to your party?" I said. "Should be some enchanted evening."

Emma held out her hand to me. "Give me the cane, Claire, and let's go do this."

I followed her into her office and we closed the door. She tore off the outer wrapping on the sperm package. Inside the package was a Styrofoam container, inside that were some small slabs of dry ice, and nestled inside those was a tiny little plastic vial holding the frozen sperm. It was about the size of a bottle of extremely expensive French perfume, only it was even more expensive than that. Emma gingerly picked up the vial, holding it with the just the tips of her fingernails. With her other hand she held up the cane and she looked back and forth from vial to cane.

"How does this work?" she asked.

"How would I know?"

"Well, I guess the sperm goes between those little prongs," she said. "Here, you hold the cane." Very slowly she slid the tiny vial into the opening between the two prongs at the bottom of the cane. About halfway down the little tube got stuck. With exquisite gentleness Emma wiggled it back and forth. "It's alright sweetie, just slide in there, Mommy's got you."

Mommy's got you?

"Theeeeere you go," she said to the little tube. With the sperm vial sitting snugly in the cane, she unscrewed the cap on the tank of liquid nitrogen, carefully lowered the cane into place, then screwed the cap back on the tank. She looked up at me with a satisfied smile. "Well, our baby is safe for now, Claire."

"Ah...yeah," I said, "that's good."

CHAPTER FIFTEEN

Three hours later 'the baby' was nestled snugly in the nitrogen tank down in our basement while I stood in the kitchen staring into some greyish-white stuff into which I was supposed to plop some pieces of crab. I had followed the instructions very carefully but that greyish stuff did not look nearly as thick as Emma's directions had promised me it would at this point. Also, I wasn't at all sure about the color. I'm not much of a cook, I admit that freely. I was taught the culinary arts by my second stepmother, Vicky, whose pedagogical methods were such that I learned nothing except to hate cooking. Still, Emma's recipes never work out for me, and I can't believe it's always my fault. Her directions are just a little too cavalier for someone whose skills in the kitchen are as primitive as mine. Before breezing out of the house some morning she'll casually say, "I left the ingredients out for semibroached, stuffed summer grouse in mustard sauce, Claire. Would you throw it together after you get home?" (That's her favorite phrase, 'throw it together.') When I start to protest she rolls her eyes and says, "It's easy, Claire, you just stuff the grouse with vegetables mixed with cloves before marinating it in the vinegar-mustard sauce, then," and there follows a set of instructions longer than the ones for assembling a stealth bomber. She concludes with, "and that's all there is to it, don't be such a wimp."

I rechecked the scrap of paper Emma had written the crab directions on. Her handwriting, as I've mentioned, is famously illegible, so there was bound to be some margin of error around what I'd put in that pot. I'd thought the directions said, 'thickens as you heat it,' but could it be, 'thickens as you beat it?' I didn't think you would beat a seafood bisque though, would you?

Cubby came in from the living room, wiping his hands on a red-checkered handkerchief. "I got a fire started, but it's kinda smoky in that fireplace. When's the last time you had a sweep in there?"

"A sweep?" I said.

"A chimney sweep. You've had chimney sweeps in, haven't you?"

"I think you're confusing me with Mary Poppins."

He made the long exhaling sound that expresses how much suffering I cause him with my careless attitude about life's little dangers. I lifted some of the grey sauce with a wooden spoon; it ran off like water. "Why don't you stay for the party, Cub?"

"Nah, I gotta go watch my daughter's kids. She and her husband are going in for 'counseling' tonight." He inflected that in a way most mental health professionals would not have found flattering.

"So, stop in when you get back."

"Maybe. If it's not too late." He gave me a stern look. "And if your house isn't on fire. See ya, Claire."

"Chim-chim-cheree, Cub."

Thick or not, I had precious little time to waste on seafood bisque. The clock above the stove said seven twenty-five, which gave me thirty-five minutes to finish preparing four kinds of hors d'oeuvres, put out three pies and two cheesecakes, set up the wine and wine glasses, lay tablecloths on three or four tables, the list went on. Maria was to have come at seven, but there was still no sign of her, and I expected little help from Cindy who was in our guest room sleeping the sleep of the heavily medicated. (She had taken three little yellow pills.) I spent a few minutes arranging stuffed mushrooms on trays to go in the oven.

I was startled by a knock at the kitchen door. Could it be one of the guests already? No, Emma had said she'd be walking the guests over from the inn at about eight o'clock. It certainly wasn't Maria, she wouldn't bother knocking. So who the hell was at the door? I had no time to play *Amal and the Night Visitors.*

It was Mrs. Leach. I found her standing there without a hat or coat, wearing a royal blue dress under a red cardigan sweater, her hands tucked under her arms to keep them warm. When I opened the door she said, "My husband's at a deacon's meeting." She stood there looking at me as if that one phrase could explain why she was standing on my back steps for the very first time in the five years we'd been neighbors. She smiled nervously.

"Ah…would you like to come in?" She came inside, rubbing her arms. She stood by the door looking around at our kitchen.

"This kitchen looks nice," she said. "I like what you've done with it. It's much nicer than when the Armstrongs lived here."

"Oh. Well, thanks."

We stood there awkwardly for a few seconds as she silently took in the kitchen decor. I couldn't think of anything to say.

"We're, uh, planning to replace this linoleum in the summer," I said. We both looked down at the slime green floor. Then another small slice of eternity ticked by in silence, so I added, "Maybe something in white or blue."

"Yes, white or blue would go nicely with the cabinets." She looked at me and smiled uncomfortably, but didn't say anything else. I wanted to ask her why the hell she was here. Had we left something to do with the sperm over at her house? She wasn't carrying anything. It seemed inevitable that she would tell me herself any minute, but I was feeling harried and the silence was starting to make me nuts.

Suddenly I remembered the bisque. "Oops, excuse me, Mrs. Leach. I have something on the stove."

"Oh," she said, "what're you making?" She followed me over to the stove, apparently glad to have this distraction.

"I'm making this seafood bisque." We peered together into the pot. "It's for a party tonight. Emma is hosting a conference at the college, and her guests are coming over any minute now. I'm way behind in getting ready."

"Oh, my," she said, "I'm disturbing you, I'll come back later." She started for the door.

"No, no, Mrs. Leach, I wasn't trying to shoo you away."

"Well, I…I just wanted to ask you something."

"Sure," I said. "Just let me thicken this stuff up and I'll be right with you." I reached into a cabinet and pulled down a box of cornstarch with the intention of dumping some into the bisque.

"You're using cornstarch?" Mrs. Leach asked. "Wouldn't you rather use flour?"

"Flour? You think I should use flour?" I frowned. "I don't know if we have any flour."

"Well, of course you have flour," she said. She came over and started looking in the cabinet next to the one I was searching. "Ah, here we are." She pulled out a blue and white bag that, by god, said flour on it and began to spoon some carefully into my pot. I stood back and watched, perfectly content to let her take command of the bisque.

Cindy suddenly appeared in the kitchen. I was surprised to see she had changed clothes from this afternoon and was wearing a black evening dress with dark stockings and a long single strand of pearls. She looked quite lovely except for some puffiness around the eyes and a general aura of weariness about her. I introduced her to Mrs. Leach, who was fine-tuning the consistency of the bisque. Cindy asked if she could help with something.

"Boy, Cindy, you sure could. Would you mind cutting up some celery and carrots for a vegetable plate?" I showed her where the cutting board was. Mrs. Leach still had her nose in the bisque pot.

The clock said seven thirty-five, twenty-five minutes before the guests were to arrive. Mrs. Leach seemed to have the bisque crisis under control so I went to the freezer down in the basement to pull out some wine I'd put there an hour ago. I was supposed to have put the wine in the refrigerator that morning, but I'd done my usual trick of forgetting all about it. So now I had to hope that a good hour in the freezer would do the job instead. Emma would've been horrified if she found out, but I figured Emma wouldn't find out, unless I did my other usual trick of forgetting it a second time and leaving it in the freezer until the bottles exploded. Pulling the wine out of the freezer reminded me that I'd also forgotten to call the liquor store to check on Kurt Burghoff's bottle of Porte Fino.

When I got back to the kitchen with an armload of wine bottles, I was surprised to see Cindy and Mrs. Leach working on the vegetables together.

"Oh," Mrs. Leach was saying, looking at Cindy with apparent surprise, "so you have a husband?"

"Well...yeah." Cindy shot me a confused look over Mrs. Leach's head. I just smiled and shrugged my shoulders.

I had stacked the wine bottles in the bottom of the refrigerator and was headed to the dining room to set out some glasses when Maria came rushing in the kitchen door, her arms wrapped around a paper sack.

"How are we doing, Claire?" She was a little out of breath. "I am sorry I did not get here sooner."

"It's OK, Maria, we're not too far behind." She hurried into the kitchen and began unpacking the bag while I went to the dining room to put out some wine glasses.

When I went back through the kitchen to get some ice from the refrigerator, Maria, now wearing a red apron she'd brought, had laid out some pita bread and hummus and was slipping a covered dish into the oven. Cindy and Mrs. Leach were slicing away.

Mrs. Leach said, "My goodness, what did you say to him when you found out?"

"Well, I told him I couldn't live this way," Cindy said, "that I'd leave him if he didn't stop."

I looked at them for a second in silent wonderment, then carried the ice to the buffet in the dining room.

The doorbell rang. Oh God, now who's that? I answered it to find Marlene from the PR office standing there with a man I didn't know. His sandy hair was thick and tousled and his complexion was kind of ruddy. He was about my height, somewhat overweight. Under an unbuttoned overcoat he wore a tweed jacket, blue shirt and mismatched green tie that was loosened at the collar. He was smoking a cigarette but casually flicked it into our front bushes when I opened the door.

"Howdy, Claire," Marlene said with inexplicable good cheer, "this is Oscar Lamb from the *Cedar Rapids Gazette*. He's been covering the story of Professor Weber's accident and would like to talk to some of your guests this evening."

I was impressed. She sounded as if she were positively delighted to have this reporter sniffing around, and as if I were a dear old friend instead of someone she'd wanted to bludgeon to death a few hours earlier. The woman had a true talent for public relations. She wore a tight-fitting maroon dress with black edging around the collar and black-trimmed pockets. She looked absolutely stunning and I told her so.

Marlene spotted the drink table in the dining room and immediately steered Oscar in that direction. I went back to the kitchen to find a buzz of activity: Maria laying shrimp on a bed of romaine lettuce, Cindy cutting carrots for the vegetable plate, and Mrs. Leach sticking toothpicks into some little cheese pastries Maria must've brought. The three of them were hip-deep in conversation.

"My son Yuri is in graduate school in philosophy at UCLA. He has a full teaching fellowship, he's just like a professor really," Maria was saying with noticeable pride. "He tried to make it as a musician in California, but he finally gave up after eight years and decided to go back for his Ph.D." She put the shrimp plate on the counter. "Do you have any children, Dorothy?"

"I have two grown-up boys," Mrs. Leach said. "My older boy, Fred, he lives in Cedar Rapids. The younger one, Ronnie, he's in Minneapolis."

"Oh, you are lucky," Maria said, "they are not so far away. I miss my Yuri all the time."

Mrs. Leach paused and looked down at the pastry in her hand. "Well, we don't see much of Ronnie nowadays. Him and his Dad don't get along."

"Oh, that must be hard," Cindy said.

Overhearing that conversation gave me a sharp pang of jealousy. Here were three women who had known each other for all of twenty minutes, whose backgrounds were as dissimilar as any three people I knew, and yet they were chatting away like the pledge committee at the Delta Chi sorority. Why couldn't I connect with other people as easily as that?

By the time I'd finished setting out the plates and silver on the dining room table it was nearly eight o'clock, which meant that the conference crowd would be here any second. I looked around the dining room to see if I'd forgotten anything.

"Maria," I called into the kitchen, "I think we can bring the food out to the table now. Would you mind doing that? I have to run upstairs for a second." I still needed to brush my teeth, comb my hair, and check one more time to see if my high-necked white blouse made me look half as fat as it made me feel. Emma says it doesn't, but I never believe her.

When I came back downstairs, the philosophy crowd was just arriving. There was a loud babble of conversation as people came pouring in the front door, piling coats and scarves in a great heap in our foyer. I had meant to do something civilized with the coats, but it was obviously too late for that now. To my great surprise, Mrs. Leach stood just inside the living room smiling broadly as she offered a tray of hors d'oeuvres to the guests streaming in.

My surprise at that sight, however, was a pale facsimile of its effect on Emma. Emma looked at Mrs. Leach with wide-eyed astonishment, obviously trying to greet her politely but mainly just staring and stammering. I came down the stairs, waved to Renee and Arnie, and headed for the kitchen. Emma immediately came up beside me.

"What in the world is she doing here?"

"Who, Dorothy? She's an old friend, I go to her house whenever I need to borrow a cup of sperm."

Emma's voice dropped a full octave. "Claire, why is Mrs. Leach here in our house?"

"I don't really know. She showed up at the back door half an hour ago, and said she wanted to ask me something."

"What?"

"She hasn't told me yet. But she really helped with that seafood bisque recipe of yours, which, incidentally, is wildly incorrect. 'Thickens as it heats,' you said. You'd have to heat that stuff with an H-bomb before it thickens."

"Oh God," Emma said, "please don't tell me you screwed up the bisque." She put a hand across her eyes. "It was incredibly simple, all you had to do was follow the instructions."

"You always say that, Emma, and it's never true. You tell me how easy it is to make something and then you leave me this very complicated set of—"

"Hello, Claire, you look very nice," Renee said. I knew she was lying. I felt like the cover girl for *Hog & Home* magazine, but from her I appreciated it. "Is there a corkscrew for the wine?" she asked us.

"There should have been one out next to the drinks," Emma said, giving me the fisheye, "but let me get one for you." She opened a drawer next to the sink and pulled out a great big corkscrew with wing handles. Renee took it, smiled and walked off into the dining room.

"Anyway, never mind about the recipe," Emma said to me. Her voice fell to a whisper. "How's Cindy doing?"

I looked over my shoulder to the big doorway between the kitchen and dining room where Renee had stopped to greet a sad-looking Cindy. Cindy had been standing there scanning the crowd as people milled through the rooms.

"I'd say her condition is stable. Did you tell Roger she was here?"

"No, of course not, I promised her I wouldn't."

"Emma," I said, "if he strolls in here with Sara Grace on his arm it could create a hellish, not to mention public, scene. And there's a reporter here, you know."

"I know. But don't worry, Roger won't come in with Sara Grace. I gave Sara Grace some errands to run, so she won't even be here tonight. Still," she glanced over at Cindy, "we'd better find a quiet place for Cindy and Roger to talk. We sure don't want them meeting in the middle of the living room."

I agreed. Separating them from the crowd at least made the plan of their meeting at this party very slightly less idiotic. Emma went to talk to Cindy and I looked for Roger.

Ours is quite a large living room, and it was completely packed with philosophy professors. I squeezed my way through the room, slipping between the backs of people involved in separate conversations. I peeked into each little group as I passed, trying to see if Roger was there. People had gotten drinks by now, and were obviously feeling warm and comfortable. They were telling each other stories, laughing at each other's jokes, occasionally arguing some point of philosophy. The voices were loud and jovial. The slight tinge of smoke from the fireplace made the big room seem a little smaller and cozier.

I couldn't see Roger anywhere in the living room, so I moved toward the dining area. Leaning against the door frame between the dining room and living room I came across Marshall standing alone, holding a glass of red wine in front of him with both hands.

"Hi, Marshall."

"Oh, hello, Claire." He straightened up and brushed a hand over his hair.

"Have you seen Roger?"

"No. Not since dinner."

"OK, thanks Marshall, see you."

"Ah...Claire? If you want I can help you look."

I paused. "Um...OK, sure."

I wandered through the crowd in the dining room. Marshall walked right behind me. No Roger. I buzzed through the foyer, Marshall right next to me, dutifully looking this way and that. Another tour of the living room, faithful Marshall by my side, then out onto the sun porch, me and Marshall, like peas in a pod. At this point I toyed with the idea of explaining to Marshall that our search would be a hell of a lot more effective if he'd stop following me like a puppy dog and look in a different part of the house. Instead I just sighed.

The sun porch had about ten people in it standing in groups of three and four. In one group was Arnie Cohen, Marlene and Oscar Lamb. Arnie was saying something to the reporter who was nodding steadily.

"The academic world is much less collegial than it seems on the surface, Oscar. It's actually full of intrigue and hostility, much of it stemming from professional jealousy." Arnie was emphasizing this point with one hand while using the other to hold a wine glass at shoulder level where he could sip it frequently. Marlene's face had her official public relations smile on it, but her eyes were darting around the room desperately. When she saw Marshall and me, she called out to us eagerly.

"Oh, Claire," she said, "come introduce your friend to Oscar." With an arm around the reporter's shoulder she turned him slightly away from Arnie and toward Marshall and me. I didn't want to stop and chat, but this might be a good opportunity to shed Marshall, who had proved absolutely useless as a member of the search team.

"Marshall Udall," I said, "this is Oscar Lamb of the *Cedar Rapids Gazette*, and Marlene Jastrow of our public relations office." Oscar shook hands with Marshall.

"Ah, now Oscar," Arnie said, pointing at Marshall with the hand holding the drink, "this is the man you want to see to get the real dirt on Erik Weber. Marshall is writing his biography."

"Oh, you're writing a biography?" Oscar said. He took a notebook and pen from the pocket of his jacket. "Maybe you could give me some background on Professor Weber. I've been told that his colleagues didn't like him much as a person." Marlene's smile remained frozen on her face, but the corner of her left eye started twitching nervously.

"Listen," I said, taking hold of Marshall's arm, "I'm sorry, but we can't talk right now, we're looking for someone." Marshall smiled apologetically as I pulled him away. I saw the muscles in Marlene's jaw relax a bit. I sensed that she had just upgraded me from Biggest-Nitwit-West-of-the-Mississippi to Run-of-the-Mill-Academic-Incompetent. It felt good to finally get some approval.

Marshall and I had left the sun porch and gone back to the living room when it occurred to me that, having dragged him out of that discussion with Oscar, I was stuck having him follow me around again.

"Marshall, would you mind doing me a favor?"

"Not at all."

"Would you call the liquor store and see if a bottle of wine that Emma ordered has come in yet? You can use the phone in the upstairs hall."

"Sure. What's the number?"

"Ummm…" I was about to tell him to look in the phonebook that was by the phone, but that was no good. In our house a phonebook might be in any one of a thousand different places, but never, never next to a telephone. Then I remembered that last evening I'd written the number on Colin's business card. "OK, listen Marshall," I put a hand on his shoulder, "the second door on the right upstairs is our bedroom. On the floor at the foot of the bed you'll find a pile of clothes I wore yesterday. In the pocket of the black skirt is a business card with the number of the liquor store on the back."

Marshall colored slightly at these instructions. "Ah…you want me to look through your clothes?"

"It's all right, Marshall, just go do it, OK?"

"Well, all right." He turned and walked away toward the stairs. As he disappeared into the crowd I remembered that I'd left a pair of panties and a bra in that pile of clothes. I hoped Marshall didn't have a heart attack.

I made one final cruise in search of Roger. Back in the living room I saw Kurt talking with a couple of older men I hadn't seen before and the youngish woman who was at my dinner table last night. When Kurt saw me coming he stepped out of the conversation and touched my arm.

"Claire, I understand I got you in trouble this afternoon by tagging along on your errand." He face was somber but his eyes looked amused.

"Oh, I'm all right. They said they'd drop the kidnaping charge if I pleaded guilty to Joyriding with a Positivist."

He smiled. "Well, I hope our adventure today leads to success for you and Emma. That would be very exciting."

"Uh huh," I said. "Listen, I'd like to stay and talk Kurt, but I'm trying to find someone. I'll see you later." He smiled again and nodded.

A final sweep for Roger produced no results, so I went back to the kitchen to file my report. Emma was standing at the table talking softly to a forlorn-looking Cindy, who had her hands wrapped around the stem of a wine glass. I told them I'd failed to find Roger.

"How could you not find him?" Emma asked in her Claire-never-ceases-to-amaze-me voice. "He's got to be out there somewhere."

"I looked Emma, he isn't there."

"Oh, you looked, did you, sweetheart?" She turned to Cindy. "She looked." She put an arm around my waist. "This is a woman who came home from the Food Mart last week and said they didn't have a produce aisle 'I looked,' she said, 'I couldn't find one.'"

I had to laugh at that. "OK, Emma, enough," I said.

"Claire's right," Cindy said. "Roger isn't here, he's with that girl. He's probably screwing her as we speak."

"No, he isn't," Emma said. "She's not with him, I'm sure of it. I sent her on some errands for the memorial service tomorrow. Even if Roger isn't here now, I know he will be." She said this with more confidence than she could possibly have felt.

Some guy I didn't recognize came walking into the kitchen. "Emma, I need to ask you if there will be an overhead projector at my—Cindy! I didn't know you were here. How've you been?"

In a flash Emma grabbed the man's arm, turned him around, and started walking him out of the kitchen. "Cindy has a hellish migraine, Zeke. Maybe you two could chat later when she's feeling better. Anyway, I've arranged for projectors to be over…" Her voice merged into the background noise as they went off together into the living room. I sat down next to Cindy and patted her back, not knowing what else to do. I leaned over her a bit to make her less conspicuous to people wandering in and out of the kitchen. We sat there for a time, me patting occasionally, her drinking steadily.

Maria came into the kitchen with an empty ice bucket. "Claire, Emma just asked me if you got a bottle of porte fino from the liquor store?"

Oops. "I just sent Marshall to call and see if it's in yet, Maria. If it is, I'll ask him to go get it."

It occurred to me that I'd sent Marshall upstairs a lot more minutes ago than it takes to make one phone call and come back down. Jeez, maybe my underwear had killed him after all. As I got up to go check on him I had a sudden image of him lying on the floor of our bedroom clutching his chest. Then came a second, even darker image, born of the paranoia this conference was making me feel. I imagined finding Marshall dead on our bedroom floor, his swollen tongue sticking out of his mouth, his eyes bulging, a pair of my pantyhose cutting deeply into the flesh of his neck. I then pictured myself coming back downstairs to the party. In a firm and steady voice I announce to the crowd, 'Everyone stay where you are! Marshall has been murdered. And the killer is in this house!' The guests all gasp at once. People are shocked and frightened, of course, but beneath their fear is a sense of confidence. They know that if there's a killer to be found, Chief Inspector Claire Sinclair will soon bring the scoundrel to justice. (Just don't let her run the press conference afterwards.)

None of this happened, of course, but what did happen was still pretty strange. At the top of the stairs I heard a loud male voice coming from our bedroom and I paused, naturally, to eavesdrop on the conversation. I couldn't understand what was being said because he was speaking in German, but the voice, though harsh with anger, sounded familiar.

I listened for a few seconds, then opened the door and stepped into the room. (It was my house, after all.) The speaker was Colin Jensen. All five fingers of his right hand were pressed firmly against the chest of Marshall Udall, whose back was pushed against the wall and whose face was bright red. When I came in, Colin stood up straight and dropped his hand from Marshall's chest. Without another a word he walked past me and went swiftly down the hall to the stairs.

"Marshall, are you all right?"

"All right? Of course I'm all right." He was breathing heavily. "I'm not afraid of him." I gathered that my question had wounded his masculine pride, a reaction that seemed typically male and kind of childish. (Or am I being redundant?)

"What was that all about?" I asked.

"Nothing, really. He takes exception to something I'm going to write in my book about Weber, that's all." He smoothed his hair, trying to shrug off the incident. "This is the sort of thing biographers have to contend with all the time. Whatever you say, somebody always gets mad."

"But why would Colin Jensen care so much about something you say about Weber?" I asked.

"I really don't know. He followed me up here to ask me what I'm planning to say about the incident of Weber plagiarizing Platburg. He got mad when I said I thought Weber hadn't plagiarized. I guess my book is going to contradict what he says in his conference paper. But I don't see why he had to get so hot about it." Still clearly rattled, Marshall straightened his tie and pulled his shirt cuffs out from the sleeves of his jacket. "I'm going back downstairs."

I touched his arm. "You sure you're OK, Marshall?"

"I'm OK," he said, "but he won't be OK if he touches me again." Marshall walked out of the room, but turned to me just outside the door. "Oh, by the way, your wine hasn't come in yet." He went downstairs.

I went down the back stairs to the kitchen where Maria handed me a plate of shrimp and asked me to refresh the one on the dining room table. In the dining room, standing next to the buffet, I saw Fritz, the young fellow I'd argued with the previous evening. I was afraid he might see me and want to start up again, but he was already conversing with, of all people, Mrs. Leach.

"No. No," she was saying. She shook her head, genuinely upset. "I'm sorry, but that just isn't true."

"Of course it is." Fritz calmly spread some brie on a wheat cracker. "It's evident throughout the New Testament. His love of the poor, his contempt for riches, the preaching of universal brotherhood. Jesus was an early communist."

Mrs. Leach glanced around nervously, as if looking for which window the lightning would come through.

On my way back to the kitchen I passed a man with blond hair and a reddish beard trying to cut a virgin cheesecake with the butt end of a plastic fork; it wasn't a pretty sight.

"Oops," I said to him, "there's no serving utensil for that, is there? Let me get you one." He smiled and nodded. In the kitchen doorway I met Renee. She was carrying a little paper plate with a few grapes and a piece of spinach quiche on it. I winked at her and was about to walk past when she took hold of my elbow.

"Come here, you," she said. She pulled me off toward a far corner of the dining room, away from the noisy crowd. "So tell me, what's the big fight about?"

"What big fight? Did Emma tell you we were having a big fight?"

She smiled at that. "No one had to tell me. It's about Emma trying to get pregnant, isn't it?"

"No, it isn't," I said, maybe a bit too quickly. "It's mainly about Emma tying up my time with this conference of hers when I have my own work to do. She's being really self-centered."

"She's under a lot of strain, Claire, what do you expect? She'd help you if the situation were reversed."

"I know, I know. But anyway it's not about her trying to get pregnant." Renee looked at me as if she were watching my nose grow longer. "Well, OK," I said, "maybe it's partly about her trying to get pregnant."

She held the slice of quiche between two fingers and took a nibble off the end.

"So, what's the problem about the baby?"

I shrugged. "I don't know. There are some things that still have to be worked out, that's all." I looked down at my shoes.

"You don't want a baby, is that it?"

"No," my head came up, "that's not it at all."

She raised her eyebrows and chewed on the quiche.

"All right," I admitted, "maybe I'm not as enthusiastic about this baby thing as Emma is. But I agreed to it and I'll stick by my agreement."

"So why aren't you as enthusiastic?"

It took me a few seconds to answer her. "Look, the thing is, Renee, if I'm going to have a child I want to be the kid's mother. Not an aunt, or a friend, or a guardian. If Emma has a baby I'm going to have to do an amazing amount of work believe me. Emma will give me a full share of the burden but what will I get in return? I'll be the other mom." I looked across the room to where the guy with the blond hair was standing patiently next to the uncut cheesecake. I'd forgotten all about him. "Do you know," I said to Renee, "that I won't even be able to legally adopt the baby? If something happens to Emma I'll have no claim to the child, no legal rights, nothing." I shook my head. "I'm just not sure this baby project has a good cost/benefit ratio."

Renee laughed. "Oh, well then! I'm glad you're considering this problem as an economist and not as a human being."

"Hey, I gotta be me."

Renee put her plate down on a table behind her. "Well, Claire, to use an economic metaphor, I'm not sure I buy all this."

"Buy what?"

"This business about being the 'other mom.' What's really going on here? Are you afraid that the baby won't love you enough or that you won't love the baby enough?"

My voiced sounded a little high when I said, "Why would I be afraid of that?"

"I think," Renee said, "that what you're really afraid of is that you won't be able to love a child that isn't truly 'your own' from your womb. Isn't that it?"

"Of course that's not it. I could love any child if I actually wanted it…her, him."

Renee stared at me for a second. "OK, if you say so, Claire. But I'll tell you something, if you're worried about loving a baby you didn't give birth to, believe me, I know how you're feeling. I went through something like this myself."

I saw the blond-haired guy by the cheesecake looking toward the kitchen, and I moved closer to the wall so he wouldn't see me standing there with Renee. "You did?" I asked.

"Yeah." Renee suddenly looked tired. She leaned her back against the wall as if trying to get some support. "You probably don't know this, but I can't have children. The effect on my life has been horrible, really horrible. I mourned the loss of my unborn children for years, I'm still mourning them." For a few seconds she stared down at her plate and pushed a little crust of quiche around with one finger. "But the thing is, Claire, I didn't have to be childless. I could have adopted. I had plenty of opportunities when I traveled in Eastern Europe."

She looked past me over my shoulder. "I almost did adopt a couple of times. Once I even had a child picked out, a little boy in Hungary, about four years old. He had dark hair, very curly. All the nurses called him Umi." She shook her head. "But I always got cold feet. These children weren't mine. I kept thinking, what if I couldn't love them? I just couldn't get past that feeling." Her eyes came back to mine. "And now I'm forty-nine years old, Claire, and it's too late. Now I realize that I could have loved an adopted child. That little boy in Hungary will be eighteen this year. I could've been driving him off to college in the fall." Her eyes drifted downward. "I left him sitting there in that orphanage."

There was a long, painfully uncomfortable pause. It was a sad story, and I felt for her, but it had nothing to do with me or my feelings and I wanted her to know that.

"Look, Renee…I'm sorry about what happened to you, I know it must really have hurt. But what you just described is not what's bothering me, OK?" I felt angry at her without really knowing why.

She rubbed her fingers lightly along my forearm and gave me a sad-eyed smile. "OK," she said, "I'm glad."

"Well, I'd better get back to the kitchen," I said. "There's a bunch of stuff to do." Renee nodded.

I suddenly noticed that the advance team for one of my tension headaches was setting up shop in the back of my skull. Over by the dining room table, the blond-haired guy had disappeared and the cheesecake looked a bit like the first victim in the movie *Jaws*.

In the kitchen Maria was busy taking some pies out of the oven. "Claire, are there any serving utensils for these?" Now she asks me. I told her to look in the bottom drawer next to the refrigerator. Cindy was sitting at the kitchen table with a glass of wine looking even more miserable than before, and a little drunker to boot.

"Cindy, would you feel better if you went out in the living room and mingled a bit?"

She was staring into her wine glass. "No, I don't think so, Claire. I know people out there. I don't want everyone to start asking me where Roger is."

She had spoken the devil's name, and at that moment he appeared. Over the din of the crowd I heard the front door slam and took a step backward to peer out toward the living room. Roger came in from the foyer. It was fortunate that from the kitchen table Cindy couldn't see her husband arrive, because two steps behind him, looking young, slender, and just generally gorgeous in a flowing print skirt and skin-tight top, came Sara Grace Harper. Damn, I thought, he was with her after all. I knew I had to pull Roger away from Sara Grace and into the kitchen before Cindy had a chance to see them together.

"Excuse me a minute, Cindy, will you?" I reached over and patted her shoulder. "Maria," I said, "would you mind coming to help me for a second?" I wanted her to keep Sara Grace out of whatever fracas was about to erupt. Maria gave me a puzzled look, but when I jerked my head in the direction of the living room she understood immediately. As we walked into the living room my eyes were searching frenetically for Emma. Did she know it was show time? I couldn't see her.

Before I could cover the few steps between him and the kitchen, Roger was engulfed by a small crowd of people.

"Oh, come on, Roger, don't be so damned coy." It was Arnie Cohen speaking. "Hand out the copies like you're supposed to so we can read the paper before your session."

"I haven't even made copies yet," Roger said. He tapped his breast pocket. "There's only one copy in here on a floppy disk." Arnie rolled his eyes.

"Would you mind answering some questions about the paper?" Oscar asked.

"Not at all," Roger said, "as long as we restrict ourselves to background information. The essence of my findings will have to wait until tomorrow."

Before Roger had a chance to tease the media again I slid my arm through the crowd and grabbed him hard by the shoulder. I forced my way in and whispered in his ear, "I need to see you in the kitchen right away." A look of irritation crossed his face. I whispered again, "It's important."

I took his arm and dragged him roughly away from the group and toward the kitchen, stopping just outside the kitchen doorway.

"Claire, what the hell—?"

"Roger, Cindy's in the kitchen."

He blinked. "Cindy? My wife, Cindy?" I now had his undivided attention.

"The same," I said. He frowned and twitched his nose twice like a rabbit, apparently considering. "There's more, Roger," I said. "She saw you with Sara Grace this afternoon, and she's very upset."

He straightened up and looked at me sideways. "Saw me with Sara Grace? Who's Sara Grace?" No kidding, he actually said that. I wanted to smack him.

"Roger," I pointed to the kitchen, "just get your ass in there and talk to your wife." I put heavy emphasis on that last noun. He walked into the kitchen without another word.

"Hi, honey. When did you get here?" he said. Cindy, who'd been staring down at the kitchen table, turned and saw him, held his gaze silently for a few seconds, and then looked back down at the table again. "Is everything all right, Cindy?"

Before Cindy could say what I would've have said—No, everything is not all right, you adulterous, cradle-robbing canker sore— I jumped in with a suggestion.

"Why don't I take you two upstairs where you can talk in private?"

Without looking at each other, Roger and Cindy silently followed me up the back stairs. Two of the four bedrooms on our second floor have been converted into studies, and I took them into Emma's. It's a good-sized room with an ancient wooden desk, an old typewriter that Emma still uses and an old beige sofa that she brought with her from Boston. Bookcases take up all the available wall space. Unlike her office at the college, Emma's study at home is a perennial mess. I turned on the light for Roger and Cindy, picked up a stack of blue books from the middle of the floor and cleared some philosophy journals and empty Pepsi cans off the sofa.

"You guys will be comfortable in here…um…if you need anything, just ah…" Shut up and leave, Claire, I thought. I closed the door behind me. Out in the hallway I felt a strong temptation to eavesdrop on their conversation but I'm happy to report that I fought it off.

And when I came downstairs the house was empty.

Startled, I stopped on the bottom step and looked around. There was nobody in the living room, dining room, or kitchen, nobody at all. Not a soul. I couldn't even hear anyone talking. It was as if the entire Weber conference had been beamed aboard some alien spacecraft and whisked away to a distant galaxy. (I didn't think that was a likely explanation, this was not my lucky day.) I heard the faint sound of the TV set coming from the sun porch.

Our large (thank goodness) sun porch was crammed to the rafters with professors of philosophy all staring at the TV in the corner of the room. Close to the set there were about four rows of people who were sitting on the floor so that those in the back could see. Our blue patterned love seat was filled to overflowing, three people on the cushions and one on each arm. People stood everywhere against the walls of the room. Emma, holding the remote control in her hand, sat next to Renee on the couch facing the TV. Marlene stood directly behind them, and Arnie and Oscar were on either side of Marlene. To be able to get any kind of view I had to squeeze behind the crowd and work my way over to the windows.

The TV screen showed a black and white photo of Erik Weber, probably supplied to the station by Marshall. The announcer extolled Weber's reputation in the field of philosophy, predicted a dire impact of his death on the academic world, and exaggerated the importance of this conference as a scholarly event. (All of which bullshit, no doubt, had been fed to the TV people by Roger Stuhrm). They switched to a shot of Roger being interviewed by that really attractive blonde newswoman who reports for Channel Four.

"Why do you think Professor Weber came to this conference without telling anyone he would be here?" she asked, holding a microphone in front of Roger's chin.

"This conference is going to be a definitive analysis of Erik Weber as a man and a scholar. I think things will be said at this conference that will forever alter Weber's gigantic reputation. I believe he came here to hear what would be said and defend himself, if necessary."

The picture cut to a very nervous-looking Marshall whose name and affiliation were printed under his face. Marshall was talking but we couldn't hear his words: the voice-over was describing him as the biographer of the dead scholar. When the sound cut in Marshall was saying, "It was, uh, unusual for Professor Weber to, uh, come to a conference. Any kind of conference. He isn't, uh, usually very communicative with his colleagues."

The camera went back to the reporter. "We asked Hammond Police Chief Peter Gammon if there was any suspicion that Weber's death was not an accident."

Pete Gammon flashed onto the screen, his face professionally solemn. "Well, of course, we're, ah, not ruling anything out, naturally. But at this point in time, we aren't, ah…we're not officially calling this anything but an accidental fall."

With the camera still on Pete, the reporter's voice said, "Channel Four has learned that the county coroner's report says that Professor Weber died from a heavy blow to the right side of the head, a blow that is not necessarily consistent with an accidental fall. What do you make of that, Chief?" In my peripheral vision I saw Marlene wince. There was a brief murmur from others in the room.

"The blow to Dr. Weber's head could've come from a fall onto the rocks…or possibly something else. All I can say is we're still investigating at this point."

The scene switched back to the reporter who summarized the report, and assured the viewers of Channel Four's commitment to stay completely on top of this fast-breaking story.

Finally the anchorman came back. "Thank you, Janet. In the light of what is, at the very least, a tragic accident, tomorrow Channel Four's Ted Phillips will file a special report: 'How Safe are Iowa's Campuses?' Coming up next, Phil Jacobs tells us how the Hawkeyes did against the Wisconsin Badgers—"

Emma clicked off the set.

"Hey!" Arnie said, "I want to hear how the Hawkeyes did against the Badgers." A few people laughed. But the general mood was not particularly jolly. It was beginning to sink in: there were lots of loose ends in the Weber case that should easily have been resolved if the death was accidental. And if his death was not accidental, then the murderer was almost certainly in this house. Standing in this room.

People started filing off the sun porch talking softly to each other. I pushed my way over toward Emma and Renee.

"You looked good, Claire," Renee said. "You may have a future in television."

"Oh no, was I on? Thank God I missed that part," I said.

"Lipstick, Claire," Emma said, "what have you got against lipstick?"

I gave her a level gaze. "Good tip, Emma. I'll pick up a tube in case some more of your colleagues drop dead." I lowered my voice. "Anyway, listen, Roger's here. I took him and Cindy upstairs to your study to talk."

Emma nodded. "Maria told me. Did Cindy see him with Sara Grace?"

"No, but we'd better get her out of here."

"It's done. I asked Maria to drive her back to the dorm."

"Well, that's good, anyway. I guess we'll just have to wait and see what happens."

When we got to the dining room Emma frowned at the buffet. "I hope we aren't going to run out of wine. How late does the liquor store stay open?" She hurried off into the kitchen with a worried look on her face. Renee patted my arm and then followed Emma.

I stood alone in the dining room. Suddenly, to my great amazement, I had a moment to myself. Sensing immediately that my brain wasn't busy, other parts of my body started phoning in complaints: my feet felt pinched by the tight dress shoes; the headache team had finished moving into the back of my head; my stomach rumbled to remind me that I had served a lot of food but hadn't eaten any. That was a timely reminder, actually. Right in front of me on the dining room table was a bright yellow cheesecake with strawberry topping. It had a deep brown crust made of cookie crumbs and its interior looked all rich and creamy. Yum. I prepared to cut a slice with the butt end of a plastic fork, a method I knew to be crude but effective.

I felt a tug at my sleeve. It was Mrs. Leach. To my surprise, in her left hand she held a half-empty glass of red wine; her expression was one of deep concern. "Did that man die? The one who was at your house yesterday?"

"Which man?"

"The one on television."

"Oh, him. Well, he wasn't actually at our house, he was just found on campus after having a fall. And yes, I'm afraid he did die."

"But he did come to your house yesterday. He knocked on my door because he couldn't figure out which one was yours."

I breathed in sharply. For a few seconds the room seemed to rock. I couldn't even say anything. But someone else did, someone asked the question that I wanted to ask.

"When was that, Ma'am, that he came to this house?" I turned to see with instant horror that the inquirer was Oscar, the reporter from the *Gazette*. Where was Marlene? Why the hell was this guy on the loose?

Mrs. Leach looked at Oscar and said, "It was about ten or eleven in the morning, I guess." To me she said, "It was just a little while after your package of frozen stuff came to my house."

"Frozen stuff?" Oscar asked.

I fought an urge to clamp a hand across Mrs. Leach's mouth. "Emma and I were out most of the morning," I said. "I don't think she's aware that Professor Weber came here."

"Oh. So," Oscar said in a smooth, professional voice, "Dr. Harrington did know Dr. Weber personally, then? I had understood that she didn't." There was not a hint of accusation, but the gist of the query was glaringly apparent: was Emma lying about her relationship with Weber? Yeah, I had understood that too, I thought.

"Mr. Lamb, I don't really have time to talk now. Mrs. Leach, will you help me cut up some more vegetables for the snack plates?" I smiled apologetically and guided a confused Mrs. Leach off toward the kitchen. It may have been a mistake to disengage with Oscar in so clumsy and transparent a manner— no doubt it just made his suspicion stronger—but I was flustered and it was the best I could do at the moment. It felt like the headache guys were throwing a housewarming party at the base of my skull.

"Mrs. Leach," I said. We paused in the kitchen doorway. "Did you tell the police that you saw Professor Weber here yesterday?"

"I haven't talked to the police. I didn't know anything about this until I saw the TV just now. Do you think I should call them?" She looked up at me, her face all innocence.

"Well…" I wished I had more time to think about this. "I suppose you should tell them, but…I'm sure it could wait until tomorrow."

She nodded. "I guess so." She drank some more of the wine in her glass. "You know, your friends are really nice." She looked behind us at the people hanging out in the dining room. "Really nice." After a pause and another sip of wine she said, "Not all of these people are…are they? I mean many of them don't seem to be…"

"Gay?"

"Well, yeah."

"No, most of them aren't." Had she really thought they would be? I felt like asking her if all of her friends were born-again, right-wing, Bible-thumping homophobes.

We walked into the kitchen. Emma was standing at the sink rinsing off a china plate, and I decided that this time I was going to have to talk to her. Weber had come to our house, for godsake, so how could she say she didn't know him? I was about to take her firmly by the arm and invite her to an immediate and intimate little chat with me on the upstairs landing, away from the party. But Mrs. Leach suddenly let out a gasp. Standing in the back doorway, tall and wide with his broad shoulders rigid, was the stark figure of Mr. Leach. His thick grey eyebrows were set above gunmetal eyes. His face was a frozen mask. Only the eyes showed his anger and disgust, staring at the small figure of his wife, drink in hand, consorting boldly with the people in this house.

"I saw you through the window," he said. "Get your coat."

"I…I didn't bring one." Her wine glass nearly toppled as she set it quickly on the counter. She scurried to the back door which he held open for her. Just before stepping through it she turned slightly toward me and mouthed the words, "thank you." Her husband followed her out without a glance at anyone.

Emma and I stared through the back door together watching them disappear into the dark backyard. "You don't think he'll hurt her, do you?" Emma said.

I shook my head. "No, I don't think so. He's pretty sour, but he doesn't seem like the type to be violent."

"Did she ever tell you why she was here?"

"Nope, she didn't. She just said there was something she wanted to ask me about."

"What could Mrs. Leach possibly want to ask you, 'Claire, did you know Jesus would prefer it if you'd stop being a lesbian'?"

"Beats me, I'm just telling you what she said."

We kept peering out the window, though the Leaches were long gone.

A voice behind us said, "Did I miss the evening news?" Roger was standing there alone. He had his hands in his pockets and was glancing around the kitchen, trying to look casual, but there was an unmistakable grimness on his face.

"Are you all right, Roger?" Emma asked. "Where's Cindy?"

"Cindy's gone."

"What do you mean 'gone,' Roger?" she asked. Her voice got louder. "Where did she go?"

"Home, I suppose. In any case, I don't consider it my business anymore. Where Cindy goes is her concern."

"Roger," I grabbed his sleeve, "Cindy's been drinking, and she took some medicine this afternoon. It isn't safe for her to drive."

"Cindy is an adult," he said coolly. "She can handle herself." He shook my hand off his arm and walked away into the dining room. Emma and I stared at each other for a second.

I turned around and raced to the front door, thinking maybe I could catch Cindy before she drove away. Too late. A few seconds later I stood in our front yard, heart racing, snow spilling over the tops of my shoes, staring at the empty space where Cindy's rental car had been. The fog from my breath rose slowly in the still air. I turned around and walked slowly back to the house. I was suddenly in the mood to see another dead philosopher.

I did not have to wait long.

CHAPTER SIXTEEN

Emma got up earlier than I did, for a change, in spite of having gone to bed much later. When I excused myself around midnight, there was still a small group of philosophers lingering by the fire, drinking and talking about Weber and his death long into the frigid hours of the prairie winter night. When I felt Emma finally climb in next to me, I remember groggily wondering how she would function in the morning on such a short stretch of sleep.

In the morning I went downstairs to find the kind of scene at which you expect to see Red Cross workers handing out food and blankets. Glasses, bottles, and half empty plates covered every available surface, including lamp tables, chair arms, footstools, even the edges of bookshelves. Stacks of pots overflowed from the kitchen sink. The aroma in the air was a nauseating melange of stale wine, cold quiche, vegetable dip, and cigarette smoke.

I tried to estimate how long it would take me to get the place cleaned up working alone, since Emma would be tied up with the Weber Follies all day. About six hours, I figured. Another of my working days would be sacrificed on the altar of Emma's damned philosophy conference. But that was not the main thing on my mind this morning.

I found Emma at the dining room table, still in her bathrobe and slippers and wearing her wire-rimmed reading glasses. She had cleared a spot amid the empty bottles and dirty paper plates and was writing something on one of the yellow legal pads she uses for her lecture notes. I came up behind her, kissed her on top of the head and looked over her shoulder.

"What are you writing, love?" I asked. The sobriquet was deliberate. I was determined to discuss some heavy stuff this morning and I wanted to start off on an affectionate note.

"The opening remarks for the memorial service. Kurt Burghoff agreed to give the eulogy, but I have to give an introduction. Marlene called up at six forty-five to make sure I was taking care of this, can you believe her?" She erased a couple of words and scratched in some new ones.

"Yeah, she s something," I said in a distracted sort of way. There was one item of old business to discuss before we got to this morning's primary topic. "Listen, do you think we should call Cindy and see if she made it home all right?"

She stopped writing and gave me a worried look. "I tried. No answer."

"Really? Well, it was late when she left, she probably couldn't get a flight out until this morning."

"That's true. We should wait a few hours and call again." Emma went back to writing and I stood there deciding what to do next. How would I begin the discussion I had planned? I needed some innocuous kind of opening.

"Have you seen my navy blue skirt, Emma? I laid it out to dry yesterday morning." A slight deception on my part.

"A skirt? When have you ever worn a skirt during winter break?"

"I'm having lunch with Renee at Amelio's." That was true, and I would wear the skirt, but I didn't actually need her to tell me where it was. Without answering, Emma penciled in another line on her pad. "I thought maybe you'd seen it yesterday morning when you were here waiting for the sperm." I paused. "You were here all morning, weren't you?"

Emma kept scribbling away. She stopped, stared at the wall for a few seconds, her lips moving silently, then started writing again.

"You know, that reminds me, Emma, thinking about yesterday morning. Mrs. Leach said something last night that surprised me." I waited. Emma was still staring down at the yellow pad, tapping her pencil eraser against it, which is a signal that she's stuck on some particular thought.

The subtle approach was apparently not working. I reached over and put my hand on her shoulder. "Emma!" She stopped writing and looked up at me. "Mrs. Leach told me that Weber came to our house the day before yesterday."

Her eyebrows came together. "Mrs. Leach said that? How would she know that it was Weber?"

"She saw his picture on TV last night. She said he stopped at her place to ask which house was ours."

Emma pulled her glasses down her nose a bit and looked at me over the rims. "Your new pal Mrs. Leach is a few hymn books short of a gospel choir. I was here all morning and I certainly never saw Weber."

"But wait a minute," I said. "You weren't here all morning. You went to see the president's secretary, remember?"

"Well, OK, I suppose he could have come then." She frowned. "But why would he come here? She's got the wrong person." She pushed the glasses back up her nose and turned back to the legal pad.

"Yeah...ah...now that you mention it, that's kind of what I was wondering about too. I mean, you told me that you didn't know Weber at all. You didn't even know he was coming to this conference."

She stopped writing, her hand still poised above the paper, and looked at me sideways, eyebrows raised. "So?"

Well, I thought, it's now or never. Out with it Claire. "Look Emma, I didn't tell you this before, but when I found Weber lying on the bridge Monday night, I also found a note next to him."

"A note?" She put the pen down and turned toward me.

"Yeah, I showed it to you yesterday. It was the note you'd written Weber, telling him to call Hans Gustav."

"The note I'd written to Weber? Telling him to call Hans Gustav?" She stared at me intently now. "Who the hell is Hans Gustav?"

I must say that question surprised me. "I thought you would know. He's apparently a friend of Weber's. He lives here in Iowa."

She squinted at me, incredulous, like I was a student who'd asked if Aristotle wasn't the guy who married Jackie Onassis. "You're babbling, Claire. You're saying you found a note from me that said....said what? 'Dear Erik, Call your Iowa friend Hans Gustav. Love, Emma?'" She leaned back a little and folded her arms.

"Well, no, not exactly. Just wait a minute." I turned and hurried up to the bedroom, fumbled in the pocket of my black skirt until I found the note, came back downstairs and handed it to her. She examined it carefully.

"Yes, I remember you showed me this, and it is my writing," she said. "But it doesn't say anything about a Hans Gustav."

I explained about finding whose number it was by searching for the phone number on the CD-ROM at the library. I didn't tell her about my little visit to Gustav's house.

She stared down at the note for a long time, than slowly reached out and handed it back to me. When she spoke her voice was soft and quiet, but deep behind it I heard the rumble of thunder. "You amaze me, Claire. You really amaze me." She shook her head. "You find a note that I wrote blowing across campus, a note I could have written to anybody, and you assume there's some kind of secret behind it?" Now her voice began to rise. "You don't just ask me about it. No, you start some kind of investigation, for heaven's sake!" She looked at me hard, the hurt and fury glowing in her eyes.

I couldn't say anything. She was right. What she had just said was absolutely true, and it made me feel like some vile little creature that one monkey at the zoo picked out of another monkey's fur.

"What is it that you think, Claire?" she said. "That I'm lying? That I knew

137

Weber was coming all along? Why would I lie about a thing like that?"

"Well, of course I don't think you were lying. But you've been...well, under a lot of stress lately, and I just thought that, ah,...you know."

"Oh yes, I know Claire, now I see it quite clearly." She stood up from the chair. "You think I'm crazy, don't you?"

Ouch. "Of course I don't think that."

"Yes you do." She held up her hands. "And why not." She got louder. "I was in a mental hospital, wasn't I? I was institutionalized. So why shouldn't you think I'm nuts."

"Emma!"

She nodded her head. "And that's why you don't want me to have the baby." She pointed an accusing finger at me. "You don't want to have a baby with a crazy person...with a...lunatic!" She burst into tears and ran away from the table, through the kitchen and up the back stairs.

"EMMA! Come back."

Well, I thought, that went smoothly.

CHAPTER SEVENTEEN

I was walking to campus to go to my office. Finally. Of course, I wasn't headed *directly* to my office. No, after our fiasco of a conversation in the dining room I'd had to coax Emma out of the upstairs bathroom by submitting to a relationship talk, through half an inch of wood no less, and offer sincere reassurances about my faith in her and my commitment to having a baby. (Actually, the wood came in handy for that last part because she couldn't see my face.) Then I had cheerfully agreed to do her yet another favor: to drop off her speech to get typed up by Maria, who is one of maybe three people on the planet who can read Emma's handwriting. Meanwhile Emma was staying home to take a shower and get dressed. Personally, I didn't think there was nearly enough time for Maria to type up those notes, but that, I reasoned, was not my problem. Nor did I have any incentive to point out such difficulties because the mood in the household was still pretty fragile. The place was a wreck, but it was tacitly agreed that cleaning the house would be postponed until either we were getting along better, or Hell froze over, whichever came first.

Maria wasn't in the philosophy office. I was afraid to just leave Emma's notes lying there on her desk. If for some reason Emma's notes didn't arrive at that memorial service there would have to be another service for me later in the week. And Weber's service was to begin in half an hour. I decided I'd better go over to the college chapel and see if Maria was already there working on the arrangements.

Just outside Emma's building I met Marshall. His puffy coat was hanging open and his face was red.

"Claire," he said, out of breath, "there you are. There wasn't any answer at your house or office, I thought you might be here."

"What's up, Marshall?" I kept walking toward the chapel, I needed to get there, fast.

"Look at this." He fell in beside me and handed me a card, Colin Jensen's business card. "This is the card that was in your skirt pocket last night, the one with the phone number of the liquor store."

"Yeah?"

"The name on it is Colin Avignon Jensen, right?"

"Uh, huh." I was walking pretty fast. Marshall puffed along beside me.

"You remember that Colin was harassing me about the Platburg thing, the plagiarism stuff, right?"

"Yeah?"

"Well, when I saw that card something seemed funny to me about that name." His coat flapped open as he gestured with his hands stuck in its pockets. "I looked in my book notes this morning; Platburg's name was Colin Avignon Platburg. That's an awfully big coincidence, don't you think?"

"I suppose so." We cruised along past the fine arts building.

"So this morning I called this friend who was in Platburg's department when this whole plagiarism thing happened. Well actually, the plagiarism thing happened over about a two year period, and this guy left in the middle of it. No, wait. ...it was really more like toward the end of it because he was actually on leave—"

"I get it Marshall, the guy knew Platburg." Jeez.

"Right. So anyway, he said Platburg had a son who was named after him, which I presume means he was named Colin Avignon Platburg, Jr."

"So you're about to tell me that Colin Jensen is Platburg's son?"

"I'm sure of it."

"And I assume you can explain the Jensen part?"

"My friend told me that about two years after Platburg's death, his widow remarried."

I slowed my pace. "To a man named Jensen?"

Well," Marshall said, "my friend didn't remember her new name. He thinks it could have been Jensen."

"Uh, huh," I said, "and it could also have been Von Hindenburg."

"All right, but let's just assume for a minute it was Jensen, OK?"

"OK." Sure, why not? I was in a hurry.

"Do you see the implication of this?" Marshall said.

"What implication?" He looked at me with his eyebrows up. I stopped walking. "You aren't going to say Colin murdered Weber, are you?"

He shrugged. "I'm not saying it, but..."

"Oh, come on, Marshall." I didn't want to hear this. Basically I liked Colin, and I hate it when people I like get sent to death row. "Look, even if Colin is Platburg's son, so what? Why would he murder Weber anyway? Revenge? For something that happened twenty-five years ago?"

"Well, who can say? Platburg got pretty messed up over it." I turned and started walking again, not as fast. "I don't know, Claire," he said, "it just seemed awfully odd to me that he never let anyone know he's Platburg's son. And he's also the only one I can think of who really benefits from Weber's death."

"Benefits how?"

"With that paper of his. If Weber were at this conference he wouldn't get away with that plagiarism crap. Erik would blow him right out of the water." There was pride in his voice, the loyal biographer championing his subject.

"But I thought you said it was an old debate. If Weber could have refuted it before, why didn't he?"

"He wouldn't bother. Not in print anyway. Erik never acted liked he cared about what people said about him. But in person? To his face? Oh, he delighted in skewering people if he could be there to watch them squirm."

"A charming guy."

"Yeah. He'd chew Colin to bits if he were alive." Jesus, Marshall sounded like he was Weber's dad at a little league game.

"OK," I said, "but still, you wouldn't kill somebody for a lousy paper, would you?" Unless, of course, I thought but didn't say, you were counting on that paper to get you a new job. "Besides," I said, "Colin isn't the only one around here whose paper would get slammed if Weber showed up."

"You mean Roger?"

"At least Roger. There are probably others." Then another, happier thought occurred to me and I shared it with Marshall. "Besides, Colin has an alibi. He was at the opening talk when Weber died."

Marshall was quiet for a few seconds. "Hmm. Well, I guess you're right about that."

As we came up to the chapel, I stopped outside the rear door, wanting to put a close to this nasty business before we went in. I put my hand on Marshall's arm. "I don't think you should tell anyone about this, Marshall. I mean, if you're wrong about him being Platburg's son, it's just going to embarrass everyone."

He gave me a shallow nod. "OK," he said, "I suppose that's best."

We were about to go inside when it occurred to me to ask him an unrelated question. "By the way, Marshall," I said, "do you know anything about a friend of Weber's named Hans Gustav?"

He looked puzzled. "That isn't a friend of his. That's the name Weber used when he was hiding from the Stasi."

The college chapel is a large stone church built around 1850, and it sits directly across the street from the inn. Its vaulted ceiling and granite floor give it the feel of a gothic cathedral in miniature. The pews are all dark wood and red fabric, and the walls are filled with memorial plaques for alumni who died in the Civil War. The number of such deaths from this one little college in this one little town is simply astonishing. Up at the front of the church is a kind of stage that the pulpit sits on. The stage makes this building handy for all sorts of events in which numbers of visiting dignitaries (read rich alumni) need to sit in a row facing the audience.

Before I even saw them, I caught the sickly-sweet smell of the carnations that lined the stage. The back of the church echoed with the clanking and snapping of metal rods as technicians set up lights for TV cameras. A bunch of reporters were milling around, talking to each other, looking at the wall plaques, or, in the case of one seedy-looking guy in a pea-green overcoat, taking a nap in one of the pews.

I felt shaken and disoriented. What Marshall had told me about Hans Gustav had confirmed a suspicion that had been gnawing at the edge of my brain: Erik Weber had been living here, in Iowa. That's why the police couldn't find out how he'd gotten here to Hammond. He'd been living up the road, for heaven's sake. And Emma was maintaining that she hadn't invited him, didn't talk to him, knew nothing at all about what he was doing here.

I really did not want to think about this now. I wanted to give Emma's notes to Maria and get the hell out of there. Then I could go sit quietly in my office and try to figure all this out. There was no sign of Maria, but Marlene was standing in front of the stage adjusting two large wreaths of purple and white lilies.

"Marlene, have you seen Maria?"

She ignored my question. "Is Emma here yet? We're supposed to begin in fifteen minutes."

"She was getting dressed when I left, she'll be here any minute."

Marlene tugged a dead leaf off of one lily. "She's going to make sure Kurt Burghoff gets here to give the eulogy, right? We need a good eulogy, there are TV cameras here, you know." The tension in her voice was quite apparent. She stopped fussing with the flowers, picked up her clipboard, which was lying on the stage, and turned to me. "Since Emma's not here for some reason, I'll tell you this. Please be sure and tell her. There are four chairs up there." She pointed behind her at some gold brocade chairs sitting on the stage. "These will be used by the chaplain, the president, Emma, and Dr. Burghoff, in that order. The president will be here at nine o'clock sharp. Tell Emma to make sure everyone else is ready." Before I could even nod, she strode off to my left and disappeared through a side door.

I saw Sara Grace near a side entrance taking programs for the service out of a brown cardboard box. (Programs? Marlene had programs overnight?) The sight of Sara Grace made me feel a flush of anger. I wondered whether she'd reconnected with Roger last night after he had chased off his wife, his wife who had come all the way out here to be with him. I knew that I shouldn't blame Sara Grace though, because she, after all, was just a kid. She was just another victim.

"Sara Grace, have you seen Maria or Emma?"

"Sorry, I haven't." Damn, I thought. Up at the front of the church I saw Colin Jensen talking to Fritz. Maybe he knew where Maria was.

"Sara Grace, would you go up and ask Dr. Jensen if he's seen them? I'm going to—"

"OK, what does he look like?" That question surprised me.

"You don't know him?"

"I did off-campus study in Holland last semester."

"Oh, I forgot." I pointed at Colin. "There he is."

"Oh, he's Dr. Jensen?" She giggled. "I thought he was a student. I'll go ask him."

I sighed as Sara Grace hurried up the aisle. I wondered when was the last time someone said, "Oh, she's Dr. Sinclair? I thought she was a student." Hell, in a few years they'd be saying, "Oh, she's Dr. Sinclair? I thought she was Whistler's Mother." Now feeling old as well as anxious to get out of there, I went back down to the stage.

Renee and Kurt came strolling down the main aisle of the chapel and I noticed other conferees coming in as well, but no Maria. Or Emma. There were also lots of non-philosophy faculty and staff taking places among the pews: Bob Johnson from history, Sandy Brodsky from Russian, Louise what's-her-name from the admissions office. I was amazed. Marlene must have recruited them this morning just to puff up the crowd for the sake of the media.

Sara Grace came back and reported that Colin hadn't seen Maria or Emma either. I figured that it was too late anyway to worry about finding Maria; Emma would have to read from her handwritten notes. But that was not my fault. It felt good to be able to say that for a change.

"Good morning," I said, as Kurt and Renee came up past the first pew.

"Hi, Claire," Renee said. "How's Emma this morning? She looked very tired last night."

"She's going to be more than tired if she doesn't get here soon. Have you seen her?"

"No, she didn't come to the inn this morning. I thought she said she'd meet us here."

I looked around anxiously. "They want to start soon. Oh, Kurt," I pointed up at the stage, "you're supposed to sit on one of those chairs up there." He nodded and climbed the few steps to the stage, slowly, seeming to drag his stiff leg a bit.

I pulled Emma's notes out of my coat pocket. "Listen, Renee, can you do me a favor? Give these to Emma and tell her I couldn't find Maria. I want to duck out before this thing begins."

"You're not staying for the service?"

"Staying for the service? Renee," I said, a little louder than I should have, "in the mood I'm in, if I hear somebody eulogizing Weber I'm likely to stand up and start blowing raspberries." As I said this, something about the way she was looking over my shoulder told me I wouldn't be happy when I turned around. Marlene and the president were standing right behind us.

"Are we ready to begin?" Marlene asked. She tapped her clipboard against the palm of one hand. "The president has a very busy schedule this morning."

Shit! I couldn't tell them Emma hadn't shown up yet. "Yes, we're almost ready." I forced a smile and gestured toward the stage. "Jack, you'll be sitting up there next to Professor Burghoff." I said this as if it had been my idea. "I'll go tell Emma that we should get started." I hooked my arm through Renee's and pulled her along with me, off toward the side of the chapel where we would be out of earshot of college administrators. "What're we going to do? Emma's not here!"

"Shall I try to call her?"

"No, it's too late for that." I glanced at the stage where Jack was leaning over talking to Kurt. He was nodding gravely, his face showing the kind of earnest concern that a good college president can always fake. "Renee," I squeezed her arm, "I hate to ask this, I know it's a huge imposition, but do you think you could stand in for Emma?"

"Well…Yes, sure. I can do that."

"I wouldn't ask if it weren't an emergency."

"That's all right. I suppose I could just read Emma's speech."

She unfolded the notes I'd given her. She took one glance at the first of the yellow pages and looked back at me, her eyes filled with horror. Emma's handwriting! I'd forgotten about Emma's handwriting. Renee would never understand those ridiculously scribbled notes; she'd have a better chance of speed reading the Dead Sea Scrolls. Slowly, and with undisguised pity in her voice, she said to me, "Claire, I think you're going to have to stand in for Emma."

"Me? Renee, I can't do that. I didn't even know Weber. I have nothing to do with this conference. I'm not even dressed for this." I looked down at myself. Actually, for once, by some miracle or tragedy, I was wearing a skirt.

"You look fine, Claire."

I looked frantically around the chapel. "Listen, Emma will be here any second, I know it." I lapsed into what someone like Mrs. Leach would probably call silent prayer. Please let her come in now. Please let her come in now.

"Claire," Renee said gently, "I think you need to do this for Emma. It'll be OK. Just go up there and sit down. I'll see if I can find Emma before the service begins." She squeezed my hand and hurried up the aisle.

No, no, not again. This could not be happening to me again.

Up on the stage the president made a furtive glance at his wristwatch. There was a substantial crowd seated in the pews now, and the chapel gently hummed with their muted conversations. Great big lights blazed behind the rear pews. Bright red dots on TV cameras told me they were starting to film.

I trudged slowly back down the aisle of the chapel. Do this for Emma, she says. I stomped up the stairs that led to the stage. Do this for Emma.

I walked on stage and whispered news of the switch to the college chaplain, who nodded evenly. I passed a puzzled looking Kurt and sat next to a slightly frowning president. Jack cleared his throat but didn't say anything to me. Marlene was seated in the very front pew, and the look on her face showed clearly that, while her full set of emotions might be too complex to sort out, it was certain to include a) unpleasant surprise, b) morbid fear, and c) unshakable determination of homicidal intent. I knew because I felt the exactly same way.

The service began. While our portly old chaplain gave a benediction, I scanned the audience for signs of Emma. Still nothing. Now I had time to start wondering what had happened to her. Emma could be careless about getting to places on time, but she knew this service was a command performance. I didn't think she would be casual about a function being held at the order of the president, a function at which she was supposed to talk. I was starting to get scared for her. Normally she and I don't worry if either of us is late in arriving someplace; the streets of Hammond are not especially mean. Moreover, in a town this size, if someone you loved were to be seriously injured you would almost certainly hear the ambulance siren. But this day was different. Weber was dead, maybe even murdered, and now Emma had failed to show up for his service. A frightening image flashed in my head: Emma lying dead on the floor of our kitchen. Why the kitchen, I didn't know, but something was very definitely wrong. She should've been here.

The image was dispelled by the sound of my name being pronounced by the chaplain. Uh, oh, my turn. I walked to the pulpit, slowly, with deliberate steps, trying to look solemn but feeling very shaky. A couple of flashbulbs popped in the front pews and I squinted into the TV lights. The cloying smell of the carnations at the pulpit gave me a sudden wave of nausea.

Should I explain why I'm the one introducing Kurt? I decided not to bother since it quite obviously defied rational explanation. I unfolded Emma's notes, smoothed them against the podium, looked down at them, and felt my heart skip a beat. God, I should've looked them over first. Did this really say, "Good morning, we are cornered in this chapel…?" No, no, "gathered in this chapel." Whew.

Well, there was nothing for it but to jump in and start reading. So I did.

Actually, my performance didn't go too badly. I (or rather Emma) briefly praised Weber the scholar, mourned Weber the man, introduced Kurt Burghoff and sat back down. It was over in a about a minute and a half. I made only one mistake: I said, "Weber's genius is hard to defend," instead of, "Weber's genius is hard to define." And I'm not sure my version wasn't more accurate. In any case, I was greatly relieved to be back in my seat.

Kurt stood up and limped to the pulpit. Without reference to any notes he began. "Mr. President, honored faculty and students, fellow admirers of Erik Weber. We gather here in memory of a great scholar." He embarked on a long (and frankly, rather boring) eulogy of the man who'd been his friend and colleague for so many years. I stopped paying attention almost immediately and resumed looking around the chapel for Emma. Had she come in while I was speaking? I could see Marshall and Arnie sitting with Oscar the reporter in the third pew back, Oscar scribbling away in his little notebook. Over on the side I saw the black beret, with Fritz sitting under it. Colin was there too. I recognized various faces from last night's party, and I knew some of the gathered faculty and staff, but there was no Emma. No Renee either, she must still have been out searching for Emma. It was hard to see the back of the church where the television lights were beaming at the stage and I wondered if Emma could be hidden in that glare.

Scanning the pews, my eye caught someone moving along the extreme left aisle headed toward the back of the chapel. It was Roger. Sara Grace was following behind him. I thought it highly suspicious that they were walking out (together!) in the middle of the service, but I didn't have time to think about that. I just wanted to know what had happened to Emma. I looked around for Maria, thinking maybe I could somehow pass her a note or something asking her to go find out about Emma. But there was no sign of her either.

During the course of my search, I'd been vaguely aware of the increasing intensity of the sound of Kurt talking. Without hearing the words, I felt the emotion surge in his voice, growing stronger, louder, and more strained as he spoke. I sensed, without considering it, that the little chapel was filling up with the booming, rasping power of his speech.

"...ideas, insight, the mind itself. THIS is the moral sphere of the great thinker, not the office, or the bedroom, or even the classroom. Let us judge Weber THERE, in that place of his GREATEST ACHIEVEMENT. To his critics I say—"

Kurt got my full attention when his voice suddenly stopped. I turned to see him bending over the side of the podium, coughing fitfully into his right hand, his left hand pressed against his chest. At that moment, everyone in the chapel shared the exact same hideous thought: he's having a heart attack. In a flash all of us on stage were up and over to him. Marlene appeared as if by magic. There was a moment of great confusion and many in the crowd rose to their feet as the group at the podium obscured their view. Marlene and the president tried to make Kurt sit down, but he shook his head at them and made a final cough. He stood up straight, wiped a hand across his mouth, and whispered something in the president's ear. Marlene held Kurt's arm in both her hands.

After a few seconds the president nodded solemnly and spoke into the microphone.

"Professor Burghoff says there is no cause for alarm. He assures me that he will be all right in a moment. He asks that we continue our homage to Professor Weber."

Marlene, still holding Kurt's arm, led him carefully down the stairs on the left side of the stage. They were joined by a man from Marlene's staff who escorted them out the side door of the chapel. On his way out, Kurt gave a little wave and a weak smile to the crowd to tell them he was OK.

In a minute or so, the audience had settled down again. The president, already at the podium, started his speech. He began by expressing the college's official institutional sadness at the passing of Professor Weber. He didn't mention that the college was especially sad that Weber hadn't picked some other campus on which to die. He talked for a while about the fellowship of all scholars, how we are all brothers and sisters in the search for truth, how the death of any one of us, whether or not we knew him personally, leaves each one of us a little poorer. He quoted John Donne and Thomas Hobbes and Keats (I think). It was an incredible speech. Jack had never even met Weber, and he practically had everyone weeping in the aisles. I was truly impressed. I would have been even more impressed if he'd said these things in a third of the time.

All during Jack's speech I kept looking around for Emma. Part way through, my heart jumped when a woman came in through the back of the chapel. I leaned forward and squinted. It wasn't Emma, it was Sara Grace. She was alone.

I began to squirm. When would this service end so I could go find Emma? Unfortunately, when the president sat down, a student choir in full choral regalia came marching through a door at the rear of the stage. I was not only annoyed by this, I was stunned. It was winter break, for godsake! Where the hell did Marlene come up with a student choir? They climbed some creaky risers that I hadn't even noticed behind the pulpit. Their young faces were somber and they looked striking in their deep purple robes with white collar and cuffs. A silver torch, the symbol of Hammond College, shone on the left breast of each robe. For a minute there was only the sound of their rustling as they arranged themselves in rows and prepared, presumably, to sing a hymn.

I wanted to pull my hair out. For a moment I considered just getting up out of my chair and walking nonchalantly down off the stage. Maybe they'd think I was going to check on Kurt. But then I glanced at the president, sitting there with his hands folded piously on his lap, and quickly lost my nerve.

As it turned out, the choir did not sing a hymn, it sang a series of hymns. They seemed like really long hymns too, about four verses each. And between the hymns the choir director, a white-haired old man whom I'd seen but didn't know, would wave his hands and mouth some long quiet instructions to the students on the risers. When they'd all flipped to the correct page in their hymn books he would pause, hands in the air, waiting until every one of their eyes was focused on his before beginning the next song. All the while I sat on stage fighting off a screaming fit.

But then something remarkable happened. Right in the middle of the fourth hymn—I think it was "A Mighty Fortress is Our God"— Emma walked into the chapel. She just bopped in. I happened to look back there just in time to see her squeeze past a couple of seated mourners (if that's the right word) and sit down in the middle of a pew.

Was she all right? I looked hard. Of course, few people would trust a medical exam conducted by an economist at a distance of forty yards, but she seemed OK to me. If she was all right, why the hell hadn't she shown up until now? She obviously hadn't been murdered. (Although the way I was feeling, she was in a high-risk group.)

The choir finished their final hymn and the chaplain closed the service with a benediction. Seconds after the amen, while the president was still shaking hands with the chaplain, I scooted off the stage. I hurried up the center aisle to meet Emma coming down. Before I could say a word, she held up both her hands as if to say, 'Don't hit me.'

"I know you're angry, Claire. I'm really sorry, I just couldn't get here."

"Couldn't get here? You couldn't get here? What, were you stuck in one of those notorious Iowa traffic jams?"

"Please don't be sarcastic." She looked over her shoulder. "I had something important to do."

"Here!" I said." You had something important to do here!" Emma cowered while I took a deep breath and held it for a few seconds. More calmly I said, "What happened, Emma? You scared the shit out of me."

Her voice fell to barely a whisper. "I'm ovulating this morning. I had to inseminate myself."

"That's it?" I said. I lowered my voice when I saw her wince. "That's it? That's why you came late? You were supposed to give the opening speech," I reminded her firmly.

"I know I was, but I thought Renee could do that for me. I figured you'd give her my notes. I tried to call to tell you that but everyone was already here."

I shook my head. "I couldn't find Maria to get the notes typed, Emma. And you didn't leave enough time to get them typed, anyway. I had to give your speech myself." That made her wince again. "You could've waited to inseminate later, Emma. You didn't have to do it the second you started ovulating." I must have said that too loudly because she quickly looked around to see who heard it.

"I know, I know. I'm sorry, Claire. I just got scared, that's all. I've been having all of these problems getting it done. I was afraid if I didn't do it then it wouldn't happen. This service was the only block of time I had today."

"But why did it take you so long? You missed the whole service."

She whispered very softly. "You have to lie with your legs up for half an hour afterward, you know that." She took my hand. "I'm sorry, Claire, I really am."

I gave her one last heavy sigh for good measure, then I nodded to show her it was OK. Renee came up to us. She was a little out of breath.

"Emma, are you all right? I've been looking all over for you."

"I'm fine, Renee. I'm sorry for all the trouble." She repeated her explanation as the three of us walked up toward the front of the church.

Before we reached the front door, I made a clear and firm announcement to Emma. "When we get outside this door, Emma, there will be a lot of reporters. I will not talk to them. You will disabuse them of the notion that I am the college's spokesperson, and you will do all of the talking. Are we clear on this?"

"Yes, yes, very clear. You won't have to worry about talking to any reporters."

As it turned out, she was right. When we got outside the chapel I didn't have to talk to reporters because there weren't any reporters there. Like everyone else in sight, they were rushing across the street to the inn, where three police cars had come screaming up.

CHAPTER EIGHTEEN

I have a weakness for television cop shows and I particularly like the scenes where they're back at the station house. There are usually ten or twelve phones ringing and a hundred people milling around while the good-looking young cop and his middle-aged partner convince the lieutenant that it was a clean bust and he just can't turn that scumbag back out on the street again. There is invariably a prostitute or two somewhere in the background. I like how the shell-shocked witnesses, when they come in to be questioned, are always offered coffee by the shirt-sleeved cop.

Hammond's police station was nothing like this. And that was too bad because I could really have used a cup of coffee. In Hammond's police headquarters, visitors waited on molded plastic chairs with thin metal legs in a brightly lit room, while a receptionist sat behind a glass window next to a grey steel door leading into the interior of the building. The very young-looking blonde woman typed and chewed and looked out into the room occasionally to smile at the visitors. The floor was beige linoleum with sparkling flecks of red and gold. The cinderblock walls were a shade of green that was chosen, I'm sure, because the paint was on sale.

Soon, I knew, I would have to go behind the grey steel door.

I did not have to sit in this depressing place alone, I had to sit there with the president of the college. Though I had been knocked off my pins by the most recent disaster of Emma's conference, Jack was as under control as ever. Concerned but calm, that was Jack.

He leaned toward me and said confidentially, "I'm sure it won't be necessary, Claire, but if for any reason Emma would like to consult an attorney, I can have the college provide one immediately."

An attorney? "Well…I appreciate that Jack. I don't think it will come to that though."

"Oh, yes, I'm sure you're right." He crossed his legs and laced his hands across one knee, staring thoughtfully at the opposite wall. Marlene came crashing into the station, hair flying, her huge bag hanging off one elbow, her coat wide open to the cold morning. She wore neither hat nor gloves. Her lipstick stood out deep and red against a very pale face as she came over and stood in front of the president. She brushed the bangs away from her face.

"Jack," she said, "I think for the time being you should stay in here. There are reporters all over outside, and some others are camped out at the administration building."

Jack nodded without looking at her. "The trustees have called an emergency meeting at noon," he said. "I'll need to be back for that."

Marlene came to rest in the chair next to Jack and pulled off her coat. Underneath she wore a green and yellow plaid skirt that came to just above the knee, and a matching green blazer over a yellow silk blouse. "I'm afraid we've gone from local to national news," she said. "Five minutes ago I was questioned by someone from the *Washington Post*."

"Really?" I said. "How could a reporter from Washington get here so fast?"

Marlene looked at me like I was a glob of something brought in for a biopsy. "The reporter doesn't come all the way from Washington, they use someone from a local bureau."

"Oh. Yeah, of course," I said. She glared at me in apparent amazement.

"Jack," she resumed, "I think this time you'll need to talk to the media yourself." A glance at me. "It's going to be important that this thing be handled competently." Jack nodded again, and I knew then that my short career as the college's spokeswoman was now completely on the rocks. I felt sure I'd be able to live with the loss.

"Have reporters started talking to the conference people yet?" Jack asked.

"I don't think so," Marlene said. "The police have them all holed up at the inn for questioning." She smoothed her ruffled hair back into place. "But that won't last long." She reached down, rummaged around in her big bag, drew out the ever-present bottle of ibuprofen, and took three straight, down the hatch, no chaser. "My god," she said, hand to her forehead, "I don't even want to think about what this will do to enrollments."

"I don't think this is the time or place to be worrying about that, Marlene," Jack said.

"In the future, Jack, I think the administration should screen the participants before approving any conferences. We can't have people bringing murderers to campus." She gave me a look that singed my eyelashes. What was the look for? I hadn't brought any murderers to campus. And even Emma had probably brought only one murderer to campus, at worst, only two.

"Right now we need to concentrate on cooperating with the police," Jack said.

Marlene went on as though she hadn't heard him. "This is a public relations disaster," she said. She got out of her chair and started walking back and forth. "We are a rural institution, a very rural institution. Why would anyone send their child to us instead of Pomona or Penn or Wellesley?"

"Marlene—"

"What do we have to offer that they don't? Better opera? More theater? A really good subway system? No!" She waved the hand with the medicine bottle which rattled like castanets. "Safety! That's what we have that's special, safety. 'Hardly any crime here,' we tell the parents, 'your child can walk the streets any hour of the night.'"

"Marlene, this is not the time."

"Now what do I tell them?" She stopped walking and stood in front of us, arms wide open. "What do I say? 'Oh don't worry about that little episode you saw on TV last winter. Murderers only come here by faculty invitation. We don't have any scheduled for at least six—'"

"Marlene, sit down and be quiet!" No one seemed to recognize the harsh voice that spoke that line, though it had clearly come out of Jack's mouth. After a second he added, "Please."

Jack's outburst turned Marlene to stone. For a long time she stood like a statue, her eyes fixed on the wall above our heads, lips pressed thin, cheeks flushed. Slowly she stepped over to her seat, turned around, and sat back down. The receptionist looked up briefly from her typing and smiled.

Jack returned to the voice of calm authority. "I promise you, Marlene, I will take steps to make sure we can avoid this sort of incident in the future." A jolt of fear zipped along my spine. What sort of steps might those be, Jack? Maybe some personnel changes? Perhaps a subtle shift in budget priorities like refusing to endow chairs for people who bring nationally-televised bloodbaths to campus? For a while we all sat without talking.

The grey steel door opened and Pete, the police chief, stood on the threshold. "Jack, I'm sorry I haven't been able to brief you yet. I'll send someone out in a few minutes to tell you what we know. Right now I have to talk to Claire." I was up. I was surprised that Pete would be questioning me; I wondered who was questioning Emma. I tried to get a glimpse of her through the doors we passed as Pete led me down a long narrow corridor, but couldn't see her. At the end of the corridor Pete took me into what looked like a small lunch room. There was a little round table with a white tablet on it, pine cabinets hanging over a steel sink, and a coffee maker on the Formica counter top. Taking up one whole corner was a great big pop machine with PEPSI on the front. I was nervous as hell and could really have used a drink, but I was afraid to ask and they didn't offer. I say 'they' because Pete was not the only other person in the room. Seated at the table was another officer, this one wearing a brown uniform instead of a blue one like Pete's. Even sitting, it was obvious he was tall, and his shoulders looked a yard wide. He had a square jaw, deep blue eyes and short blond hair. Very short blond hair. The collar of a white undershirt showed through the V in the neck of his tan uniform. "Claire Sinclair, this is Sergeant Christenson from the state police barracks in Newton." The sergeant responded to my hello with a barely perceptible nod of his head.

Pete and I sat down at the table. I needed to ask them a question before they started in with the rubber hoses. "Has anyone been able to contact Roger's wife and tell her about…his death?" The term 'death' was a euphemism in this case. Death is what comes quietly one night in the sleep of old age; it's what finds you in the hospital, weak and exhausted after a long bout with emphysema. It was something meaner than death that had found Roger in his room at the inn that morning. A student worker, coming in to change the sheets, had discovered Roger lying on one of the inn's thick oriental carpets, staining it red with the blood from his broken skull. There was no speculation that this death was accidental.

"No, we haven't contacted her," Pete said. "That's part of what we need to talk to you about. When did Mrs. Stuhrm leave your party last night?"

"Well…Cindy left the party around nine fifteen or so. I didn't actually see her leave."

"That's kind of early to leave a party, isn't it?" Pete asked.

"Well, I understand that she and Roger had an argument."

"What do you mean 'you understand'?" Sergeant Christenson asked. His was a titanium steel voice and it fairly hummed with impatience.

"I wasn't present. I took Roger and Cindy up to Emma's study so they could talk privately." I was sure Emma was already telling them all this, but I knew they'd also need to hear it from me. They would compare our stories.

"How did you know when Mrs. Stuhrm left the party, Claire?"

"Roger told us. It was obvious that they'd argued and he said she was leaving. I ran out to try to stop her, but she had driven off before I could get outside."

"Where do you think she went when she left?"

"I assume she went back home."

"Why do you assume that?"

"Well…she had a rental car, for one thing. It makes sense that she would've gone back to the airport." Pete glanced at the sergeant, and for a second neither said anything.

"She never showed up at the airport, Claire. Her rental car wasn't returned and the airline says she didn't fly out of there. Not last night or this morning."

"Good Lord," I said, "she could have been in an accident. She'd been drinking before she left the party."

"No," Pete said, "if she'd had a wreck the state police would know about it."

This made it obvious, of course, what they suspected Cindy had done. For me it was a truly incredible thought. "Are you going to ask me if I think she could have killed Roger?" That's what the cops on TV would do. A brief guttural sound from the sergeant showed how much he would value my opinion on this subject.

"Right now, Claire," Pete said, "we just want to know where she could be."

I shook my head. "I really have no idea, Pete. She knows a number of other people at the conference, could she have stayed with someone else at the inn?"

Pete assured me that they had checked that possibility. He said they had not yet checked all of the local motels or those near the airport, but they were in the process of doing that. There were a few more questions on the subject of Cindy's whereabouts. Then the discussion moved on to the inevitable issue of Emma's activities at the time of Roger's murder. I told them the whole story: how Emma was trying to artificially inseminate, how the sperm had arrived when Emma wasn't ready for it, how we'd been struggling for two days to keep it frozen, how Emma, discovering that she was ovulating this morning, seized the opportunity to inseminate, thereby making herself late for Weber's service. It sounded pretty goofy when you strung it all together.

"So Emma asked you to give her talk so she could, ah, do this other thing with the sperm, right?"

"Well, she didn't actually ask me to do it for her. I decided to do that myself when she didn't show up." Boy, that didn't sound good.

"So you didn't know she wasn't coming. Then how'd you know what she was doing?"

"Well, she told me afterwards why she hadn't come."

"Uh huh." He jotted on a notepad that lay on the table. "So when she didn't show up, you just made things up to say, sort of off the top of your head, huh?" "Well, no. I had Emma's notes for the talk." He shot a glance at the state trooper.

"But if you weren't planning to talk for her, then why'd you have her notes?"

I could feel my blouse getting damp around my underarms. "You see," I said, "I was supposed to get her notes typed by the philosophy department secretary, but I couldn't find her. So I still had them when the service started. When Emma didn't show up, I asked Renee Amundsen to read Emma's speech. But then Renee couldn't read Emma's handwriting, and I can. Read Emma's handwriting, I mean. So when the service started, and Emma still wasn't there, I had no choice but to read Emma's notes myself." It's surprising how improbable the truth can sound when it's told to men wearing skeptical expressions and police uniforms. We all observed a moment of silence, as if in memory of my late credibility.

Pete wrote something on his pad and then changed the subject. "Claire, can you think of anyone at the conference who might've wanted to kill Professor Stuhrm?"

"Not really, but then I don't know these people very well. I'm not actually a part of the conference."

Next, Pete and his colleague wanted to hear about Emma's past relationship with Roger. We spent a long time on that one. They also showed substantial interest in my own attitudes toward Roger, my lover's ex-lover, a man whom I myself had recently fantasized about killing, though I don't believe I mentioned those thoughts to Pete. Then we went back to more recent events.

"You picked Professor Stuhrm up at the airport, right? Did he say anything about someone having it in for him, anything like that?"

"No." I thought for a second. "He did say he had some big revelations to make about Weber in the paper he was delivering. I can see why that might make Weber mad, but not anyone else."

"What kind of stuff did the paper say about Weber?"

"I don't know, he wouldn't tell me. In fact, he refused to send in a copy of the paper to Emma before the conference like he was supposed to. He was very secretive about the contents of the paper."

Pete made another note on the pad. "So, has anybody had a look at this paper, anybody you know of, that is?"

"No, I don't think so."

"Can you think of anyone at the conference who was not at the memorial service?"

Only one person—Emma. "Not really, but I don't know all of the participants. I only know a few of them." That statement was true and it gave me some comfort. After that we arrived at a subject that I had been dreading all along.

"Did your housemate know Dr. Weber pretty well?" Pete asked.

"Um, not personally, I don't think."

"You don't think?" Sergeant Christenson said.

"Well, it's only for the last ten months that we've been living together."

"But she knew him professionally, right?" Pete said. "She knew how to get in touch with him."

"Get in touch with him?" I asked. I was stalling to give myself a few seconds to think.

Pete studied me for a moment. "Emma knew where Dr. Weber lived, didn't she?"

"Ah... well, she never told me that she did."

"She didn't know Dr. Weber lived around here?"

So they knew. Oh, Jesus. I tried not to let my fear show in my face. "He lived around here?" I said, trying to sound surprised. More stalling, and not very smart, because now they'd find out that I was hiding something.

Pete looked briefly at the state trooper. "Dr. Weber had some personal effects that make us think he was living here in Iowa, Claire. Don't you think it's kinda funny that Emma wouldn't know about that?"

My terror ebbed just a smidgen. Apparently they hadn't found his house, so they hadn't talked to his housekeeper, so they didn't know that Kurt and I had been there. Of course, it was only a matter of time until they did. I shrugged at Pete and made a statement that, while not exactly forthcoming perhaps, could certainly be classified as absolutely true. "Emma and I don't talk much about philosophy, Pete. It's not something I'm interested in."

He nodded and scribbled something on the pad.

There were more questions, lots of them. We went over, in quite meticulous detail, how I had found Weber lying on the bridge that first night of the conference. They asked about who I saw and didn't see at the memorial service, about Roger and Sara Grace, another iteration on Emma's old romance with Roger, and generally about how I'd spent the last two days. The interview lasted a solid hour. When it was over, no one offered to show me out. I just got up, said good-bye to Pete, gave a nod to the sergeant, which he declined to return, and headed back down the deserted hallway. The waiting room was empty, save for one key person. There sat Emma Harrington, woman of many occupations and talents: scholar, conference organizer, prospective mother, murder suspect and the only person who had ever managed to give tiny Hammond, Iowa a national reputation. (As an easy place for philosophers to die.) The cumulative effect of these recent events was summarized in a single aspect of her appearance: her hair was a frizzy mess. She sat there, pale and limp, with her coat on her lap, staring at the wall. For some strange reason she had her gloves on.

When I came through the grey steel door she tried to say, "I waited for you," but couldn't even get it out.

I went to her, wrapped my arms around her neck and held her face against my chest. I said, "Come on, sweetie, let's get out of here." We pulled on our coats, I took her arm, and we walked out of the station house.

I held her arm tightly and she leaned against me as we walked toward her car. "Claire," she said, in what was almost a whisper, "they think Weber was living here. Here in Iowa."

"Yeah, I know."

"They think I knew it, Claire, and that I've been lying to them all along."

I didn't say anything. I walked with her around to her side of the car and opened the door.

She looked right at me with those puffy, bloodshot eyes and said, "I didn't Claire. I swear to you that I had no idea that Weber was living in Iowa."

And I knew right then that she was telling me the truth.

CHAPTER NINETEEN

It is widely acknowledged that to an academic there is no sound more melodious than that which emanates from his own throat. We professors love to hear ourselves talk. In faculty meetings, for example, it is quite common to spend two hours discussing each and every nuance of a minor curricular issue that everyone already agrees on and no one cares about anyway. We're willing to talk on any occasion, for any length of time, on any given subject, whether we know anything about it or not. This isn't so surprising, of course, since talking is what we do for a living. But the odd thing is that we don't even have to be good at talking. After all, we don't really have to please our listeners—student audiences are hopelessly captive. No doubt we'd be better speakers if we faced the same constraints as, say, lawyers do: 'Objection, Your Honor, the professor's comments are boring and incomprehensible.' 'Sustained. Ms. Sinclair, you will confine your remarks to things that interest the students.'

But that's not how it is. I make this point about academic loquacity to emphasize how unusual it is to sit in a room with six or seven college professors and have no one be talking. A bunch of us sat in such a room at the Hammond inn. A colleague, more likely two colleagues, had been brutally murdered for reasons that no one as yet could fathom, and that was enough to trigger a silence. (It was also enough to trigger a lot of drinking, though in this conference crowd that was less remarkable.) Normally, of course, I would not have been able to tolerate so much silence, but even I was feeling too listless to say anything.

I sat on a long sofa with Marshall Udall and Rupesh, the Pakistani man who had been at my table the first dinner of the conference. Across from us, in matching armchairs, were Renee and Colin Jensen. Young Fritz, still wearing his black beret, was standing by the fire into which we were all staring. There were similar groups staring at similar fires scattered about the first floor of the inn. It was about two o'clock in the afternoon. The silence was broken when Arnie Cohen came walking up carrying a glass of red wine in one hand

and a nearly empty bottle in the other. He stood for a moment surveying the silent group, then dragged a chair over and sat down next to Renee.

"So where's Emma then, still being grilled by the cops?" His voice sounded huge in that quiet room.

"She's with the police chief looking at Roger's room," I said.

"Why on earth would he need Emma for that?"

"They're looking for Roger's paper. The one he was supposed to give here. He had been carrying it on a disk in his pocket."

"Huh! Waste of time," Arnie said. He poured the last of the wine into his glass. "It was the wife, what's her name? Cindy. Had to be."

"How could you possibly know that, Arnie?" My voice was much sharper than the occasion called for.

He looked at me calmly. "It's simple, Claire. If she didn't do it, where is she? She's not here in Hammond and she's not back home. If she were innocent she would be one of those places. It has to be she." He gave a pedagogic wave of his hand. "It usually is, you know. A family member, I mean. Murder is mainly a crime of passion, always has been."

"I disagree with you Arnie," said Rupesh. "To me this is looking like a double murder, Stuhrm and Weber, both killed for the same reason."

"What reason?" Marshall asked.

"We do not yet know," Rupesh said, "but we can be fairly certain that one is to be discovered. Two deaths at this one conference? It cannot be a coincidence. They surely are somehow connected."

"Oh they're both murders, Rupesh, I've been saying that from the start," Arnie said. "An accomplished drunk like Weber doesn't stumble over a stone wall, for chrissake. Hell, he could drink all night and then dance *Swan Lake*, old Erik could. But connected? No. That's the wife's angle, you see. She wants us all to think they're connected—throws suspicion away from her."

"Excuse me," I said, "didn't you just tell us it was a crime of passion? So when did she have time to think up an 'angle?'"

Arnie pointed at me and gave a self-satisfied smile. "Ah, Claire, your question betrays an unwarranted presupposition." In a flash I realized what a mistake I'd just made: I had started an argument with a philosophy professor.

"You see, passion," Arnie explained with admirable patience, "is not the absence of rational thought, it is an emotional complement to rational thought. Of course its external product, the passionate act, may appear to an observer to lack rationality."

Fritz jumped in with obvious relish. "You're missing the point, Arnie. Labeling the murder a crime of passion says nothing about the rationality of the act. It merely speaks to the criminal's intent. Emotion is passionate only in its negation of rational intent, hence the confusion with irrationality."

Arnie was shocked. "Are you going to stand there and suggest that an act of passion is at all times an act of negation?"

Sadly, we never discovered just what Fritz was prepared to stand there and suggest because I interrupted. "Rupesh," I said, hoping I'd heard the guy's name correctly, "what connection do you see between the two deaths?" This was not a subject I was anxious to talk about, but anything was better than Whether Passion is Negation.

"I cannot be specific, but we have every reason to suspect that there is one. I suppose," he said, "it must be related to the paper of Professor Stuhrm."

"But this was someone Roger knew," Arnie said, "someone he let into his room. There was no forced entry."

Renee broke her silence and in a solemn tone said, "Roger would have let any one of us in, Arnie."

"You mark my words," Arnie said, "this is a black widow case, the female destroys her mate. Happens all the time."

"There's a problem with your theory, Rupesh," Colin Jensen said. "Roger was killed while all of us, almost all of us, were at the memorial service."

"Why wasn't Roger at the service?" Renee asked of no one in particular.

"He was there at the beginning," I said, "but he left pretty quickly."

"You could see him leave from the stage?" Colin asked.

"Yeah."

"Was it before or after Kurt got ill?" Everyone turned to look at Colin. After a few seconds I said, "It was before."

"How about that girl," Renee said, "the one Roger's been seen with?"

"Sara Grace? They left together," I told her. "I haven't talked to her. I don't know why they left. The police haven't arrested her so I assume she wasn't there when Roger was killed."

"Is she one of our majors?" Colin asked me.

"She's one of your majors, yes," I said.

"Well," Arnie said, "there's one good thing that will come out of all this. Now Marshall can sell movie rights to his book." That remark landed like a crystal vase on a tile floor.

For a moment no one said a word. Then, slowly, without looking at any of us, Marshall got up out of the overstuffed sofa and stood silently, his face passive, his hands at his sides. He stared down at Arnie, who was sitting across from him, slunk casually against the back of the armchair. "You drink too much, Arnie," Marshall said, and walked out of the room.

No one said anything, so shocking was this outburst on Marshall's part.

From Marshall Udall that simple statement was a slap with a glove, it was a verbal horsewhipping, it was 'pistols at dawn.'

Arnie appeared to have no trouble handling it. "Well, then," he said. He rose from his chair with some difficulty, and frowned at the empty bottle in his hand. "If you find me lying on the rocks by the river, tell Marshall for me that he was absolutely right. Meanwhile, I'll go see if I can find some more wine." As he moved toward the door I noticed him listing a few degrees to starboard.

The rest of us, now feeling embarrassed as well as sad, resumed our examination of the flickering fireplace. I started thinking about what Rupesh had said. How could the two murders be connected? The circumstances of the deaths made it highly improbable. The timing issues were not complex here. If you were at the opening talk you hadn't killed Weber; if you were at the memorial service you hadn't killed Roger. It was that simple. And almost everyone at the conference was at one or the other.

So who connected with the conference missed both events? Emma wasn't at the memorial service, but she was at the opening talk. Well, she wasn't at all of the opening talk, she said she'd been in and out. But in any case, Emma could not have killed anyone, much less two people. I absolutely knew that, however much the icy fingers of doubt might poke and prod my faithless little brain. So who else could have done both murders? Maybe someone at the conference I didn't know. It had to have been.

Actually there was one other person who was connected with the conference and had no alibis: Maria. She hadn't been at either event. I couldn't imagine a possible motive for her, but who knew? She was European, after all. And from what I learned in the last two days, it was clear that if she, 1) had lived in Europe in the early '60s, and 2) was a human female with a beating heart, she had almost certainly slept with Weber, and he had almost certainly dumped her. If Weber had lived here in Iowa it made sense that someone local would have helped him arrange things. Maria had been hired by John Marchak, who knew Weber. Maybe there was a connection there that we didn't know about yet. But then why would Maria kill Roger?

No, the two-connected-murders theory just didn't have enough wheels. The alternative hypothesis, that the two deaths were unrelated, required two separate murders or one murder and one accident. Either of those cases, unfortunately, looked really suspicious for Cindy Stuhrm-Lawson.

I heard someone talking softly in the hall; it sounded like Emma. I listened. It was Emma. I stood up, excused myself from the group and scurried out after her. In the hallway just outside the door were Emma, Pete, and Sergeant Christenson, the state trooper. All three standing there peering down the corridor, listening intently. They looked like they were about to spring a drug bust. I came up quietly behind them. Maybe a little too loudly I said, "What's going on?" The two men whirled around and Emma gave a little yelp. "Sorry," I said. The sergeant looked as if he were about to slug me.

Pete said, "Claire, would you mind checking to see if the lobby is still filled with reporters?"

"Sure." I walked a few feet down the hallway and made a right turn into the main room of the inn. Yes, the lobby was definitely still filled with reporters. There must have been at least a dozen of them standing around the room looking bored. Camera equipment was everywhere, and one corner had been given over to a small mountain of coats, hats, scarves and mittens. These people had not been permitted to walk around the inn collaring and interviewing conferees, they'd been required to sit on their hands in the lobby. This apparently did not make them happy. Jack had wanted to keep them out of the inn entirely, but Marlene had explained the public relations implications of making journalists stand outside in Iowa in January. She said we might as well turn the dorms into chicken coops and plow the quads for corn and soybeans. So here they all were: newspapers, radio, television, you name it, unhappily camped out in the lobby of the inn. I caught sight of Marlene carrying a tray of cookies through the crowd, smiling gamely, trying to soothe their seething impatience. I went back down the hallway and reported to my SWAT team. "There are reporters all over out there," I said. Emma suggested they go out through the kitchen, and the three of them turned around and headed down a hallway toward the back of the inn.

"Where are you going, Emma?"

Over her shoulder, she said, "To the department," before Sergeant Christenson shushed her.

To the philosophy department? Why? I decided to find out. I started to run back to the lobby to get my coat from the main cloakroom. I slowed to a walk as I rounded the corner, the sight of the college's former spokeswoman dashing outside with her coat half on might be regarded by the media as mildly interesting. I was not craving media attention. Walking with as much nonchalance as I could muster, I took my coat from the rack in the lobby, tucked it casually under my arm and walked back toward the kitchen exit. No one seemed to notice or care. I went out through the kitchen. Outside, I headed around toward the front of the inn, crossed Park Street and headed toward Emma's building. Just as I was crunching through the snow on the front lawn of the inn, a man stepped out from the bushes at my right. I jumped.

"Claire, isn't it?" he said. The man was Oscar Lamb, the reporter from the *Gazette*. He was standing there in the same brown blazer he'd worn at the party last night. An unlit cigarette was stuck between his fingers. "Where ya headed?" He asked this in a way meant to sound chummy and folksy, like something old-time Iowans would call out to one another as their buggies passed on a dusty road. But I was not in a folksy mood.

"Over to my office, I have some things to do."

He smiled. "Your office? You get your coat from the front of the inn, then slip out the back of the inn, so you can go to your office?"

I do not like being made to feel stupid. (Though you'd think by now I'd be getting used it.) "If you'll excuse me, Mr. Lamb," I said, and walked away. He followed me, but I ignored him, thinking I'd show the snotty bastard. I had a coat and he didn't, so how long could he stay with me?

"OK, Claire," he said, "I'm sorry. I won't ask where you're going. Could you just give me some background on Dr. Stuhrm and his wife?"

"For godsakes, Mr. Lamb, Roger's wife doesn't even know he's dead yet. I'd hate like hell for her to read about it in a newspaper."

"She knows he's dead."

That slowed me down some. "How do you know?"

"The police took her into custody about twenty minutes ago."

All I could do was suck in my breath. After a second I said, "Where'd they find her?"

"All I know is that she's at the police station."

So she hadn't left Hammond after all. My God, what's she still doing here? I could think of an answer to that question, but it was not an easy one to stomach. "Did they arrest her?"

"I don't know yet."

This looked really bad for Cindy, no question about it. I began to think the unthinkable—that maybe she had actually killed her husband. But was that a genuine possibility? She couldn't even leave him, was she really capable of cracking his skull open? No, I didn't think so. No, something else was going on here, something other than a marital tiff. There had to be.

"All right, Oscar, I'll tell you what, I'll answer your questions if you answer one of mine."

"Shoot."

"On Monday night you called my house less than two hours after Weber's death. How did you hear about the accident so fast?"

"Sure, I'll tell you that." He stopped walking and flicked a disposable lighter at the tip of his cigarette. "Dr. Stuhrm called me."

CHAPTER TWENTY

When I came in, Emma and the sergeant were sitting idly in chairs over by the department's desktop computer, Emma looking very nervous. Maria was at her desk answering a call. Pete's muffled voice came from behind the closed door of Emma's office. I gathered he was using her telephone, no doubt being told that they'd brought in Cindy. Amazing. Oscar had known about it before the chief of police. Obviously the *Gazette* had a mole at the police station.

Maria hung up the phone and handed a message to Emma, who held up the little pink slip at me. "Maria has taken thirty-two messages for me today," she said. She looked at the one in her hand. "Thirty-three. People have been hearing about this on the news all over the country. My mother has called six times."

"I'm surprised," I said. "I would've expected your mother to call twelve times."

Emma smiled wanly and nodded.

Pete came out of Emma's office. "Sorry," he said. He went over and stood by the others at the computer. "I gotta be back at the station soon, so let's try and get this done, OK?" Get what done?

In his hand Pete held a computer disk which presumably had come from Roger's room. Since he wasn't wearing gloves, I supposed it had already been dusted for fingerprints. He handed the disk to Emma who slid it into the PC. Christenson and Pete stood behind her, each looking over a separate shoulder. Emma tapped away at the keyboard while the two men stared intently at the screen. When Emma paused to look at the monitor, I fought a desperate urge to go stand between the two cops. Emma started tapping again, then stopped and looked. Tapped some more, stopped and looked. Neither of the cops so much as flickered. Eyes still focussed on the screen, Emma slowly shook her head. "There aren't any files on this disk," she said.

"What?" Pete looked at his trooper colleague. "The paper's not there?"

"When I ask for the directory of this diskette it says 'no files found.' The directory tells you what files are on the disk."

Pete's voice fell to a low growl. "Now look, Emma, this is the disk from Stuhrm's pocket—"

"I don't understand it either, Pete."

"—the one you said had the only copy of the paper."

Emma swallowed. "That's what he told people at the party."

"And now you're telling me the disk is empty."

Emma had swiveled around and was facing Pete. She seemed small and pale looking up from that chair at the two big cops towering above her. The trooper was leaning down toward her as if he thought he could stare the truth out of her. Emma's left eyelid closed slightly and began to flutter. I knew how scared she was feeling.

"The file was probably erased," I said loudly. "Maybe the murderer erased it."

The three of them turned to look at me. After a second Pete said, "So the paper's gone, that it? We don't ever get a look at it?"

The trooper gave a short, fierce grunt. "And so what should we do now, huh, just go home and forget about it?"

"Well...ah..." Somehow 'yes' didn't seem like the answer he was looking for.

"Excuse me for interrupting," Maria said, "but may I make a suggestion?" Please God, Maria, make a suggestion. "If the paper was erased it may still be there."

"Yeah?" Pete said.

Maria came over from her desk and stood next to Emma. Maria knows a lot more about PCs than Emma or I do. (Hell, Mrs. Leach's cat knows more about PCs than Emma does. And I do huge amounts of computing, but almost entirely on the college's mainframe computer.)

"How could it still be there if it was erased?" the trooper asked.

"Well, a computer does not actually erase information like a pencil would," Maria said. "When you tell it to delete a file, it just relabels the file space as being available for writing over. As long as the disk has not been written on, the information in the file is still intact."

"So the paper's still there?" Pete sounded skeptical.

"Unless the disk has been written on since it was erased. Here, let me try." She shooed Emma away from in front of the computer, lowered her big frame down into the chair and tapped away at the keys for a few seconds. The rest of us huddled behind her chair. The disk drive clicked and whirred. "There." She pointed at the screen. "There it is. The 'undelete' command shows that two files were erased from the disk. One is called '?eber.txt' and one is '?eber.bib.' The question mark character is put there by the undelete command." Someone had erased those files, I was right.

"To recover the files we need the first letter of the filename. It seems pretty obvious that it is a W." Tap, tap. More whirring and clicking. "There we are," she said, "the files are back." Maria smiled up at them.

"Wonderful job, Maria, thanks so much," Emma hugged her from behind. "Now could you print out four copies, please?"

Maria brought coffee in to Pete, Emma and me. The sergeant had gone back to the station, probably to start interrogating Cindy. The three of us sat in Emma's office reading Roger's paper, which was entitled *The German Word for Weaver: The Spider Who Betrayed Anton Spengler*. In spite of having spent a decade as the whenever-possible-lover of a renowned philosophy professor, I'd read very few papers in that field. (This was not an oversight.) So reading Roger's paper was a new experience for me.

The first thing I noticed was that Roger's manuscript, though only forty pages long, appeared to have hundreds and hundreds of *words* in it. This probably wouldn't have surprised most people, but we economists seem to be moving away from words. A comparable-sized paper in my field might get by with, maybe, fifty of them. For example, a paper from the *Journal of Economic Theory* might look like this:

> *In this study we extend Fung's Theorem on the existence of multiple equilibria in bilateral monopolistic trade. First we define the production function f as: [there follows six pages of equations]*
>
> *Now, letting P be the equilibrium price vector, we can show that: [eight pages of equations]*
>
> *Substituting expression (22) into inequality (9), (and using Euler's Theorem) we find that: [ten pages of equations]*
>
> *In conclusion, the implications of these findings for an export tariff will be obvious to the reader.*

Naturally, economists embrace the axiom shared by all academics since the days of the Lyceum—if what you're writing doesn't manage to be useful, at least make it incomprehensible. Also, it's always important to make your paper boring, lest the reader pay enough attention to discover that it's just a lot of meaningless jargon. Roger, who was a good academic whatever his faults, made sure his paper adhered to these principles. Nevertheless, the main point of his thesis (when he finally got to it) was pretty startling. He hadn't exaggerated about that part.

After reunification of East and West Germany, a wealth of secret material from the former communist government became available to scholars.

Roger searched these materials acting on a hunch. On page four of his paper, after the requisite summary of all the related literature, Roger wrote:

> *Weber's timely exit from East Berlin has been hailed by philosophers as an event of great fortuity for the profession. Other East German scholars, notably Wolfgang Harich in 1957, and Anton Spengler and Kurt Burghoff in 1965, were ensnared by the regime's ever increasing intolerance of dissent. Recent evidence, however, raises questions about whether Weber's escape can be entirely attributed to good fortune.*

The paper then described in meticulous and monotonous detail Roger's search through various East German archives. It got interesting again on page eleven. Here he described the discovery of recently opened files of the oddly named Ministerium für Staatssicherheit (Ministry of Statistics), popularly known as the Stasi. This was the notorious East German secret police agency, and in its records Roger found a gold mine:

> *The Stasi file on Erik Weber, to which numerous references are made elsewhere in the archive, has either been lost or destroyed. But a very substantial file on Anton Spengler still exists. Spengler and Weber were members of the same group of dissident scholars, the one referred to by the Stasi as "die Insekton," the insects. It is this file on Spengler which proved so fascinating.*

Fascinating? Well the file must certainly have been more fascinating than the next ten pages of Roger's paper, which spared no details in describing every damned thing the file said about Spengler. We read about the surveillance logs, we read the descriptions of Spengler's movements, we read what the file said about his friends, his family, his work routines, even his clothes. (I was thankful the Stasi hadn't seized Spengler's dental records.) Finally, the plot started to thicken again as we rounded the bend toward page twenty-one. Roger described the circumstances surrounding Spengler's death:

> *On the night of October 26, 1965, Spengler and seven members of his group were entering an escape tunnel under the Berlin Wall near Chauseestrasse, when the Stasi appeared. The police opened fire, killing Spengler and wounding two other men. Later that evening, the Stasi rounded up the remaining members of the dissident group. These included Kurt Burghoff, Heinz Ostman, Angela Voos, Johan Katz, Colin Platburg, and Inga Stolz. Yet Erik Weber and another man, John Rommereim, had gone through the same tunnel the previous evening without being molested.*

Roger then embarked on a seven-page discussion of what other people had written about this incident, including Erik Weber. Just as our eyes began to glaze over, things started to heat up again.

File notations for January of 1965 provide the first confirmation of a hypothesis that Weber and others had advanced in print, that the Stasi had an informant within Spengler's group. The person assigned to run this informant was Paul Hertz, a man of thirty-five from Dresden who had been with the Stasi for ten years. Hertz gave his informant the code name 'die Spinne,' the spider.

Having said something interesting for half a page, Roger felt compelled to digress into a boring discussion about the nomenclature Stasi used for its agents and informants. He spent a lot of space providing evidence that the Stasi in general, and Hertz in particular, assigned code names that reflected some salient characteristic of the person or his life. He gave us four full pages on this, though I personally was prepared to believe him after one.

Shortly thereafter we came to the hot stuff. According to Roger, Hertz had made a deal with his informant: the Spider would be allowed to leave the country in exchange for help in arranging that the others get caught trying to escape. That would give the authorities a sound excuse for prosecuting them.

Recall that Erik Weber had successfully escaped East Berlin the night before Spengler's death, but the others were caught. Hertz had told his superiors that Die Spinne would "weave a web that would catch all the bugs at once." That web, in fact, was woven as promised.

The next sentence Roger had underlined: *I remind the reader that "Weber" is the German word for weaver.*

Roger stopped short of actually stating the obvious conclusion: that Weber had ratted on his friends. (Apparently Roger had heard about lawyers, too.) He spent another few pages summarizing his evidence and anticipating possible objections to some of his points. He concluded simply:

The implications of these findings for our understanding of Weber the philosopher, and Weber the man, are perhaps best left for other scholars to ponder. Here I will be content to call for a reexamination of both the life and the writings of this influential thinker.

When the three of us had finished going through the manuscript, Emma said nothing. She leaned her chair way back and sat there, eyes closed, one hand draped limply across her forehead. It seemed like minutes before she finally spoke. "Dear God, this is unbelievable. It changes everything." Her chair came forward and she put her head against her hands, elbows on the desk, palms covering her eyes. "We've all been duped. He's made damned fools of us all." She put her hands down from her face and looked at Pete and me. "All these years we've been writing about his ideas. All these ideas of his on…on freedom and truth and…and ethics. ETHICS!" She paused and her mouth hung open. "And the son of a bitch turns out to be a traitor. He turned in his friends so that he could get out." Then she did something that kind of scared me; she started to laugh. To actually laugh.

"But it's so obvious," she said. "We deserve to feel like idiots. Erik Weber never gave a damn about anybody he ever met or ever knew. Why should we be surprised he'd do a thing like this?" Pete and I sat there and let her go on. "Why should we? Because he wrote so many beautiful things? It doesn't matter what somebody writes, that doesn't tell you what they believe. It's what they do, it's how they are. That's what tells you." She swivelled her chair away from us and I knew she had to be crying.

For a minute the room was absolutely quiet. Then Pete spoke. He spoke so softly and in such a gentle way that it made me want to lean over and kiss him. "Emma," he said, "I know this is hard on you and I'm real sorry. But I need your help. Is this paper gonna help us find out who killed Dr. Stuhrm?" Emma turned her chair back toward us, pulled a kleenex from a drawer in her desk and wiped her cheeks. "Yes, Pete, I think it will."

CHAPTER TWENTY-ONE

For the second time that day I sat in that phlegm-green waiting room wondering what was happening behind the grey door. At least this time Emma was with me. It was about four o'clock in the afternoon, and Emma and I had gone back to the police station intending to take Cindy home to our house the minute the police finished questioning her. We weren't saying much. It seemed that neither of us wanted to broach any subject that would make us confront the hideous implications of what was happening in Hammond that day. Minutiae—that's what we talked about.

"Is everyone going to have to stay here in Hammond until this thing gets resolved?" I asked her.

"According to Pete it won't be necessary for everyone to stay." Emma's voice was muted by the strain she was feeling. "He thinks most people can leave tomorrow when the conference is supposed to end anyway."

"So what about tonight? Do things just go on as planned?"

"Well, there won't be any papers delivered if that's what you mean. I think we can still have the scheduled dinner. I don't see why not."

"So you're still going to troop out to Rube's tonight?" I tried to disguise my incredulity. Rube's is a steak house twenty miles away in the tiny town of Montour, Iowa. Rube's is locally famous for having solved the problem of customers complaining about how their steaks are cooked by having the customers do the cooking themselves. It's a fun place, with people standing around great sputtering charcoal pits, gabbing and laughing while broiling up their big slabs of steak. I had a hard time picturing these befuddled, grieving professors of Emma's getting into the swing of Rube's.

"There isn't much else we can do," Emma explained. "We already have a reservation for forty people. And I really don't have any other way of feeding them. Maria is going out at four-thirty to set things up."

I tried to be encouraging. "No, you're right, I think you should go. In fact, I can even see Rube's helping to cheer people up."

She patted my hand. "Oh, you'll be able to see it all right, Claire, because you're going to be right there with us."

I was way past arguing at this point so I just leaned back against the wall and sighed a heavy sigh.

The steel door swung open and in its frame there appeared the bedraggled figure of Cindy Stuhrm-Lawson next to the starched and pressed Sergeant Christenson. She looked awful. Her face was blotchy, her eyes were blood shot, and her hair looked like the police had skipped the legal formalities and stuck her straight into the electric chair. Emma and I hurried over and put our arms around her. She started crying the second she buried her face in Emma's shoulder. Sergeant Christenson, who apparently didn't find this group-hug scene especially moving, handed me her purse and said, "She can't leave Hammond. She's already been told that, but now I'm telling you." Emma put an arm around Cindy's shoulder and walked her to the door.

"She can't leave?" I asked Christenson. "Why? She's not a suspect, is she?"

"Why wouldn't she be?"

"Didn't Pete tell you? We found Roger Stuhrm's paper. Someone tried to erase it from the disk."

Christenson was half in and half out of the doorway, holding the grey door open with one hand. "So?" His face held no expression whatsoever.

"Oh, come on, Sergeant," I said. "Cindy would have no reason to erase that file. It's obvious that the killer erased it to cover up what was in it."

"That looks obvious to you, does it?"

"Of course."

"Well, maybe it looked obvious to her, too." The steel door swung shut.

OK, Christenson won that round on points. Theoretically, Cindy could have erased the file to make it look like that was the killer's motive. But I didn't believe it. Cindy wasn't cold and devious enough to think that clearly seconds after clubbing to death the man she loved.

Outside I saw a big crowd of people where our car was supposed to be. A pack of reporters swarmed over the vehicle shouting questions at Emma in the driver's seat and at poor Cindy cowering in the back. Someone was taking Cindy's picture through the glass. I pushed past two guys who were blocking the door to the passenger seat.

"Excuse me! EXCUSE ME! Come on, out of the way, please!"

I heard someone call my name, proving that my reputation as a spokesperson was still alive in central Iowa. I wasn't flattered. Before I had even closed my door, Emma blew the horn twice and stepped on the gas. She drove out through the tunnel of reporters, not bothering to head back to the entrance, just bumping down off the curb at the far end of the lot and heading down Park Street back toward campus.

In the back seat Cindy slumped against the door, the top of her head just brushing the window. Emma and I exchanged a look. Were we going to ask any of the questions we really wanted to ask? It didn't seem like the right thing to do. If not, what kind of small talk do you make with a woman who's just learned that her husband's been murdered? We drove a number of blocks without saying anything until I (naturally) cracked under the pressure of silence.

"Cindy, when you left the party last night we got very scared. We thought you must have gone back to the airport." Emma shot me a disapproving look, but I knew she was glad I'd broached the subject.

"I'd been drinking too much," said a small voice from the back. "I stopped at the Motel 6 out by the highway and got a room for the night. It was too dangerous to drive so I figured I'd sleep it off and head home in the morning." She sniffed.

I wasn't looking at Emma but I knew she was feeling the same relief I felt. This was a plausible explanation for Cindy's not leaving town.

Then Cindy said, "No, that isn't the truth," and started to cry.

Uh, oh.

"The truth is," Cindy said, "I was just too chicken to go home and pack up and leave Roger. I got scared. I'm afraid to be alone." She sniffed again. "I thought I'd come back tomorrow and talk to him again. See if maybe we could work it out."

I was glad Cindy couldn't see me roll my eyes. But a question sprang immediately to mind and I had to clench my teeth to keep from asking it: And did you come back and talk to him again?

Cindy continued. "I took some more dalmane—way too much—and went to sleep. I didn't wake up until the police knocked on my door."

That answered my question all right, and the whole thing sounded pretty believable. In spite of what the trooper had said, the police must have thought so too, because Cindy was sitting in the back of our car instead of rattling a tin cup against the bars of some jail cell.

Emma cruised slowly past our house without turning into the driveway. There were no reporters standing around waiting in front of the house, and we could see no news vans parked along our street. At the end of the block she circled into the alley that runs between the streets, and pulled the car into our garage from its rear entrance. I held Cindy's arm and put my hand on her shoulder as we climbed up the icy back steps.

I opened the back door and gasped. Holy shit, what happened here?

I'd seen it in movies. At the end of a harrowing day, the innocent heroine comes home to find that hoodlums have completely ransacked her apartment. They came searching for the secret papers or the bag of money, or the Maltese Falcon, or whatever it was they were after, and tore everything apart. They turned over lamps, shredded the sofa cushions, ripped down the drapes and tossed piles of debris in the middle of the floor. The place is left a tortured mess.

Well, this was just the opposite. The mess we had left had somehow disappeared. Where this morning half-empty plates and dirty pots had formed little skyscrapers, there was now an empty sink and a clean counter. The kitchen table had no empty bottles on it, only our crystal vase with a pink silk rose. The living room was not only tidy, it seemed to have been vacuumed. Good Lord, I could even smell the faint hint of ammonia. Our entire first floor had been savagely cleaned.

On the counter by the stove, the perpetrator had left a note. *I heard the news. Sorry. Call me if there is anything I can do. Cubby.*

Emma took Cindy into the living room where I heard her tell Cindy to lie down on the couch. The red error light was blinking on our answering machine which meant that the message tape had rewound to the beginning because there were too many messages for the machine to handle. I knew just how the poor little thing must have felt. At that moment I could not muster nearly enough emotional strength to push the button and listen to the messages, so I took off my coat and started making some coffee. Halfway through grinding the beans it occurred to me that I didn't know why I was making coffee. Probably because it's what my dad would have done.

"Cindy," I called out to the living room, "is there someone you'd like me to call?"

A voice that could have come from a field mouse with laryngitis said, "I called my mom from the police station. She's flying out in the morning. There really isn't anyone else."

"Claire will meet your mom at the airport," I heard Emma say. This time I didn't offer any objection.

There was a knock at the kitchen door. I froze. Better ignore that, I thought, the last thing we need is to talk to more reporters. Then it occurred to me that reporters would be likely to come to the front door, not the back, so this was probably someone we knew. Peeking cautiously through the window curtains I saw a small woman standing on the back steps holding a cooking dish with two matching potholders covered with big daisies. She had on galoshes and a long wool coat.

I opened the door. "Mrs. Leach," I said.

"I heard the terrible thing about Cindy's husband. I thought I'd better bring you girls a casserole."

A casserole? She'd brought us a casserole? For a few seconds I didn't comprehend this. "It's shaved pork in barbecue sauce," she said. "It's kind of my specialty. I make it for church potlucks all the time."

She'd made us her specialty?

I'm sure my reaction was partly fatigue, partly stress, and partly how Cubby's kindness had affected me, but the sight of this tiny woman, a woman I barely knew, standing on my back step in the January air holding out to me her own special casserole, somehow put a lump in my throat. I couldn't even think of anything to say. I swallowed hard and reached out to take the potholders. My hands covered hers for a second before she slid hers out and buried them under her folded arms.

"You might want to heat it before you serve it. Twenty minutes at 350 degrees."

I managed, finally, to croak out what a born-and-bred Iowan might say in this circumstance. "Thanks...neighbor."

She gave me a sad little smile, walked down the steps and went home, carefully stepping in the footprints she'd made in the snow on her way over. She moved slowly. Her shoulders seemed slumped and she looked tired, trudging alone across the yard. Standing in my kitchen doorway, holding that dish with the silly-looking daisy potholders, I watched her disappear through her kitchen door. I went back into the house. I set Mrs. Leach's dish on the counter and lifted the lid. Steam rose from the hot pork and sauce, and the tangy smell of barbecue made my stomach growl with hunger, I hadn't eaten all day. I put the lid back on and stared down at the dish.

Emma came to ask me who was at the door and I told her about the casserole.

"She brought us this? Really?" Emma picked up the lid and looked in the dish. "Gee, that was nice of her." Emma peered out the window toward the Leaches' house, as if Mrs. Leach would be out there in the snow. Standing at the counter I began to think about how Mrs. Leach had shown up unexpectedly at the party the night before.

All at once I was seized by a powerful urge.

"Emma, I'll be right back." I stood up and went out the back door, not even bothering to pick up my coat. As I went down the back steps I heard Emma ask me where I was going, and then yell out a protest that she needed me at home. I ran through the snow, large amounts of it falling over the tops of my shoes, and went up the back steps of the Leaches' house.

"Claire?" Mrs. Leach looked surprised and concerned to see me standing there. "Is everything all right with the casserole?"

"Yeah, it's fine Mrs. Leach, it was really sweet of you to bring it over. May I come in?"

"Oh, of course, I'm sorry." She stepped away from the door and I walked into her kitchen. It was about what I'd expected. There were blond wood cabinets over the counter, yellow window curtains with white lace fringes, and wallpaper with pink and yellow tulips on a white background. Every surface was spotless and gleaming. A plaque below the kitchen clock showed seagulls and clouds and said *In His Love Always*. Just above the stove was an enormous spice rack filled with forty or fifty matching blue jars. The place was not to my exact taste perhaps, but it was bright and warm and welcoming in its way.

"My husband is at a meeting and won't be back for an hour," she said. "Would you like to sit down and have some coffee?" It didn't seem to occur to her that placing those sentences in tandem like that could be interpreted by me as slightly insulting.

"Coffee would be nice, thanks." There was some coffee already made and she poured two cups for us at the kitchen table. From a mushroom-shaped canister she extracted some homemade, chocolate-chip things, cookie-like, but sort of clustery.

I didn't know whether I should start out with small talk, but I decided I had better get down to my business. I didn't have a lot of time.

"Mrs. Leach, last night, when you came over for the party...well, I mean when you came over and then ended up staying for the party—"

"Oh dear, I hope I wasn't butting in."

"Oh, no, no," I said quickly, "not at all. Glad to have you. You saved the seafood bisque!"

She smiled and made a dismissive gesture. "That was nothing. But don't use cornstarch unless the recipe calls for it. I'd say you should probably use flour for most of your thickening."

"Yeah, I plan to from now on, thanks. Ah...anyway, what I was going to say is that I never found out why you came over. I mean, you seemed to want to ask me something."

"Oh." She hesitated. "Well...it wasn't anything really." Her smiled vanished and her gaze dropped from me down to her coffee cup. For an uncomfortable moment she didn't say anything. Then her face turned upward toward a shelf on the wall to the left of the table. "Have you seen these pictures of my children?" she said.

Was she changing the subject, or was this relevant? I had no idea. I looked at the shelf, which was crowded with photographs: portraits, family shots, adults, children, the occasional dog, everything. She reached up and pulled down a big silver frame holding double portraits of two young men around high school age. Both were fair-haired and quietly handsome. Blue eyes all around.

"These are my boys. Of course, these are old pictures; they're both in their twenties now. Joe here is married and has two little girls, but Ron is still single."

I felt my jaw clench. Had I fallen into some kind of trap here? I imagined the next thing she might say. "Claire, I just know you could stop being a lesbian if you found the right man. Now, my son Ron here…"

Luckily that didn't seem to be her point at all. "Ron has a job in Minneapolis," she continued. "He lives in an apartment there." She looked back down at her cup again. Quietly, she said, "He lives with another fella."

I assimilated this news with no particular reaction: her son lives in Minneapolis, he rents an apartment, he has a roommate. Uh, huh. When the conversation paused it finally dawned on me what she was saying.

"Mrs. Leach, are you trying to tell me your son is…gay…uh, homosexual?"

She looked up from her cup and slowly nodded.

"How do you know, did he tell you?"

Again, she nodded slowly. "About a year ago." She looked at her son's picture for a moment, then turned the frame toward me so I could see him. "Ronnie was always a quiet boy, kind of shy, didn't talk much about his feelings and all. But he always seemed normal enough. He played sports. He had a girlfriend in high school. I don't know when he changed over."

"Well, he probably didn't 'change over,' Mrs. Leach. Many gay people have heterosexual relationships for a time before acknowledging their other feelings. I've gone out with men, so has Emma."

"Really?"

"Sure."

"Then why did you become…you know?"

"A lesbian?"

"Yeah."

"Well," I said, "I don't think I ever became one. Even as a young girl I knew that I was attracted to other girls. I guess after a while I just stopped pretending not to be."

"Emma too?"

Funny, I wasn't really sure about Emma. "I think Emma figured it out in college. When she was in college, she fell in love with another woman. Nothing happened between them, but she knew she was in love. After that she continued to date guys for a while." I held up my cup and allowed a little smile to cross my lips. "But then she met me." I winked at Mrs. Leach and actually got a smile for a second, but her face quickly sagged again.

"How did your folks feel about it?"

"Well, my mother died when I was nine, I was raised by my dad." How would my mother have felt? I'd always wondered about that. "My dad," I said, "I don't know...I never really told him I was a lesbian. I mean I didn't announce it or anything, we never sat down and talked about it. He just kind of knew. The first time I brought home a female lover he didn't act surprised."

"So you still get along with your father?"

"My dad died five years ago. He had a heart attack. But yeah, we got along very well."

"Oh, I'm sorry." She looked away from me, embarrassed, as if she'd committed a faux pas. For a few seconds we both just sat there, and I started remembering all over again how much I missed my dad.

"Would you like some more coffee, Claire?"

"No, I'm fine, thanks. But tell me, when did you first find out about your son?"

"Well, about a year after he moved to Minneapolis, Ronnie said he'd started 'dating' another man."

"Did he tell this to you and your husband both?"

"Yeah." Her eyes met mine. "And Bob said he couldn't ever come home again." She looked away. After a second, she turned back and stared down at the picture of her son. "You know, when my boys were little we used to go camping. Couple of times a year. One summer, we were out at the Grand Tetons and Ronnie disappeared. He went off into the woods and didn't come back. In those days we didn't think much about kidnaping, things like that, but I thought he might've fallen and hurt himself. Maybe gotten mauled by a bear or something. Anyway, while everyone was out looking for him, I just prayed and prayed and prayed. And the Lord told me to just feel Ronnie," she tapped her chest with two fingers, "inside here. And I could feel him. Like I knew he was OK, and we would find him soon. And that's just what happened." She looked at her son again, her thumbs caressing the edges of the picture. "I know this will sound silly, you being a professor and all, but I still try to do that sometimes. Try to feel Ronnie." Two tears rolled down Mrs. Leach's face now. "But anyway, the thing is, I can't feel that now. It's like he's not there anymore."

I tried to put the next question as gently as I could. "Is your son ill, Mrs. Leach?"

"You mean AIDS?"

I nodded.

She shook her head. "No. He said he wasn't." Mrs. Leach took a lacy white handkerchief from the pocket of her dress and wiped her eyes with it. It occurred to me that after all she had told me, I still wasn't sure what she wanted from me.

"What is it you wanted to talk to me about?"

"Well," I could see how difficult this was for her to say, "my Ronnie was always a good Christian boy. He was a junior deacon at thirteen." She paused to see if I was impressed by this and I raised my eyebrows as if I had been. "Anyway, Ronnie said that this thing, you know, being homosexual, wasn't something he chose himself. He said God made him this way. He said God gave him these feelings, and so it wasn't a sin no matter what the Bible says."

She stopped and looked at me. "What do you think?"

What did I think? If this woman was looking to me for some scriptural authority she was seriously confused about the nature of my education. "Do you mean do I think homosexuality is a sin?"

"No, I mean what do you think about Ronnie not choosing this? About God making him this way?"

I thought it important to point out that as an interpreter of God's will my credentials were unimpressive. "I don't know much about religion, Mrs. Leach. Are you asking me whether I think I chose to be gay myself?"

"Uh, huh."

"No, I didn't. It wasn't like deciding to become a smoker or to start drinking. I don't think sexuality is an acquired taste. I suppose some people would say that even if you can't help having these different sexual feelings, it's wrong to act on them. You should just deny them. But that would be asking a lot, wouldn't it? I mean, what if someone had told you that you were allowed to love your two boys, but never hold them. Never kiss them or put them on your lap. You would have had a hard time doing that, wouldn't you?" I am normally not comfortable speaking in platitudes, but under the circumstances it seemed appropriate.

"Yeah," she said, "I sure would have." She was staring hard into my eyes now, and I saw that she was trying desperately to understand her son. She really thought I might offer her some help. I didn't know if I could. I did know that I truly wanted to help her, this sad woman, my neighbor, maybe even my friend.

Softly she said, "Oh, Claire, I wish my husband was hearing this. He won't admit it but he really misses Ronnie, too." Personally, I wasn't much lamenting Mr. Leach's absence, but I could believe that he was the one who needed convincing. It seemed obvious that what was separating this woman from her son was not her convictions or her religion, it was her husband.

"Why don't you tell him," I suggested.

Staring down at her coffee mug again, Mrs. Leach squirmed uncomfortably. "Well…I don't know if I could…"

"I think you could, Mrs. Leach. Dorothy."

She raised her head. "Do you?" I nodded at her. She picked up the picture of her son again, stared at it for a few seconds, then met my eyes again. "You're right, Claire, I need to tell him this. I'm going to. I don't care if he gets mad. I'm going to talk to him and tell him what you said." She smiled at me, clearly pleased with herself for making this decision. I inferred that this small gentle woman did not often find herself standing up to her spouse.

Come to think of it, neither did I! I knew I'd better get my ass back over to our house before Emma began tossing my clothes out in the snow. "Listen, I really have to get back to Emma and Cindy now Mrs. Leach. Thanks for the coffee."

"Thank you, Claire."

With my hand on her back door, I had another of my sudden and stupid impulses, and I resisted it as effectively as I usually do. "Dorothy, when you talk to your husband…well, if you want, I could come over and talk to him with you." I felt instantly foolish for having made that suggestion and I winced imagining how she might respond. "That's a lovely idea, us all getting together, Claire, but let's wait for a time when Bob's chain saw isn't working."

Amazingly, Mrs. Leach didn't seem to think I was nuts. "Would you do that? Really?" she asked. Her eyes got wide and hopeful.

"Yeah, I really would," I told her. "As soon as this mess is cleared up about the murder and all, I'm coming over and we'll talk to your husband."

I walked out the door. As I trudged along the path she and I had worn in the snow between our houses, I saw Dorothy's face at her kitchen window. She gave me a smile and a wave, which I returned. I noticed that there was also a face at our kitchen window, though it wasn't smiling and it wasn't waving.

CHAPTER TWENTY-TWO

Before I'd even closed the kitchen door, Emma asked in a harsh whisper, "What the hell were you doing over there?"

"I just wanted to ask her why she came to the party last night," I said. "No big deal, I'll tell you later. How's Cindy?"

"All right, I guess. Still pretty much in shock."

I nodded. "What are we going to do with her, Emma? What are we supposed to do in a situation like this?"

"I don't know. I suppose we can do little more than just stay with her until her mother arrives tomorrow afternoon. Speaking of which, we have a problem. Who will stay here with Cindy while the rest of us go to dinner at Rube's, in," she looked at the wall clock, "oh God, half an hour?"

That was no problem. I knew just the woman for that job!

She held up a hand. "Don't even say it, Claire, please. I really need you to come to Rube's with me. I absolutely cannot handle this event without you. Please, I really need you tonight."

"OK, OK, I know. Why don't we ask Renee to stay with Cindy?"

"Good idea. Will you call her, please?"

Emma went back into the living room and I called the inn and asked for Renee. When Renee finally came to the phone she said she'd be happy to come right over. I hung up the phone and came back to the kitchen wondering if I should bother changing for dinner. Given all that had happened today did it really matter what I wore?

In my peripheral vision I saw something move just outside the back door. Someone was standing there. Had there been a knock? I didn't think so. A reporter? Mrs. Leach again? I didn't want to go to the door in case it proved more convenient to pretend we weren't home, so I went over to the window above the sink and peeked out sideways through the curtains.

Standing on the steps was a slender figure in a blue dress who wore no coat, only a battered black sweater that wasn't even buttoned. She wasn't looking through the glass in the door, but seemed to be staring down at her feet. I hurried over and opened the door.

"Sara Grace?"

She was shivering and her lips were thin and tinged with blue. Her gaze met mine, but her eyes were glassy and unfocused, her expression void. I wasn't even sure she knew where she was.

I was suddenly faced with a nasty dilemma. Should I bring Sara Grace into the house? At that very moment Cindy Stuhrm-Lawson was lying on the couch in our living room. While I didn't know the exact protocol for handling a grieving widow, I was certain that arranging a meeting with the girl her late husband just had a fling with was pretty far up the list of Don'ts. On the other hand, I could hardly send Sara Grace back out in the snow in an obvious state of emotional crisis, dressed like the Little Match Girl. I grabbed Sara Grace by the sleeve and pulled her inside, admonishing her to silence with a finger across my lips. The poor child accepted this without any reaction, as though it were a typical way to enter someone's kitchen. I sat her down at the table.

I whispered, "I'll be right back."

In the living room, Emma was seated on our old leather footstool next to the couch where Cindy lay. Cindy had a cloth across her forehead. "Emma, why don't you take Cindy upstairs and put her in our room? I think she'll be more comfortable there."

"I'm fine, Claire, really," Cindy said. "I don't want to be any more trouble than I've already been."

"Cindy, don't be ridiculous, you're no trouble," I told her. Emma patted Cindy's shoulder and gave me a puzzled look. I glanced over my shoulder at the kitchen, jerked my thumb up toward the stairs, and mouthed the word 'now.'

"Claire's right, Cindy, let's get you settled upstairs. We can put you in some pajamas. One of us will still sit with you, don't worry." She helped Cindy up off the couch and held her arm as the two of them climbed the stairs together. Emma shot me a worried look but I made a reassuring gesture with my hand.

Back in the kitchen Sara Grace was sitting with her shoulders hunched over, staring down at her lap. I reached underneath the table to pull off her wet shoes and felt that her feet were ice cold. So were her hands. I sat down in the chair next to hers and put a hand on her arm.

"Are you all right, Sara Grace?"

It took her a few seconds to answer me. "I came to apologize to Emma." Apologize? For a second I imagined she was about to apologize for killing Roger, but that was crazy. "And to say good-bye," she said. "I'm quitting school."

"Apologize for what, honey? What makes you think you did anything wrong?"

"For wrecking the conference." She started to cry. "For being such a slut and getting Roger killed."

"Sara Grace, I don't think Roger was killed because of anything between you two." You don't *think*? Good Claire, very reassuring.

"Wasn't he murdered for cheating on his wife? Didn't she kill him?" Good Lord, had this girl been talking to Arnie Cohen?

"No, she didn't kill him, Sara Grace. I can't talk about it right now, but she didn't kill him." Boy, did I hope I was telling her the truth.

She looked at me hopefully with those soft brown eyes.

"We didn't do anything," she said. "Roger and me. I didn't, like, sleep with him or anything. He wanted me to, but I didn't."

For some inane reason I was relieved to hear that, though I couldn't see how it could matter now. I had the selfish urge to ask Sara Grace a question, selfish because I should have been relieving her guilt, not satisfying my own curiosity.

"Sara Grace, what did you tell the police about you and Roger? Did they ask why you two left the memorial service?" I couldn't resist.

She rubbed one sleeve under her nose. "I told them what Roger said to me. That he had something important to show me back at the inn. He was going to show me what was in his paper." She looked up toward the ceiling and shook her head. "I can't believe I fell for such a stupid old line."

"What do you mean 'stupid old line?'" I wanted to keep her talking.

"When we got outside I asked him why I couldn't just wait to hear his presentation; it was coming up right after the service. He just laughed and put his arm around me." She wiped away tears with the heel of her hand. "He just wanted to take me back to his room and screw me while everyone else was at the service."

We were getting close to the part I wanted to hear about, and I pushed on shamelessly. "But you didn't go to the inn with him, did you? I saw you come back into the chapel."

"No. I finally saw, I'm so clueless, that that's all he wanted me for. He wasn't impressed with me or my work, he just wanted to screw me. Oh God, if I hadn't been such a ditz, maybe none of this would have happened." Tears again, hard this time.

I sighed and put one of my hands across hers, "Sara Grace, people like Roger know exactly how to exploit their students. They're very good at it. It isn't your fault you fell into the trap."

Speaking of exploiting students, I continued to press my interrogation.

"So you didn't go to the inn with Roger?"

"No, I got mad and told him I wanted to go back to the service. The service was for Professor Weber! He'd just died the day before yesterday." By her look, she was obviously expecting me to confirm the importance of honoring dear old Professor Weber, so for her benefit I nodded slightly. She leaned her forehead against the palm of her hand, exhausted by this one small burst of outrage.

After a few seconds she continued. "Anyway, I turned around to go back to the service. But I was crying, so I waited a few minutes before going back in."

I would like to report that, having satisfied my curiosity about why they left the service, I returned the conversation to a higher purpose, that of making Sara Grace feel better about herself. I can't. I desperately wanted Sara Grace to answer one more question before Emma came down the stairs and stopped me from grilling this poor tormented child. With one ear I listened for Emma's return.

"Sara Grace, there's something I've been meaning to ask you. On Monday evening, during the opening talk of the conference, you were standing at the door handing out conference schedules."

"Yeah?"

"And yesterday you told the police that the only people you saw leave that talk were students. Right?"

"Yeah, that's right."

I heard footsteps on the stairs. "Are you sure they were all students?"

She thought for a second. "Well…"

"Is it possible that someone came out who you thought was a student, but wasn't?"

She frowned at me. "Well, I'm pretty sure that—"

"Sara Grace! What are you doing here?"

Damn.

"Are you all right?" Emma said.

Time to let the subject change. "Apparently she's not all right, Emma," I said matter-of-factly. "Sara Grace feels responsible for what happened today. She says she's quitting school." I knew Emma would put this nonsense to bed.

Emma put a hand on her hip and stared down at the sniffling girl. "You think you're responsible? That is utterly absurd. And there will be no more talk of your quitting school, young woman."

She sat down beside her star pupil and started doing the thing she does best.

About a half hour later I was in the driver's seat of a large brown van with Hammond College painted on the side. I had eased it quietly into the small lot behind the kitchen of the inn, and was sitting there waiting with the motor running. Two similar vans were parked beside mine, their drivers as tense and alert as I was. We were about to launch a secret mission, which I will call Operation Prairie Feed.

It was Marlene's idea, and a little silly if you ask me. When Marlene heard that we were going to lug all the conferees out to Rube's Steak House, she got panicky that the press would follow, and was horrified at the thought of dozens of reporters mingling with two score philosophers making wild speculations about the deaths on campus. She said she didn't want to 'lose control' of the media situation. This struck me as an odd thing to say; while I could think of many colorful phrases to describe the media situation on campus, 'under control' did not suggest itself. In any case, Marlene's plan was to distract the media with some official statement while Emma smuggled her colleagues out through the kitchen and into the waiting vans. I sat at the wheel of one of those vans. Mine was not to reason why.

In a few minutes they all came trudging out, some of them looking a little disheveled, all of them noticeably somber and tense. Most of the crowd piled into the vans, but a few climbed into private cars. My vehicle took ten people, the last one being a tired-looking Kurt Burghoff, helped into the van by Arnie Cohen. I was glad to see Kurt was up and around and I told him so. He thanked me as he slid into the seat directly behind me.

Our little convoy crawled out of the lot. Emma drove the lead van, Sara Grace drove the one in the middle, and I took the rear position as we headed down Lincoln Avenue. We made a left on Park, a right on Seventh, and drove out onto the frozen prairie. I kept checking our tail for media bandits, but apparently Marlene's little ruse had worked. It was very dark now, with light snow falling, and Emma set a cautious pace as we headed north toward Montour.

When we were rolling along on Route 146, I felt two fingers tap my right shoulder.

"Claire," Kurt was leaning forward so he could talk near my ear, "how is Emma? This must be very difficult for her." His voice sounded raspy.

"She's OK. It hasn't been easy, but she's coping." I had to speak more loudly than I wanted because I was afraid to turn my head too much. The driving was making me really nervous. A strong wind across the open fields buffeted the van, and a powdery mist of blowing snow did a snake dance on the highway.

"Claire, I want to apologize for having to leave the service this morning.

I hope I did not embarrass you."

"No, no, not at all. We were worried about you, that's all. So you're feeling better?"

"Much, thank you. Once I got outside the chapel I felt better. I took a walk for a while." He sighed. "I got to the inn just as they were taking Roger's body out. Horrible."

I nodded. There wasn't much you could say about it.

We stared at the road for a while. On a midwinter evening, with snow falling, it's fearfully lonesome on those rural highways. We passed a farmhouse every half mile or so, and here and there across the fields a single bulb would twinkle in the distance. Other than that, the two sets of taillights from the other vans were about all I could see up ahead of us.

A voice from the back called out, "Is Emma coming with us tonight, Claire?"

"Sure," I called back, "she's driving the van ahead of us."

"Oh. I was thinking she might be sick since she didn't come to the memorial service this morning."

Another voice asked, "Yeah, what happened there, Claire, was she tied up with the police or something?" It sounded like Fritz of the black beret.

I did not think this was the ideal topic for highway chit chat—where Emma was when Roger was murdered—but I wanted to make one thing absolutely clear.

"Emma was at the memorial service," I assured them. "She just missed the beginning, that's all."

"I didn't see her there," Arnie said, "and you gave the introduction."

"She was definitely there. She came in about halfway through," I said, adjusting the truth by a couple of percentage points. "She came over as soon as she'd finished inseminating, and got there in the middle of the ceremony."

A sudden silence. There was only the squinching of the windshield wipers.

"After she had finished what?" Fritz asked.

Uh, oh.

"Did you say 'inseminating'?" Arnie called out. "As in artificial insemination?"

My knuckles turned white as I clenched the steering wheel.

"I didn't know you and Emma were trying to have a baby," said a female voice that sounded familiar. "That's wonderful." It was the young woman who'd been at my table the first night; I think her name was Melanie. There were several other approving noises.

"What are you hoping for, a boy or a girl?" someone asked.

Oh, my. Not good, not good.

"Well, ah…we haven't thought much about that. This is, you know, just a first attempt." I wondered if the cringing was evident in my voice.

"Oh, I'm sure it will work out," said Melanie, whose face I saw smiling through the rearview mirror. The whole group seemed relieved to have something cheery to talk about.

"Hell of a lot of work, parenting is," Arnie said. "Still, worth it overall."

"So will you adopt the baby, Claire, to be a legal parent?" Melanie asked.

Fritz chimed in without waiting for me to answer. "I doubt she'll be able to. Adoption laws are made for the benefit of so called 'normal' upper-class white families. They're not made to accommodate lesbian households."

"Is that true, Claire?"

"Ah…well, I don't really know, I haven't checked it all out yet."

Fritz continued in the pedantic tone I now saw as his trademark. "No, I'm afraid the only way you'll be a recognized mother, Claire, is to have your own biological children. The capitalist world will always be hostile to lesbian motherhood because it's too empowering of women. Capitalism needs a class of docile females producing workers for the industrial reserve army."

"Oh, for godsakes, Fritz," Arnie said, "you're not still shoveling that pabulum to your students, are you?"

Fritz laughed. "'Shoveling pabulum,' Arnie? Well I'd rather shovel pabulum than mix metaphors. And that pabulum, as you call it, is what the corporate sponsors of university research want to keep your students from hearing."

Arnie, of course, had an answer for that, but I didn't bother listening to it. My eyes stayed focused on the tail lights ahead of me while my thoughts wandered away. Away from the conversation, away from the van, away from these people I hardly knew. 'Off to the land of wishes,' my dad would've said. I wished I hadn't blabbed Emma's secret. I wished this goddamned conference was over. I wished I understood why I just couldn't quite connect with this baby plan. By the time I was done wishing we were pulling into the parking lot at 'The Best Little Steak House in Montour, Iowa'—where it would become clear that we had not eluded all members of the press.

CHAPTER TWENTY-THREE

I saw him the instant I came in the door. The inside of Rube's is dark and smoky, the air heavy with the smell of charbroiling beef. It's a big place with a couple of huge dining areas and a special room where customers grill their steaks. We could hear the hissing and sizzling of the charcoal pits as soon as we stepped inside. There weren't many patrons on this snowy evening, just a few tables of two or three scattered through the room. There was one big party of square dancers: about twelve people sitting around a single table, most of them in late middle-age, the men in bright matching vests and cowboy hats, the women in bushy skirts and petticoats.

He sat alone at a table in a deserted corner of the dining room. While Emma's crowd was still busy finding hangers and hooks for their coats and hats, I crossed the room and stood next to his chair. He looked at me sideways, casually chewing on his garden salad.

"Well, there's just no end to your web of informants, is there? First someone at the police station, and now someone at the conference. You're too good for little old Cedar Rapids, you should be working for the *New York Times*."

He smiled at my sarcasm. "Web of informants? Nothing so clandestine, I assure you."

"So how did you know we were coming here, Oscar?"

He wiped his mouth with the napkin from his lap. "I asked the staff at your inn when dinner was and they told me none was planned. It only took a few phone calls to find out where you were headed. There aren't many restaurants around here that can handle a crowd this size. And it stood to reason you'd bring them here, Rube's is the quintessential Iowa experience."

"Well, congratulations." I looked over my shoulder. Emma was lecturing her weary band about the procedure for selecting steaks from the refrigerator cases and cooking them on the open grills. They filed after her into the grill room. "I'll tell you, Oscar, philosophically I'm not a media-basher. I think people blame the media for things that are really the public's fault. No one wants to say out loud that it's the audience that's so ghoulish and star-

188

struck. As we say in my business, the media is just satisfying demand. So I know you're going to do your job. But I think you could give these people some consideration, couldn't you? Maybe let them settle in a few minutes?"

He smiled at my little speech. "OK, sit down, I'll start with you while they're cooking their steaks."

"I've already told you everything I know," I said. But I sat down at his table. At least I might be able to stall him a little.

"Would you like to order a drink or something?"

"No. I'm a designated driver tonight."

He nodded and shook a little pepper on his salad. "So, Claire, do you think the killer is in this room?"

"No, I don't. I think the killer's in that room." I pointed to the next room where the conferees were selecting their steaks from the huge glass cases lining the walls. I decided that there wasn't any point in trying to snow this guy.

He leaned toward me. "You really think one of those people is a double murderer?"

"No," I told him. "There is no double murder. I'm convinced there was only one murder, Roger Stuhrm's."

"Why?"

"Because no one could have committed both murders. Everybody has an alibi for at least one of them." I did not identify Emma as a notable exception. "For there to be two separate murders there would have to be two separate murderers. And what's the probability that a small group of wimpy old philosophy professors would have two killers in it? Damned small I'd say. No, Weber's death was an accident, I'm sure of it."

He nodded. "Interesting. OK, Weber was an accident. Then why was Stuhrm killed?"

I raised an eyebrow. "No doubt you already know all about Roger's paper." He smiled sheepishly and shrugged his shoulders. "Well," I said, "I think Roger was killed to keep that information from coming out."

"Why?" He took another bite of salad, wiping off the dressing that dripped on his chin. He didn't notice the drop that fell on his tie.

"Well, at first I thought Weber's killer had done it to cover up his motive, which was revenge for Weber's betrayal of his friends in East Germany."

"But now you don't think so."

"No, I don't. There's only one person here who had that motive, and he couldn't have murdered Weber. I think there was another motive for killing Roger."

Oscar pushed away his plate and leaned his chair back on its two hind legs. "Another motive? The wife, the mistress, that whole thing?"

"No! Roger's wife did not kill him." My defensiveness made him laugh. "Look, Oscar, I'll spare you the usual speech about how I know this woman and she couldn't do a thing like that, blah, blah, blah. All of that stuff certainly applies in this case, but never mind. The thing is this: Roger's paper was erased. Cindy wouldn't have had any reason to do that, would she?" I didn't bother expounding Sergeant Christenson's theory, that Cindy erased the file to draw suspicion away from herself. "I now believe the paper was erased not to protect Weber's killer, but to protect Weber himself."

That brought Oscar's pudgy little eyebrows up. "Somebody killed Roger Stuhrm defending Weber?"

"Yep. Weber came to this conference to defend his reputation, but he died before he could do that. Now someone else has stepped into the breach."

Oscar took a pack of cigarettes out of his jacket pocket and shook one out. "Like who?"

"I don't know yet. But the guy was an icon for lots of young philosophers, and he had more former lovers than this restaurant has ribeyes. He could no doubt arouse some pretty passionate loyalty."

It surprised me to hear myself say this. I wasn't aware that I had formulated this theory until the exact moment that it jumped out of my mouth. Apparently this discussion had unconsciously caused wayward strands of evidence in my head to coalesce, to fit together into a radical new way of viewing the erasing of Roger's paper. It was a bold hypothesis. I knew that it would soon be proved to be either: a) a revolutionary insight, or b) the sort of stuff Iowans step in when they walk around the barnyard.

I felt kind of proud of this theory and was about to elaborate on it, but Oscar seemed to have stopped listening. He held a cigarette in one hand and a lit match in the other, but was making no attempt to bring them together. He stared at something straight over my head.

"Claire doesn't have time to talk you, Mr. Lamb." Emma's voice came from really close behind me. "She needs to help me attend to my guests. So if you'll please excuse us—"

"Emma." I turned and gave her a frosty look, feeling a little tired of being bossed around. "I'm talking to Mr. Lamb. I'll be with you in a moment."

She sighed. "All right. But will you please hurry, some of these people don't have a clue about how to cook a steak." She shot Oscar a baleful glance and walked back toward the other room. I started to get out of my chair.

"I really should go in and help her."

"OK, just let me ask you a couple more things. The official word is that Dr. Weber had gone into isolation, or into hiding, about two years ago. Does that mean your roommate knew where Dr. Weber was living before he came to the conference?"

That question nearly made me gasp, but I checked myself because I was afraid he might notice. So they were all finding out, as of course they would, that Weber had actually been living in Iowa. I'm proud to say that in answering his question I was not, technically, lying through my teeth. "I never discussed with her whether she knew where he lived or not."

There was just a glint of amusement in his eyes when he said, "I see. Well, did you know that the police suspect that Dr. Weber actually lived around here, somewhere in the vicinity of Hammond?"

"Really?" I said, trying desperately to look surprised.

"Professor Weber lived here?" Another voice from behind me, this time Maria's. She looked hard at me as if for some kind of explanation. Oh, Lord. At that moment there was almost nothing I would rather not do than involve Maria, and thereby eventually the entire conference, in this particular conversation.

"Do you need something Maria?" I asked.

"Emma was looking for you a few minutes ago."

"Thanks, Maria, please tell her I'll be right there." I turned back to Oscar as she walked slowly away. "Look, I'm sorry, but I've really got to go now." I turned away much too quickly and headed into the next room, restraining myself from breaking into a run. Yikes.

I found Emma by one of the big charcoal pits silently counting up the number of lambs in her flock. "Claire, help Maria get them going with their steaks, will you? I'm going to go make sure there's proper seating."

She walked away and I glanced around. I didn't see anyone who needed help, things seemed pretty under control to me. Maria was already over by the refrigerated cases helping a woman pick out a piece of meat. Colin Jensen was fussing with Kurt Burghoff's steak and talking earnestly to the old scholar, who just smiled vaguely and nodded now and then. The rest of Emma's people were mostly crowded around the four great cooking pits, poking thick slabs of meat with long steel forks and pairs of tongs. They were flipping, turning, and seasoning their steaks, all the while advising each other about whose was done and whose wasn't. Every now and then a glob of fat would drop down into the fire, sending flames shooting up a foot above the grill. This would make the crowd ooh and aah, while someone spritzed the flames with water from a handy spray bottle. The professors joined in the local custom of soaking inch-thick slices of bread in pans of melted butter, then laying them on the grill to fry up golden brown.

Considering the circumstances, Emma's people were having a pretty good time. Maybe Emma had just dragged me in here to get me away from

Oscar. I figured I might as well pick up a piece of something for myself and slap it on the fire. I chose a thick slice of pork and laid it on the nearest big grill, across from where Marshall was sprinkling seasoning on a sizzling T-bone. I kept an eye out for people in trouble, but no one appeared to be having any. After a while people started pulling their steaks off the grills and wandering into the dining area. By the time my pork chop was done I was almost alone.

Along one wall of the room, about twenty feet from where I was grilling, stood a long salad bar. I noticed Colin Jensen cruising along it, looking at lots of things but not picking up much. No one else was there. I watched him for a while, remembering the conversation Marshall and I had had about him that morning. The memory brought on a sudden craving for salad.

"Hi, Colin." I came up behind him at the bar.

"Hi, Claire." He was carefully examining a single leaf of lettuce from a huge overflowing bowl. "Some salad bar, huh?" He shook his head. "Classic Iowa restaurant, two food groups: fat and sugar. A place like this wouldn't stay open long in Berkeley."

"I can see why. Who'd want to be standing near a charcoal pit when an earthquake breaks the gas main?" He smirked at that. I needed to ask Colin a question, but had to let a few seconds pass so that I didn't appear eager to ask it. I picked up a plate, put some lettuce on it, threw on a few bacon bits, shook on some shredded cheese.

"Listen, Colin," I said, "I'm sorry I barged in on your conversation with Marshall at the party last night."

He turned and studied my face for a moment. "No problem," he said, and went back to the condiments.

I picked up a couple of croutons and pretended to examine the tomatoes. "Say, what was that about, anyway?"

"Oh, just a philosophical discussion."

"A philosophical discussion?"

"Uh huh."

I followed him as we passed the dressings and moved to the side dishes. There was coleslaw, potato salad and cherry Jell-O with fruit inside. "You guys sounded pretty mad at each other," I said. "I mean, for two people who were just talking philosophy."

"Not uncommon. You wouldn't understand, Claire, economics doesn't arouse passion like philosophy does."

"Oh, yeah? I once decked a guy for saying my covariance matrix wasn't block diagonal."

"Yes," he said, smiling, "I'm sure you did. Well, I'd better go find myself a seat while there are still some left. See ya, Claire." He walked briskly off toward the dining room.

That conversation hadn't told me much. I guess I was hoping he'd say something more, something like, "I got so angry at Marshall, Claire, because I'm really the son of Colin Platburg, and though I've kept that a secret from everyone at this conference, I've decided to confess it to you here at the salad bar." Oh, well.

The conference people were seated at six tables in the enormous main dining room, sawing away at their great hunks of steak. Their mood was improving as the evening progressed. Emma was at a table with two open seats, so Colin and I sat down there. Also at the table were Arnie, Kurt, Rupesh, and, I noticed at the last second with considerable dismay, Fritz. Arnie, not surprisingly, was leading the conversation. It was surely not happenstance that the topic was something academic and innocuous, entirely unrelated to the conference itself.

"You're swallowing the sociobiological argument hook, line and sinker, Fritz," Arnie said through a mouthful of sirloin. "You should read Kurt's piece in the *Journal of Western Philosophy*. He shows that the whole thing is just a logical loop—circuitous pseudo-reasoning. Tell him Kurt."

Kurt, who was carefully trimming the fat from his steak, hardly noticed that Arnie was talking to him. When he did look up, he only smiled faintly.

"You're a dinosaur, Arnie," Fritz said. "You can't accept the changes that have come in this field because you're afraid of them. If philosophy ignores the biological roots of behavior we're doomed to irrelevance."

"Relevance?" Arnie said. "Good God, Fritz, when was philosophy ever relevant to anything? If you want relevance you'd better switch over to Claire's department." He turned to me and winked. "Stocks, bonds, making money. Nothing more relevant than that, eh Claire?"

"Well that's what it says on our recruiting posters, Arnie. 'Economists: The Few, The Proud, The Relevant.'" I looked over at Emma to see how she was doing. She had barely touched the food on her plate.

"Admit it, Arnie," Fritz said. "You're scared by biological determinism because it means that all those theories of morality you learned in grad school are a lot of crap. You're afraid to acknowledge that the gene is the moral center of the universe."

Arnie's fork clattered on his plate. "The gene is the *what*?" Apparently dumbfounded, he looked around the table at his colleagues. "Is he serious? Is this man serious?"

"I'm quite serious. The need to produce fit offspring is the driving force of evolution." Fritz held his steak knife aloft like a scepter. "Love, sex, marriage—everything is a slave to it. Why is romance so important to culture? Why do we put up with snotty adolescents?" He pointed the knife at Emma. "Why did Emma miss the memorial service this morning? Reproduction!"

Uh, oh. Well there it was. Emma now knew that the pregnancy cat had crawled out of its little bag, and she would have absolutely no doubt who untied the string. When I gathered enough nerve to look over at Emma, there was no reaction that the others would've noticed. But her mouth was pursed and the skin between her eyes was showing extra wrinkles. Not a good sign.

Meanwhile Arnie was trying to set Fritz straight. "Turnips reproduce quite successfully, Fritz. They don't seem to require cities and symphonies and surrealist paintings. So how can you argue that all of our culture is based on reproduction?"

"I don't. I'm not saying everything was created for reproductive purposes. All I'm saying is that reproduction leaves its fingerprints on all human activity. Look at capitalism: it's about making money, not making babies, but see how it mimics our reproductive behavior—the capitalist as dominant male, the working class as subservient female. And look at the accumulation of wealth for status' sake; it's just like the siring of sons to prove virility. The analogy is too powerful for that to be accidental."

Rupesh joined in. "I do not understand, Fritz. I thought you Marxists believed that all of society was governed by relationships of production."

"Production relations govern the behavior of institutions, Rupesh. Among individuals the key is kinship."

"Oh, twaddle," Arnie said. "Are we gathered here tonight because we're kin? Is this a clan meeting?"

"I didn't say there couldn't be other kinds of relationships, but they will never be as strong as family ties. Protecting one's genes is always the main thing. Take Emma for example."

No Fritz, please don't take Emma for example.

"Emma will make all kinds of sacrifices for her new child when it comes. Claire may make sacrifices too, but mainly as a way of helping Emma. It won't be the same between Claire and the child because there won't be true kinship. Is a stepparent like a real parent? Just read the fairy tales if you want an answer to that."

He was doing it to me again, this guy. It was simply impossible for me to keep my mouth shut.

"How the hell could you know how I will feel about Emma's child...our child?"

"You see, you gave yourself away, Claire." His smile was so smug I wanted to hurl my baked potato at him. "Even though you may love the baby, it will always be Emma's child. In our hearts we know that our real kin are different than other people. You won't be the same as the child's mother."

Now I was steaming. "You know nothing about how I'll feel towards that child. Emotional bonds aren't based just on kinship. Did you know that unrelated children raised on the same kibbutz rarely ever marry? Why? Because they're raised like brother and sister and so they feel like brother and sister." I read that years ago, how did I remember it now? "And that's how I would feel about a child I helped raise: like a parent."

Before Fritz could respond, Emma stood up at her chair. Her voice quavered, and she looked away from our faces. "I'll be right back," she said. She walked quickly away, out of the dining room.

The table fell silent. No one seemed to know what to say. All the others looked meekly around at each other, as if hoping someone else knew what had just happened. "I, ah, better see if she needs some help," I said and hurried off after her.

Emma was moving fast, but where was she headed? She went past her colleagues at the other tables, walking stiffly, not looking at anyone, like someone who had just been called to the witness stand. I saw several people notice her. Their expressions changed from curious to concerned as they watched her face, and their heads turned to follow her as she passed. No doubt they were afraid that there'd been more bad news. I struggled to catch up with her, fighting the urge to break into a trot. She sailed out of the dining room, made a left into the lounge, and was whizzing past the long bar when I finally caught up with her and grabbed her by the arm. "Where are you going, Emma?" She stopped walking, but she wouldn't look at me.

"I don't know," she said, "outside."

Was she angry? Sad? I couldn't really tell because the room was dark and she kept her head turned away from me. The lounge was empty except for us and a tall bartender wearing a red vest and a white shirt with black garters on the sleeves. The bartender was carefully wiping a tiny shot glass. More carefully, in fact, than any tiny shot glass had ever needed to be wiped.

"I don't want to stand here," Emma said, and she started moving again. I followed her as she went past the kitchen and pushed through a door at the back of the restaurant. We went out into a big rear parking lot completely empty on this slow Wednesday evening and stood under a large overhang that kept away the falling snow. The wind had stopped blowing and the air was a bit warmer than when we'd come in. Now the snowflakes were big and wet. They were like the flakes I remember as a kid in Brooklyn, the ones I used to catch on my tongue as I walked home from school along Flatbush

Avenue. The streets of little Montour were dark and quiet.

"Are you OK?" I said. "Look, I didn't mean to blab about your trying to get pregnant; it slipped out while we were driving. I'm sorry."

"It's all right. People are going to find out anyway."

The only light came from a streetlamp at the far end of the lot. I could barely see Emma's face. "Well, if that's not why you're upset, why did you storm out of the restaurant?"

"That stuff Fritz was saying. About genes and all. God, Claire, is that how you feel? Is that what's been bothering you, that the baby won't be yours?"

The look on her face made me embarrassed, ashamed. I turned away from her and stared out at the streetlight, watching the snowflakes gleam white as they fell through its arc of light then turn dull grey again a few feet from the ground. "I don't know," I said. "Maybe. Maybe, a little." Another few hundred flakes touched ground. "Maybe more than I wanted to admit," I said.

"Why didn't you say anything?"

What could I say in response to that? I stepped out from under the overhang, closed my eyes and turned my face up to the sky. The falling flakes gave me little wet kisses and I just stood there feeling the snow for a while. "I've been scared Emma, and it's not a feeling I'm very proud of."

"You're afraid you wouldn't be a good mother?"

"Any kind of a mother." I looked at her. "I don't know a lot about mothers because I never really had one. But I know about non-mothers. I know about a woman who's married to your parent, who lives in your house, who runs your life, but who isn't your mother."

"You mean like Vicky and Eleanor?"

"Yeah," I said. "I don't know what to call what passed between me and those women, Emma, but it sure as hell wasn't motherhood. I don't want to have another relationship like that. Not even from the other side, when I'm the adult and have all the power."

What Emma said next came out as a whisper. "I wish I had known this." She shook her head. "Maybe this can't really work. Maybe Fritz is right."

"No, Emma, no he isn't. I may be unsure about a lot of things. Maybe even my own feelings sometimes. But this much I know: that guy Fritz could never be right about anything. Fritz is the one who showed me I was wrong." I stepped back in under the overhang. "I was just scared, that's all. I really like kids, you know that, I always have." All at once I felt released from my fears. I could see what a fool I'd been to be afraid, my body tingled with the sense of relief.

In Emma's eyes I saw a trace of new hope. "Of course, I know that. Do you think I'd make a baby with you if I didn't know that?"

"And that's another thing that bothered me," I told her. "You weren't really 'making a baby with me.' This insemination thing, you left me totally out of it. A straight couple would have done that together, and we could have, too. You could have made me part of it. And I don't mean just running around getting the liquid nitrogen, either. I mean helping you, being there when it happened. If it's going to be our child, then I should help conceive it, even if only symbolically."

"Yes." Emma was nodding her head up and down and crying softly. "You're right, Claire. I'm really sorry. I wanted you there too, but you seemed so distant, and everything has been so hectic...."

I sighed. "Anyway, that's not important. The important thing is that I was being an idiot, I wasn't trusting myself. I think I would make a good...you know, parent, quasi-parent, whatever you want to call it."

Emma took a step towards me. "Mom," she said, "I want to call it 'Mom.'"

I laughed and felt a rush of giddiness. "OK. Mom it is then."

Little tears rolled down Emma's cheeks as she reached over, put her hands on my face and kissed my lips very softly. That made me want to cry, too. I felt how much the anger between us in the last three days had made me feel tired and tense and isolated from Emma. I wrapped my arms around her and put my face against the nape of her neck, like I do sometimes when I really need comforting, like I did the morning of my father's funeral. But I wasn't sad right now. It was odd, I suppose, to be feeling happy at such an unhappily remarkable moment in our lives, standing in the eye of this great hurricane of murder and betrayal and dark, ancient secrets. But I did feel happy in those few moments I stood there holding Emma.

Too many moments, really. We stayed there longer than we should have maybe, in the dark and the cold, without any coats, away from all of her colleagues and guests. But it was good. "We should go back inside," I said.

"Yes." Her eyes were red but she was smiling. Then her face darkened again and she took my hand. "There's one more thing, Claire," she said. "This conference is a complete fiasco, you know that. The college is never going to give me a permanent chair now."

"Well golly," I said, "that's just a shame." I opened the door to the restaurant and breathed in the rich aroma of broiling beef. "Because wherever we end up raising that kid, there will never be as good a steak house as this." I held out my hand for hers and we walked inside.

On the way back to the table Emma peeled off into the women's room to rinse off her face. I met Oscar Lamb on my way through the lounge.

"I have to go now, Claire, but I wanted to tell you something before I left."

"Yeah?"

"I liked your theory about the murder, but there's something you don't know. I tried to tell you earlier but you rushed off."

"What?"

"The forensic report on Roger Stuhrm said that his head wound is identical to Weber's. The police say they were both killed by the same object. It looks like both men were not only murdered, but murdered by the same person. Well, got to meet a deadline, good night."

I couldn't speak. I stood there dumbstruck and watched him walk across the empty lounge, push open the front door and go out into the snowy darkness. This was incredible. The nice little theory of mine had turned out to be nonsense. Crap. Buffalo chips. A big pile of stable pudding. It seemed so unfair, really, that after I'd come up with such an elegant explanation for how these deaths had occurred, that the actual evidence should be so uncooperative. (I may not be the first economist to whom this has happened.) It made no sense now. None of the people who might have wanted to would have had the opportunity to kill both of those men. It didn't add up.

I walked slowly back to rejoin my table. What the hell was going on? As I often do when I'm thinking hard, I looked down at my feet as I walked—a really bad habit. I almost knocked over a little boy trotting through the dining room carrying two pieces of chocolate cake. "Oops, sorry," I said as the kid scooted past me. He looked back and smiled. A cute kid, about five or six, wearing oversized blue jeans and a yellow rugby shirt. His hair was straight and blond and hung down across one eye. He reminded me of someone, but I was too distracted to think who it was.

There was no one at our table but Arnie and Rupesh, talking to each other in low tones. As I got near them I heard Arnie saying something about Cindy. Ha! Now there, at least, was a bit of good news. Cindy wasn't in town when Weber was murdered, so if there was a single killer, it couldn't have been Cindy. Guess what, Arnie? You can go stuff your black widow theory.

I stopped walking. The black widow. That phrase went through me like an electric shock as I suddenly realized who the little boy reminded of. Oh Jesus, what an awful thought I was having. I wanted to kill it. But before I could kill the thought, it was joined by other thoughts, thoughts that folded neatly together in a tight, vicious little pattern. Now I had a new theory, a theory that explained the data all very neatly, a theory as smooth and simple as it was mean and nasty. A theory I would be happy to see collapse.

Maybe I could disprove it. It all rested, really, on one flimsy little datum, something small and incidental, something hanging around in the back of my memory. Maybe I could show that my memory was wrong.

But I couldn't do it here. Not in Rube's. I looked around frantically. Where was Marshall? There he was, sitting two tables down talking to Sara Grace. I hurried over, put my hands on his shoulders and whispered in his ear.

"You brought your car, didn't you? Can you drive me home?"

He turned around, startled. "What's wrong?"

"Oh, it's nothing serious." I gave Sara Grace a reassuring smile. "Can you do it, Marshall?"

"Yeah, sure, OK." He hastily wiped his mouth and fumbled to his feet. I grabbed his sleeve and tugged him along to the coatroom. "What's this about?" he asked.

I bent toward him, "I can't tell you right now. Is that OK?"

"All right."

Colin Jensen was coming back from the salad bar again and I waved him over. I held up the keys to the college van. "Colin, can you drive my van back to Hammond? I have to leave."

"Sure I can." He frowned. "Are you all right?"

"Yeah, fine, no big deal."

I had my coat on in a flash and was ready to leave, but Marshall was standing there fussing with his mittens when Maria appeared looking very concerned.

"Claire? Colin told me you're leaving. What's wrong?"

"Oh, Maria," I scrunched up my face and patted my stomach, "I should-n't have eaten that pork steak. I'm feeling pretty sick. Marshall's going to take me home, but Colin will drive my van. Would you tell Emma for me?"

Maria looked surprised. "You mean you haven't told her?" Maria's sur-prise, I knew, would be nothing in comparison with Emma's. That seemed like a really good reason to get going now.

"Oh, if I told Emma she'd just start fussing over me, Maria. You tell her. Say it's nothing serious, I just don't think I can drive, OK?"

"All right," Maria said. She looked very doubtful.

Outside, crossing the parking lot, we heard only the muffled steps of our feet in the fresh snow.

"You made that up, right?" Marshall asked. "You aren't really sick."

"No," I said, although my stomach was flopping like a flounder in a fish-ing boat.

"So why are we leaving?"

"Because I just realized something."

"What?"

"A black widow is a kind of spider."

CHAPTER TWENTY-FOUR

To a city kid, it's amazing how many stars are visible in the sky above Iowa. A long thin curtain of them opened up on the western horizon as Marshall and I drove south from Montour. It had stopped snowing. For most of the drive I'd been staring off at that wedge of clear sky, my breath fogging up Marshall's side window. I remember the first time I saw the night sky in Iowa. It was the end of that hot August day five years ago when my dad had helped me move out here from Chicago, towing a U-Haul loaded with way too many books and not nearly enough furniture. I was sad that day, sad and scared. Sad because my dad was about to leave. Scared because I was beginning to suspect that my first major career decision, to accept a job at Hammond College, was going to prove to be an egregious error. Could I really make a life for myself out here in these cornfields? I'd never lived in a place like this. I recall that there was a storm that night, way out across the prairie, and to try to cheer me up, my dad and I drove a mile out of town on Route 6 and sat on the hood of his Volvo watching great lightning bolts leap out of the clouds. While we sat there on the dark road, every car that came along, every one, stopped to ask if we needed help. No, I realized, I had definitely never lived in a place like this.

Driving back to town with Marshall I thought about those people who'd stopped to offer help. Was that what I was doing now: helping out, being a good friend and neighbor? I mean, what if I was wrong? If my new theory turned into a cowpie like the last one, I would have infuriated Emma, inconvenienced Marshall, and looked stupid in front of the entire conference. Again. On the other hand, what if I was right? That, of course, would be considerably worse.

"Can you at least tell me why we had to leave so suddenly?" Marshall, the old sweetie, was being very patient.

"Because what we're doing is probably dumb, and if it is, you and I will be the only ones who'll know how stupid I am."

"Well, where am I taking you?"

"Back to the inn. I need to look at your photo album."

"My photo album?"

"For your book. The one you were showing us that first night at the inn. It had all those pictures of Weber in it." Marshall took his right hand off the wheel and draped his arm over the back of the seat, arching his body to extend his reach. After fumbling a few seconds he pulled up the thick album. "I packed up this morning thinking I'd be heading home tonight after dinner."

"Oh great! Turn on the dome light."

"Um…You're not supposed to do that when you're—"

"Marshall!" He turned it on. Where was that picture? The one with Weber and Spengler seated at the table, and the little boy playing on the floor. I flipped some pages. There. When I first saw that picture I'd noticed something familiar, though at the time there was no reason to attach any meaning to it. Now there was.

"Which one are you looking at?" Marshall craned his neck to see over the album cover. "Weber, Spengler and Spengler's son. Ah! Does this have something to do with Roger's paper?"

"You heard about that?"

"There were rumors going around the inn. All I know is that it was about the incident in Berlin when Spengler got killed."

"It was. Roger's paper said that before the escape from Berlin, Weber had… ah…" my voice trailed off as I realized where we were. We were on Route 146, about four miles north of Hammond, and I recognized, up ahead on the left, the unpainted wooden shed sitting behind a rusted gas pump by the side of the highway. I knew that past the shed a gravel road ran off to the west, and that if we went down that gravel road a little way…and stopped at the old house…a quick stop, really, maybe five minutes…then I could be absolutely sure. Sure that Emma was not hiding anything. It wasn't necessary, of course. I had figured the thing out; all I had to do now was call Pete and tell the police everything I knew.

Still. It would only take a couple of minutes.

"Slow down, Marshall, we want to make a left up here."

Marshall slowed the car to a crawl before turning onto the side road, which was still covered with a couple of inches of snow since the gravel roads are the last to get plowed. He leaned forward a little and squinted over the steering wheel. "We aren't going to get stuck out here, are we?"

"Nah. Just stay on this road for another half mile."

I could see how tightly he was clenching the wheel. "There seems to be a ditch on both sides of the road, Claire."

"Well, stay on the road and you won't go in the ditch, Marshall. Jeez." I studied the picture again as we crept along.

"Am I to understand," Marshall said, "that our driving down this very primitive country lane is somehow related to Roger's paper?"

"It might be." I put the picture back in the album. "Roger found evidence that the Stasi had an informant in Spengler's group. The informant was code-named the Spider. Roger quoted some Stasi guy as saying the Spider would 'weave a web' and trap Spengler's group."

Marshall's head turned. "Weber was the weaver!"

"Right. Roger's paper implied that Weber had made a deal with the Stasi: if they let him go, he'd arrange for them to catch the rest of the group trying to escape."

"What?" He stared at me for a couple of seconds, then realized what he was doing and looked back at the road. "You're saying Weber turned Spengler over to the Stasi? No." He shook his head. "No. I don't believe it."

"You don't?"

"Absolutely not. Look, Erik Weber was not a nice man, everybody knows that. But you're saying he betrayed his closest comrades? Worse, that he betrayed his most cherished principles? No, Erik Weber would not do that."

Our turnoff was just ahead. "See that driveway on the left? That's where we're going, but don't pull into it."

"Don't pull into it?"

"Right. Go on up the road about a hundred yards, just over that crest. Park on the side."

"There's a ditch on the side."

"So park next to the ditch, Marshall, next to it." Yeesh.

The reflector on the mailbox gleamed red, looking like a lone channel buoy in a great white ocean of snow. It was very dark out here among the empty cornfields, the nearest neighbor probably a thousand yards up the road. A single light burned on the porch of the old farmhouse. Marshall let the car roll slowly past the mailbox, the snow crunching loudly under the tires, and went up the road until it started down a gentle slope. When I could no longer make out the mailbox through the rear window, I said. "OK, this is good enough." I didn't want to take a chance of anyone seeing a car pulling into or out of the driveway of the old house.

Marshall turned off the engine, and we climbed out of the car. "Come on," I said, "It's just over this rise."

"How will we get across this ditch?" Marshall said.

I threw up my hands. "What is it with you and ditches, Marshall? Did your nanny abandon you in one as an infant? In your previous life were you wounded at Verdun? Come on."

We walked through the ditch (with no casualties), ducked through a barbed wire fence and started trudging across the snow-covered field. The snow was deeper here in the field and the sound of our tramping footsteps and the soft wind were all you could hear.

"Whose house is this?" Marshall asked.

"Erik Weber's."

Marshall didn't even say anything in response to that, he just looked at me sideways, his eyes slightly fearful, like he had suddenly recognized the situation he was in. He was alone on a dark country road with a madwoman, a delusional lunatic who thought Weber lived in Hammond, a psychotic who lacked the normal human fear of ditches.

"I'm not crazy Marshall, I wish I were." I told him about finding the slip of paper with the number on it, about Kurt and me coming to this house in the country, about how a foreigner lived there named Hans Gustav. He thought for a long moment, then nodded slowly.

"Well," he said, "it's not so implausible, really. Weber could have come here because of John Marchak. He liked to hide out when he was finishing a major work and this would probably have been a good place for that. You know, I wonder if this is where he always came on his little disappearing acts? He could trust Marchak to keep his secret. He probably came this last time while Marchak was dying."

"That's what I figured. And I need to get some evidence that he lived here. And that he knew the person who I think killed him and Roger." We walked about two hundred yards, and had to plow through one drift that came up to our knees. I got winded quickly and great clouds of my breath drifted off behind us. We came over a slight rise and there stood the old house, dead still, no lights on, no smoke from the chimney. The apple orchard appeared as a dark smudge on the gentle slope behind the house.

"Why don't we just go to the police?" Marshall said.

That's a really good question, Claire; why don't we just go to the police? But this would only take a few minutes, and I just really needed to be sure: sure that Emma wasn't involved, sure that I wasn't getting her into trouble, sure that... well, OK, sure that the woman I was apparently planning a family with was not dangerously mentally ill. Was that so unreasonable?

I could say none of this to Marshall, of course. What I said was, "Let's go in the back door."

"How will we get in?"

"We're in the rural Midwest, Marshall, nobody locks their doors. Didn't you ever see *In Cold Blood*?"

"Well, this door will be locked," Marshall said.

I turned the cold brass handle. He was right. I looked at his face and searched it for a moment. "How did you know that?"

"I know Erik Weber. He was paranoid."

"Well, here goes," I said. Standing on one foot like a flamingo, I took off my left shoe and whacked the heel against a small pane of glass in the door, thereby adding Breaking and Entering to Withholding Information and Obstructing Justice on the rap sheet I was rapidly compiling for myself. I held my breath, listening. Had that sound brought anything in the house to life? Nothing.

The door opened into a small utility room that had an old coat hanging on a wall peg and a pair of boots standing near the entrance.

I stepped just inside the door and stopped, letting my eyes adjust to the darkness. There was a light switch on my left but I dared not turn on a light. Marshall was still outside meticulously kicking the snow off his shoes.

In a loud whisper I said, "Marshall, we're burglars. No one expects us to wipe our feet."

"I just don't want to get—"

"Will you get in here and close that door!" He came in and stood next to me in the small dark room. My brain, trained in such logical fields as differential equations and the calculus of variations, was telling my heart that there was no reason to be pounding as it was. My heart was not listening.

"What are we looking for?" Marshall said.

"Something that proves this was Weber's house, and something that tells us who knew he was here. In Iowa, I mean."

"Didn't Emma know?"

"NO!" We both jumped at the loudness of my voice. Whispering again, I said. "No, Emma didn't know he was here." Boy, did I hope that last statement was true.

I had no idea what I was searching for, but my instinct told me to start in the kitchen, which is the heart of any Iowa farmhouse.

We felt our way slowly along the dark hallway that ran down the center of the house. The wallpaper was rough against my fingers, textured with some kind of raised pattern. The stillness in that big, isolated farmhouse was so sepulchral we heard only the floorboards creaking under our shoes.

As we approached a doorway, I saw something ahead of us move out into the hall. Oh, God. I sucked in my breath and flattened against the wall, trying to check the scream that clawed at my throat. My eyes strained into the darkness to see what could be coming at us. A slate grey cat appeared at my feet, blinked up at me for a second, then scampered past us toward the back of the house. I let my breath whoosh out and pressed a hand to my heart.

Marshall leaned toward me and whispered, "Weber liked cats."

"Oh, did he?" I said, "How sweet."

Feeling a little foolish, but unable to help myself, I reached back and took hold of Marshall's hand. We found the kitchen on the left side of the hallway, about midway through the house. It was pretty dark in there, with only a little starlight coming in through the lattice framework in a window over the stove. The room was pretty typical of houses built somewhere around the turn of the century. The cabinets and sink looked like they might even be original. There was space enough in the middle for a round oak table and four chairs. The place was pretty tidy, because, I remembered, Weber had that housekeeper, the one I'd met when Kurt and I had stopped here. On the wall next to the refrigerator was a calender and a bulletin board with some papers stuck on it. I walked over to have a look at them. It was hard to read anything in the dark kitchen and I felt a renewed temptation to turn on the light. "Marshall, look in some of these cupboards, and see if we can find some matches or candles or something so we don't have to turn any lights on." This far out in the country there would almost certainly be some provisions against power failure. I continued squinting at the bulletin board in the dark.

"Here," Marshall said, "some candles." He lit two short squat candles from the gas stove, put them on saucers, set one on the table and handed the other to me.

The kitchen was a disappointment. The stuff on the bulletin board was just notices from the owner to the tenant about paying utility bills, servicing the furnace, putting up storm windows in the fall and whatnot.

"We need to find his personal papers, an address book, something like that," I said. "He must have a study somewhere; let's find it."

"The study will be whichever room has the best view of the sunset," Marshall said.

"More Weberama, huh?" I had to think for a second which direction was west. "OK, upstairs, back of the house." Besides the one we came in there were two doorways off of the kitchen, one led up the back staircase, one led down to the basement. We started climbing the narrow stairway, still trying to walk softly, though by now we were sure there was no one else in the house.

"Claire," Marshall said. He spoke quietly but in a normal voice. "I'm trying to figure out what this is all about. You said Roger's paper accused Weber of betraying Spengler. So your theory is that Weber was killed in revenge for Spengler, and Roger was killed to cover up that motive, right?"

"No, that isn't why Weber was killed. Roger's paper was erased to make it look like revenge was the motive for the killing."

"Erased? Wait a minute. If Roger's paper was erased, how do we know what was in it?"

"It was recovered from the erased disk," I said, "it was 'undeleted.' Which is kind of strange, isn't it? Think about it. If you want to destroy the information on a disk, why bother to erase a file? Why not steal the disk? Or just step on it? And besides, what good would it do? Surely Roger had a backup copy of the paper somewhere."

At the top of the stairs I paused and looked around. The faint light of my candle showed us a hall running to our left toward the front of the house. Directly across from us was a door to the room that most likely had windows facing west, toward the sunset, which could indeed be beautiful out here on the rolling prairie. "Let's try in here," I said.

Marshall was right, it had to be the study. The room was bare save for a battered wooden desk and straight-backed chair. It was apparent that the housekeeper was not allowed to disturb this room. The desk was buried in sheets of white paper with scribbly handwriting. Several books with yellowing pages lay open on top of the papers, and more books formed tall precarious piles around the edges of the desk. I set my candle on the edge of the desk and started rooting through the papers.

"So, why?" Marshall asked.

"Why what?"

"Why did the killer erase the file and not smash the disk like you said."

"Oh. Because the murderer wanted the paper to be recovered. Wanted it to appear that the paper had been erased to destroy some incriminating information. After all, why would Roger's killer want to suppress his paper if the information it contained wasn't true? Erasing the paper seemed to validate Roger's theory."

"But his theory was wrong?"

"Yes it was. Roger was so anxious to make a big scoop about Weber that he leapt to a false conclusion about the Stasi files. He assumed the informant, the so-called 'weaver,' must have been Weber. But it wasn't Weber."

"So who was it?"

There was a loud crack from the front of the house and then the sound of tinkling glass. Marshall and I froze where we stood.

We heard the front door creak open and then footsteps on the hardwood floor in the living room. Neither Marshall nor I moved an eyelash. Slowly, the steps came forward, paused, then came forward again. There was another pause and a slight scratching sound, then the footsteps began to ascend the front staircase. Marshall looked at me wide-eyed. I quickly wet two fingers and snuffed out the candle I had set on the desk. The footsteps came up to the top of the stair. I was about to gesture to Marshall to snuff out his candle but I realized the room was already dark. He didn't have a candle. Oh, my God. Pushing down my fear I mouthed to him: WHERE IS YOUR CANDLE? He grimaced and pointed down with his finger. He'd left the candle burning down in the kitchen, which meant there was absolutely no chance we could avoid getting caught. And whoever was about to catch us was sure as hell not the housekeeper.

The footsteps were irregular, tentative, but still coming toward us down the main hall. They stopped just a few feet shy of the study door. I held my breath and braced myself for the shock of discovery. A moment passed. No movement, just that slight scraping sound again.

Suddenly, unexpectedly, there was the sound of splashing. For some reason water was being poured on the floor of the hallway.

The steps moved back toward the front of the house again and stopped, more splashing sounds, then moved back a bit further, more sounds of splashing water. Within seconds, of course, we realized it wasn't water, the acrid odor was absolutely unmistakable. Marshall's eyes, improbably, got even wider. He silently mouthed the word to me. "GAS-O-LINE."

Well that certainly clarified the options for how to end our burglary. I hazarded a whisper. "We have to get the hell out of here." I waited until the footsteps started back down the front stairs, then, quietly as I could, I slipped around the door of the study and crossed the hall. Marshall was right behind me as I started down the back staircase, stepping carefully, trying not to make noise, which is virtually impossible in a creaky century-old Iowa farmhouse.

I just hoped the sound of the splashing would drown out the noise. But it didn't much matter really, because whether we were caught or not we quite obviously couldn't stay in the house.

I whispered to Marshall, "We have to get out before she lights it."

"She?"

I pushed open the door at the bottom of the staircase just as a dark figure backed into the kitchen, spreading some gasoline along the linoleum. We froze again. Once inside the kitchen she suddenly noticed the lighted candle. That made her stop cold and she straightened up, her back still towards me. It occurred to me that there was really no sense in continuing this farce. I spoke to her.

"Maria."

She screamed and let go of the can of gas, which fell with a great splatter, and whipped around toward me. Her face was pale as a gravestone in the flickering candlelight. She seemed unable to get any words out.

"It's Claire, Maria, don't be afraid."

"Claire…" She tried to suck in some breath. "Claire… what? I…" She looked hopelessly at the gas can on the floor which she must have realized was utterly unexplainable.

"I know what this is about, Maria. You wanted to burn this place down so no one would connect you with Erik Weber. Didn't you, Maria? Or would you rather I called you Mrs. Spengler?"

"How did you…" she trailed off, her face drained of any life. The cat skulked into the room behind her.

We were standing in a house that reeked of gasoline talking to a desperate woman who was sure to have matches, so I knew I'd better keep her mind engaged lest she do something crazy that would get us all killed.

I asked a question.

"Weber got you your job here, didn't he, Maria? After you escaped East Berlin. He was afraid the Stasi would still be after you, so he got his friend John Marchak to give you a job out here. Out in the middle of nowhere where they wouldn't find you."

"How did you know he lived here?" She seemed to regain some composure, but her eyes still looked frightened, even wild, like those of a bird caught in a net. "How did you know?"

"This is where he hid, wasn't it. Whenever he did his disappearing act to write another book, he came here to Iowa, where you and John lived."

"Yes, but how did you know that?" Slowly I reached into my pocket and pulled out the slip of green paper I had found on the ground. I held it out to her. "I found this note on the ground next to Weber's…body. I recognized Emma's handwriting. I thought Emma had written this note to Weber, and Weber had dropped it. So I traced the number to this house. But the note wasn't to Weber, it was to you. He must have called you at the philosophy office and she took the message, not knowing it was Weber who called. I figure you must have dropped this yourself, accidentally, after you, ah, hit Weber on the head."

She stared at the note for a moment without trying to touch it. "It fell out of my purse when I got the…I didn't have time to pick it up when I…heard you coming."

She looked up at me. "I didn't want any of this to happen. I never wanted anyone to get hurt."

"I believe you Maria," I said. The smell of gasoline was making it hard to breathe. "But I don't think we should talk about it here. Let's get out of here. We'll sort it all out." She looked down at the palm of her hand which held, as I had feared, a white-tipped kitchen match, the kind of match that lights with just one stroke against any rough surface. Maria took a step away from me, which was in the wrong direction because it put her out in the puddle of gasoline.

"I had to protect Yuri. It would have killed him if he knew." I was not the least bit sure what her son had to do with this, but I was getting very afraid at how she kept staring at that match. I moved closer, making sure I stayed on the edge of the pool of liquid.

"Maria, come on now, let's go home and get this sorted out." I leaned toward her and reached out my hand, trying to keep my feet clear of the gasoline, which made me lose my balance and have to take a short sidestep. My shoe came down on something soft and squishy.

There was a great screeching howl as the cat leapt from the floor to the kitchen table and skidded into a vase, knocking it sideways so that it rolled toward the edge of the table. The vase rolled, then slowed almost to a stop, but not before brushing the saucer that held Marshall's candle. The candle teetered on the edge of the table, seemed for a second to be about to right itself, then tipped forward and fell toward the floor. In a split second I grabbed Maria's sleeve and yanked her toward me with all my might.

FROOM! The whole place ignited in an instant. You could hear the flames rush out into the living room and up the front stairs, racing along the stream of gasoline. A great wall of fire rose between us and the hallway which led to the front and back exits from the house.

Marshall, who had not moved a muscle since we came downstairs, suddenly became quite mobile. He looked up the back staircase and said, "We can't go back up, that hallway is on fire." It was hard to hear him over the roar of the flames.

"The window," I yelled. As one being, Marshall and I ran to the single window over the stove, each grabbed a handle and tried to pull it open. It didn't budge. We pulled hard again, Marshall grunting. No movement.

"We have to break it," Marshall said. No, that would take too long, I thought. The window had a wooden lattice that looked pretty solid, and already the smoke and heat in the room were unbearable. Behind the table the door to the cellar began squeaking open as the fire sucked up the air in the kitchen.

"The basement," I said. "Come on!" An old Iowa farmhouse will have two floors to live on, an upstairs and a downstairs, and two floors to store things on, a large attic and a full basement. In rural Iowa at the turn of the century, one could not just zip out to the mall to do a little shopping; many things had to be stored in the home.

I had to grab Maria, who seemed to be in a state of shock, and pull her bulky form down the cellar staircase. The cat sailed past between my legs. The basement was even darker than the rest of the house, with a only a few tiny windows high up the walls at ground level. I hit the switch at the top of the stairs, and luckily the lights still worked down there. Despite the fire raging above, the cellar smelled damp and musty. The stairway led down to a large center room with several smaller rooms leading off it. Entering the house I had seen the characteristic metal doors leaning at an angle against the east side of the house. They would cover a stairway where a load of coal, a piece of equipment, or some other large item could be brought directly into the basement from outside the house. So I had dragged us all into the cellar because there was an exit down here. I remembered those outside doors.

What I forgot was what a crazy bastard Weber was.

"He chained them," I said. "Shit! He chained the goddamned doors shut!" I looked at Marshall as if he, the biographer, with his intimate knowledge of Weber's mind, could somehow make this not be true. He just stared back at me, breathing hard. Wordlessly, we both turned to look up the cellar stairs we had just come down to see that the kitchen above us was now an inferno. In that instant it suddenly hit home that the three of us were in very real danger.

"What about the windows?" Marshall said. We ran over to one.

"Give me a boost." I stood with my foot in his hand and banged hard against one of two little windows along the top of the wall. "Painted shut." Marshall lowered me down. "Besides," I said, "I'm not sure you and Maria could squeeze through one of those." Marshall nodded. Drops of sweat beaded up on his forehead.

"Break the window, Claire." His breath sounded raspy. "You crawl through it. We'll be OK down here until you bring some help."

The cellar lights suddenly flickered and went out. Upstairs the inferno was roaring like a freight train, and over our heads some flames already licked through the basement ceiling from the main floor above. I knew there would never be time for me to bring back help, and I was sure that Marshall knew it too. "I'm not leaving you, Marshall. We're going to get out of here." I pulled his arm. "Come on, let's look around. There's an orchard out back, there should be some tools around here someplace."

In the patchy light from the fire above us Marshall and I scurried among the small rooms of the basement, looking for something that would open those doors. Passing the stairs I inhaled some smoke and had to stop for a moment, coughing violently. When I finally recovered, my hands were shaking and my mouth was cotton dry. I was not in a panic. But I felt the panic, felt it in my chest, felt it slowly expanding, like a soap bubble being blown, and I sensed, without thinking, that when that bubble finally burst, all my composure would burst along with it. And then I would surely die.

As I hoped, in one of the rooms I found equipment that had been used to care for the orchard, and among the equipment was a set of pruning shears. They had small curved blades of only two or three inches, attached to great thick handles nearly three feet long. The blades could fit around tree branches which could then be clipped off by closing the handles. They were made to cut green wood, not metal, but I tried not to think about that. We ran back to the doors, put a link of chain between the blades and put the handles of the shears between our two bodies. I held the handle that was against Marshall's chest and he held the handle that was against mine. We pulled the handles with all our might. There was a crunching sound but the chain didn't break, and we could tell that the blades of the shears were being gouged by the chain.

"Once more," I said, "hard." Marshall puffed out his cheeks as he strained. I pulled until my arms ached from wrist to shoulder, but I didn't let go. After a few very long seconds, the chain snapped and clattered to the cement floor. In a flash Marshall shoved hard against the two doors and they pushed open out into the night. The sudden blast of cold air felt electrifying against my sweaty face as we rushed out of the cellar, followed closely by the cat.

A few yards away, both panting, we turned to look at the holocaust of the farmhouse. The fire had reached the attic and flames were shooting out of parts of the roof. A long trail of sparks rose up in the black sky like a parade of fireflies. We stood there mesmerized. It took several seconds before I realized she was missing.

"Where's Maria?" I looked around. "Oh, God," I said, "she's still in the basement." For a moment I stood staring in disbelief. My stomach churned at the thought of what I knew I had to do now. Had to do because it was partly my fault, because I had hidden important information from the police, because if I had not interfered, Maria would not be underneath a roaring inferno. But I couldn't think about it. I just had to do it.

I took off running through the snow, headed back to the cellar doors. Marshall's voice called after me in protest.

I ducked back into the basement and immediately started to cough from the smoke.

"MARIA." There was plenty of light from the fire, but the smoke made it hard to see. "MARIA!" Would she hear me over the roaring and crackling of the flames overhead?

"Claire, come out!" Marshall shouted from the top of the cellar steps. He squatted low and used the flap of his coat to shield his face from the heat.

"Help me Marshall, I can't find her."

"Claire, come out, the ceiling is going to collapse."

I didn't have time for another argument with a philosopher. I turned and pushed on deeper into the cellar.

I felt my way along the cellar wall, where there was less danger from falling debris, and worked my way back toward the kitchen stairs, which is where I had last seen Maria.

"MARIA!"

It seemed like a very long time before I found her huddled against the cellar wall, her face pushed down into her knees. I reached down and grabbed her thick upper arm. "Maria, hurry, the door is this way." Her head came up, her face smeared with soot, but she made no effort to rise. She stared at me glassy-eyed, seemingly oblivious to the heat, the smoke, and the noise all around us.

"I did not want Yuri to know, Claire. What happened back in Berlin. I could not let them tell, it would have hurt him too bad." There was a crashing sound as a large chunk of the main floor fell into the cellar a few yards to our right.

"Come on, Maria. We'll talk about it outside." She shook her head and pressed it back into her knees. I got angry then and tried to pull her to her feet, but Maria is a big woman. She barely seemed to notice my tugging on her arm.

I felt Marshall's hand, pulling on my own arm. He shouted, "Claire we've got to get out of here. NOW!"

"She won't come!"

"Then we'll have to leave her, there isn't any time!"

He pulled on my arm but I shook him off, bent down and put my mouth right against Maria's ear. "Maria, whatever it is you don't want Yuri to know, if you die here, who will tell him? He'll have to hear it from strangers. You're his mother, Maria. You have to be the one to explain it to him."

Her head turned and she looked at me, searching my eyes. Suddenly she grabbed my arms in a strong grip and pulled herself up from the cement floor.

"Hurry!" Marshall yelled. We each took one of Maria's arms and, ducking low against the heat and stepping over burning pieces of the living room floor, moved as fast as we could back to the cellar doorway. We ran up the few steps, half dragging Maria, and out into the snow, staggering forward ten, twenty, thirty yards from the house. Behind us there was a great crashing sound as the second floor fell through the first and down into the cellar. We stopped and gently lowered Maria down. She stayed on her knees on the snow-covered ground.

Out on the highway I heard sirens blaring.

CHAPTER TWENTY-FIVE

By the time the firemen arrived I had pulled Maria's old Buick station wagon off the driveway so the trucks could get in, and the three of us sat in it, the engine running, the heater on full blast. We had to leave a window open because of the smell of gasoline from Maria's shoes. I had assured the fire chief that we were OK and that it would be a good idea for him to call the police. I declined his offer of a couple of blankets. Maria and I were in the front seat, Marshall was in the back, and Mrs. O'Leary's cat sat purring on his lap. It was a long while before Maria, staring out the window at the blazing house and the scampering firemen, finally spoke.

"How did you know who my husband was?"

"Marshall has a picture of Weber and Spengler and Yuri." I said. "He showed it to us on that first night at the inn. Yuri is playing with a spotted horse. I saw that horse on the shelves at your house when I went there with Roger."

She sniffed. "He carried that horse out through the tunnel. I told him not to bring any toys. But he hid it in his knapsack." A long moment passed. "And you know about what happened in the tunnel?"

I nodded. "When I finally figured out why Roger was killed, I knew what must have happened," I said. "Roger said Weber was the Stasi informant, the Spider, but it was really you." The black widow who kills her own husband, I thought.

"It couldn't have been Weber because he only knew the people in his cell. Kurt told me your husband was the head of the group, only he would have known all the people in it. He and, obviously, you."

A heavy sigh from Maria. "I did not want my husband to be killed," she said. "They were supposed to catch him, that was all. They came late and started shooting." She nodded her head toward the hulk of the steaming, smoldering house. "Anton was just like him, you know."

"Like whom?"

"Like Erik Weber. Arrogant, self-absorbed, absolutely confident in his own brilliance. 'You are lucky to be with me,' he would say. Only Anton was worse, Anton was violent." She rubbed a hand against her lower jaw as if the memory sent a twinge through an old wound. "It was bad enough in East Germany without him joining the underground. He was going to destroy us with all his politics! He wanted to play the hero, the freedom-fighter. But what if he was caught? What would happen to Yuri and me?" She shook her head. "He just did not give a damn." She gazed into her lap, her hands holding onto her knees. "When the Stasi approached me they said Yuri and I could go, could get out. They already knew my husband was planning to escape—all I had to do was say where and when. If I told them that, then Yuri and I could go through the tunnel and Anton would be caught. No one would know what really happened."

"If they knew he was going to escape, why didn't they just arrest him?"

"They could prosecute," she said, "have a big show trial, brand the dissidents as traitors to the republic. It would be good propaganda." She looked back out the window and her voice began to trail off. "They were not supposed to shoot anyone."

After a pause, Marshall spoke up from the back seat quietly. "Did Weber know you'd been the informant? Before now, I mean?"

She shook her head. "He had his friends in Berlin look at those files himself after he heard that Dr. Stuhrm had been snooping around. When they told him what they found he figured it out. He called me and said he wasn't going to be blamed for my 'treachery'—that was the word he used. He said if Stuhrm accused him of the betrayal, he would tell everyone it was me."

"This happened that first morning of the conference, didn't it?" I said. "I knew something was odd about your activities that morning. You said you couldn't pick up Roger at the airport because you had to go straighten out your son's student loan. But at the party last night I heard you tell Mrs. Leach that your son had a full teaching fellowship. He wouldn't need a student loan. You came here that morning to meet Weber. It was you who drove him to the college."

"I tried to reason with him. There was no point in stirring up the past. I tried to get him to go see Emma, to have her make Stuhrm show us the paper before it was delivered. He went to your house, he could not find her."

"So you killed him."

"I didn't mean to! But he wouldn't stop! He was on his way to the inn, and I was trying to talk him out of it, but he would not listen." Her voice sounded teary now. "I hit him with a piece of pipe I carry in my purse. I have carried it since a man attacked me once back in Budapest."

"And that's when you dropped the slip of paper with Weber's number on it," I said. "It came out of your purse when you got the pipe. Where did you hide when you heard me coming?"

"Under the bridge."

I nodded. "Then when I ran for a phone you dragged him to the edge and threw him on the rocks. My arrival was convenient, it made the whole thing look more like an accident." It was very nearly the scenario Arnie had suggested when teasing Marshall that first night at dinner. Maria didn't say anything. "What about Roger?" I asked.

Now her voice was angry. "I did not mean that, either! I just needed to look at the paper, to see if he knew what really happened. I had to know. He should have sent the damned paper in like he was supposed to, the pompous fool!" After a few seconds she turned back toward the window. "Anyway, I waited until I knew he would be at the memorial service then went to his room to look at it."

Of course, I thought, she'd have a master key to the inn for the conference.

"I heard him unlocking his room," Maria said, "just as I got the paper up on his computer screen. I tried to make up some excuse—I told him I just wanted a copy of the paper."

"But he didn't believe you."

"No," she said, staring out through the windshield. "He figured it out." She looked at me, a look of disbelief. "He figured it out! He knew that Erik's death was not an accident. When he saw me reading the paper he guessed who I was. I denied it and started to leave, but then I panicked again. While he was looking at the computer screen, I hit him from behind."

"You came here to burn this house down to destroy the evidence," I said. "At Rube's you heard Oscar tell me that the police were trying to figure out where Weber lived. And there was something in this house that linked you to Weber, right? This house was the only thing that would link you to Weber."

Maria ignored my question. She put her hand across her eyes and bent forward a little. "I do not know how it got so out of hand. All this killing, I can't understand it."

I couldn't understand it either. "Maria, why was it so important? That your secret not get discovered, I mean. It was almost thirty years ago. You couldn't be prosecuted for anything, not now. Not here in America."

When she finally answered, her expression was pleading. "I told you, Claire, it was my boy, Yuri. I could not let him find out I had gotten his father killed. He still worships his father. He is following in his footsteps, studying philosophy. He would never forgive me." She turned away from us and started crying, keeping her head down so we wouldn't see. "He is all I have now."

"But couldn't you have—"

"You do not understand, Claire!" Her head came up and she looked at me fiercely. "You have no children, so you do not know what it is like. What I did all those years ago was to give Yuri a chance, a chance for a real life—a life he could not have in East Germany. A life like you had when you were a child. You never had to live behind a wall." Quietly, as if to herself, she said, "It has been a good life here, too."

Good Lord, I thought, is that what all this comes down to—Motherhood? Is simple motherhood really as powerful as all that? Could it drive quiet, orderly Maria to burn down houses and commit multiple murder? Whatever would it do to a woman as volatile and passionate as Emma? To what lengths might motherhood drive her, I wondered. Well, one thing was obvious; she definitely needed me around to help her raise that kid.

In a few minutes Pete showed up with a couple of patrol cars. I will not describe the conversation Pete and I had when he found out what I was doing there, except to say that before it was over, the cop car I sat in became somewhat hotter than the cellar I had just escaped. Eventually I was released with a very severe warning. I used Pete's police phone to call Emma, whom I was sure would be frantically wondering about what happened to me.

They had already taken Maria away when Marshall drove me back to the house.

"Marshall?"

"Yeah, Claire."

"Remember what you told me about Emma's old roommate at Freiburg? That she'd killed herself when Weber dumped her?"

"Yeah?"

"Is it possible that Emma doesn't know that? I mean about the connection with Weber?"

He took a moment to think about it. "Well, the suicide happened in the spring—April, I think. The scandal broke in, let's see, mid-June. Actually, you know, it was a couple of months before anyone knew about Weber being involved. If Emma had left Freiburg before that part of the story came out, she might not know."

Yes, Emma had come home shortly after Karen's death and that explained why she hadn't known. I felt a hot flash of guilt at the thought that I'd had any suspicions about Emma. Of course I hadn't *really* had suspicions about Emma. I mean, not honest-to-God suspicions. It would be more accurate to call them concerns…or worries…or bouts of anxiety, perhaps. Yes, that was a good way to look at it. I'd had a few little bouts of anxiety about Emma, which, though they had almost gotten three people incinerated, were relatively minor in the scheme of things, and now they could be completely forgotten. No need to even mention them again.

"Marshall," I said, as he swung his car into our driveway.

"Yeah?"

"I'm sorry that I almost got you killed tonight."

"It's OK." He stopped the car and smiled at me, just for a second, then he turned away and looked out over the steering wheel.

"And thanks, Marshall. Not just for helping me tonight." I put my hand on his shoulder. "For being such a good friend and all." I reached over, wrapped my arms around his neck and gave him a solid, heartfelt kiss on his cheek. Even in the dark I could see him flush.

"For you, Claire," he said, "anything."

I climbed slowly out of his car and walked up our front walk. When I got to the steps I turned to wave at Marshall who was still sitting there idling in the driveway. He waved and slowly backed the car out to the street.

Before I reached the front door Emma came rushing out, barefoot and in that hideous blue bathrobe again. She threw her arms around me and squeezed me to her. "Are you all right? Are you hurt?"

"You mean, aside from the cracked ribs you're giving me?"

CHAPTER TWENTY-SIX

It was a bright morning in early May and I was trying to do two things I'm really bad at: mow the lawn and mind my own business. It was the first mowing of the year, and I'd gotten impatient with a thick clump of crabgrass and shoved the mower a little too hard. It had shot into Emma's tulip bed and sucked under a few of the yellow ones. Oh, well. I hadn't been paying close attention because with one eye I was watching the goings-on in the Leaches' front yard where two little girls were playing with the wooden lawn ducks. A young man in shorts and a polo shirt was standing with them. Since I couldn't hear their voices this seemed like a good time to shut off the noisy mower and pull weeds at the base of the hedge between the yards.

The bigger of the two girls picked up a mallard. "This is Bridget, she's the oldest one."

"And this is Lulu," said the smaller girl, "she's the babiest."

"Her name is Lucy, not Lulu."

The little one shook her head. "It's Lulu."

"It's Lucy! I named her, and I—"

"What's the daddy duck's name?" the young man asked. He pointed at the biggest duck.

Both girls looked at him and the little one cocked her head. "That's the mommy, Uncle Ron," the older girl said. The little one nodded in agreement.

"Oh, the mommy. Of course."

So that was Uncle Ron, huh? I was very glad to see him there. After the conference, as planned, Mrs. Leach and I had a little powwow with her husband on the subject of their son's homosexuality. It wasn't the sort of chatty gathering we Iowans might have over coffee down at the feed store—there had been a certain amount of anger and yelling. But there had also been a certain amount of listening. And since my eventual exit from the house had been unassisted by Mr. Leach's foot, I had figured the meeting was less than a disaster.

And there was Uncle Ron standing in the next yard.

All of a sudden, a great grey-haired figure rose up out of nowhere, towering above the hedge in front of me. He wiped some dirt from the trowel in his hand.

"Oh," I said, "good morning, Mr. Leach."

He nodded, taking work gloves from his back pocket and putting them on. "Good morning, Claire." He gave me something like half of a smile, maybe three quarters, then disappeared below the hedge again.

I was about to restart the mower when Emma's car came rolling up the driveway just behind me. I went around and opened the passenger door. One of Emma's legs came out, then the other leg came out, and when they were both on the cement, she sat there for a time taking deep breaths. She wore a sour expression.

I reached down and took hold of her elbow. "Need some help?"

"OK, but give me a second."

Cubby came around from the driver's side. "Doctor says it shouldn't last but three months. Gets real bad, she can come back."

"Yeah, they say it goes away after the first trimester," I said.

"Not always, though," Emma said. "It's not uncommon for this to go on for all nine months." She held out a hand to each of us. We gently pulled her to her feet and walked her into the house.

In the kitchen I asked Emma, "Can I get you some crackers?"

"Oh, God, crackers don't help. Whoever started that stupid cracker myth?"

"Probably Keebler," I said. Cubby poured himself some of the coffee I'd left on the warmer.

Two quick knocks came from the back door, which swung open. Colin Jensen walked in.

"Well, guys," he held his arms open wide, "I'm outta here."

"Right now?" I asked. "I thought you were staying for graduation."

"I'm not leaving this minute, but this afternoon sometime," he said. "I can't stay for graduation, Claire. It'll take me three days to drive to Irvine." Colin had gotten a new job in California.

"At least sit down and have some coffee, Colin."

"I can't, Emma, I still have to pack my skis." He laughed. "I'm finally going someplace I can use them."

Emma held her arms up to him. "I'll miss you, Colin."

"You too, Em. Having you as a colleague was the best thing about this place." He bent and hugged her. "You take care of yourself. And send me a picture of the baby." He leaned over and pecked me on the cheek. "Take it easy, Claire."

"See ya, Colin, keep in touch."

"And it's been nice knowing you, Gabby."

Cubby nodded. Colin vanished through the back door.

"So," Cubby said to me, "that's the guy you first figured for the killer?"

"What? No, I never said that."

"You did, too."

Emma groaned. "Cubby, please, not again," she said. "Why are you so obsessed with those murders?"

"'Cause I've lived in this town for sixty-six years and they're the only interesting thing's ever happened." Cubby pointed his coffee cup at me. "You did say you suspected him."

I sighed. "No, I didn't. I said he was one of several people who appeared to have a motive and, possibly, opportunity for the first murder. That's all I said. He's the one person I knew of who could have left the opening talk—him and maybe what's-his-name, with the beret. They both looked young enough to be mistaken for students."

Emma put a hand on her forehead. "I really do not want to hear this again."

"Why'd you think he'd wanna kill Weber?" Cubby asked.

"I think he really is the son of that guy, Platburg, the one Weber plagiarized."

"You know, I hate to say it, but I think so, too," Emma said.

I looked at her. "I thought you just said you didn't want to hear this?" she shrugged. "Anyway," I said, "Colin is very ambitious. He wrote what he thought was a great paper, and Weber might have been able to make a fool of him. It was enough to make me suspicious."

"So he's the only professor who could've killed Weber."

"No, I thought maybe Roger was a possibility."

"But wasn't he at the talk?"

I went over to the sink to wash the grass stains off my hands. "Well, it was Sara Grace who said no professors left the talk, but she was infatuated with Roger. She might have lied to protect him."

"Uh huh. But then who'd you think killed Roger—Colin?"

"No, he couldn't have, he was at the memorial service. Same with Fritz the beret guy, I saw them there myself."

"So who else would've wanted Roger dead," Cubby asked, "besides Maria?"

"Obviously his wife was one, but any number of other people too. Remember, all anybody knew about Roger's paper was that it had some dark secrets to show. Lots of people around here had dark pasts with Weber. Kurt

Burghoff and Renee Amundsen, to name two. And both of them had the opportunity to kill Roger."

"Why would Renee kill anybody?"

Emma interjected, "She wouldn't. Miss Marple there just suspected everybody. And people thought Weber was paranoid! Hey, I just had a thought, Cubby. Maybe Claire is Erik Weber's illegitimate daughter." Cubby laughed.

"That would certainly explain my love of philosophy," I admitted.

"Well, in any case," Emma grimaced and rubbed her stomach. "I'm going upstairs to lie down. Maybe I can finish grading my exams." She stood up, took a deep breath, and wobbled slowly toward the living room. I waited until I heard her feet on the stairs.

"Renee was Weber's ex-lover," I told Cubby. "I wondered if maybe he had fathered her aborted child. That illegal abortion messed up her life. Then again, maybe she still loved Weber, and killed Roger to protect his name." I spread my hands. "These were pure speculation, but they couldn't be ruled out. What cleared it all up was the discovery that Roger and Weber had both been killed with the same weapon. Then just about everybody got eliminated. None of them could have done both murders."

Cubby swished the coffee around in his mug and stared into it as if he saw a bug. His little elf's face wore the hint of a smile. "Of course, you suspected Emma too, didn't ya?"

"What?" I looked over my shoulder toward the kitchen door, then leaned toward Cubby. My voice came out as a harsh half-whisper, "I never said a word to you about suspecting Emma."

"That's how I know," he said.

"Look, I did not suspect Emma." I paused. "But there are a few things that can't be denied. She was the one obvious person with the opportunity to commit both murders."

"And motive, right?"

"Motive? I never said she had a motive."

"Didn't need to."

I came back to the table and sat across from him. "I didn't suspect her, Cubby, I was just worried that other people would suspect her."

"OK, Claire, if you say so." He wore his not-quite-a-smile look.

I shook a finger at him. "Don't you say a word to Emma about this."

"Don't worry," he laughed. "Anyway, I don't blame you—she's high strung, she's been in the looney bin."

"Her being at Marlborough House had nothing to do with it," I said. "And by the way, the term 'looney bin' is no longer endorsed by the American Psychiatric Association."

He started fishing around in his breast pocket, then stopped suddenly. "Oops, forgot, can't smoke in here while she's pregnant. So, anyway, you're the big detective in town now."

"I'm the big dope in town—I should've stayed out of it. My meddling almost got several people killed and me sent to jail. I'm sure the police would have figured it out from the forensic evidence, they usually do nowadays."

Cubby folded his brown, knuckly hands together on the table and we sat quietly for a bit. "I still don't see why you all're leaving," he said. He gestured toward the kitchen door. "She worries about getting a regular job here and the minute she's got one she up and leaves."

"Just for a year," I said. "She needs this sabbatical, Cub. She needs to put this stuff behind her. Have the baby, get back to her book."

"And where is it you two're going again?"

"She's going to George Washington University and I'm going to the Fed…the Federal Reserve."

He nodded. "Just as well you won't be here, I guess." He got up and walked over to the counter and put his cup in the sink. "Don't know if I remember how to take care of an expectant mom."

"Excuse me? Did you say 'an expectant mom?'"

His smile came back. "Sorry," he said, "expectant moms."